INTERFERENCE!

T5-BQB-624

Paul F. Hammond

PublishAmerica
Baltimore

First printing

ISBN: 1-4241-0401-7
PUBLISHED BY PUBLISHAMERICA, LLLP
www.publishamerica.com
Baltimore

Printed in the United States of America

For Paige

JULY 1998

ONE

"*Foremast watch, on deck! Right now, on the double!!!* Ashburn, are you dead? You look like a goddamn mummy. Climb out of your shroud, man; join the living! Move, move!"

OK, OK, stop shouting. The person next to me immediately swings his torso up to slide out of his hammock. Smack, his head slams into the big beam barely above his hammock. "Ohhh shit…ohhh, shit." He falls backward, one hand holding the top of his bleeding head. The other arm is flailing out to grab something, anything to stop from twisting out of the hammock and crashing to the deck. He falls backward, but manages to grab my right knee, twisting me upside down in the hammock. His grip slips off my knee. He lands with a groaning, flailing thud.

"Clumsy matey, very clumsy," shouts Tony, our Captain-of-Tops. "The t'gallant yard should be special fun. Into your beautiful 'slops', mateys; she's raining a bit more than a gentle sprinkle!"

Still hanging upside down I slide gracelessly down the hammock after finally untangling my legs, my knees landing hard on the deck. A great start. It's a madhouse around me. Somebody falls out of his hammock, cursing and groaning. Someone else yells, "Where the hell is the foul weather gear?" Another complains, "My shoes, who's got my shoes?"

*　　　　　*　　　　　*　　　　　*　　　　　*

Tony shouts, "Get into layers, mateys; it's nippy tonight. But hurry, damn it, time's a-wasting! 'Slop chest' is over there, next to the companionway. Grab pants, a jacket and a hat. You'll love 'em; they fit beautifully, smooth and soft as a baby's bum!"

I fumble under the head of my hammock to find the bag in which I stuffed my pants, sweatshirt and docksiders. Got it. How do I get this stuff on? The area is barely lit by a distant emergency light. People all around are stumbling into tables, chests, hammocks, banging their heads in the dwarf headroom, cursing a blue streak. The ship must be in a nasty storm; she's rolling hard side-to-side. Sit down...pull the pants on, sweatshirt and shoes. Stand up, bending low, follow someone headed in what seems like the general direction of the companionway.

"Queue up here for slops." We shuffle forward. Tony hands me a lumpy, sodden brown oilskin jacket, greasy brown oilskin pants and an absurd yellow slicker hat.

"Tony, this stuff is...."

"Ah, the dead has arisen. You have the very best available...off with you, on deck for some fun!"

You bet, anything to get out of here. It's like being in a cave, with too many people. It feels a little panicky. The space is too small, too dark, nobody has much idea where they're going or what to do when they get there.

Two of us lunge for the companionway (stairway) toward the late night fresh air. The ship rolls hard to port, a loud thud, a body crashes into me, we fall backward down the companionway in a bruised and battered tangle. I sit up. Head hurts a little from a whack once I hit the bottom of the companionway, right shoulder stings some. My butt hurts the worst, must have landed on it when the body crashed into me.

"Ah nicely done, mateys." Tony peers down at me. "Again I ask you, Ashburn, are you dead?"

"I'll live."

"OK then, on your feet. You'll probably not dash madly up the companionway from now on, eh?!

"You, Spasiano, will you live?"

No answer. Finally, the other body moves a bit, rolls over on its back moaning loudly.

"Can you hear me Spasiano?"

"Ohh, man, ohh man…sort of."

"Can you sit up? Sit up man, let's go!"

Spasiano slowly rocks to his side, pushes himself up with an arm to a wobbly sitting position. "Ohh man, everything hurts, ohh, Jesus!"

"Stand up, walk over to that chest, sit and rest a minute." Tony resumes tossing slops as fast as he can to other members of the Foremast watch.

"Everybody gather around me!" As eight of us gather around Tony, he exclaims, "You'll love this! T'gallant needs putting to bed. Wind is freshening fast; it's too much sail."

It's raining hard, gusty winds blowing sheets of it across the deck. The *Endeavour* is rolling violently. It is really dark. We're headed for the fore topgallant yard (a.k.a. yardarm; a cylindrical wooden spar, slung horizontally, from which a sail is suspended), more than 100 feet up to furl the topmost sail on the foremast.

"Just remember what you learned this morning. Let's crack on, mateys! Margaret here will lead you up. I'll be right behind…no worries!"

Margaret, a tall, thin, red-faced, red-haired Australian deckhand, beams brightly at us and scampers easily up into the starboard rigging.

Suddenly I receive a sharp slap on the back, turn and see a familiar face smiling at me. I can't remember his name. He shrugs, "What the hell; time to go, I guess!"

"Yeah, seems it is. I'll follow you."

We climb onto the starboard railing, step up to the low ratlines (rope steps horizontally fixed to the shrouds), hanging onto shrouds (strong ropes extending from high on each mast to the side of the ship), just below Margaret. Up she goes, we follow. Climbing here is steep, but not impossible. At the moment the ship is heeling to port, so the climbing angle is easier than tied to the dock this morning in Norwalk when we first climbed to the foretop (a platform on the foremast). In the very dim light of a lantern hung under the maintop (the platform on the mainmast), I can see Margaret now standing on the foretop peering down as we slowly climb the ratlines. I'm careful to pull myself up by the tar-covered shrouds, just stepping on the much smaller ratlines. As we approach the futtock shrouds that support the foretop, Margaret shouts to us, "Wait a moment, gauge the roll." Gauge the roll, what does that mean? In its back-and-forth rolling, the ship is now rolling past vertical, toward starboard. What was an easy climb now isn't. We're clinging to the shrouds as the *Endeavour* keeps rolling to starboard, making us hang on to keep from falling in the water. Finally the ship starts to roll back. Margaret shouts, "OK, first guy, climb now!"

He starts to climb, heading out and up. The futtock shrouds support the foretop by securing it to the foremast. They are attached to the outside of the foretop platform. The lower shrouds are attached directly to the foremast. He transfers from standing among the lower shrouds next to the mast, to the futtock shrouds by grabbing the latter and heading out, literally hanging by his hands and feet while climbing up toward the edge of the foretop.

"Next man, get climbing!"

Alongside and slightly below I grab the lower portion of the futtock shrouds. Slowly, one hand at a time, I grab up on a futtock shroud, and take a step up on the lower shroud ratlines. Next hand, next step. Shortly I'm fully on the futtock shrouds, hanging there like a huge, ungainly spider. If either hands slips, I'm done...right on the deck, or in the water. The *Endeavour* continues to roll to port.

"Hurry," yells Margaret, "use the roll, get up here!" The other guy has reached head-up on the platform. He pauses...what's he doing? Got to keep moving, or stop and grab hard hugging the shrouds to wait out the roll. Is there enough space for two of us to pull ourselves up to the platform?

Margaret has leaned far down so her face is right in front of mine. "Don't stop, keep moving up here". She looks at me, her eyes widening. "Where's your belt?"

Oh, damn, I didn't hook my harness belt onto the safety line.

"Move up a little more, grab the platform, that's it." She leans down, unhooks the hook on my safety line from my belt loop, hooks it on the nearby vertical safety line.

"Thanks."

"No worry. Keep moving, grab the base of the topmast shrouds, pull yourself up and climb with your feet."

Damn, the strain on my arms is intense. I'm still hanging past vertical, but the roll is going to port and it'll get easier. Rest a moment. OK, slowly I scramble my left knee onto the platform. One more hard pull, then the right knee scrapes onto the foretop. Slumped there, rain pouring on me...made it.

The familiar face leans over. "That was something, huh!"

Yeah. Meanwhile, Margaret is leaning over yelling instructions and encouragement to the others as they one-by-one struggle onto the foretop.

Tony bounds onto the platform. "OK mateys, I need four to keep going up, four to stay here. First four, you're the most rested, let's go. Margaret, if you please!"

I start back up. Whoa, much smaller here, fewer shrouds, narrower, and very steep. The friendly face follows Margaret. I follow him this time hooking my climbing belt on the adjacent safety line. Friendly face seems to be getting stronger, or I'm getting slower. I don't know, but the gap is getting bigger each step. The ship is rolling to starboard, and as I get higher the roll is evermore exaggerated. Holy shit, can I hang on? It keeps rolling, I stop, looping both arms around the shrouds, they bite into my biceps and underarms. Stop! Stop the goddamn rolling! Finally the roll slows, stops and head back to port. Thank God! Get moving…one hand up, one foot up a step, one hand, one foot. Suddenly a figure looms out of the darkness. It's Margaret.

"Want you to stop here for a moment. Now, still pulling up with your hands on the shrouds, step up one more ratline. OK, can you see the topsail yard right in front of you? I want you to swing around the outboard shroud you're holding onto, while turning first your left foot, later your right foot onto the ratline but on the other side of the shroud. Then turn your torso around the shroud so you'll be holding onto the shrouds and ratlines but on the opposite side. Once there, you'll be able to grab the line running along the top of the topsail yard and step onto the foot line. OK? Got it?"

You must be kidding! I'm shaking like a leaf, and the ship is rolling hard again to starboard, in what seems like a huge sweep. No way.

Margaret points in the near total darkness. "You'll stand on the foot line on the other side of the topsail mast from Harry."

Oh yeah, I remember…the cop from DC.

"Look, Jack, there's not enough room on the crosstrees up there. Tony and I will go on up to the t'gallant yard to make sure you can work it OK. Tony's got a pocket flashlight to check it. Go ahead get on the topsail yard foot line."

I can see a little now, there's the yard. I unhook the safety line, re-attach it on the other side of a middle shroud.

As the ship rolls back to port, I reach my left arm around the opposite side of the shrouds grabbing the second shroud. Next I step around to the opposite side with my left leg, eventually following it with the right leg and finally reverse my right hand grip.

"Simple enough huh?" says Margaret. She's facing me standing backward on the foot line. "Step over next to me and as you do it, grab the top of the yardarm.

Put your foot right next to my right foot so you're standing on the foot line (used to stand on when working sails attached to the yard), but please don't step on it. I'll be very unhappy if you do. Don't forget to unhook your safety line. You'll hook up to the line running along the top of the yard."

It's a small step, but I feel nearly paralyzed. As I numbly unhook my safety belt, and turn toward Margaret, the *Endeavour* lurches a little and Margaret commands, "Step now!" She leans out to me grabbing a handful of my oilskin jacket and commands again "My foot!" Slightly pulling me she again says "foot". My right foot lands on the foot line next to her and I grab for the yardarm, but it's at waist level. I belly-flop over the yard, my leg shaking violently on the foot line. I wrap both arms around the yardarm to steady my body a bit, and in a great piece of luck my left foot touches the foot line so that after several frantic probes my foot finally settles onto the line.

"Fasten your belt. Welcome to the topsail yard! Happy to be here?"

"Give me a second. I'm hoping my heart will start to slide back down my throat."

"Here comes Tony, I'm going to leave you for a minute and meet him just up there on the crosstrees. Follow me there. Harry, stay on the foot line for now."

"OK."

Tony bursts into view exclaiming "One left, Spasiano insisted on joining us but spewed all over the foretop, asked to forego the next scamper. Top's a might slippery, have to watch your step. Ah, but no worries now, up we go."

Tony's easy to spot with his bright yellow jacket. All day he's been a bundle of madcap energy. Now he climbs into the crosstrees, an absurdly small platform three wood planks wide. Margaret is already there.

"Jack, you'd better stay on the foot line."

Makes sense as the other crewman, unrecognizable in his foul weather gear, slowly follows Tony, stopping in the shrouds just below the crosstrees.

"Off we go, Margaret. We'll check to be certain the t'gallant is presentable to these dainties! Right back…tahtah!"

As they scamper away, for the moment it's quiet. Again the *Endeavour* lurches, this time to starboard. Up here the swaying motion is fearsome. What did they say in the briefings? The top of the mast moves five times as much as the deck? The problem is the lurching makes the motion inconsistent, really frightening. A smooth swaying is one thing; this seems impossible to get used to.

A voice, broken up in the wind and rain, comes from my right. "Hey, Jack, isn't it?"

"Yeah. Harry, right?"

"That's me. You OK? This is un–friggin'-believable, absolutely nuts. I love it…I must be crazed! I don't know if I'll laugh or cry! What the shit are we doing here?"

"Don't know man, I'm just trying to hang on."

Harry turns to our new companion standing motionless in the shrouds. "How you doing, buddy?"

"I'm OK, thanks."

There's a thump on the crosstrees. Tony smiles down at each of us as he repeatedly pushes his blond-streaked, long brown hair out of his face. "Here's the plan. Harry, you follow me up, Jack behind Harry. Professor, you climb into the crosstrees and wait for us. When we get to the t'gallant yard, Harry you follow me out to port (left), we'll work together. Jack, you go to starboard (right), Margaret's already waiting for you. We'll just grab the t'gallant and tuck it to bed, no problem!"

Still belly-flopped over the yardarm, I slowly stand up holding onto the yard. I've got to reverse that stunt I did with Margaret, back onto the shrouds, so I can climb past the crosstrees and on up to the topgallant yard. Not sure I can do that again.

Just then a dim light comes on, straight down the topsail mast.

"OK mateys," says Tony, "here's a little light on the subject to help you on your way."

Without thinking I lean out to grab the nearest shroud with my right hand. I step as far as I can with my right foot. My right foot brushes past a ratline but my right hand has a death grip on a shroud. My left foot follows my left arm into the shrouds, landing on a ratline. I'm slightly tangled, my right leg over but dangling from the ratline I missed with my mis-aimed right foot. Still I'm safe…sort of. I slowly stand up and crawl the few ratline steps up onto the cross trees.

Harry's already there. "I'm off…do not think, Jack, just act."

Right. Hell, I'm not thinking, somebody just tell me what to do. Can't stop, that'll be a huge mistake. Just keep going, doing, whatever. Jesus I'm soaked. Damn, my ugly yellow hat just blew off! Now, I'll really be soaked. I take another step up. My head bumps into shoes. Harry must have stopped.

Tony is standing on the port foot lines, shining his little light on the topgallant sail. Good idea, the grayish whiteness of the sail, slightly reflects the flashlight beam, lighting up the yardarm and foot line a little.

"Harry, OK, step out on the foot line and grab the yard." Harry's weight makes the foot line jump and vibrate furiously, but Tony rides along like a high wire performer.

"Hook on. Your job, Harry, is to reach down and gather sail, section by section. I'll help and tie off the gaskets. Slide out a bit, we'll start outboard and work back toward the mast."

Harry clearly is better at this than I am. He quickly attaches his safety hook to the line on the yard and slides each foot along the foot line. Tony hands the flashlight to Harry and he on to Margaret. She lashes it with a gasket to the yardarm. The gaskets are short pieces of line used for gathering the sail hanging down from the yardarm. She angles it to face Tony and Harry. Quickly they are gathering the sail. Tony loops the gasket line under the bunched up sail and cinches it tight to the yard. Harry slides right a little and they do their act again.

Margaret is sitting on the yard starboard of the mast. "You and me, Jack. Let's tidy this side up."

Slowly, while still hanging onto shrouds, I step to the right of the mast and onto the foot line. Next I shift my left foot onto the line, then release my grip on the shrouds transferring my hands to the yard. Margaret still sits on the yard. The foot line does not droop far underneath the yard. I'm nowhere near belly flopped here as below on the topsail yard. Really a difficult position—the yard is only at my thigh, so I can't bend over the yard without feeling certain I'll lose my grip and flip over forward into space.

Margaret slides backward on the yard out into the dark. "Twist your body along the yard, Jack. Sort of lie on the yard and gather sail for me. Keep one foot on the foot line, the other draped over the yard."

Amazingly as the ship rolls and lurches, she sits on the yard quickly looping the line under the portion of the sail she and I have gathered. She cinches it tightly to the underside of the yard. Next she slides forward to the next gasket, flicks it over her shoulder so it drapes free and easy to work with, then repeats the process. For much of the first part of our work, I'm almost motionless, lying on the yard gathering sail with an outstretched right arm while holding on fiercely with my left. When Margaret has cinched the gasket I awkwardly slide backward toward the mast and repeat the same sail gathering.

The ship lurches hard to starboard. For a wild, terrifying moment I think I'll come loose and fall. But, by half lying on the yardarm, my legs are on either side of it, so they instinctively clutch me to the yardarm as *Endeavour* lurches.

A light shines in our general direction. Harry and Tony must be done.

As we get closer to the mast I have no room to lie on the yard. With both arms around the yard and Margaret shouting guidance instructions I manage to get my left foot to join my right on the foot line. In minutes, as I feebly gather chunks of sail and Margaret deftly grabs, loops, cinches, we're done.

Tony and Harry already are in the shrouds, and descending with the light.

Margaret shouts, "Tony, shine the light into the shrouds for us."

Nice touch. Not for "us", but for me.

Slowly we descend ratline by ratline, Tony, Harry, me, followed by Margaret. I hear Tony telling the "professor" to follow him. Tony has tied the flashlight somehow so while it wobbles wildly, it shines generally upward.

"That light's not much use," I complain.

"It would be on anybody but Tony. But he goes ten directions at once."

I can smell the foretop before I arrive. The stench is revolting. Tony stops us in the shrouds well above the platform. He shines the flashlight down on the foretop. Tony's light together with the mainmast fixed light clearly show Spasiano on his knees, with vomit and water all over the platform. Nobody else is there. The four left there earlier have been smart enough to depart the mess.

Tony tells the professor and me to keep going. I pass Harry clinging to the shrouds just above the top. I stop at the severely-angled futtock shrouds. Crouching down a little, I thrust my left leg inward desperately trying to reach a ratline. A firm hand grabs my foot and shoves it onto a ratline.

"Thanks."

"You bet." It's the professor, waiting just below in the lower shrouds to help as I make the past-vertical descent down the futtock shrouds. I see the welcome deck.

"Jack, run and get a broom from the locker next to the crew mess companionway and bring it up. Hurry, that's a good matey!" Tony bends over Spasiano now sprawled motionless, lying on his side.

I step on the starboard railing ready to jump on deck, but someone runs up thrusting a broom at me. I scramble up to the futtock shrouds yelling, "Broom here," as Tony reaches down grabbing it from me.

"Watch out below!" Tony madly sweeps the foretop of Spasiano's spew as I duck and flatten myself against the shrouds. Some of it lands on me.

"Go stand under the main course; the rain water coming off it is like a shower," suggests the professor.

Sure enough, once on deck I stand under the mainsail. In a moment I'm thoroughly wetted down.

The professor and I stand on deck shielding our faces from the rain. "How the hell will they get Spasiano down? He looked totally crapped out up there."

"Listen," says the professor, "Tony's yelling to Harry to come down to the top."

We hear snatches of Tony asking Harry about lowering and carrying Spasiano down.

"Lowering Spasiano? How?"

"Harry's pretty good size and he's a cop...maybe he can handle it."

"But Spasiano's a heavy guy. He must weigh 200 pounds or more and he looked helpless, so it's dead weight."

More talking and gesturing. "Jack and professor...climb the shrouds up here. Go around to the inside of the futtocks, stay there," orders Tony.

We're just into the shrouds next to the railing when a body emerges from the "lubber's hole", a space in the middle of the foretop onto the shrouds and ratlines just under the platform. We can hear Tony shouting at someone, so must be Harry.

Tony shouts down to us, "Climb up on either side of Harry. Margaret and I have tied off Spasiano under his arms and will lower him onto Harry's back. We have a second line tying his wrists together. We'll use that after Spasiano is on Harry's back to drape his arms over Harry's head onto his chest. You two position yourselves on either side of Harry. Grab each other's wrist under Spasiano's butt helping Harry with this dead load. Spasiano is conscious but out of it. Got it?"

"OK." We scramble up next to Harry who has flattened himself against the shrouds just under the lubber's hole.

"Harry, you OK? Can you handle this?"

"Half-ass fireman's carry. Just because I'm a cop, Tony tags me. Here he comes."

Harry ducks his head between shrouds as Tony and Margaret slowly lower Spasiano by running his line over the edge of the platform thereby gaining slight help controlling Spasiano's dead weight. As he slides down Harry's back, the professor and I grab each other's wrist under Spasiano's sizeable butt. The deadweight strain on our arms is immediate and intense. Our grips are already slipping.

As the arms come over his head, Harry roars into Spasiano's ear, *"Grab my belt goddamn it!"* Spasiano's eyes blink open he shudders and grabs a little handful of Harry's shirt. Harry hooks his left arm around a shroud, with his right hand quickly yanks Spasiano's hands down onto his belt. "Here, damn it!" The strain is a little less.

One step and my feet bump into futtock shrouds heading from the foremast out to the foretop. We're on the inside of the futtock shrouds. We've got to get this whole crowd around those shrouds to the outside.

Tony calls out to the deck, "Need some more hands up here." Quickly two bodies clamber up the port shrouds to the foretop.

"Harry, we'll pull Spasiano up slightly. Jack and professor let him go. Harry then move around the futtocks onto the lower shrouds and we'll re-settle him on your back there."

With the extra help from the deck, Spasiano is lifted up a few inches. The professor and I let go as Harry scrambles onto the lower shrouds and ratlines. The professor and I join him, reassembling into our strange little group, now surrounded by several others who've joined us in the shrouds. Four or five sets of hands are now on Spasiano's bent, soaked body as we descend slowly, step by step. The *Endeavour* lurches yet again. But with so many hands on Spasiano and each other, the dead weight load is minimized, and the effect of the lurch is nothing. As we reach the railing, gently we turn Harry and Spasiano inboard. Hands reach up to grab the nearly inert body, lift it off Harry and carry it toward the mess deck companionway.

I start to jump off the railing onto the deck. No, no, bad idea, way too tired and shaky. Demurely, I sit on the railing and slide gently off for a short jump/ fall on my feet to the deck.

Margaret arrives on the railing, calls out to the Spasiano procession moving across the deck, "Michael, take him below, have him get cleaned up in a hot shower, new clothes and up here on deck. Find a sheltered spot amidships. He'll survive, though presently he surely doubts it."

A booming voice commands "All hands to sailing stations! Let's move, children!"

*   *   *   *   *

Tony's suddenly standing next to Harry, pointing at me. "Jack, you and Harry come here." A few quick steps and he's standing next to the portside rail, his hand resting on a formidable looking line tied in a figure eight to heavy wood crosspieces. "Listen carefully, you're going to have to learn fast. This line is the fore course brace." Pointing to a strong-looking post mounted on the deck, "This is a 'bitt'. Loosen the brace to two turns around the bitt and be ready, both of you holding the line. You're going to be hauling in on the brace. Hauling and taking turns of the line onto the bitt will swing the sail to the left. We're shifting course to the right, so first we'll be spilling some wind, then getting it back by 'bracing up' this lee brace. Doing this will re-fill the sail with wind. Got it?"

"That means we're heading more south, no longer east, right?"

"You're bloody James Cook himself, Ashburn, what a navigator! This is a hard pull. I'll send you some help if I can. Keep several turns of line on the bitt once you start hauling. Listen for the commands. When you hear 'belay', one of you hang on, and the other tie off the line to this cleat. Take the line down its left side, make three figure eights over the cleat, run it around the back and loop it. Got that?"

A quick nod from Harry and Tony's gone. We can hear him talking animatedly with the professor and Andrew, a tall, sharp-featured, skinny guy. I've already noticed Andrew because he has talked by far the most among our Foremast group, seemingly very confident of what he knows about the *Endeavour*. They quickly walk over to Tony standing next to the ship's bell, itself framed by a short but sturdy arch, painted red, just behind the foremast. The heavy red frame for the bell has several cleats on it. Tony is gesturing and yelling loud enough for Harry and me to hear, "Haul in on this fore t'gallant brace on command, to properly align the t'gallant. Listen for the commands, I'll relay them."

Tony and the other captains-of-the-tops keep scurrying around shouting instructions to their crews. It's a din of bewildering shouts. Belay this, hold that, haul away on some other line—"crojacks", "downhauls", "buntlines", "truss tackle", "jeer bitts"; quickly it becomes meaningless.

The stern-faced, heavy-set First Mate yells, "Easing on starboard, hauling on port, haul away." Tony goes through a series of specific commands, one of which is "haul on fore course lee brace".

Harry exclaims, "That's us!" Starting to haul, we quickly feel the hard tug of the wind in the fore course sail. Holding it from slipping out of our hands is hard enough. "We could use a winch handle", says Harry.

"Sure could," I say, "but not likely; let's take another turn." Such a modern sailing aid is surely not going to be part of a painstaking replica like the *Endeavour*.

Andrew bellows, "You've got too much luff in the fore course!" None of his business. Tony appears suddenly, pulls violently down on the line. That gives us some slack in the lower portion of the line, enabling us to wrap a loop of line onto the brace. Tony moves quickly off to another sailing station.

"Keep going!" shouts Andrew. "You need to haul in much more."

"No shit," grumbles Harry. He grabs the line above the brace, and jumps in the air to hang all his weight from his grip on it. I feel a little slack in the line, and struggle furiously to get one coil of line onto the brace. We repeat this maneuver several more times, gaining scant inches each time.

Andrew appears next to me, "Can't you guys get this done?"

"Go back to your station."

The professor yells out, "Andrew, get back here."

He continues to glare at me. "Get the fore course around!"

Harry glances at me. "That was helpful."

An Australian voice in my ear shouts, "Could use some help, mate?"

"Sure could."

The Aussie crewman is covered head-to-toe in slops, so impossible to recognize. He smiles at Harry. "Join your mate behind the brace." He climbs up on the railing next to our brace. Grabbing the line, he jerks down hard on it as he leans far over the deck keeping his feet on the railing and pushing off with his legs. "Grab it," he yells, as Harry and I frantically haul at least a foot of tension-free line onto the bitt.

A moment later the First Mate orders, "Belay!" With the Aussie we manage to tie off the brace to the cleat below the bitt. He's immediately off aft toward the mainmast.

"Check your fore course brace!" thunders the First Mate.

I start to say, "It seems OK…" as Tony arrives at our station and unties the line from the cleat. Carefully, with Harry's help he eases the brace one turn on the bitt.

"You mateys are too strong for the gentle *Endeavour*, too taut!"

The wind is sheeting the rain almost sideways, drenching me. The *Endeavour* continues to roll sickeningly. For the first time I notice the nasty sound of people retching. Peering into the dark I make out figures scattered on the deck around me. I realize they're crew members being sick into buckets, or directly over the side.

The same Aussie crewman walks by. "That's the 'spew crew'. Best you ignore'em, too easy to join'em."

Thank God I haven't been sick…yet. I've usually been OK while boating, but then again I haven't been on a boat tossing around like this. Maybe the distractions help.

The crewman tells us to "Take ten minutes. Go grab a cup of tea in the 'twentieth century'."

The *Endeavour* is a nearly exact replica of the HM Bark *Endeavour*, the converted collier Captain James Cook, in 1768-71, sailed around South America. His journey took the ship through the southern Pacific to New Zealand, the east coast of Australia, the Dutch East Indies, the Cape of Good Hope in southern Africa and home to England. On this epic voyage Cook made extraordinarily accurate charts of all his travels, which were later renowned for their exceptionally precise usefulness to generations of navigators. Our version of the *Endeavour*, while a faithful replica built as much as possible using the original method of construction, also necessarily contains some modern equipment—auxiliary diesel engines, top quality navigation electronics and communications gear, and a modern galley nicknamed "the twentieth century".

The ship has four decks—the weather deck on top; below it running basically beneath the quarterdeck portion is the after-fall deck which contains the great cabin where officers and accompanying "gentlemen" gathered, the Captain's cabin and gentlemen's cabins; lower down is the "mess deck" where the seamen sleep, with numerous storage lockers; finally below that is the hold which houses the galley, two diesel engines, electrical generators, showers and heads, watermakers and various ship supplies.

Harry and I stumble down through the "sailors' mess" where all the crew hammocks are slung. The noise is startling—all matter of snorts, whistles, full-blown snores, grunts, several people murmuring curses at the hammocks as they flop around trying to scramble into them. They must be the off-watch crewmen. We descend to the next deck down. Here we suddenly leave the eighteenth century behind and emerge into a brightly-lit stainless steel galley with wood benches and long tables all fixed to the deck. Everything is neat, spotlessly clean, warm and smelling of fresh-baked breads and coffee.

"Jesus, Jack, I'm requesting kitchen duty! This is where I belong!"

A chunky blond woman smiles brightly at Harry. "I'll be sure to give you some special project when it's your turn here. But for now, how 'bout a nice cup of tea?"

"Any possibility for something stronger? Can I claim my 'grog' rights?" I know it's a useless request, but it's a chance for a little light moment which I sure could use now.

She replies, "Ah these insurance companies, no sense of humor or history! They have no respect for the rights of sailors now. You'd think a bunch of amateurs sailing an eighteenth-century square-rigger would be an acceptable risk to allow alcohol and selected other vices, wouldn't you? It's a wonder we love them so."

"Well, if you'll lead the protest movement against the insurance carrier, I'll follow you. But for now tea it is."

"How about a little Vegemite on toast? Always plenty of Vegemite in my galley!" Vegemite is the incredibly bitter Australian spread that looks as appetizing as soft tar.

"No, thanks, had some earlier and don't want to take more than my fair share!"

She smirks. "Right, I'll make sure you get plenty when you're on duty here; don't want you to be deprived after all!" Thanks.

Harry sighs. "What an incredible night! I wasn't sure I wouldn't fall or quit or cry! The motion up above the foretop was un-goddamn-believable. I didn't know whether to look up or look down, and either way I couldn't see shit! Maybe it was better in the dark, at least we couldn't see much. I'll tell you though, Tony and Margaret are very cool and very quick. Without them, forget it, I'm on the deck, period."

Surprised, I looked at Harry. He's a pretty formidable-looking man, well over six feet, blocky, almost square, big arms and hands. He wears his dark hair in a short, military-style haircut like lots of cops, but has an open, friendly face with surprisingly bright blue eyes. "Man, you got to be kidding! You looked like you knew what you were doing, looked solid. I was barely functioning. If I thought at all it was what an incredibly stupid mistake it was to be there! Didn't you say in this morning's intro meeting you were a cop, I think, in DC?"

"Yeah, wasn't a lot of prep for this, huh? What about you?"

"I've been in executive search for years. Absolutely no training there."

Margaret strides into the galley. "Hi, Annie—have a quick cup to go, please. Hey mates, Tony wants all Foremasts on deck. Captain will give us some poop."

Tony gathers the Foremast crew around the Captain, standing in what little "lee of the storm" there is, behind some canvas put up around the companionway to the sailors' mess. With help from permanent crew members holding flashlights, he unfolds a big chart, holding it down on the deck. As we squint through the sheeting rain he describes our position at the far eastern end of Long Island Sound. The sail adjustments we made enable us to head southeast past Plum Island at the tip of Long Island, toward the Atlantic Ocean. He explains we'll continue southeast into the Atlantic Ocean then slowly sweep around to the east, later changing our course north toward Martha's Vineyard, and eventually west into Rhode Island Sound and on into Newport Harbor, our final destination. He goes on to say we'll get three more days and nights of "blue water sailing". The *Endeavour* will track back and forth in this large, open sea area. By the morning of the fifth day, we'll be in Rhode Island Sound heading for Newport. "You people signed on for five days of square-rigger sailing and you'll get them. Weather should moderate tomorrow, but this little squall with its 25-30 knots of wind will be with us 'til the Forenoon watch. Pleasant news for the spew crew."

We sailed out of Norwalk, Connecticut yesterday noon. Along with twenty-six other "voyage crew" members, I've not only volunteered but paid $750 for the privilege of sailing on the *Endeavour*. We've been divided into three watch crews—Mainmast, Mizzenmast and Foremast. My Foremast watch was on duty as we left Norwalk. Yesterday we powered and sailed amidst—what from my station on the mizzen top, a small platform midway up the mizzenmast—looked like maritime pandemonium. Dozens of power and sailboats of all sizes and shapes accompanied us in a narrow channel. Some darted in and out like maddened insects. All were waving and shouting and blowing horns. The *HMS Rose*, a locally refit replica of a naval frigate, sailed with us for a time once we cleared Norwalk Harbor. Much faster, she quickly sailed away. We made our slow, stately eastward passage up the Sound, passing Bridgeport and New Haven. Our large crowd of escort boats slowly diminished as the wind picked up from the southwest, and sheeting rain arrived. Darkness fell and the accompanying boats finally dropped away to none.

Enthusiastic plans to build a replica of the HM Bark *Endeavour* had materialized several times since the 1960s, usually to stall and ultimately fail. Whitby, England, the port in which the original was built as a collier, was the first to try unsuccessfully. Ten years later, the Aussies tried to capitalize on the James Cook Bicentennial celebrations in Sydney without any better results. In 1988 the Australian government approved plans for a national maritime museum. The trustees of the new museum agreed to support the building of a replica ship. The Bond Corporation of Australia, famous in sailing circles for Alan Bond's sponsorship of the victorious America's cup yacht *Australia*, offered to fund the project as a gift to Australia's 1988 Bicentennial. In keeping with earlier support for the replica, even here the idea stumbled before final resolution. First, the Bond Corporation, then reeling toward insolvency, pulled out. It was replaced by Yoshiya Corporation of Japan. They quickly thought better of it and abandoned the project after five months. Finally, a foundation, created with the support of Britain's National Maritime Museum, finished the project in 1994.

Building the *Endeauvour* replica was something of a spectator sport. She was constructed in a Fremantle, Australia shipyard with a gallery. Visitors were able to virtually peer over the shoulders of the project team. The romantic nature of the project was powerful lure, a magnet for passionate interest. Shipwrights, artisans, trades people came to the project as true believers. While grudgingly conceding the need for dependable power, along with first rate communications and navigation systems, the ardor for a replica true to the original was intense. The project team however was faced with the ever-present dilemma of such projects—the reality of available materials, skills and funds versus the worthy aspirations of passion and purity. Not surprisingly, the project constantly was forced into compromises. Right away, the project was faced with what materials and tools could be used. Building the replica with the exact same materials and tools was a noble concept which simply could not be done.

Researchers burrowing in naval archives found the plans describing the refitting of the collier (coal-carrying ship) *Earl of Pembroke* into the *Endeavour*, plans commissioned by the Royal Navy and endorsed by King George III himself. They learned the original was built of oak, with an elm keel and apparently Baltic pine for decks, topsides, masts and spars. Unfortunately, oak is fine for sailing in cold northern waters. However, it is given to rot in tropical waters in which the replica likely would spend much of its life. Local hardwoods replaced northern woods—jarrah replaced oak, Douglas or Oregon fir replaced pine. Here even the compromise failed. The fir was cut and shipped from northern hemisphere forests in winter. The timber arrived in hot summer Australia only to crack. As a remedy, the project team ingenuously devised a sophisticated laminating process. Each spar and mast was finished with an extremely strong sheath of planking.

Not unexpectedly, the passion to do the right thing included a preservationist's zeal for tree protection. Recycled wood was used wherever possible, often from wonderfully strange sources—an old timber bridge, a wartime munitions factory, even an abandoned nunnery. The team collected timber felled during road construction work. Some timbers literally were manhandled out of state forests in which vehicles and work animals are banned.

Other clever, well intentioned and workable compromises appear all over the ship. All planking was fastened using wooden nails. However, below the waterline, coach bolts were used. Each timber was treated with a preservative and coated with red lead. Modern paints and varnishes were used with preserving chemicals, but matched by research to original eighteenth-century colors. The ship's miles of rope were a major challenge. The original used hemp rope, unfortunately long out of favor for marine purposes. Eventually three different ropes were used—polyester, polypropylene and pre-stretched manila. The standard eighteenth-century European sail material was flax, also no longer used. Flax was replaced with a Scottish man-made material, Duradon.

Despite the constant push-pull of compromise and ingenuity, the overall effect seems startlingly authentic. The smells, motion, noises all seem associated not with the twentieth century, but with an earlier time.

The Captain says, "Tony, put two new people at the wheel, the rest to the fore course yard to take a reef in her. Mainmast will be up shortly, I'll have them reef the main course."

Tony responds, "Harry and Jack, you had so much fun before, let's let the others get to play. You take the wheel, everybody else with me to our spanking clean top!"

Great! This is a moment I've been looking forward to…steering the *Endeavour!*

The voyage crewman at the wheel motions me over. "You better keep a careful eye on those lights well off the port bow. See 'em? They're big and seeming to get bigger. Don't know what the hell they are, but we're pretty sure the Officer of the Deck hasn't seen them yet."

TWO

The Officer of the Deck points to me, "Muscle", and to Harry, "Brains". Just as I start to suggest he reverse the descriptions, I realize he's pointing for me to stand next to the wheel. OK, who cares if the descriptions need reversing; I'm at the wheel.

"Your job is simply to hold the course. 'Brains' will tell you the adjustments that need to be made. He'll tell you a certain number of spokes to left or right." He smiles. "As an alert crewman you will have noticed the wheel has spokes, and your counting skills quickly will enable you to change course correctly."

Harry now is standing behind the port side instrumentation lectern and binnacle. Like other deck furniture and fixtures, it is painted an incongruous bright red. It has several gauges each virtually unreadable in the nearly black gloom. On top is the binnacle in which sits a large compass. Harry's staring at its faintly visible horizon, back-lit by a dim light. The officer steps over to Harry. "Your job is to constantly watch the compass. You'll notice it gyrates a bit so you can't make precise changes. You give course changes when you see the needle stray more than five degrees from our directed course. Let's watch together, shall we?

"New 'Muscle' takes over from old 'Muscle', by standing to his right. Place your hands on the wheel exactly as his are. Old Muscle shifts away by sliding out to the left as New Muscle slides in to the left. Ready? Go!

"Such a sweet shuffle, you two will make wonderful dance partners. Ah, 'Brains', look—it turns out they're not good dance partners, what a disappointment. What's happened to the course?"

Harry, staring at the needle, says, "Well, we were on SSE, south-southeast, 165 degrees; we're now closer to S, south, 180 degrees."

"Yes, right on. This is not good. Our course is south-southeast, so we must get back there. Do you agree?"

I catch a glimpse of Harry glancing at the officer with a slight nod. Harry does not look particularly happy.

The officer continues, "So, I suggest, generally make little changes, not big ones. You'll tell 'Muscle' here what to do in the number of spokes to move right or left. For now, we want to 'fall off' the wind so we should turn the wheel to the left. Don't make exaggerated changes. We don't want to yaw, which is the same thing as fishtail, along our course. Captain would not be thrilled. So, let's correct by moving the wheel two spokes to the left, see how that works. 'Brains', give those instructions to 'Muscle'."

"Course correction, two spokes to port."

The wind remains strong, rain still sleeting diagonally at us. Squinting into the rain, bound up in my miserable slops, slipping on the wet deck, even turning the wheel two spokes is a struggle. I bend my knees, then move around to the left of the wheel, trying to pull down the two spokes amount. Slowly I get two spokes to the left, with a little help from the officer. I turn to Harry, "Two spokes to port."

The officer smiles and says, "See, the course is correcting slowly toward south-southeast. Watch it carefully, that it settles within five degrees of south-southeast. Now for the fun part, 'Brains', you have to remember not only your last command, but how many spokes you've moved from 'midships', the wheel's original position. Being kind and caring people, we've given you a prompt. When the wheel is at midships, the spoke straight up and down has a wrapping of heavy thread on it. 'Muscle', feel around the wheel to that spoke, tell us where it is."

I fumble from spoke to spoke finally feeling it to my left, three spokes from the top. I tell Harry where it is, "Midships three spokes to port", as the officer sternly warns, "You must know that at all times. Also, 'Brains', you'll help 'Muscle' shift the wheel if needed." He wanders aft as we settle in, me grasping the ever-tugging wheel, Harry staring at the compass.

Soon it is apparent the *Endeavour* has a "weather helm". While it moves with a heavy, sluggish feel, it keeps turning toward the wind. I can't hold it from this constant thrust to starboard, so every few minutes Harry orders a correction back to port.

Our concentration on our constant small course corrections has our total focus. I jump as a loud voice right behind me demands, "Damn it, what are those lights on the port bow?"

Shit, forgot all about what the previous 'Muscle' said. How'd I lose sight of the lights? Now they're suddenly looming out of the darkness only several hundred yards distant. It's a distinct frame of lights, with one lower green light just visible on the lower right of the higher lights. Must be a large ship headed toward us. How far away is it? What's it doing here? Can't it see us on radar?

I recognize the voice right behind me, as he commands, "Helm, ten spokes to starboard!" It's the Captain. Wearing only a blue slicker and shorts he has appeared without warning. He's right behind me and moves up next to me, "Come on, man, bend into it." He's a slight man whose receding brown hair is being whipped around by the wind. Scowling he grabs the right side of the wheel and together we start to move the wheel to the right. I stand on its left pushing spokes up toward the Captain as he pulls them down on the right side, all the while counting spokes. We get to ten spokes surprisingly fast, but the *Endeavour* hardly seems to move. After a moment, slowly she starts to turn slightly starboard.

I look up at the ship lights and they seem not to have moved left or right, but definitely are bigger, taller. "Five more spokes to starboard." Pushing and pulling we move five more spokes up and to the right side of the wheel.

"She's well clear," says the Captain looking to port. Sure enough, we start to see the lights differently. The ship is well away and bearing off. Lights now are visible along the side of the ship.

I can hear the deck officer laughing with the Captain. "I bet that skipper crapped the bed when someone finally noticed us on radar! When's the last time he saw anything along his course into New London at night in a squall!

"OK, 'Brains', join in with 'Muscle' at the wheel; let's get back on course."

The rest of the Foremast watch arrives back on deck from reefing the fore course, the lowest sail on the foremast. Tony jumps up the steps leading to the quarterdeck where the helm is located. He's trailing two voyage crew members.

"Switcheroo, my mateys. Time's up, your watch mates Christopher and Alice are relieving you. Pray they can sail a safe course after you mateys tried to collide with a tanker! And before we've learned our 'Abandon Ship' procedures no less."

I'd chatted with Christopher Peoples intermittently during our morning briefings yesterday. Short and chunky, nearly bald except for a fringe of dark brown hair, wearing thick rimless eyeglasses, he is a quiet, serious Department of Justice attorney. This sail is his retirement present to himself, a little adventure travel before he settled into an early retirement from government service. I watched him approach wondering how he viewed his choice of adventure travel now. He smiles ruefully at me. Alice Chatham is the only female member of our Foremast watch. Young and attractive, she has an athletic look and short brown hair. She was the fastest climber when Tony took us yesterday on our brief introductory climbs to the foretop. Smiling at Harry, she asks, "How was the t'gallant yard, Mr. Cassis?"

"It's Harry, Alice. A piece of cake, you shoulda been there. Lots of laughs."

"You're not smiling, Harry," grins Christopher.

"Nope."

The Officer of the Watch steps forward. "OK then, Alice, in deference to your feminine wiles you'll be 'Brains' and Christopher 'Muscle'. Let me explain."

As we hand over helm duties Tony tells Harry and me to "kickback" for fifteen minutes, but stay within "shouting distance".

Harry considers this, saying, "Guess that means stay on deck. Let's find some shelter."

"How about we go next to the companionway where the Captain briefed us?"

Harry turns to acknowledge my suggestion and walks smack into the replica carriage gun mounted on the quarterdeck. He falls over the gun but grabs onto its slippery iron surface before falling to the deck.

"I'm gonna turn into one big goddamn bruise on this ship, Jesus!"

We reach what little shelter the companionway canvas provides. Struggling around to its lee side, we crouch down trying to get somewhat out of the rain.

"So Harry, what provoked this madness for you?"

"Hah, madness is right. I don't know...needed a break from all the garbage I have to deal with in DC. Saw the *Endeavour* when she was in Alexandria. A few years ago I saw the *Eagle* and some tall ships in Baltimore, and got all fired up about crewing on one. I sail a fair amount; I've got a little day sailor on the Potomac. So, all together I guess it 'seemed like a good idea at the time'. This thing is sure as hell out of my league! It's my own fault, I love doing this kind of stuff. I always seem to get in trouble volunteering for 'real' experiences like this!"

"I'll tell you I'm really looking forward to dawn. Climbing around this thing is tough enough, but in the dark, it's off the charts."

"Jack, if we're still up here at dawn I'll be one whipped puppy. And I'm afraid that may be the case. You know what time it is?"

"No idea."

"I have 3:30 in the morning."

"You're joking me!"

"Time flies when you're having fun, Jack. So, what got you here?"

"I saw it down in Florida a few months ago. I was down to see a friend in Palm Beach, do some fishing, catch a couple of spring training games. He had to work one of the days so I went down to Fort Lauderdale to this place on the water for lunch. Right there they have a good size launch that takes people on little cruises. Big sign says they're departing at two o'clock to view a square-rigged ship sailing along the coast. That sounds like fun, so I order a couple beers and a sandwich and jump in the launch. It turns out it's the *Endeavour* we go to see. The skipper of the launch gives us a running commentary including how you can sign up to sail on her. It's a beautiful day, light air, looks like fun. The masts look tall as hell, but I figure I probably can climb at least part way up and maybe I won't have to. But, I just liked the idea of being on the ship…like you, having a real experience, not just looking at her. I've been reading the great Patrick O'Brian naval history novels. Being on a replica of a ship of the same era seemed a way to better appreciate the novels. But most of all I could just see myself on the *Endeavour,* having an adventure, a terrific experience."

"Sounds like a kinda macho thing for you a little, huh?"

"Maybe some, but I just wanted to see myself part of it, not just watching. I tend to think that way, for better or worse, often worse! Sometimes I go out of my way to find something a little different to experience, something a little special."

Tony walks over. "Mainmast will be on deck in fifteen minutes. You're going to get a fine two hours' sleep, my beauties!"

My first try at sleep earlier tonight, however, had been, at first, a little piece of slapstick comedy, later uncomfortable misery. Tony had shown us where to hang our hammocks in the crew's mess. There is virtually no swaying room, each hammock about eighteen inches apart from its neighbors. In his typically funny, casual Australian style, Tony quickly showed us a knot for securing both ends of the hammock. "Use this, or lots of half hitches, or just lots of knots, whatever, you won't enjoy falling on the deck."

After finally getting his knot and repeatedly jerking on each end to insure it will handle my weight, I hoisted myself into the hammock. I teetered wildly kneeling in the hammock, and promptly fell out the other side. On the next try I settled into it on my back as the hammock wrapped itself around me like a mummy cloth. My arms were force folded tightly across my chest, shoulders tightly bound, feet far above my head. After much pulling and shoving, my head was at least as high as my feet. Something lightly bumped my head. Turning slightly to my left, I was face-to-face with someone's feet. Turning to my right, a watch mate was still fumbling and grumbling over knotting the hammock securely. I apologize to him, pointing to my little bag of extra clothing and a pillow under my hammock, explaining I needed to get hold of it. "I'm afraid I'll never get back in the hammock if I unwrap myself now."

Sweating profusely, he smiles. "At least you're in," and hands me the bag.

The noise of chatter, the occasional falling body thudding to the deck, crewmen clambering up and down stairs to the heads in the ship's hold, laughter and groans, were to make sleep utterly out of the question. Never having slept on my back, I experimented with modest changes in my sleeping position. Slowly, hesitatingly, I rolled onto my side, carefully shoving the little pillow I'd brought along under my head. Not too bad, might be able to sleep a little like this.

"I'm in!" exclaims my neighbor. But he bumped me, then again and again...something's wrong. He's not swinging like I am. Regularly his shoulder bumps into the foot end of my hammock. Not helpful for sleeping. Pointing to his other side he moans, "There's a stanchion right here. I keep bouncing off it."

Great, a hammock mate with the wrong rhythm.

The Mainmast watch musters on the quarterdeck and Foremast is released from watch. We all head directly to the gloom of the sailors' mess. Exhausted, I drop my foul rain gear next to the slop chest, then holding onto stanchions, bulkheads, beams, whatever helps for balance, I search for my hammock. There's no chatter now, but the noise is similar to what we heard on our way down to the twentieth century—snorts, snores, whimpers, the ship's timbers creaking and groaning, even the thrumming rattle of the rigging. I see my hammock, number ten, and carefully hoist myself up to a sitting position, turn slowly on my back, then even more slowly on my left side.

"Foremast hands, Foremast…you're wasting a beautiful day! On your feet, we're first breakfast seating."

Shocked and stunned, I jolt awake grabbing the edge of the hammock. It's too late. I'm twisting upside down and falling to the deck. All my grabbing does is slightly break my fall. Dizzy and disoriented, I hear someone say, "Morning there!"

Looking up I see it's my arrhythmic hammock mate grinning down at me. "Graceful. By the way, you make some serious noise when you sleep."

Really, never been told I snore. "It must be the hammock."

"Whatever, you'll need to muffle that hole, man, too much."

Damn I'm sore. My hands are black with the tar that coats all the rigging. My body is sore all over. Leg and arm muscles feel miserable, feet hurt, everything tender or just plain hurting. Why do my feet hurt? I had noticed my docksiders didn't seem to give much support in the rigging. I'll try sneakers today, they have thicker soles, might help. For now though, I've got to get a shower. Grabbing my soap and towel I head for the showers forward on the next lower deck. Half way down the stairs I can hear Andrew, "Two minute showers, no more than two minutes!" Anything will do. Arriving in the showers area I join a line of men undressing and shuffling along toward the little showers. Finally in one, I wash my filthy hands and face and just stand there water beating on my face. "Time's up, next!"

A few minutes later, dressed in the same dirty shorts and "*Endeavour* World Voyage" jersey, I spot the professor and Andrew at the end of a booth in "the twentieth century". Taking a heaping bowl of "porridge", toast and tea, I sit down with them.

The professor is saying, "This galley was such an incredibly welcome place coming off watch. I really didn't want to leave it last night. I still don't!" He's slumped well over his porridge, eating by bending his wrist only. His posture suggests he feels as tired and sore as I do. Younger, maybe late forties, he's small and wiry, has longish, thinning sandy hair, curling down his neck. I notice his

31

hands, very long fingers, so long I can hardly see the spoon he's using to slowly, regularly scoop up the dark brown porridge.

"But it's so out of whack with the experience we're supposed to have," complains Andrew. "It's 1998 and we're supposed to have an eighteenth-century experience. We only have a 'sort of' eighteenth-century experience when you have this place, the showers and heads, and all the other modern conveniences. Couldn't they have been a little cleverer, or at least honest? Did you see the '"nav" station' off the great cabin?"

"That's not a very realistic complaint, Andrew," says the professor. "Obviously the replica has obligations—safety, a schedule to keep, good food for the crew. Besides it seems silly not to have modern systems that are available, as long as she still sails like the original *Endeavour*."

Andrew exclaims, "That's exactly the point! It's not sailing like the original sailed when you have two Caterpillar diesels, generators for electrical power, this fancy galley, computers, electronic navigation and communication systems, showers and heads, and all the rest. It's a false premise!"

"Andrew, I said 'sails like', not meaning the whole voyage, just the actual sailing."

A slight pause allows me to break in. "Hi guys, Jack Ashburn."

The professor turns to me, "Yes, hello Jack, I'm Walter Buckingham. Sorry I didn't introduce myself during our early morning adventures. This is Andrew Braun."

"Why does Tony call you the professor, Walter?"

"I teach colonial history at the University of Rhode Island. I got onboard early yesterday morning and was telling Tony a little about colonial Newport before everybody else arrived. He decided to call me 'the professor'."

I stick out my hand to Andrew, who looks at it for a second, glances at me and shakes hands, "Hi". He's young, maybe late twenties, has a startlingly thin face, long patrician nose, thinning blond hair, and round, rimless eyeglasses, all topped with what appears to be a brand new black "Princeton" baseball cap with an orange "P" on the front.

Andrew continues, "It's a false premise because the Aussies went to such great lengths to make the replica like the original. All this modern equipment flies in the face of that effort at integrity. I mean, they had the drawings and plans of the ship when she was refit from being the collier *Earl of Pembroke* to the bark

Endeavour. They followed the plans as closely as possible, only replacing European woods with those found in Australia. The dimensions and measures are the same, all fastened and caulked with traditional stuff like wood trunnels and caulking made of oakum and pitch. All the bolts and spikes and blocks and hinges, even cannons, and rigging made of manila coated with tar, reflect their efforts at building a true replica."

"How do you know all this, Andrew?"

"I read all about it in a design magazine, then went online to look at it, and visited it on vacation. They should have been more honest, do it entirely right or don't do it at all. It's too much of a compromise."

"Pretty harsh review." I sprinkle more sugar on the porridge. It wasn't tasting very good, probably because there's no skim milk so I was mixing water and whole milk together, failing to get even close to a skim milk taste.

Andrew stands up. "Either do it or don't, just don't do it halfway." He turns away, dumping his tray in a nearby bin.

"So why'd he sign on?" I ask the professor.

He smiles. "Fair question, why don't you ask him? I'm a little tired of having breakfast with an irate bumble bee. I keep fending off little stings, about this and that of eighteenth-century ship design. What do I know? I'm an archeologist used to teaching history to bored undergraduates, not to a know-it-all architect. Sorry, that wasn't very fair. I guess I'm little short of sleep, and too tired to be understanding.

"We better go, have to stow away our gear and hammocks before 7:00."

I bolt a few more gulps of porridge, two pieces of cold toast with terrific blueberry jam, steaming hot tea, and head for the stairs back to the sailors' mess.

The Foremast crew members are rolling all the possessions they brought aboard into their hammocks. They're tying the hammocks tightly, each with a piece of line provided. Then they're checking the hammock for proper size by passing it through a twelve-inch-diameter rope loop. The hammocks are then to be stored in a forward corner of the sailors' mess.

"Foremast on deck!"

With no chance to pass my hammock through the rope loop, I bend over, scurry forward barely under the low beams of the sailors' mess, toss my hammock in the Foremast pile. Turning, I remember to duck, trotting up the companionway stairs. Tony has the Foremast watch assembled next to the carving of a very large, bright red head mounted just aft of the foremast.

Christopher turns to Harry as I reach the group, patting the head, "Who is this red man?"

Harry replies, "Don't know, but he's either very embarrassed or very sunburned!" The group titters, as Tony announces, "He is a fierce and mighty Foremast sailor who eats voyage crew for snacks. First Mate's inspection will be next. We're assigned to clean the entire sailors' mess, because we're not on deck 'til the forenoon watch at 0800."

A shout is bellowed from deep inside the ship. "Hammock 10! Who the hell has hammock 10? Report here immediately!"

Damn, that's mine.

The First Mate is hunched over my hammock poking at it with his foot. "What is this clumsy mess? It looks like a huge fat snake with a pig in its belly! Did you bring a snake and a pig onboard my ship? Why would you do that to my ship?"

No sir, sorry sir, I'll fix it up, sir.

Thankfully, he moves along, bellowing out another hammock number for attack and embarrassment.

Tony, trailed by the entire Foremast watch, is crouched in the half light of the forward hold, smiling at me. "Stay away from the fierce Foremast head; he's mighty pissed at you, and ready to take a big bite out of your sorry ass!"

"Stay here," he says to me as he assigns cleaning tasks to the watch—sweeping, scrubbing, washing every surface area of the mess. "Here's a toothbrush. Your reward for such good behavior is to scrub the seams between each deck plank. By the way, what's the 'pig' in your hammock?"

"My foul weather gear and a sleeping bag."

"Obviously you didn't read our meticulously prepared instructions sent to all voyage crew. If you had, you'd have seen we take care of all that gear including the beautiful garments you got to wear last night and will again today. So pull the pig out of your hammock, take it forward to the locker just aft of the "gentlemen's quarters" and stow it in there. Nary a word to anyone about the locker."

"Thanks, Tony."

Slowly going up and down the mess deck plank-by-plank actually is pleasant. I occasionally dip the toothbrush in a little jar of detergent. Each stroke makes a modest difference slightly brightening a seam. All my body parts are for the most part at rest except my right hand and arm. I'm too sore to kneel, so I slide along on my butt. Tony later hands Andrew a toothbrush to help. Andrew finished his dusting task too early, and glowers as he furiously brushes a seam.

"All hands finish your jobs in ten minutes and prepare for inspection. No sitting, stand over here by the companionway."

Soon the First Mate bounds down the companionway. Running his white-gloved hand along and under a table he thunders, "Who cleaned this disgusting table…look at my glove!" Sure enough it's a bit soiled. Tony gestures to a watch mate who furiously rubs a cloth all over and under the table. "This deck isn't clean; there are dust balls everywhere!" as he points to one drifting along the starboard edge of the deck. Christopher scoots over to the offending area broom in hand. The First Mate reaches up, running his hand along the top edge of several beams as Tony smirks happily. Apparently Tony's knowledge of this trick has worked. No comment from the First Mate.

"This work warrants only a barely passing grade." As he turns to leave, the First Mate glowers at Tony who, remarkably, winks back at him.

Harry growls, "How smart are we? We're paying $750 each to have as much fun as recruits at Parris Island boot camp."

Tony replies, "Ah, but your instructors are so much smarter, more handsome and generally better company, don't you agree? Grab your slops; we're due on deck in twenty minutes."

It's barely light out, gray sky and sea, rain still pelting down, wind still blowing hard.

"Vincent, isn't it?" I notice that Spasiano is among the cluster of us pulling out foul weather gear. "Feeling any better?"

He looks up with a sad half smile. "Thanks for asking. You're the first person who's even spoken to me. A little better, nothing left to throw up that's for sure. I took two Centrum multi-vitamins to get some good stuff back in me and drank a bunch of water. So far, not too bad. I gotta try to get back with the watch."

He's very pale, his hands are trembling. Bent over, he keeps stumbling back and forth as the ship continues its ceaseless rolling.

"You sure? You could wait 'til our next watch. It's not as though you've been impressed by the British Navy."

He smiles slightly, "I suppose. But I feel like such a schmuck."

"Hell, I'd guess half the voyage crew is seasick." Ugh, that sounds patronizing as hell. I easily could be next.

"Well at least it's daylight. I told Tony I'd do anything on deck, amidships if possible. But I prefer not to go aloft."

Andrew, standing just behind me, says "Geez, I thought you'd want to make up for last night! You need to have more fun up there!"

"Andrew, you ever been seasick?" I ask.

"Nope, no intention of it either."

"I very much doubt anyone intends to get seasick. But once you do, its true misery. I suggest you go easy on people who are seasick."

"I don't remember asking for your advice. I'm just kidding Spasiano anyway, right Vincent?"

Spasiano, glancing up at Andrew, turns to finish pulling on his slop jacket.

I'm not at all anxious to go on watch for the next four hours in the rain and roll. Peering up the companionway the sky is low and dark gray. I can see sheets of rain gusting past the hatch. Crewmen that walk by are crouched over bent into the wind, or being pushed along by it, forced into a foolish-looking, arms-flapping, skipping gait. I follow a few Foremast members up onto the deck. Each of us is slapped in the face by the wind and rain as we clear the shelter of the companionway.

I've got to "suck it up" here. Sure I'm tired, and more than a little apprehensive that I can go through more of last night's trials. But, it's clear you have to move ahead. No way I can drop out. I may not like it, but that can't be an option. This trip is entirely my choice. I just have to get through this, not take stupid risks, but not "wimp out" either.

"You four, come with me." Tony starts to herd four of us forward.

"Tony…." It's Spasiano.

Andrew slaps him on the back. "Looks like you're going to get your chance!"

Tony turns toward Spasiano. "Yeah, OK, you need to stay here."

"No," Spasiano says, "I'll go."

Thankfully I see Harry near Spasiano.

"We're gonna fly the sprit topsail," says Tony. "That's up there," pointing to the sail farthest forward whose yardarm is hung from the jib-boom, an extension to the *Endeavour's* huge bowsprit (large spar projecting forward from the bow). "As we release the sail from the gaskets, your mateys will sheet it home. They're hauling in on the sprit topsail lift now. You can see the sail's yard lifting forward on the jib-boom."

Jesus, here we go. We'll be right out over the water just under the jib-boom, forward of the bowsprit. Since we're just releasing the gaskets and shaking out the sail it won't take long, but what a place to be. Simply can't think here. This is not a reasonable act. Don't imagine what would happen if I fall. I'm not going to fall. Just do what Tony tells me to do.

Harry turns to Spasiano. "Come with me."

Tony is crawling out on the bowsprit, turns to wave us along. "Best thing to do is to crawl along the top of the bowsprit, then shimmy along the jib-boom here."

It's a long way out. Tony must be at least twenty feet away.

Harry turns to Spasiano. "Go ahead, mount up, cowboy. I'm right behind you."

Spasiano slowly crawls up the big bowsprit, around the maze of lines, rigging blocks (pulleys used to assist in handling sails), and furled staysails (fore-and-aft sails). Harry is right behind him. Spasiano gets to the jib-boom, an extension on the bowsprit from which the spritsail and sprit topsail are mounted. Here he stops. Harry sits down while grabbing Spasiano by the waist. They both get their legs in position straddling the jib-boom, which is far smaller than the bowsprit.

Andrew jumps up on the bowsprit ahead of me, turns. "Are you coming or not?"

Screw you. I start crawling on hands and knees along the top of the bowsprit. Lots of obstructions, particularly lines everywhere. I have to carefully pick my way through. The motion here is very different than aloft. While there's some roll, I'm more aware of a pitching up and down in the ocean swells. I keep reminding myself not to grab lines for balance. Some lines will be taut, but others loose. I spread my knees and hands out farther, hoping for a little more stability. The inboard end of the jib-boom is lashed on top of the bowsprit. I slowly settle myself straddling the jib-boom and inch my way out.

Ahead Tony is standing on the sprit topsail yardarm foot line just to the left of the jib-boom. He has his hand on Spasiano's safety belt, saying to Harry, "He can't move. I've got to get him out of the way forward a bit, then I'll stay with him, you go starboard."

As Harry maneuvers to the foot line right of the jib-boom, Tony motions Andrew to stop. He gently pushes Spasiano into a nearly prone position on the jib-boom. Next, he tries to loop Spasiano's safety line around him under the jib-boom, but it's just short. Patting him on the back, he clips it to the safety line running along the top of the jib-boom. "Wrap your arms and legs around the jib-boom. We'll go back together in a minute." He walks along a foot line hanging directly under the jib-boom, turns and faces us.

"Andrew, go to port. Ashburn, follow him. Spasiano, try to pull yourself forward little bit."

I sit still in my straddle position, leaning forward with hands on either side of the jib-boom. Andrew slides forward a few inches and stops. There's no motion from Spasiano's prone body.

Harry reaches over, puts his hand on Spasiano's back. "Bend your knees up, Vincent."

Apparently that's enough because Andrew slides forward some more. The foot line is now just below his dangling feet. Holding onto the jib-boom safety line he leans over, places is foot on the line, grabs the safety line running along the top of the yard, then brings his right foot over.

I notice he towers over the yardarm. Just like last night at the t'gallant, the line doesn't droop down far enough to put the yard at your waist. Following Andrew, I slide forward, lean slightly left to get my left foot on the line, and grab the yard safety line. As I put my weight on the foot line it sways and vibrates furiously. Desperate, I wrap my left arm around the yard, hanging on fiercely. Immediately though I realize I must have both feet on the foot line. Balanced on one foot I'll fall. I twist and lurch slightly forward and left, lifting my right leg while still hanging on to the yard. My right foot grazes the line, but the next moment is on it. Still clinging to the yard for dear life I finally find my safety hook and snap it onto the yard line. Slowly, gasping and hugging the yard, I try to stand slightly upright.

"Move left a little," I say to Andrew. The yard is at mid-thigh level, and the foot line still is jumping and wiggling like a thing possessed.

"What for?"

"I'm too close here, need more drop to the line."

Tony's watching. "Move a bit, Andrew; help out your matey."

The *Endeavour* pitches down into a large wave trough. I pitch violently forward. My right hand has a firm grip on the yard safety line, my left hand flails out uselessly. My body twists to the right as my left foot slides off the foot line. Instinctively I slam my flailing left hand down on the yard grasping for anything. Suddenly, Tony is beside me. "OK, Jack stay still…Now, touch your right leg with your left and put your left foot down next to your right…you're fine."

My fear is overpowering, close to panic. But the act of getting the left foot back on the foot line is immediately reassuring.

"You look like a pretzel all turned and twisted every which way! Take your time and straighten yourself up. We'll untie a few gaskets and be done with it. Right? Let this beautiful sail loose to the wind, mateys." I turn to ask him how he got there, but he's gone back to Spasiano.

My breath seems to come in rapid bursts, short and shallow…is this hyperventilating? After a few moments it begins to slow. OK, take another moment to calm down with larger, slower breaths. There…breathing still slowing…I feel somewhat more under control.

Right below me is a gasket. I reach down and untie it; shuffle slightly to the right and untie its neighbor. Andrew has untied the gaskets outboard of me. Glancing to my right I see Harry has untied the gaskets starboard of the jib-boom. The sail flaps madly for a moment but quickly becomes taut as it is sheeted home by the Foremast crew on deck.

"OK beauties, let's not forget the spritsail. What we do for one we must do for its mate, it's only fair."

Harry is already down on the bowsprit crawling toward the spritsail yardarm, inboard and below where I stand on the sprit topsail foot line. Below on deck I watch Margaret herd two watch mates over to haul on the lower sail's sheet once its gaskets are untied and the sail set free. I take another few breaths exhaling deeply. Next I slide along the foot line to the jib-boom, turn and flop over onto it, slowly lifting my left leg onto its starboard side so I can straddle it and slide down to the big bowsprit. As I do so, suddenly Spasiano sits up.

"Well, hello there, Mr. Spasiano", says Tony. "You've decided to rejoin us; how very kind."

"I want to help; what should I do?"

"Jack, keep going, get to the bowsprit, and turn around. You'll be Mr. Spasiano's one-man welcoming committee. Spasiano, just slide backward along the jib-boom, turn around when you get on the bowsprit with Jack. I'll follow behind Spasiano, Andrew behind me."

I feel elated when I crawl onto the bowsprit from the jib-boom. It seems an absurd reaction, almost giddy and joyful. It must be a response to the near terror of the sprit topsail yard. I turn around to watch Spasiano slide backward along the jib-boom. He doesn't seem to have made any progress at all. Then I see in fact he is sliding backward, just very slowly, in tiny increments.

Andrew says, "Can't you move any faster? This is ridiculous!"

"No special hurry," replies Tony, "he's rather stately and deliberate."

I laugh; that certainly is the best spin possible on Spasiano's painfully slow progress. Finally he arrives to the point where the jib-boom is lashed on top of the bowsprit. Here his feet touch the bowsprit. He picks up his pace, reaching the end of the jib-boom.

Harry is nearby standing on the spritsail foot line, suggests Spasiano just keep going, pointing out a strong cable to step on just below his left foot and a line he can pull himself along on top of the bowsprit.

"Great job, Vincent."

It's true, got to give Spasiano credit. He looked out of it and in real trouble, yet here he is on his way to the deck.

"I'll stay here and watch you guys," he says.

I join Harry on the spritsail foot line and release the few gaskets on the starboard side. Christopher goes to the port side, joined by Tony, as Andrew ignores us and continues down the bowsprit to the deck. Shortly the spritsail is sheeted home (by pulling on "sheets", lines used to control the sail's attitude to the wind) as we slide and crawl down the remaining portion of the bowsprit, jumping down onto the deck.

"Jack, relieve the professor on mizzen watch. Rest of Foremast, kickback here for a moment."

Tony and I walk aft (toward the stern), up the steps to the quarterdeck, he heading over to the Officer of the Deck. I climb the rigging into the mizzen top, the small platform above the fore-and-aft mizzen sail just aft of the wheel.

"Hello, Walter," I announce my arrival on the mizzen top.

Startled, he turns, "Who's that? Oh, hello, Jack. How was the sprit topsail?"

"Survived it," I reply, "what's going on here?"

"There's lots of rain and very little light. So as far as I can see, very little is going on." The professor pauses and adds, "You've had your share of adventures so far, huh?"

"Wrong place, wrong time."

"Maybe, but so far you're always in the middle of the action. You seem to be seeking it out."

"Not really."

"Well, for me so far this has been an amazing experience. Despite what Andrew said, when you're on deck it seems like what I expected, sailing like they did hundreds of years ago. I want to get as much of it as I can. Seems like you do too."

"Yeah," I reply, "that's kind of the point of being here I think, to live the experience."

The professor looks sharply at me. "You're right, you're absolutely right!" He pauses, starts walking toward the edge of the mizzen top. He looks back. "You know, maybe it could be made even better…maybe we can make the experience far more powerful…make it go beyond what it is now." He nods. "I better get below, but let's talk some more soon."

I watch the professor cautiously kneel down on the mizzen top. Hanging onto the shrouds leading up the mizzenmast from the top, he very carefully steps out and down feeling for a ratline to stand on below the mizzen top. Eventually he disappears from view as he cautiously descends.

What was that all about? He thinks the *Endeavour* experience can be changed. How?

THREE

Three days later, I'm "Brains" watching *Endeavour's* northeast course through light ocean chop on a cloudy, humid late summer day. Since the miserable wind and rain of the first twenty-four hours, we've settled into a pleasant stretch of summer days and nights. Repeatedly, we sail far south in the Atlantic only to "wear" the ship around and return north within sight of Block Island or Martha's Vineyard. The fear, exhausting physical effort, and close calls of that first day, slowly fade in memory as we sail in typical New England summer conditions. The wind blows from southwest, the sea consists of regular swells of three to four feet passing under the hull. Evenings are cool, days quickly turn hot and humid. Each day we've been doused by a rain squall, accompanied by heavy wind cells. Each lasts only a few minutes and serves barely to wet surfaces, yet demands sail work aloft. All in all, while not a tourist idyll, the experience is more than matching my expectations.

The Officer of the Deck has given me a course of 040 degrees, just north of northeast. As usual, the *Endeavour's* weather helm requires periodic correction. I turn to the professor at the wheel. "Muscle, two spokes to starboard; you're heading too high again."

"Aye-aye," grins the professor, "two spokes to starboard."

Gradually I've come to enjoy the professor's company over the last days. He's been all over these waters as well as nearby Rhode Island Sound, Vineyard

Sound, and Nantucket Sound. He doesn't own a boat, but crews in sailboat races, cruises with friends, and fishes on party boats. Generally he manages to avoid classroom assignments part of each summer. Off the water he is utterly devoted to ferreting out eighteenth-century documents, especially letters. He has an apparently unquenchable passion to understand how ordinary people lived then, particularly seafaring people. The smallest detail of home life, or life at sea, anything that reveals eighteenth-century reality thrills him. His devotion is so consuming that each week he looks through local papers for tag sales and estate sales. Whenever a sale is held at a house originally built in the eighteenth century or even at a neighboring house, he rushes off in the usually fruitless hope of buying old household documents.

I hand him a plastic water bottle filled with tepid, sour-tasting tap water. Taking it, he grumbles, "Damn, this stuff is awful. It seems to me I'm sweating out sweet water and taking in toilet water. That is definitely a bad exchange."

"Short of tying a sponge to every extremity of your body to collect your dripping 'sweet water', I have little to suggest."

As he wipes his gleaming forehead he mutters, "Some better weather would eliminate the need to consider sponges."

"There you go again criticizing the weather. First it's too cold, rainy and windy. Then it's too sunny and hot. Then it's too humid. It's a good thing the weather pays no attention to your criticism. He—or more likely, she—would have real problems coping."

The professor laughs, "Well then please pass along my apologies to your friend the weather. Actually I guess it has both good and bad parts to it. The good part is, overall the last two to three days have been nice sailing days. The bad part is you haven't had any more hair-raising adventures. You must be bored!"

"You've got to be kidding! Here we go again—your nonsense about me chasing after dangerous situations."

"Come on, Jack, admit it. You're always ready to go. Always in the best position to go up to work sail. I bet I've been up half the times you have."

"Not likely. By the way, your good news-bad news point reminds me of what a doctor said to his hospitalized patient. He comes into the patient's room and says, 'I have good news and bad news.'

"'What's the bad news?' the patient asks. The doctor replies, 'You have a terminal disease and about three months to live.'

"'My God, give me the good news,' exclaims the patient. The doctor says,

'You know that beautiful nurse who comes into your room every morning? I'm having sex with her!'"

"You're avoiding the issue." The professor goes on, "I remember when we first talked it was about the importance of the experience. I was struck by how emphatic you were. Now your experience seems different than mine. I want the sensation of eighteenth-century sailing. You just want the physical risk."

"Walter, I'm fifty-five years old, physical risk is hardly a focus of my life!"

"Right, I'm forty-eight, myself. Obviously it's logical and sensible to avoid physical risk at our age. I've no reason to doubt you. But I just don't see it on this voyage. Watch after watch you race aloft whenever Tony is looking for people to go. Is this some sort of test?"

"Not at all. Going aloft is the most intense part of experiencing the voyage. At first it scared the hell out of me; to some degree it still does. But, it's the unique event on the *Endeavour*. It's what makes the trip special. The ship itself is remarkable. Its precise replica accuracy seems extraordinary. But the drama and excitement are aloft."

"So, Jack, you're in fact supporting my point. You're saying what turns you on is not so much the experience but the exciting moments within the experience. Now, since most of the exciting moments come from being aloft, and because being aloft has inherent risk, it seems to follow that the excitement you seek comes from risk. Yes?"

"That's too narrow a view and your logic seems a little jumpy. I focus on the entire experience. I believe our experiences drive the quality of our lives."

The professor starts to reply as Tony pops out of the companionway from the "gentlemen's quarters" slightly forward of our position at the wheel. "Passed inspection in the quarters, but just barely as usual. What a noisy helm! You two are jabbering like a tree full of rhesus monkeys. Are we on course or wandering aimlessly in the Atlantic Ocean?"

I check the compass to see we're fairly steady just above 040 degrees. "We're OK, Tony."

Tony lets out an exaggerated sigh of relief, "Thank goodness." Pointing to two approaching Foremast mates, "Help is on the way; your relief arrives just in the nick of time. After you're relieved, go forward and see Margaret by the ship's bell for another 'make and mend' task."

*   *   *   *   *

Apart from regularly standing watch and irregularly sleeping, the rest of each *Endeavour* day is a reminder this is not a cruise, not even a sail training trip, but hard and nearly continuous work. We've been aloft again and again for sail or course changes. We've repeatedly cleaned the gentlemen's quarters where on the original *Endeavour* Captain Cook, his officers, the famous naturalist Joseph Banks, his colleague Dr. Daniel Carl Solander, the astronomer Charles Green, and their servants lived and worked. On our voyage several passengers had paid fat sums of money to occupy cabins in the gentlemen's quarters. They could join us in our tasks if they wanted. None that I saw ever did. We've washed the galley, swabbed the deck, cleaned the heads and showers. Over and again we've scoured, wiped, scrubbed and polished. When not at cleaning stations we were assigned jobs—painting or staining sections of the ship, putting protective tar coating on the rigging to prevent it from rot, and given myriad specific tasks from the seemingly endless number of things that needed to be fixed, maintained, or cleaned.

The professor and I reach Margaret who points to Harry sitting on the starboard side of the main deck surrounded by small woven rugs. "All those rugs have sections that are loose, or twisted, or have frayed ends. Sit with the dexterous Harry there and make the rugs tight, flat and trim."

Grinning widely, Harry tosses each of us a rope rug. The ropes in mine are loose and the edges frayed.

Margaret, handing each of us a pair of scissors, continues, "Find the beginning of each rope and gently pull it taut through each point where they overlap, and wherever there are knots, retie them. When it's done right, the rug should lie flat. Then use these scissors to clip it square."

Not so bad…to sit leisurely on the deck and pull on little sections of rope seemed for once an easy, non-taxing assignment.

Harry says, "So guys pull up a rug! Where've you been? I've got all these screwed-up rugs for you to fix!" Still grinning, he asks, "Is this a good trip or what?"

After some nodding in unison from the professor and me, Harry laughs "Yeah, pretty good!"

The professor looks up from his rug, "You know how an eighteenth-century sailor would have described a good ship having a good voyage like the *Endeavour* is giving us? They would have called the ship a 'barky'. It meant they liked the ship, sort of an endearment."

"Professor," says Harry, "you've got a damn ton of miscellaneous knowledge. Maybe then you know something I'm curious about."

"What's that?"

"The reading material we got before boarding the *Endeavour* says it was Cook's ship for his first voyage. Apparently he used another ship for his next voyages. What happened to the *Endeavour*?"

"Harry, that is a great question, with, I think, a very interesting answer. When Cook returned to England in 1771, Banks, Solander and the others brought back thousands of samples of plants and animals collected on their three-year voyage. They were treated as heroes of London society. Cook was even received by the King and promoted to Commander. The *Endeavour*, though, was re-assigned by the Navy as a transport ship to the Falkland Islands. Later, according to extensive research into British naval records by the Rhode Island Marine Archeology Project, she was sold out of the Navy and renamed the *Lord Sandwich*. A cynic might claim the name was a bit of a ploy to curry favor with the Navy. Lord Sandwich himself was then First Lord of the Admiralty. The ship was employed in the late 1770s ironically as a troop carrier for British troops coming to fight the colonialists in the American Revolution. Near the end of her service she became a prison ship. Finally, after the French joined the Revolution, they sailed a portion of their fleet to attack their long-term British enemy in American waters. In one attack by the French fleet on the British, the *Lord Sandwich* was scuttled to blockade a British harbor. That harbor is where we'll be tomorrow afternoon...Newport."

"The *Endeavour* is at the bottom of Newport harbor?" Harry is staring at the professor, the rug forgotten.

"Yes. Our replica will sail nearly right over the remnants of the sunken original."

Tony walks up to Margaret. "We need a couple of your rug weavers aloft. Squall's coming in, the Captain wants us to reef (reduce by pulling the sail closer to the yard and tying it in place with small lines attached to the sail) the main and fore topsails. I've got these fine gentlemen for the fore. Alice is 'powdering her nose' and will be here directly to join you."

Christopher, Andrew and Wes, a bearded, young software engineer I've gone aloft with several times, are climbing into the shrouds directly above us. Wes, as usual, is behind the others. He's at least 6'4", all legs and arms and so

46

ungainly in the rigging it's painful to watch. Andrew, who seems incapable of simple pleasantries, looks down at us. "Looks like the first team is headed aloft while the scrubs are deck-bound idlers intent on making rugs!"

Harry stands up, "Careful, boy, Daddy might have you eat this rug!"

"Now boys," Margaret says quietly, "make nice. Who wants to come?"

"Where Alice goes, I go," says Harry. "I like to watch her climb."

"What a nice man, so pure of heart," Margaret laughs.

I put the rug down to stand up. The professor looks at me, smirking with eyebrows raised, he shakes his head. "I rest my case."

As I turn toward the windward shrouds of the mainmast, Harry, eyes sparkling, slaps my back, "Once more into the fray, eh matey!"

Alice appears on the stairs of the sailors' mess companionway as we start climbing the mainmast shrouds. Margaret, waiting in the lower shrouds for Alice, tells us to stop at the maintop. The *Endeavour* is turning slightly into the wind to luff (reduce the pressure on the sail by bringing the ship closer into the wind) the sails so they can be worked. The ship is still heeled over to starboard, so climbing in the port shrouds is relatively easy. Even the futtock shrouds now seem manageable, and I climb quickly up and onto the maintop. Certainly should be getting easier, by now I've had enough practice.

The professor surprised me with his observation. While much of the action aloft has been nerve-wracking and scary, repeated climbs have somewhat overcome my fear. I just need to keep going up. I now have some confidence in the rigging, so eventually I'll feel good about…what, the challenge, some sort of self-imposed test? That's just what the professor said. So what? I am getting better at this and that's the point—truly have the experience. Is that so silly? No, it's always the experience that counts. Actually, to be honest I rather like his notice. Why though? Why is he paying such attention to what I'm doing?

"OK everybody," says Margaret, "the girls are now going to show the boys how to take in a reef fast and neat. Harry and Jack, I'm so nice to you, go to the easy port side of the mast at the topsail yard, we'll handle the starboard side."

Oh-oh, Margaret is a professional crewperson and seems utterly fearless in the rigging. Alice is much faster and more agile than either Harry or I. How do we get an edge? Edge? What the hell am I thinking?

Harry says, "Wait, I'll ask Spasiano to come up; he can be on your team!"

"Not nice, Harry," says Alice, "not nice."

"Just a thought."

Margaret claps her hands. "Tell you what. The far outside reef is a little tricky. I'll take care of yours, then join Alice on the starboard side. That will give you a nice head start. We'll all start once we're at the yard together. Most important…safety first, nobody takes any chances. Just work fast, neat and safe. Fair?"

"How about two reefs?"

"Not a bleeding chance, Harry."

Margaret, sinewy arms and legs a blur of motion, quickly climbs onto the topmast shrouds, and in moments is on the topsail foot line left of the mast. Sliding quickly out to the end of the foot line, she bends over, grabs the edge of the sail gathering it up to the yardarm. Holding that clump of sail in her left hand, she reaches down and gathers some more sail. She then is able to reach the "reef-point", a short line used to gather the sail when reefing. She wraps first one reef-point then a second around the yardarm, tying each off. As she slides amidships Alice is finishing the climb in the starboard shrouds, followed by Harry and me climbing in the port shrouds near the yardarm.

"How nice am I?" shouts Margaret. "Two reef lines instead of one! Everybody out and ready. You've done this before; just grab sail until you can reach the reef-point then tie that off around the yard."

Harry reaches the topsail yardarm, leans over to grab the yard. He then unsnaps his safety belt and holding the yard with his left hand easily steps onto the foot line, using his right hand to snap the safety belt onto the safety line running along the top of the yardarm. He slides left along the foot line, puts both hands on the yard and turns to face me. "Come to Poppa, Jack."

Slowly, but fairly steadily I climb the last few ratlines, turn slightly to my left, step on the foot line and lunge to grab the yardarm. This time my right foot follows obediently onto the foot line next to my left. Wobbling madly I stand up awkwardly.

"OK, the gang's all here!" laughs Harry.

Margaret gives each of us a serious look. "Remember where you are; don't take any chances. One hand for you, one hand for the sail. No quick movements, plan your actions ahead."

As always, I have to remind myself not to look down. Even though I'm bending over the yardarm facing the deck directly, every time I've focused on the deck I've immediately been disoriented. I've got to focus my eyes just on the sail and reef-points.

Harry slides a bit out to port. He turns his head toward me. "I count about fourteen reef-points for us to gather and wrap, sort of in pairs. Because we've got to grab and lift the sail it seems better to work next to each other. Let's try to do it each handling a pair. That way we're pulling on the same section of sail together. Do two pairs, then shuffle toward the mast and repeat. OK with you?"

"Aye-aye, boss!"

Margaret waves to get our attention, signals thumbs up, and shouts, "Start now."

The topsail is luffing back and forth. It is heavily wrinkled from repeatedly being gathered to its yardarm. Harry and I easily grab sections and pull them up to the yard. Despite Margaret's instructions, I quickly find the heavy sail easier to handle by bending over the yardarm and pulling with two hands, as apparently does Harry. We fall into a natural rhythm as we gather enough sail around the yardarm that we can reach a reef-point, then wrap it around the yardarm, move on to the next set of reef-points. Rather than bunch the sail into an unsightly lump, we remember to fold the sail into itself as we pull it up thereby making little folds within the sail that are cinched to the yardarm by wrapping the reef-point.

Slowly we work our way inboard to the mast. Totally absorbed by our grabbing, folding, cinching task, I'm startled when I realize the sail I'm gathering is no longer hanging down but slants up to the right.

Margaret reaches over and touches my shoulder. "Our feelings were getting hurt. We thought you'd never come to say hello."

I'm astonished. "You're done?"

"So it would appear. But you boys are surprisingly neat reefers, you may even be neater than the clear winners of this contest! Look Alice, we have to admit their reef is smooth and flat, not bad."

"Yes, but will they ever finish, Margaret?"

Margaret smiles. "Right, finish up and we'll meet at the main top."

Harry grumbles, "Not even close. Whipped by two women aloft in a square-rigger. Not exactly a personal triumph."

Moments later we're finished, tying off the last reef-point. Harry starts to descend in the port shrouds. I stop and look a moment at our sail work. The reef does look flat and clean. Harry's wrong. We actually did a seamanlike job so I'd say it was a little triumph…at least for me it was.

We reach the maintop where Margaret and Alice wait. Margaret says, "We forgot to select a prize for the winners. We'll let you guys do that!"

"OK", replies Harry, "the prize is Jack and I will provide free wrestling lessons to the winners."

"I don't think so, though it certainly is a gallant offer!"

I suggest, "How about a gallon of Vegemite to the winners."

Alice counters, "Better, a gallon of Vegemite to the losers."

"I guess we'll waive a prize and simply savor the victory," concedes Margaret. "Yea for the victors!"

We scramble onto the maintop futtock shrouds and down onto the deck. I walk forward toward the professor still sitting with a rug in his lap. Harry and Alice follow behind laughing together. All around us crew members are belaying and furling lines as the *Endeavour* returns to her set course.

The professor looks up. "You're beaming like a lighthouse, so's Harry. Must have had a good time up there!"

I reply while turning around toward Harry and Alice, "Actually it went very well. I almost made it to able seaman rating." Watching Harry I continue, "Harry apparently had a great time too."

"So it seems."

"All hands, Captain's briefing in the lee of the long boat in fifteen minutes."

Harry says to Alice, "Right back, pit stop."

"He puts things so delicately, don't you agree?" She looks down at me as I squat down to take up my rug task.

"Yes, I understand he's the 'Miss Manners' of the DC police department."

Smiling she goes on, "That was fun just now, not too much motion, you guys did really well."

"If we did so well, you and Margaret must have been phenomenal. You beat us handily."

Alice replies, "I didn't, she did. All I did was follow along, sort of mimic her. She did most of the work."

"Maybe, but you seem to move around the rigging well. Have you done this before?"

"My father lifted me up in a bosun's chair on our Cal 25 a few times. I did like tumbling and gymnastics in school, but I wasn't a gymnast. You seem to go up a lot, often with Harry. Are you two like a team, did you know him before?"

"No, met him onboard. We're not a team; it's mostly chance I'd say."

"He's a lot of fun." Alice is grinning broadly, nodding her head.

"Yes, Harry is that," I answer.

"Damn, it's raining," the professor grumbles getting up.

As he does, Tony announces all Foremast to the sailors' mess to pick up slops. The briefing is being moved there. Since we're still on duty, we'll only hear the start of it before going back on deck.

We walk forward to the lower deck companionway. Harry, already there, hands Alice a set of foul weather slops as he puts his on.

"Very nice, Harry," I say. "I assume you've selected gear for me, too."

"Well no, we lost. Now I'm only going to associate with winners, not losers." He and Alice laugh loudly together.

"The cute new couple," grimaces the professor.

Moments later the Captain comes down the companionway with several charts rolled up and a weather fax. "By sunset we'll make one more run south, turning north again about midnight. We're supposed to enter Newport Harbor mid-morning tomorrow. There's a big celebration, a re-enactment, a boat parade, TV coverage, lot of nonsense. Unfortunately, the wind will collapse to nothing during the overnight hours so to keep the schedule we'll have to motor for some hours tonight. Assuming the wind doesn't change much and the weather people don't expect it to, it means we'll have little if any wind until at least daybreak. I do intend though, if at all possible, to sail into Newport Harbor."

I hear Andrew muttering behind me, "A less than glorious voyage end."

The professor next to me turns to glare at him. "But on schedule."

"OK, Foremast on deck. I'm pleased to announce we've arranged to have the rain stop so you can resume your critical tasks on behalf of our dear *Endeavour*!"

We start up the companionway as the Captain laughs at the First Mate's comment about Tony being "incorrigible" and continues his briefing. Sure enough the rain has slowed to a drizzle. Here and there a hint of blue sky peeks through the cloud cover.

The professor and I head back to our now wet rugs, followed by Harry and Alice.

Harry says, "Alice has agreed to join us to add a much-needed feminine touch to our clumsy efforts at rug weaving."

"Feminine skills are always welcome by me…" I start to reply when I notice the professor looks sour. He doesn't like Alice, or doesn't want her here?

Harry doesn't seem to notice as he hands Alice a thoroughly tangled rug and laughs, "Here's an easy one."

"Thanks a lot," she replies. "You're too generous!"

Maybe Alice senses the professor's unease, or simply because she's sitting next to him, she smiles at him. "That's a pretty taut rug Walter, very handsome. I'm not at all convinced I can make this mess look like that. Can you help me get started? I don't have any idea what to do first."

The professor leans over and takes hold of an edge of her rug. "I'll have a look."

Watching Alice, you have to be impressed. Bright brown eyes, pleasant smile, tall, trim figure with a nice overall appearance, she's spotlessly clean and groomed but not in any way coiffed. Harry's right, she is fun to watch. Wonderful long and lean legs nicely tanned, taut but not overtly muscular. Short, light brown hair slightly curved up at the ends and parted on the left side, it has some subtle blond highlights. She's sitting with her legs folded under her looking directly at the professor and occasionally glancing at the rug. She seemingly is fully absorbed by what he's saying. I look over at Harry, who's watching her with a slight smile. He looks up at me, flicks his eyebrows up and smiles broadly.

I laugh, "What a group, a collection of thumbs for the most part, when suddenly the professor emerges as 'rug weaver extraordinaire' and now he has a young acolyte. Strange things happen on the *Endeavour.*"

"Walter's rug is really nice. I'd have it at home. Yours, on the other hand," Alice smiles at me, "is not quite ready for prime time, though it does show some definite potential, Jack."

"Right, potential in rope rugs is a highly valued quality. Thankfully I still can buy one rather than make it."

The professor looks up. "Ah is there an opportunity here for a cash sale?"

"Professor, let's consider the finer points of ownership for a moment…."

"Jack, you're spoiling my highlight moment in handicrafts with a highly legalistic complaint."

Harry glances over at the professor, "I remind you sir, I am an officer of the law sworn to protect the citizenry against all crimes great and small. Your right to sell this rug—cash or not—rests on, if I may use a relevant term, a very thin thread of evidence."

"Ohhh," groans Alice. "What thread?"

"Possession and causing a change in the nature and value of a product. Little help in court though."

The professor, now fully engaged in the conversation, smiling asks Harry to "Disappear for a moment. What you don't see didn't happen, right?"

"Sorry, my duty is solemn."

"Jack, you raise my hopes of cash reward for my newly discovered handicraft, and the brutish Harry dashes them. How cruel and mean-spirited!"

"Sorry, professor. Maybe I can redeem your shaken faith in the capitalist system on shore. You could open a little roadside handmade rug shop. I'll come by and make a purchase."

The professor eyes me curiously, "You keep talking about buying things, Jack. Where do you get all this money?"

"From the bank, professor."

"I've mastered that notion, but who or what puts the money in the bank for you?"

"Grateful clients favor me from time to time."

Alice interrupts, "What is this? Do you guys have an act? Will you be performing later? I'm getting neck strain following your 'bon mots' back-and-forth!"

"'Bon mots', Jeez, that's the best review we've had!" laughs Harry. "Nope, no act. It must be the spirit of the moment, or the quality of the company."

Alice leans over and messes Harry's hair, shakes her head. "Impossible, you guys are a little cute and a lot impossible!"

"Back to the professor's question," Harry says, "you all know I'm a cop, the professor is—you guessed it—a professor. What do you do, Jack?"

"I'm a principal in an executive search firm in Hartford."

"Oh oh, everybody hold onto your job; a headhunter's among us!" whispers the professor.

"Relax, Walter, we don't do cops or teachers."

Harry grimaces, "Probably 'cause fees for us don't exactly measure up to those for the corporate honchos who dance around from job to job, right?"

"Headhunters don't hunt pygmies, do they?" asks the professor. "What kind of people do you hunt for?"

"Giants! We search for nobody but giants! Actually, we're in the construction industry, our clients are mostly big civil engineering firms and construction companies doing large manufacturing and public works projects.

We staff project managers, engineers, superintendents, some corporate positions, a few others."

"Who's we?"

"I have two partners and three associates, a junior assistant and an office manager."

"So, you conduct searches?"

"Actually I sell our services some of the time and manage searches."

"Are you the boss?" asks Harry.

"Usually each job has an associate do some preliminary search work, identifying prospective candidates, learning details of the job's circumstances. Once that's done if it's my project, I conduct the search with help from the associate. I have a young assistant works full time for me developing prospective sales opportunities which I work to convert to search opportunities."

"Jack the rainmaker," says the professor.

"Only sort of, my partners have longstanding clients who come back to us somewhat regularly. My job is to grow the business with new clients."

Alice stops pulling on her tangled rug. "Where do you find the people for the jobs you're asked to fill?"

"It's all about contacts, finding them, staying in touch, maintaining really good database information about them."

"Do you select candidates from your contacts?" she asks.

"Sometimes, but usually the candidates come from references, suggestions, comments by contacts. We're always developing contacts."

"It must help to concentrate in a certain region," suggests the professor.

"Probably initially it was useful, but by the time I showed up, the company was doing searches all over the US, and a few in Canada."

"What'd you do before this?"

"I ran the US sales for a road-building equipment company. Gave me lots of contacts in the industry which is why the search firm opportunity made sense."

"When did you become a headhunter?"

"Five years ago."

Alice leans forward looking at me. "Jack, you're not exactly verbose about this job. I think maybe we're prying too much."

"No, not at all. It's just not particularly interesting. We offer a good service, clients have been using it for years. That's it…no startling moments, no great stories to tell. It allows me to make decent money, meet and talk to lots of people, now and then help somebody who appreciates it. Besides, Alice, it allows my wife and me to bring up two daughters at least within shouting distance of the manner in which they'd like to become accustomed."

"Really, how old are they?"

"One's a junior at BU, the other a freshman at Mount Holyoke."

"What do they think of your sailing on the *Endeavour*?"

"Dad is certifiable."

"And your wife?"

"Exactly the same, with less laughter."

"Mine was thrilled," interrupts the professor. "Five days without going to tag sales and hearing me complain about the minuscule academic effort of summer school students were described as a blessing, a surprise vacation, a chance to run off to the Cape with some friends. She thanked me again and again. Was there a message there?"

"No," laughs Alice, "couldn't possibly be!"

Harry is fidgeting, "Sorry Jack, but interesting as headhunting is, does anybody mind if I change the subject of our little weavers' caucus? The professor knocked me over earlier when he told us about the original *Endeavour*. Incredibly, Alice, it was sunk in Newport of all places!"

Alice looks from Harry to the professor. "You're kidding! That's absolutely amazing. The new one will be in the same place as the 200-year-old one? What a wild coincidence! How'd this happen? How'd the original end up in Newport of all places?"

The professor replies, "As I told Harry and Jack earlier, after Cook's first voyage on the *Endeavour* throughout the Pacific, it was sold out of the British Navy. It ended up renamed the *Lord Sandwich*, and did troop transport duty to America during the Revolution. Newport was a British base during much of the war, so it delivered troops there. Once the French allied themselves with the Americans, they dispatched a fleet to attack the British blockade of the colonies. One attack—frankly a botched plan—was on Newport. The British scuttled the *Lord Sandwich* and numerous other ships to prevent the French fleet from getting close enough to Newport to fire on the city."

That's a slightly different take, so I ask, "Walter, before you didn't mention the attack was botched. What do you mean?"

*　　　　*　　　　*　　　　*　　　　*

The professor pauses for a moment, then continues. "220 years ago this month, the French fleet under Count D'Estaing—like most French commanders, a member of French nobility—entered Newport harbor with the British in a panic. Lord Howe was supposed to arrive with a British fleet to challenge the French, but hadn't shown up at this point. Desperate to defend Newport, the British took advantage of the harbor's shallow waters. They burned, sank—including the *Lord Sandwich*—and ran ashore numerous ships in an attempt to blockade the French from approaching the town. The French didn't attack immediately but remained poised off Newport. Eventually they sailed a portion of the fleet up and back in Narragansett Bay firing on Newport from a distance. Shortly thereafter finally Lord Howe did show up with a formidable British fleet. The French broke off their attack on Newport and sailed out to battle the British fleet. To complicate an already too complicated strategic situation, in the midst of these fleet actions an American militia force moved south close to Newport, dug in and prepared to support the French invasion of Newport. The French fleet and American army were trying to create a pincer movement on the British.

"This was some American force. Under Brigadier General John Sullivan there were 1500 regulars and an ever-changing number of militia, roughly 8,000. Apparently they were something to see. A French officer described the militia as a 'laughable spectacle'. All the tailors and apothecaries in the country must have been called out, I should think.... They were mounted on bad nags and looked like a flock of ducks in cross-belts.

"In any case, the two fleets began a furious engagement, but were soon dispersed by a violent storm. The French fleet promptly departed to Boston to refit its damaged ships, leaving the British still in control of Newport. The American troops, now badly exposed to both British army and naval forces, hastily retreated to await the return of the French fleet, which never showed up. General Sullivan was so outraged at D'Estaing he called him a traitor. For a while there was a furious exchange between the French and Sullivan, Lafayette even threatening to challenge Sullivan to a duel. George Washington eventually smoothed all the ruffled feathers but it was an early mess in the Franco-American alliance.

"Back to the Rhode Island campaign. After some skirmishing with the Americans slightly north of Newport, the British army simply retained its occupation of the town. This likely was a little disappointing for the most of the locals who had lived a nasty, harsh existence under British rule, particularly at the hands of Hessian mercenaries. Some Loyalists to the crown lived in Newport, others took shelter there. The brutalities of an occupying army, however, made Newport a different place than it was in its pre-war cosmopolitan elegance and sophistication

"This confusing, futile set of events is not uncharacteristic of Rhode Island's history. It's a marvelous blend of eccentric characters; of odd, often amusing, even screwball events. Generally it was out of step with regional or national events and trends. Frankly, it's wonderful stuff to study and discover."

Alice has settled back, clearly intent on hearing some stories. "What was Newport like then?"

"Wonderful question. I've spent—at least so many of my friends and family would say—far too much of my time picking up tidbits, little nicks and knacks, snippets of information on eighteenth-century Newport and the coastal towns. I do tend to go on and on, often far too long, on that subject."

Sensing the professor is just warming up I break in, "Maybe a kind of 'Cliff's Notes' version, professor. What do you think?"

Alice is scowling at me as the professor responds, "Yes, OK. I'll give you a few anecdotes so you have a flavor of this odd little corner of America.

"You get an immediate sense of the place by how it got started. It was founded by disgraced clergy for the most part run out of Massachusetts. Roger Williams first left England just ahead of persecution. Later, settled in Boston, he had to sneak away in peril of jail or worse in the middle of a snowy night. Other clergy leaders followed, virtually all forced out of Massachusetts for not adhering to rigid Puritan doctrine. My favorite is Samuel Gorton, who was kicked out of three colonies. Even the tolerant-to-a-fault Roger Williams couldn't stand Gorton and forced him out of his Providence colony. Somehow Gorton talked the Earl of Warwick in England into supporting his settlement in what is now, not surprisingly, the town of Warwick, Rhode Island.

"The name is another oddity. Its full name is 'The State of Rhode Island and Providence Plantations'. Yet it is neither an island nor a set of plantations. The explorer Giovanni Verrazano, in what seen now was a woefully misguided attempt, in 1524 was seeking a passage to China. Lots of explorers used that gambit, maybe it was an easy pitch to pick up some exploring money. He sailed up Narragansett Bay. He recorded in his diary that the island on which sits Newport looked like Rhodes in the Aegean.

"It's a place of spectacular contradictions—Newport was the colonial center of the American slave trade. For most of the eighteenth century, upwards of fifty to sixty Newport ships hauled African slaves occasionally to be purchased there, more often in the Caribbean. The city fathers paid for street paving and bridge-building with a three-dollar tax on each slave passing through Newport. Yet, the first black regiment ever formed in North America fought under General Sullivan in the skirmishes with the British. It was made up mostly of slaves who, if they stayed through their enlistment, were freed.

"By the Revolution, Newport was a place of remarkable wealth, concentrated by then in the control of a few dozen families. Arguably it exceeded New York in concentrated opulence and splendor. The wealth, however, did not come from nice sources. Largely it came from slave trading, smuggling, piracy and privateering. Moreover, for many rich Newport merchants, their wealth came not only from what they earned in mercantile trade. It also came from their obsession to protect it. They were famous—the British likely would have said 'infamous'—for going to extraordinary lengths to avoid not only custom duties and other taxes, but most trade regulations and navigational law as well.

"Newport was a principal port in the infamous 'triangular trade'. One corner of the triangle was molasses from the West Indies. Another was the nearly two dozen distilleries in Newport in which molasses was transformed into rum. The third corner of the triangle was western Africa where the rum was traded for slaves. Yet despite its unsavory commercial connections, Newport unquestionably was a cultural center of the colonies. It was a haven for free thinkers, dissidents, Jews escaping the still-powerful and very scary Inquisition in Spain, and Quakers fleeing from persecution in Connecticut and Massachusetts.

"My readings of colonial Newport repeatedly describe its affluence, even excess. Magnificent homes, churches and commercial buildings; goods from all over the world. It was described as a society of 'scarlet coats and brocade, lace ruffles and powdered hair, high-heeled shoes and gold buckles, delicate fans and jeweled swords, delicately bred women and cultured men.' Chocolates, the finest brandies and jams, ornamental jewelry and elegant fabrics, leather-bound books, all manner of imported goods were found in the finest Newport stores.

"In an amusing cluster, within a few minutes walk of each other in Newport are the oldest continuously operated tavern in America, the oldest continuously operated library, and the oldest Jewish synagogue. You'll love this…the son of the founder of the tavern was a famously notorious pirate. When his father died in the early 1700s, he took over as tavern keeper and apparently the authorities couldn't or at least didn't do anything about it!"

"Ah," says Harry, "a tavern. At last my true destination on this voyage is identified!"

"Harry, you can focus on the tavern. As a 'delicately bred' woman I'll take the lace ruffles, high-heeled shoes and delicate fans, even a cultured man," exclaims Alice. "Sounds wonderfully charming."

"Yes," continues the professor, "I think it must have been an incredibly fascinating place, at least until the British occupation." Oddly, he glances at Harry and me. "Two more little anecdotes and I'll stop."

"No, this is great fun, let's hear more."

I notice Tony striding across the quarterdeck toward us. "Seems likely we may have to rejoin the twentieth century, Alice; here comes Tony."

"Quickly then, two characters. One was Pero Bannister, an owner of Bannister's Wharf on the Newport waterfront. You'll probably get there sometime while you're in Newport. When he died he was measured for a coffin. Unfortunately it was not built properly to one of his measurements. The lid would not close over his rather over-sized nose. So the coffin maker cut a hole in the lid. Old Pero was laid to rest with his nose peeking out.

"The other story is about Reverend Clap, pastor of Newport's Congregational Meeting House in the 1720s. His preaching and behavior eventually caused great distress in the congregation. A committee was formed to confront him with the congregation's demands for change. Rev. Clap listened to the committee's complaints. He handed each member a fig. He then left the room shouting, 'A fig for you all.'

"To be continued."

"And here's our rug crew. Damn if the rhesus monkeys are not still about, the chatter here is deafening. Let's have a look at your weaving skills, shall we? Yes, some are clearly better than others. Professor, surprisingly that rug likely will pass muster with the First Mate. Jack—no chance, Harry—even less chance, Alice—some potential. So my duty is clear. Professor and Alice, stay with the rugs. Jack and Harry come with me. Your weaving days are over."

Harry and I follow Tony as he strides forward. Passing the fierce red head, he reminds us to "Be careful, he still isn't very fond of this crew—talks too much, can't be serious 'before the mast' sailors. One of you take the bow watch. Slide out to the end of the bowsprit. Keep an eye out for buoys, logs, small boats, long distance swimmers, any debris that the *Endeavour* should avoid. When you see something, explain where it is by points, as 'buoy, three points to starboard'. The other of you is the 'runner'. Take that information to the Officer of the Deck. You can share, switching jobs. You'll have it 'til the end of Dog Watch, about an hour."

Harry says, "Go ahead, Jack. I'll be your runner and relieve you in half hour."

I shinny out to the bowsprit's end, and lie down facing forward. I prop myself up on my elbows. The wind is fairly fresh. The late afternoon sun gives the ocean a sparkle. A few seagulls swoop by peering at the ship as she moves at her slow, stately pace through the ocean chop. Scanning the ocean directly in front, I see nothing that conceivably might obstruct or damage the *Endeavour*. The only object on the water is a boat with a small forward cabin hundreds of yards off the port bow. In the haze just on the horizon I can spot the low, humpback shape of land. It must be Martha's Vineyard. No distinct shapes are visible, but seeing it gives the overall scene dimension and perspective. A few small fish jump off to starboard, patches of seaweed drift by. After a few minutes I notice the wonderful variety in the look and texture of the water— little whitecaps almost everywhere, surface ripples scurry by driven by the wind. The water color is surprisingly varied, sometimes dark green, sometimes almost black.

I hear Harry call, "Look below!"

Two sleek grey shapes are just below the surface almost touching each side of the ship's bow…dolphins! They seem motionless, just gliding along next to the bow. Suddenly they're gone. The *Endeavour's* plodding pace must be maddeningly slow for such beautiful, boisterous creatures.

It's almost hypnotic, lying on the bowsprit watching the water pass under me. I force my gaze away occasionally to look forward for things to report. The ocean ahead seems empty. I'm falling into a spell, surely made easy by being bone-tired, easily sleepy, and always slightly hungry.

Suddenly I'm startled by a yell, after a moment I realize it's Harry. "My turn, wake up, Jack!"

"I'm awake…be right there." I slide along the bowsprit, and clamber down onto the deck as Harry climbs on the foredeck railing headed for the bowsprit.

Leaning on the railing I watch Harry settle into a similar position as mine, lying forward on the bowsprit. From here the ship's pace seems even slower since I'm less aware of the water passing directly underneath. Looking from any visual angle other than directly down, there is very little sense of motion. Her blunt nose obviously is a factor, as is her wide beam (twenty-nine feet). But her sail rig is quite extensive, the masts tall (our written material claims the main mast is 127 feet tall). She carries square sails on all three masts, topgallant, topsails and course (main) sails on the fore and main mast and a topsail plus fore-and-aft course on the mizzen mast. Since her sail plan is principally square-rigged, the *Endeavour* can't sail close to the wind. In fact she can sail only within about eighty degrees of it. Typically she wears around away from the wind rather than tacks into the wind thus makes leeway (slips laterally) whenever she turns.

But, that's far from all the sails. The big bowsprit supports the much smaller jib-boom, from which hangs the sprit topsail and spritsail. In between the masts are numerous fore-and-aft sails permanently attached to various stays. Finally, for foremast and mainmast courses and topsails, the ship has stunsails that can be rigged alongside. In all, she can set a total of seventeen sails.

The *Endeavour* is very dry. While I've been wet over and again, it has always been due to rain, not seas coming onto the ship. It is now apparent she sails best in heavy winds, over twenty-five knots. In the light winds of summertime New England, she tends to feel slow, plodding.

After a while, Harry slides backward along the bowsprit. While he can still look for obstacles ahead, he's close enough to talk.

"I was recruited by a headhunter last year. He was looking for a guy to run security at a DC bank. Very coy approach. He wanted to know if I knew anybody who might be interested, obviously including me. I told him to 'take a hike'. Not too smart huh? Probably never get another call from that guy."

"Harry, I don't think I'd worry. Lots of large companies are looking for security people. It's a hot search category. If you got one call, you're bound to get more. Be nice on the next one, you never know."

"Yeah, I gotta start looking around, come up with something better than what I have. I've been at my game way too long, thirty years on the force next year. That is goddamn enough. I absolutely have just had it. I hardly can cope with the idea of leaving this to go back.

"I know a lotta guys who jumped into security jobs. Boring as hell, no action, but at least they don't have to put up with all the crap and nonsense I still get.

Once we wrap up this useless task force I'll get on the stick, figure out my next move."

Harry is a District of Columbia police officer. In fact, he's a captain heading up a task force with a purpose he's grown to hate. Despite his mostly upbeat style, when he's occasionally talking about himself I haven't been able to dislodge him from an intense bitterness and frustration with his current assignment. I've no doubt his rank, experiences and natural storytelling can produce some fascinating tales. But he is mired in the mud of squatters and the homeless.

Harry heads up a police task force created under heavy pressure from the Federal government. The task force is supposed to make squatters and homeless go away. In Harry's admittedly jaundiced view, suddenly after complete neglect of the District, the administration now wants to clean up DC. As they get ready to spend scarce budget money on new federal buildings, they have to deal with hundreds of squatters. Telling me this story, Harry loudly reminds me 2000 is a national election year.

Apparently several new federal building projects are going out for bid all total packages to build-lease-manage the federal facilities. The Feds want nice neat deals. Usually a deal will take the form of a guaranteed rental period at fixed costs plus interest escalators, generally for at least ten years. The Feds put several sites on a short list for a facility, usually in run down, decaying areas of the city. "See how your government is working to make the District a better place to live and work!" Developers bidding on the project feverishly grab enough cheap real estate in the area of the planned project to have sufficient land to build the facility. The District owns dozens, if not hundreds of cheap buildings— abandoned warehouses, condemned housing complexes, boarded-up old row houses. And the District is broke. Not surprisingly, since the District always needs cash, the bureaucrats will listen to offers, often for fractions of the buildings' nominal value.

Very frequently the buildings house squatters. As the deals for the fancy new federal buildings go together, the squatters have to be evicted. They're in public buildings so the police are called on to throw them out. Police don't like squatters. They have little or no training to work with them, and very little sympathy. The squatters are dirty, smelly, often mentally ill and frequently consumed by booze and/or drugs, especially crack. They have no rights at all, not even the right of notice. As a result, the evictions usually are tense. The police are rough with the squatters. It is grubby, nasty duty.

Evicting squatters in city-owned buildings is only part of Harry's task. The Feds have been complaining for months about the seeming increase in homeless in the Mall, and areas immediately within White House-centric Washington. They're cluttering national monumental spaces, making tourists uneasy and an embarrassing the federal government. Since Harry's force is already handling squatters, his commanders assigned it to clean up the Mall homeless as well.

Harry is surely no "bleeding-heart liberal", but his constant exposure to the homeless has left him in a rage at the stupidity and heartlessness of both tasks. He claims there are 10,000 homeless in DC. The lucky ones are squatters. The rest sleep on the ground, or park benches, under bridges, in alleys, wherever they can find a little refuge. There are very few public shelters, and those still open are scary as hell. The broke city is closing existing shelters, not opening new ones. The homeless have to be someplace, but often it's the wrong place. Harry's cops are ordered to move them. All they can do is sweep up the homeless and evict the squatters. The cops can put them in jail or move them somewhere away from where they were picked up.

The jail option is senseless. The criminal justice system is hopelessly clogged as it is—adding the homeless just clogs it all the more. Moreover, if they are put in jail, they are tried for vagrancy, or panhandling or being a public nuisance or other charges, and have to pay a fine. If they have no money they add to the ludicrously over-burdened prison system. If they have a little money, they then are released back on the street to be homeless again but with less money.

The other option, to move them, is equally absurd. The cops sweep through the Mall area picking up hundreds of homeless. They deposit them in other areas of the city, usually at already over-crowded shelters or charity food centers. The problem of homelessness is not addressed, just pushed around.

Harry has little sympathy for the homeless, though incessant exposure apparently has forced him to revise his blanket opinion of them as habitual bums. His rage is at the ludicrous futility of his task force's responsibility for squatters and Mall homeless. For him, it is a waste of manpower and a degradation of police value. It is an utterly useless and demeaning task.

Harry's wife divorced him years ago. His blunt explanation is it wasn't so much him as his rank. The higher in rank he rose, the less time he was home. There were no kids, then no time, eventually no marriage.

Yet, on the *Endeavour*, Harry is charged with energy, enthusiasm, and fun. It's as though the ship is a badly-needed respite from his DC life. It's almost a sanctuary for him, into which he has plunged headlong. The Foremast crew, even most of the Aussie professional crew seek him out, clearly want his company. His laughter, "wise guy" humor and transparent joy with all the *Endeavour* activities are infectious. This in fact seems to be the "real" Harry, not the malcontent police captain. Certainly it is the Harry to whom the effervescent Alice clearly is responding.

Harry turns back toward me, "Margaret and Alice sure whipped our butts on the topsail yard. I continue to be amazed at how good Alice is in the rigging, very quick and agile."

"Yeah, she mentioned she'd done some sailing and a little gymnastics in college."

Harry grins. "I think she's remarkably graceful. Margaret got on me earlier when I said I liked to watch Alice climb. But, I do. She does it so easily and smoothly."

"You've spent a fair amount of time with her. How'd she get to the *Endeavour?*"

Harry smiles. "She lives in New York, saw it there and signed up. She teaches English and writing in a New York City prep school. She's single, thirty-three, says she goes out casually with a few different guys, nothing special. She lives in the Gramercy Park district in what she says was advertised as a small, one-bedroom apartment. Alice claims it's better described as a studio with a bed in a closet. She's a serious singer, active in a New York choral group. She's into pottery and jogging. Alice spends lots of time at the 92nd Street Y making pots and whatever. She jogs every other morning along the East River. I told her at least that must be safer than Central Park. She said probably is, but that's offset by noise and smell from all the cars on the East Side Drive, plus whatever delights the river churns up or deposits alongside her route."

Harry pauses for a moment, looks over at me and continues. "We've spent a lot of time together in the last couple days, talking, telling stories, arguing politics. She still likes Clinton; can you believe it, after all his asinine shenanigans with women! Mostly she distrusts the Republicans' interest in education and in women's health issues. The funny thing is she and I sure aren't a natural fit, that's damn obvious," he laughs. "But, we just talk and talk, joke around and laugh. It seems to flow non-stop. Tony calls us the 'jackdaws', cackling together all the time."

I grin at him; he's almost bubbling now. "Tony will have to make up his mind. You can't be a rhesus monkey with me and a jackdaw with Alice. He'll have to choose one."

Harry looks forward over the bowsprit. "I can see people on the fishing boat off the port bow. Maybe they caught a fish, lots of moving around.

"I asked Alice if she wanted to hang around Newport for a couple days after we finish with the *Endeavour*. She said sure, sounded like fun to wander Newport, get to know it. There's a lot to see. How good is that! I was thinking, maybe you'd like to join us for some of that time. You and she get along. We'd have fun together maybe get the professor to come along as a guide. Trouble is we may never get him to stop talking!"

"I'm not sure you want me along, kind of classic 'third wheel'."

"No," replies Harry, "not at all. It's just to have some more time, enjoy a landlubber's vacation after our days at sea. Hell, we won't even be able to walk straight the first day!"

"OK, I'll check in at home when we get in to see if I won't be missed for one more day."

Harry keeps glancing forward at the fishing boat, now just a few hundred yards diagonally ahead. Pointing at the boat he says, "Something's wrong. There's a guy standing on the bow waving furiously."

I look carefully at the boat, the man waving. "I'll go report it to the helm. See if you can figure out why he's waving at us."

I arrive at helm, as the First Mate climbs up the adjacent companionway. "Fishing boat, two o'clock on the starboard bow, about 300 yards out. Someone is waving hard in our direction, apparently trying to get our attention."

The First Mate replies, "Right. Captain is on the radio with them now, some sort of medical emergency." Holding a big set of binoculars he climbs into the starboard mainmast rigging. After a few climbing steps he stops to focus on the boat ahead. Moments later he looks down at Tony now standing with me on deck. "Get your first aid kit, Tony. There's a medical problem, and the guy waving on the bow looks frantic."

Tony turns to me. "Ask Harry to meet me here." He dashes down the great cabin companionway, nearly running over the Captain as he comes up.

The Captain shouts to the First Mate, "Adjust our course to the boat. Bring her up to full engine speed. Damn fools apparently were fishing for sharks. They tried to bring one onboard and a crewman got his leg nearly severed by the shark. They say there's blood everywhere, sharks in the water, a total disaster. They're scared witless."

As I run forward toward Harry, I see he is looking back at the commotion around the helm. I wave to him to come quickly. Tony arrives with a huge box, much like a very large fishing tackle kit.

The Captain puts his hand on Tony's shoulder. "Sounds bad. Crewman got bitten in the lower leg just above the ankle. Apparently he was standing on a swim platform attached to the boat's transom, helping to boat a big shark. He and one guy in the boat each managed to gaff the shark. They and the guy reeling the line the shark hit were trying to lift it into the boat, when the line snapped, and the shark fell backward landing on the platform. It thrashed about wildly and ripped a big section from the crewman's leg. They just dragged him into the boat, but there was so much blood there are other sharks in the water all around. You've got to assume lots of blood loss, a dirty wound, maybe some form of shock. Make sure you've got all the stuff you need. Margaret is your aide, right? Where's she?"

"Coming, sir. I'll bring Harry Cassis here along. He's a policeman, should be helpful."

"Good." Turning to the First Mate, the Captain orders, "Bring us right alongside; no point in wasting time lowering a boat. Get lines ready to lash the fishing boat tight to us. You're in charge here. I'll radio the Coast Guard what I know, and give them our position. We're going to need their help.

"Tony, the fishing boat is still on the radio with us. I told them to elevate the leg, and apply direct pressure on the wound with whatever they have, at least a clean cloth if not a compress. Anything else? The guy on the radio is nearly hysterical, so I don't know if he will get that done. Get the bullhorn in the great cabin, go forward and start repeatedly telling them to apply pressure."

Tony rushes forward, climbs the foremast starboard shrouds. The bullhorn amplifies is voice as he says, "You must apply direct pressure on the wound with the heel of your hand using a large thick bandage, a clean towel, or a clean t-shirt. Do it now, right now."

He repeats the order again and again as we rapidly close in on the fishing boat. It is about thirty feet long, a little pilothouse cabin forward, its hull is dirty white, and slightly scuffed up, a dark green stripe just below the gunwale, another on the water line. The name *Sarah Tess* is spelled out in big square letters on her transom. She's apparently powered by an inboard engine, no outboard is in view. There are two small outrigger poles on either side of the cabin, a short radio antenna on its top. As we approach and the *Endeavour* slows, I see one person is in the little cabin, another bending down in the cockpit. Moments later, the *Endeavour* is looming over the much smaller fishing boat. Our engines are reversed momentarily as we stop alongside. I see the victim lying on his back near the transom. The cockpit is awash in blood, as is the water around the boat. Bloody water flows in and out of the boat's scupper drains (openings just below the boat's deck to allow water to run off). A dorsal fin flashes between us and the fishing boat. The man in the cabin hands a towel to the crewman bending over the victim. He then turns toward the *Endeavour* grabbing at a line tossed across. He's dressed in cutoff blue jeans, black sneakers, a baseball-style cap with a long black bill. His large, protruding belly is barely covered by a faded red, collarless shirt with a drawing of a black dog, above which in small black letters reads "The Black Dog". He ties the line to a mid-ships cleat. A crewman jumps with another line from the ship into the smaller boat, tying off to a forward cleat. Other crewmen swarm onboard to make the two vessels fast together, as Tony, Margaret and Harry jump down into the fishing boat.

The First Mate angrily shouts, "Careful, damn it, you want to be shark lunch?"

The Operations Room radio operator at Air Station Cape Cod strides over to the door as the jeep pulls up from the helicopter flight line. "Lieutenant, I've got the GDO on the line…a medical emergency on a boat south of Martha's Vineyard."

Lieutenant (j.g.) Francis Ondishko steps from the jeep and walks quickly inside. Speaking into the radio's small, handheld mike, "Lieutenant Ondishko here."

"Franny, Lieutenant Norris here, Group Duty Officer. This is a pre-alert for a Jayhawk MEDEVAC launch, rescue swimmer with a litter hoist. Already got a 'Go' from D1 (First Coast Guard District D1 in Boston). No doubt we'll get the same from the Flight Surgeon. Situation is this: major trauma from shark attack twenty-two miles SSE of Gay Head. Crewman on a fishing boat had his leg severely bitten, apparently massive tissue damage, blood loss, probably moderate to severe shock. The Aussie three-masted ship *Endeavour* is on scene with some first aid capability. Your people have to move fast, go get him, deliver to Cape Cod Hospital."

"Sounds nasty. Permission to hit the SAR Alarm?"

"Permission granted, but standby for final authorization, out."

"Roger, out." Franny reaches across the console alongside the radio, lifts a cover to reveal a button. Pushing the button sends a loud "*Whoop...Whoop...Whoop*" alarm crashing through the intercom. Soon afterward, Franny steps to a nearby microphone. Careful to sound firm and urgent, not too excited, he announces, "Now put the ready aircraft on the line, MEDEVAC southeast of Martha's Vineyard—Rescue Swimmer Provide."

Silence for a moment, then pounding feet as the two duty pilots charge up the stairs into the Operations Room. First they dash over to the flight planning area to check weather and get information about the case. Clear visibility, two- to three-foot seas, southwest winds at ten to fifteen miles per hour. Franny briefs them on what he's learned, sternly reminds them to check the aircraft first aid equipment, especially to be sure there's plenty of sterile gauze, large compresses, tourniquet elements, blankets. Make sure warm fluids are on board.

The pilots scramble downstairs to put on their dry suits, then followed by Franny, rush out the door as several aircrew roll the big HH-60J Jayhawk helicopter out of the nearby hangar, onto the flight line. Though Franny himself is a pilot, he remains impressed, even slightly awed by the Jayhawk. It's a brute—sixty-five feet long, two big gas turbines, one for a huge fifty-four-foot-diameter rotor blade, the other the whirling tail rotor, black snout and bright orange forward section and tail. Franny thinks she is some formidable beast.

The pilots jump in, one to check the on-board gear including looking over the litter basket, the other checking the helo's gauges. As they settle into the two forward seats, Franny orders, "Start up, wait for my signal to launch!"

Both flash thumbs-up signs. Franny steps away from the cockpit as the rescue swimmer arrives. With a big grin, a large, broad-shouldered, very fit middle-aged man with short black hair salutes Franny. "Boatswain Mate Lubas reporting, sir!"

"Mickey...glad you got tagged! But be careful, could be messy—shark bite, shock, bloody mess. Don't get your feet wet, probably sharks in the water. More details en route. Get it done…you're the man!"

One more crewman jumps into the helo's open doorway, the flight mechanic.

The swimmer is the only crewman wearing a wetsuit in the summer heat. All four are now seated in the helo, the rescue swimmer strapped into a little jump seat next to the open sliding door.

Before Franny reaches the Operations Room door, the radio operator slams the door hard against the building as he rushes out. "GDO just got final approval for launch."

Franny turns to the helo, strides toward its nose, gesturing thumbs up, and pointing skyward. The pilot salutes as the Jayhawk lifts off the ground, tilts slightly left and roars off to the south. Located at the Otis Air National Guard base, eight miles south of the Bourne Bridge onto Cape Cod, the Jayhawk, flying at an airspeed of 140 knots will reach the *Endeavour* in less than fifteen minutes.

Alice, then the professor, join me next to the great cabin companionway as we stare horrified at the scene below us on the fishing boat.

Pointing in the water around the boat, the professor says, "Thresher sharks, you can tell by their extremely long, arching tail and large round eyes."

Tony and Harry kneel on either side of the victim, Margaret behind his head, unfolding a small blanket and placing it over his torso. Tony has a pair of tweezers in his right hand, picking out chunks of flesh and what appears to be bone from the wound, as Harry shakes a mercurochrome solution directly on. Quickly after they apply the solution they place a large piece of gauze on the wound, then a thick bandage on which they're applying pressure with the heel of each's left hand. I can hear the Captain talking on the radio. Suddenly he climbs halfway up the companionway yelling, "Give me a status report! What's the victim's condition?"

Tony shouts back, "Trying to get the bleeding to slow, but not stopped yet. Huge blood loss…arterial bleeding…blood is spurting. Tibia appears bitten nearly through, lots of damage around the ankle. Pulse is erratic. We're losing him into shock."

Harry adds, "It's a nasty wound, too wide to cover with one compress. I've got another one on, but still losing blood. We did some cleaning and were able to pack the wound with sterile gauze before applying pressure. It's likely he'll go deeper into shock. We've *got* to stop this bleeding completely. Probably need a tourniquet. Agree, Tony?"

"Yeah, don't like it, we could lose the leg. The trouble is, it may be now as long as ten minutes since the bite occurred, and there's been blood loss through much of that time. These guys slowed it for a moment, then lost it."

The Captain replies, "Wait one." He ducks back down the companionway. I can hear him on the radio, apparently with the Coast Guard.

He returns to the companionway. "Coast Guard is scrambling a chopper with full gear to lift him out. They say to try pressure for full blood stoppage for another two or three minutes, then if still anything but a trickle of blood, apply a tourniquet just above the wound. Can we do that, Tony?"

"We have the materials, but I've never done it."

Harry turns toward the *Endeavour*. "I have. Tony can take up full pressure on the wound I'll set up for a tourniquet. Likely we'll need it. Margaret, please give me a triangular bandage from your kit."

She hands him the bandage, then lifts out a six-inch piece of wood. "We put this in to use to turn the knot tight."

"Good work," says Harry, "terrific first aid kit."

Tony peers down at the wound. He's applying pressure with both hands, one on each compress over the wound. "Still bleeding, though less. I think we go with the tourniquet. Coast Guard is at least minutes away no matter how fast they make it here. It's our only chance. We still could lose him."

Harry wraps the bandage around the victim's leg twice tying the ends with an overhand knot. Then using the free ends of the bandage he ties the wood stick on top of the triangular bandage with a square knot. He starts slowly to rotate the stick around the square knot, tightening the bandage.

Tony exclaims, "That's got it, bleeding has stopped." He and Margaret examine the wound carefully as Harry holds the stick motionless. He then ties it in place with the ends of the bandage left over from the square knot.

Tony, turns to the victim's head. "We've got to treat for shock. It's the 'ABC's'—right, Margaret?"

"Yes, airway—breathing—circulation. Get behind his head and use the jaw-thrust technique. Put your fingers under each side of his jaw, lift up and forward without tilting his head back."

Tony performs this little maneuver, peers into the victim's mouth, sticks his index finger and middle finger in the victim's mouth. "Seems OK, can't feel any obstruction, tongue's OK."

Margaret leans over the victim, puts her ear over his mouth, lightly touches his chest and abdomen. "Breathing seems sort of shallow, and it's definitely fast; each breath is short."

Tony says, "Not good, shock is getting deeper. I'll check circulation." He slides his index and middle finger down alongside the victim's neck muscle feeling for a pulse. "I'd say it's weak. Feel it, Harry."

Harry does so, nodding. "Yeah. Let's get ready to do CPR."

I'm startled as the Captain appears right next to me, leaning over the railing. "Coast Guard chopper pilot says he less than five minutes from our position…amazing! He's got a visual on us."

We all look up trying to spot the helicopter. The first recognition is the noise. We turn in the direction of the well-known *"whomp-whomp-whomp"* sound.

"There it is," Alice shouts, pointing over the top of the foremast.

Co-pilot Warrant Officer Jimmy DeForest, "Tree" to all who know him, establishes radio guard with Group Woods Hole, the Coast Guard area command stationed at Woods Hole on Cape Cod. The GDO tells him to access the *Endeavour* on marine radio channel 83. Moments later into the microphone on his headset he says, *"Endeavour,* we have a visual on you. Our position is approximately eight miles northwest, closing fast. We will be on site in five minutes. Please provide a detailed description of your vessel and the fishing boat."

Listening to the *Endeavour* captain's reply, "Tree" is fidgeting to stretch out his lanky frame as he interjects, "Sir, please have the fishing boat lower its two outriggers all the way down. Turn your vessel along with the fishing boat forty-five degrees to the right of the windline. Do that now. In your current position, you are facing approximately due North, turn ninety degrees to port. Also, please prepare both vessels for severe downwash, securing all loose gear and materials. The helo has 80 to 100 knots of downwash. Anything loose will be blown right off both vessels.

"We will conduct a direct deployment of the rescue swimmer onto the bow of the fishing boat. He will be preceded by a 'trail line'. Have two or more crewmen on the bow of the fishing boat to grab the line. It's made of orange nylon, easy to spot. They will help steady the rescue swimmer as he's lowered down. They must protect the line from becoming wrapped in the fishing boat's rigging and gear. Once the swimmer is down, they should stand by to tend the trail line as we will retrieve it, then attach the basket litter to the hoist hook and lower it right behind the swimmer. He will proceed immediately to the patient. Detach the litter from the hook on the line, following instructions from the swimmer. We will retrieve the hook, then re-position the aircraft, again lower the trail line, then the hook. The swimmer will hook the litter up to the hoist hook once he has the patient ready for hoisting. Is all that understood?"

Tree gets an affirmative from *Endeavour*, folds one long leg over the other and turns to instruct and supervise the flight mechanic preparing the line and hoist.

Harry steps across the boat's deck toward all of us leaning on the *Endeavour's* rail. "Captain, we can provide CPR, all of us. Tony, Margaret and I are trained. I suggest we tell the chopper we'll proceed on his OK."

The Captain nods and jumps down the companionway to the radio position. In a moment he returns to the top of the companionway. "He agrees. Will be overhead in three minutes; have a swimmer down within two minutes after that, then lower a litter onto the fishing boat right thereafter."

"Captain," says Tony, "negative on the swimmer; sharks all around here."

"Right, of course. That's just the guy's title. He's going to drop the swimmer right onto the boat. There are only small swells; our masts are only swaying a few degrees; shouldn't be a problem."

Tony kneels over the victim, again feeling his neck for a pulse. "Pulse is still there. Harry, keep your fingers on his pulse; I'll kneel over him to check breathing. You be ready to do mouth-to-mouth. I'll standby to do the chest compressions."

Margaret has walked over to a crewman, covered with blood, slumped against the cabin, head down. "Where are you injured?"

He mumbles without looking up, "I'm not, it's Lenny's blood all over me." He glances up at her, tears streaming down his black stubble beard. "Is he dying?"

She puts her arm around him. "No, he's lost lots of blood, he may or may not lose his lower leg, but I think he'll survive. These guys know first aid, and the Coast Guard will be able to stabilize him and get him to a hospital really fast. He's got a good chance."

"What a goddamn mess, all over a stinkin' goddamn shark." He slides down, squatting on the bloody deck. "Why the goddamn hell wouldn't he listen to get off the goddamn platform…why…why?" He starts to whimper, then sobs louder and louder. Margaret crouches down, puts her arms around him as his shoulders rapidly rise and fall.

The Captain has ordered the *Endeavour* to turn ninety degrees to port. Doing so enables the ship and attached *Sarah Tess* to move slightly away from the bloody site, still full of circling, snapping sharks. Some have even butted their snouts up against the *Sarah* Tess's transom where the bloody water continues sloshing in and out at the scuppers. The now-dead gaffed thresher shark also has been attracting fellow sharks hitting on its carcass. Our turn to port serves to clear us slightly away. The Captain orders a crewman to use a shipboard hose to wash the remaining bloody water out the boat's scupper drains as we make the turn.

The Coast Guard helicopter is directly overhead, the noise overwhelming, the downdraft blowing hats and debris everywhere. In what seems like scant seconds, a helmeted crewman in a wet suit steps from the door, standing on a small sling. Boatswains Mate Mickey Lubas descends, guided by two *Endeavour* crewmen holding the orange trail line. He detaches his little sling, it's retrieved and moments later a basket litter emerges attached at four points to a massive hook. The *Endeavour* crewmen grab the descending litter and detach it from the hook, carefully carrying it aft to the cockpit of the *Sarah Tess*. The helicopter shifts slightly to keep the line perpendicular. Mickey leans over the victim talking to Tony and Harry. The noise makes it impossible to hear the conversation. He checks the pulse and breathing, signals to the helicopter holding up his index finger. He over-wraps the wound and entire lower leg using a role of gauze he pulls from a pouch wrapped around his waist, secures the wrap with a large elastic bandage from another pocket of the pouch. Then he, Harry and Tony lift the victim, Lenny, onto the litter as Margaret very gently holds the wounded leg, one hand under the knee, the other the heel. Mickey quickly clips all of the stretcher's straps across Lenny's body. He signals thumbs up to the helicopter. Moments later the litter is alongside the open helicopter door, as arms reach out to bring them in. The hook is dropped back down with the small sling attached. Mickey steps on the sling and rapidly ascends to the helicopter door. The helicopter is already moving, tilting sharply off to the right, heading back in the direction from which it came. The trail line is detached and falls harmlessly in the water.

Harry, Margaret and Tony slowly shuffle across the cockpit of the *Sarah Tess* toward us. Pale-faced, their entire body demeanor slumped and slow, each of them covered with blood, they struggle on board next to us. Alice puts her left arm around Harry's shoulder, kisses his cheek gently and lays her head on his shoulder. No words, hardly a look from Harry, as he puts his arm around her and pulls her closer to him. The Captain shakes Tony's hand and lightly kisses Margaret on the cheek. "Thank you both, wonderful effort, wonderful."

He says to the crewman in the Black Dog shirt, "We'll release all lines now. Do you need assistance to make your home port?"

"No, thanks, we'll make it." He starts to walk toward the little pilothouse then turns back. "Thanks for your help. Maybe Lenny will make it. Wouldn't have without you guys."

We watch the helicopter flying northward until it's just a noisy speck in the sky.

I turn around aware of crewmen gathering directly behind me. The next watch is getting organized. Tony yells to us that we're off duty when replaced. He goes on to order us amidships, where the Captain will brief the entire crew. A few minutes later the Captain, holding a glossy, colorful pamphlet says, "First and most importantly, the patient has already been off-loaded at Cape Cod Hospital Trauma Center in Hyannis, and is in the 'OR' right now. The Coast Guard says he's been stabilized and they will let us know his condition. My compliments to Tony, Margaret and Harry Cassis for some damn fine work...probably saved Lenny's life. Everybody involved did very well indeed."

He holds up the pamphlet brightly titled, "Newport Maritime Days: Revolutionary Newport, sponsored by the Maritime Society of Newport, the Newport Maritime History Museum, and the Waterfront Merchants Association". The Captain begins by telling us the *Endeavour* is to be the star of this weekend event, the second in a series of waterfront spectacles. First was Colonial Newport and later in the summer will be Gilded Age Newport. It obviously is a chance to lure tourists, to show off an apparently remarkable collection of maritime historical memorabilia, authentic and replica. All the waterfront businesses pitch in with displays and foods and various routines. The Captain looks sourly through a sheaf of paper, goes on to say there'll be a clambake at $25.00 per person, numerous displays of maritime artifacts, open houses, Newporters roaming the streets dressed up in period costumes, a race for small wooden sailboats, street entertainers, and "on and on and on, a regular circus. One of our volunteer crew members is all involved, Walter Buckingham. Walter, maybe you can add something interesting."

Harry leans over to me. "What is the professor up to? Remember, that look he gave you and me when he was telling his Rhode Island tales?"

"No idea."

The professor gets up, again glancing over to Harry and me. "I teach colonial history at the University of Rhode Island, which is nearby, in Kingston, Rhode Island.

"Newport is not just another 'pretty face'." Some chuckles from the assembled crew. "Before it became a playground for the super rich, early on it was an important port, especially in the eighteenth century. Leading up to the Revolution it was a powerful commercial center, richer than New York. That interesting and important record, coupled with the absurd wealth of its later summer visitors made the preservation of its maritime history a slam dunk. For decades now, money has poured in to preserve or replicate. In fact, Newport itself exists as it is today because one really rich lady decided to preserve and replicate the whole downtown area. In the 1960s Doris Duke spent untold millions turning Newport into something of a New England, maritime Williamsburg. But she lived in Newport, and didn't want to be living in an outdoor museum. The city needed its daily life. So she bought and restored dozens of early American buildings, renting them back to Newporters. The result you'll see is a wonderful mix of eighteenth- and nineteenth-century architecture housing private homes, B&B's, museums, stores, restaurants, etc.

"But I digress as I often do. The waterfront events…. The sponsors have several actual eighteenth-century boats. Not replicas, painstakingly preserved originals. Since colonial history is my field and its coastal and maritime life is my particular specialty, the Newport Maritime Museum invited me to consult on the Newport Maritime Days project. As often happens to teachers, they didn't pay me. However, they did offer me a reward. My reward comes tomorrow. I'll be in an authentic late eighteenth-century tender called a 'jolly boat'. I'll be wearing an authentic English naval lieutenant's uniform welcoming the *Endeavour* to Newport Harbor. Jolly boats belonged to ships of war and were used to carry passengers and light cargo. When the ship was underway the jolly boat was hoisted at the stern. This one is quite beamy, and fitted for rowing and sailing. Boats like it—gigs, whaleboats, pinnaces—were often used by the British as 'press tenders'. These boats were used to round-up men impressed into service in the British Navy. That was a nasty business the British did constantly here and at home. In fact it was a significant cause of our next war against the British, The War of 1812. Interestingly, it seems likely this one may well have been used in the Newport area, and could have been used, among other things, to impress local men into the British Navy. Newport was occupied by the British from 1776 to 1779. It was an important naval base with thousands of British troops bivouacked there as well.

"The *Endeavour* will be escorted into Newport likely by a big crowd of boats—private boats, ferries, and who knows what else, but certainly including several America's Cup racing yachts. At the entrance to the harbor I'll be picked up and brought into the waterfront area. Along with several others in authentic uniforms, we'll later sail out to greet the *Endeavour* as you pick up your mooring. The *Endeavour* will stay on the mooring overnight then tie up at Brown & Howard Wharf the next morning."

The Captain interrupts to say, "They have us on the mooring apparently for several reasons—to spruce up the ship before it goes on display for visitors; and to do a whole series of sail drills for local TV to film. Also, Newport has a small fleet of America's Cup 12-meter sailboats. Several will be racing in Narragansett Bay tomorrow and one or two will tie up at the dock space we'll later occupy. There's also a US Coast Guard ship in the same area. The voyage crew won't be finished until we get to our dock. That way you all get to go through lots more sail handling and a major ship's clean-up. You can't say we don't want you to get your absolute fill of crewing the *Endeavour*!"

Dismissed, we head down to the twentieth century galley for dinner. Harry and I shuffle along in line, getting salad, fresh bread, a thick brown stew and milk, another hearty carbo-load shipboard meal. We sit down, moments later joined by Alice holding hands with a very subdued Harry. Silence, then the professor and Andrew join our table.

Andrew says to Harry, "You think that guy will make it?"

Harry doesn't look up. Head down, mechanically buttering his pieces of bread, he mumbles, "Hope so."

Andrew quickly asks, "How about his leg; will he lose it?"

"Hope not."

Alice looks over to Andrew. "Let's change the subject for now, shall we? Thanks."

Moments later, Andrew points his fork at the professor. "Walter, I've read Newport was a hotbed of traitors and Loyalists during the Revolution."

Alice jolts up straight, with an exasperated look at Andrew, opens her mouth, but before she has a chance, the professor waves his hand slightly.

He replies, "OK Andrew, for a minute we can talk about Loyalists, just a minute. I'll pass on the subject of traitors though, too complicated a term when a third of all Americans supported the Crown throughout the Revolution, and thousands later left for Canada, the Bahamas, even England.

"Certainly there were many Loyalists in Newport; nevertheless the British treated Newport very harshly. Residents were evicted from homes, wharves ripped up, property and furnishings seized. Most churches became stables or barracks. It wasn't a nice place to be. Patriots fled north to Providence and other towns. Merchants escaped with what the British didn't destroy. The Hessian mercenaries, accompanying the British, stole and burned throughout the countryside. Here's how bad it got. The British finally left Newport in 1779, when they were ordered to New York. That winter was terrible. The residents were desperate just to survive. So desperate they were reduced to tearing down empty houses for firewood."

"What happened to the Loyalists when the British went to New York?" Andrew asks.

"For the most part, their only chance was to go along to New York. They surely wouldn't have survived if they remained in Newport, especially after such a hard occupation by their British protectors, though they weren't always very protective."

The professor abruptly stands up, picks up his food tray and deposits it in the nearby trash bin. He nods at me and walks out of the galley.

Apparently he wants me to follow him. All this glancing and nodding seems silly, but I don't want to insult him. I get up and trudge after him. Looking over at Harry I see he's only paying attention to Alice as he munches relentlessly on one piece of bread after another.

I spot the professor leaning on a big locker in the crew mess. Walking up I ask, "Why didn't you mention the new *Endeavour* passing over the old? That's great stuff."

"It's not part of the celebration, not being mentioned. Only a few historians and marine archeologists actually know about it. Currently the old one's location is being identified by a local archeology group. I guess the rather nasty last days of the *Endeavour* as the prison ship *Lord Sandwich* don't fit the celebratory style of Newport Maritime Days.

"Jack, there's one more part of this story I'd like to tell you and Harry together, just the three of us. It could represent an amazing opportunity. But— sorry for the secretiveness—I'd like to keep it just between us."

"What is it?"

"Not now, we need to pry Harry loose from Alice. Nothing against her, it's just that what opportunity there may be can't include her. I'll explain it's not Alice herself at all. I know I'm assuming a lot here. But we've talked for days. I'm sure this will really interest you and Harry. I guess I'm asking you to indulge me. It'll just take a few minutes to explain."

"OK, OK. I'll ask Harry to meet us. Where and when?"

"How about at the ship's bell in a half hour?"

"We'll try and see you then."

I climb the companionway to the main deck. The professor is being mysterious. He's obviously nervous, all stirred up. Whatever it is, he evidently thinks it is special. Why is he so nervous?

I see Harry and Alice approaching. Alice lightly touches my arm. "I hope you can come with us on our Newport jaunt."

"I hope so too, though likely only for one day."

Alice replies, "Well I really look forward to it. Excuse me, I'm going to get a sweater, be right back."

As Alice disappears down the companionway I turn to Harry. "The professor has something he wants to tell just you and me. I have no idea what it is, but he describes it as an 'amazing opportunity'. He wants to meet at the ship's bell in a half hour. I think we should indulge him. And I must admit to being curious. He seems very excited and nervous about whatever it is. OK with you?"

"Sure, what can we lose? The professor's an interesting guy so no reason not to. No Alice?"

"No. He says it's nothing against Alice, but she doesn't fit somehow. I'm going below to take a fast shower and get out of these shorts. See you shortly."

*　　　　*　　　　*　　　　*　　　　*

Harry and the professor are already at the bell when I climb back on deck. Harry is still in his shorts and *Endeavour* jersey. The professor has put on a windbreaker. Harry pats the professor on the back. "OK professor, what's up?"

"I have complete access to the jolly boat I described earlier. Once the *Endeavour* is secure on her mooring, I'll come aboard from it along with a guy dressed in a replica uniform of a British post captain. We'll welcome the ship for the TV and newspaper photos. I'll stay on board and the others eventually will return to shore. The jolly boat will remain with the ship. The next day, I'll get back into my lieutenant's uniform and in the jolly boat lead the *Endeavour* into her space at Brown & Howard Wharf. I can arrange for you guys to be in the boat, rowing or raising the sail to go the short distance from the mooring to the dock.

"Over the years the museum has received some incredible donations from wealthy sponsors and collectors. The museum's collection includes several sets of naval uniforms and other clothing from the period, including uniforms of British sea officers, plus American and French sailors. It has some clothing which are not uniforms but likely worn by crewmen at sea during the period— American ships didn't have uniformed crews. Some of it probably came from crewmen on whalers, trading vessels, even privateers. Seamen in the British Navy in the late eighteenth century had uniforms, though they made them themselves and only wore them for special occasions. They wore sailcloth pants, collarless striped jerseys and blue jackets. There are three sets of seamen's sailcloth pants and a few striped shirts, one of which probably is large enough to fit you, Harry. There are also two blue jackets—British Navy seamen were called 'bluejackets'—one of which certainly will fit Jack. I'm sure we can put together authentic outfits for both of you. You could then have real parts in the Maritime Days activities. I'll bring them out with me when we welcome the *Endeavour* at her mooring. Seems to me it'll be great fun to do together. I want to you guys to have the first chance to do it, before I ask anybody else."

Harry turns toward me. "That sounds cool to me. But, can just the three of us handle this tender?"

The professor shrugs. "We should be fine in fair conditions. She's only twenty-two feet long, with a small gaff-rigged sail. She has two sets of big sweep oars. So we'll have you guys plus two others. I'll be at the tiller. The distance from the mooring to our wharf space is not far, just a few hundred yards. She's heavy so not exactly fast and easy to handle like a dory, but should be OK."

"What's the weather forecast?" I ask.

"Doesn't seem bad," the professor replies. "I asked the Captain. Light winds, weather shifting toward south, likely bringing in fog at night, cool early then hot and humid during the day tomorrow and especially the next day. Thunderstorms are possible."

"Like I said," Harry exclaims, "it seems like a good plan. I'd love to do it. Are you in?" He punches me lightly on the shoulder.

"Are you kidding? I wouldn't miss this!"

"Great," the professor seems not only genuinely happy, but oddly, relieved as well. "You don't actually have to do anything for now. Once you're on the mooring and I've come out in the tender, we'll check out the clothes. We'll choose the best stuff for you to wear."

I ask, "Maybe we can wear some of our own clothes, sort of fill in with the real stuff?"

"No, no, that's not possible," the professor replies heatedly. Seemingly catching himself, he goes on, "Sorry, I don't mean to make a deal of that. It's just that we've made a very big effort to be as authentic as possible. I'm sure we'll have clothes that work fine."

"OK, we're in. But Walter, I'm not sure I get what's 'amazing' about this. No doubt it'll be fun and interesting, but earlier you said to me it was an 'amazing opportunity'? Help me out. What do you mean?"

The professor leans forward toward us. "Don't you see? This is maybe an once-in-a-lifetime opportunity to have a truly authentic historical experience. Not just visiting a site, or looking at artifacts in a museum, or reading history, but nearly living it. We will be in a real eighteenth-century boat, in real eighteenth-century clothes, just having come off a virtually real eighteenth-century ship. We won't have to imagine it, for a few moments we'll have it! But here's the best part, the part I want just the three of us to share."

He's right in our faces now, eyes gleaming, some spittle plainly visible in the corners of his mouth. "So you can get a feel for the jolly boat, I'll arrange to take her out late tonight, just the three of us. It'll be quiet and dark. There will be heavy fog. The sights and sounds of modern life will be muffled and minimized…not gone, but barely part of the background. We'll go for a sail. Can you imagine how that will feel?"

Harry asks, "Where would we sail?"

"To the site where the original *Endeavour* was scuttled. Where else?"

FOUR

Once again I push the button on the top of my watch to illuminate its face. It now reads 2:19 a.m. Have I gotten any sleep? None, not a damn minute, and we're on deck for the morning watch at 4:00. Over and again I find myself coming back to the professor's late night sailing scheme. Harry's taken to calling it "Weird Walter's Great Adventure". He accepts the plan on its face value, a night-time sail in an old tender. He concedes the plan to sail the jolly boat over the site of the scuttled *Endeavour/Lord Sandwich* is a little odd, maybe even slightly spooky, but mostly harmless. He went on and on about sailing at night on the Potomac. The best sailing he insists is on a good night—there is plenty of light from the moon, city lights and especially lights on the roads adjacent to the river. It's quiet, no other boats are around. It seems you have the river to yourself. Very often, he claims, he'll sail until early morning, then sleep overnight onboard back at his marina. Most of the time he single handles the boat, sleeping in the tiny cabin forward of the cockpit. I like the name he gave his twenty-two-foot day sailor, "*Cop Out*".

Soon after he described his idea, the professor explained he had to go over details of the Newport activities with the Captain and left us. Harry and I went back and forth about him and his idea. Harry thinks it's a highly romantic notion mostly driven by the professor's devotion to colonial history. For a day or two he gets to play what he studies. It brings the dry world of history somewhat to life. You hardly can blame him for being excited and for trying to get as close as he can to a sense of place and time.

Alice came by in snug blue jeans and a baggy blue cotton sweater over a white turtleneck. She put her arm around Harry as we all walked to the stern of the *Endeavour*. Standing next to the British naval ensign, we leaned on the taffrail (rail across the stern) and watched the ship's wake trailing away. Harry explained to Alice that the professor had asked us to participate in the Maritime Days event and told her about the jolly boat and the clothing. He then looked over at me and insisted he wanted to tell Alice about our little late-night sail. Before I could object, he emphasized to Alice the importance of sharing this with no one, as the professor meant it just for us. He went on that he was telling her knowing she would respect its privacy. I was a bit surprised when he didn't include the destination, just described it as a night-time sail to "feel like eighteenth-century sailors."

As I expected, Alice's response was very positive, that it sounded like a "neat" plan, one on which she would have loved to go. Harry started to reply, but she put her finger on his lips and told him not even "to think about it". She kept her arm around him as she turned to ask my opinion of the professor's "jaunt", apparently a word she favored.

I explained my take was a little "edgier" than Harry's. I went on that I had spent much more time with the professor than had they. I said two factors made my reaction different. First, I gave them some details of the professor admitting and describing his "obsession" with local colonial history. Walter freely admits it is a consuming passion. He describes the process as though it were a giant jigsaw puzzle. He is compulsive about endlessly trying to fit pieces together. Only in his case, he concedes the compulsion is absurdly complex. He must first find the pieces, interpret and authenticate them, then fit them together. I continued that my concern was the power of his apparent fixation, and his ready admission to being driven by it. Second, I asked Harry to describe Walter while he was telling us his sailing idea. Harry admitted he looked a little "loopy". I laughed, saying that for me he was a lot more than "loopy", closer to "nuts". My fear is he has transferred his fixation with the puzzle into the night-time sail. That makes the whole idea of the sail a lot more problematic, even unpredictable. I wanted to add, especially given our destination, but couldn't because of Harry's odd omission.

Harry scoffed at that, saying even if he does go nuts, there are two of us. We can manage.

Alice added very little, rightfully saying she wasn't there for the "loopy look". Moreover, she had no idea the professor was so preoccupied.

We chatted for a while on what we might do together in Newport. I lobbied for a highly recommended restaurant in a B&B housed in an eighteenth-century home. I then headed for the "twentieth century" to find a corner spot and read a few pages in my as-yet-unread paperback, before wrestling my way into hammock 10. Harry and Alice waved distractedly as I left.

Still in my hammock, another thought creeps into my ruminations on the professor. It seems he may have been planning this adventure for a while. Several memories come together—his insistent urging that I value the "eighteenth-century sailing experience" of the *Endeavour*; his attention to Harry and me the last few days as though somehow he had selected us and wanted to get to know us better; his generally distant attitude toward Alice suggested he wasn't thrilled to have her around; his readily-apparent joy telling tales of eighteenth-century Newport. Is all this part of a plan he's cooked up? And why was he evidently so relieved when we said we'd go? Is the plan finally coming together?

Now what time is it? My watch reads 2:41 a.m. This is silly lying here with no chance of sleep. I get up and head down to the "twentieth century" with my book.

In the galley, Andrew, with his Princeton baseball cap now turned backward, is just sitting down with Tony and Margaret. All three have steaming mugs of coffee in front of them. Damn, I just want to read my book, not have another prickly, irritating conversation with Andrew.

Tony sees me. "Join us, Jack?"

"Sure, soon as I finish the chapter I'm on."

As they nod, I take a cup of water, a tea bag and a spoon, retreating to the far corner of the galley. I should have some peace for a short while. Maybe I can stay out of the conversation until our watch is called.

But the galley is too small and Andrew too loud. As I squeeze the tea bag into the cup and stir in some sugar, Andrew's voice blasts through my hoped-for peace.

"Have you guys heard Samuel Johnson's famous quote about shipboard life? 'Being in a ship is being in jail, with the chance of being drowned.' I guess that's not as true now, but sailing in the Pacific with Cook for three years in the late 1700s, I bet it was too close to the truth for comfort."

Tony looks over at Andrew. "Well, if you compare it with today's life at sea certainly yes. But for his time Captain Cook was widely praised for his unusual interest in the health of his crew."

Andrew replies, "Maybe, but I read somewhere that he returned to England having lost more than a third of the original crew."

Tony continues, "That's actually very misleading. Cook had an amazing record with his crew. For example, after two years at sea, sailing from England to the Horn, across the Pacific, around New Zealand, up the east coast of Australia, and eventually to the Dutch East Indies, he arrived there having lost only eight of the original ninety-four in crew. That's an astonishing achievement in eighteenth-century sailing when losing large numbers of crew to diseases and injuries was normal. In the Dutch East Indies port of Batavia—today's Indonesian city of Jakarta—the crew got caught up in a malaria epidemic. Several crewmen died. Cook hired replacements, but they brought aboard 'the bloody flux'—to us, dysentery—and it decimated the crew. Eventually twenty-three died during the voyage from Batavia to the Cape of Good Hope. So, while it's true Cook came home having lost thirty-six dead of the original ninety-four, the vast majority of those deaths in fact were caused by circumstances clearly beyond Cook's control."

Margaret chimes in, "Cook actually sailed from England with almost four tons of sauerkraut, of all things. The sauerkraut was used to ward off the scourge of seamen, scurvy. The *Endeavour* sauerkraut was highly fermented. It must have been dreadful stuff. In the various journals by Cook, the scientists and ship's officers, it is described as awful and foul-smelling. Cook however persuaded the crew to eat it by telling them it was being served every day to the officers. Amazingly, in an era when scurvy was still devastating crews, the *Endeavour* arrived in Tahiti seven months after leaving England without a single fatal case of scurvy."

Scurvy was an appalling disease. Its symptoms were severe depression and fatigue, disgustingly foul breath, painfully swollen joints, later hemorrhaging, eventually death. As we now have long known, it is caused by an absence of Vitamin C. Therefore it is easily prevented by vitamin supplements and eating fresh fruits and vegetables. The British Navy of Cook's time had determined scurvy could be prevented by fresh food. Unfortunately most ships were faced with the impossibility of constantly re-provisioning for fresh food. Cook however was not. His voyage was one of discovery, scientific inquiry and exploration. He stopped regularly and in doing so, rigorously collected fresh foods for the crew. They caught fish, turtles, gathered oysters, and shot birds and animals whenever they could. Likely these fresh foods, particularly greens identified as edible by the botanist Solander, were the principal reason the *Endeavour* avoided scurvy so completely. Moreover, his journals make it plain he ordered regular cleaning of the ship, crew clothing, hammocks and bedding. He insisted on bathing. He regularly took seawater baths. He went so far as to use sails to divert fresh air from the weather deck into the lower decks.

Andrew snickers, "My God that sounds awful. Not only the sauerkraut, but all the food stored in the *Endeavour's* hold for months at a time, must have been revolting."

One of the galley crew has been listening in. "No, that wasn't always true. The sailors' diet seems to have been decent, especially with all the stopping. Their basic diet was meat four days each week, a pound of biscuits each day, and a gallon of beer daily. They also had some choices here, including rum and wine rations. The favorite choice was 'grog', which by the way is rum and water. The non-meat days had fish or cheese. Breakfast daily was wheat porridge with beef stock added. The journals of Banks and the other scientists on board note it was so good they ate it every morning. The fresh foods Cook insisted on obviously vastly improved this basic menu."

I can't read in the din of conversation, and Andrew's disagreeable style of asking with a smirk is just too irritating. "Andrew, what do you think was Cook's mission on the *Endeavour*? Why take the voyage in the first place?"

He looks over at me. "He was charting and claiming lands for the British Navy and the very 'squirrelly' king at the time, George III, of American Revolution fame."

Tony stands up. "What a load of silly nonsense. Is that what they teach you in America? I doubt it. It must be some left wing, liberal slant on the voyages. Someone set Andrew straight. I'm going on deck to get ready for the watch." Muttering, he hurries out of the galley and up the stairway to the crew's mess deck and the weather deck.

Margaret slides over next to Andrew. "I'm surprised at your answer. Cook, as far as I know, is widely regarded as an extraordinary explorer, navigator and chartist. You need to remember he set out not specifically to claim land, and certainly not to colonize. His purpose was to explore and chart. Along the way he in fact did claim lands for the crown, but this was a common practice in exploration. But his principal purpose was to explore the vast unknown waters of the Pacific, the 'Great South Sea'."

Actually his first specifically assigned task was to arrive in Tahiti in time to observe the transit of the planet Venus across the face of the sun, on June 3, 1769. He and other parties sent to Norway and Canada were dispatched by the British government in an attempt to achieve precise astronomical observations that were hoped ultimately to help deduce the distance between the sun and Earth. The plan—developed decades earlier by Edmond Halley of Halley's Comet fame—was to precisely track the planet's path across the face of the sun, from each of the three positions. By comparing the angles of the three widely dispersed measures, the distance could be derived. While they did get measures, Cook and the others were frustrated by their instruments' inability to time and track the path with sufficient precision. As a result, overall the astronomical calculations did not achieve their intent.

The balance of his orders from the Admiralty was to explore, especially for an unknown "south land" thought to be necessary to balance the known land masses of the northern hemisphere. And explore he did. He did so much charting that in effect he was among the last explorers of uncharted waters. Those explorers who followed him were left—with the exception of the poles—largely to filling in remaining blanks in the charts of known seas. During the course of his three epic voyages, he spent most of his time in waters for which there were no charts at all, and with no large-scale knowledge of weather patterns to enable him to anticipate storms. Despite using primitive navigational tools not unlike those used by his predecessors for centuries—albeit with considerable help from vast improvements in determining longitude by the eighteenth-century development of a reliable chronometer, as well as notable help from an improved sextant—his prolific charts were so precise they were later used by generations of seamen. Some were even used far into this century.

Andrew replies to Margaret, "He claimed Australia for England."
She nods and sips her coffee. "Yes, and did so at numerous other islands as well. Curiously his orders stated he should make the claim with the 'consent' of the natives. How he was to gain such consent was not addressed. However, in

an accompanying document The Royal Society acknowledged the natives were the 'legal possessors' of the land. His journals indicate the concept of claim was meaningless to the natives, thereby they didn't resist."

Sensing Andrew is ready to pounce, I walk over toward him and Margaret. Before I get a word out, Andrew leans back in his chair, "But you're conceding he made all these claims for England!"

I stop in front of Andrew, "I think the point here is not so much the claims. That was an expected act when European sailors arrived at a place with no European inhabitants. The claim itself, as a practical matter, was less a form of conquest, rather more a statement of use, access. That said the downside effect of all his claims clearly was terrible. Behind Cook came the devastating effects of English and other European sailors, traders, commercial enterprises, military garrisons, colonists and missionaries. They brought diseases for which the natives had no resistance, often business and labor practices that took extreme advantage of the natives, as well as an unwanted but widespread zeal for converting them to Christianity. Yet to contend these results were his purpose is, to use Tony's word, 'nonsense'. Cook was seeking a southern landmass, and charting all that he saw, not an advance man for the South Sea Company, the British trading firm in the Pacific."

"But you can't deny the effect of his voyage ultimately was ruinous to the natives!"

"Yes Andrew, but by the same token you can't ascribe the ruin to Cook. The ruin came over succeeding decades by those who followed."

Margaret is mad. She stands up, walks to the counter to drop off her mug. Glaring at Andrew she scolds, "You need to study Cook. You seem to want to make him out as some sort of evil scout enabling the corruption of Paradise. Frankly that's a remarkably uninformed and unfair conclusion. And I don't like it at all!"

In a few strides she's out of the galley and up the stairs.

Walking back to my seat I pick up my book. Turning back to Andrew, I ask, "What was the point of all that? You just pissed off two nice people."

"They don't seem to be prepared to deal with the facts and realities of Cook's voyages."

"How does adopting such a perverse style with them help?"

"Their answers and information are so conventional. I think they needed challenging."

"That's just insulting. It's one thing to ask some questions, to have a discussion. You were being deliberately contrary, almost baiting them. It's obvious and natural that they believe in Cook. They're on a replica of his ship for God's sake! I'm outa' here…time to get on deck for watch."

"You think they're right?"

"No, Andrew, more to the point, I think you're wrong."

Reaching the weather deck, I immediately notice the fog. It's thick and makes the air cool and moist. I'm glad I still have on my long pants and added a sweatshirt.

Tony, wearing his bright yellow slicker, has the Foremast watch gathered around him. "Good, here's Jack. So…I love to play golf. Jack told me this golf joke so blame him if you don't like it! On a golf tour of Ireland, Tiger Woods drives his BMW into a petrol station in a remote part of the Irish countryside. The pump attendant, obviously knowing nothing about golf, greets him in a typically friendly Irish way, completely unaware of who the driver is.

"'Top of the mornin' to yer, sir,' says the attendant.

"Tiger nods a quick 'hello' and bends forward to pick up the nozzle. As he does, two tees fall out of his shirt pocket onto the ground.

"'What are those?' asks the attendant.

"'They're called tees,' replies Tiger.

"'Well, what on the good earth are they for?' inquires the Irishman.

"'They're for resting my balls on when I'm driving,' says Tiger.

"'By Jaysus,' says the Irishman, 'BMW thinks of everything!'"

Everybody laughs, especially Alice, leaning into Harry who puts his arm around her as they giggle happily together. She reaches out and slaps my palm.

Tony looks around, asks "Everybody here?" just as Andrew arrives.

"Captain has slowed us way down. We'll just ghost along until the fog starts to lift after sunrise. Once it lifts we'll set some of the sails so we look like a proper ship coming up on Newport. We should be at the outer marker for the harbor by mid-morning. Hopefully there will be enough wind to sail into the harbor. He expects lots of boats to come out to greet *Endeavour*."

The professor is standing nearby. "Wait 'til you see!"

Tony looks over at Andrew. "One more thing. The galley needs someone to do some extra pot and grill scrubbing before breakfast. I don't think you've had a chance to scrub yet Andrew, so I volunteered you for the job. The galley folk were very appreciative. Margaret will show you the drill. Thanks for helping out. Margaret, please get Andrew started."

"Delighted," laughs Margaret, "come with me, Andrew."

As Andrew and Margaret head down the nearby companionway, Tony's trying hard not to laugh, but mistakenly looks over at me, gives up, letting out a whoop of laughter. It's impossible not to follow, as several of us burst out in guffaws.

After an hour at the wheel with the First Mate next to me nervously peering into the darkness and fog, even posting Wes far out on the jib-boom for better forward viewing, I am relieved by Margaret taking over the wheel. She smiles happily as she grabs the wheel. "Last seen Andrew was waist deep in huge cooking pots. His fancy hat had a big grease smear on its top. He seemed most unhappy. Ah, the shame of it all." This provokes a giggle fit until the First Mate's scowls get her attention.

For the next hour, I "kick back", watching the *Endeavour* creep along at three or four knots. The steady "thrum-thrum" noise of the diesel engines was sedating me into a mildly hypnotic state so it takes a while to recognize the change. Finally I realize it is no longer entirely dark. I can see the full length of the ship, though not much else. Dawn had snuck in but not yet dispersed the fog. I hear a yell from forward, notice Tony standing next to the ship's bell whistling and waving. He's gathering the watch for our next assignments.

"We'll be changing course to the northwest shortly. There's a little puffy wind beginning to build in from the south-southwest. So we'll be able to sail a bit shortly. Captain wants us to set the topsail and course for all three masts. That'll make us look nice and ship-like. Mainmast watch will be brought on deck to handle the lines, we'll handle the sails. We'll do it mast-by-mast, mainmast first. Half of you go to the topsail yard, half to the course. We'll go aloft in fifteen minutes. When you're done scampering up and down the *Endeavour*, you'll have a great reward…pancakes and Vegemite, or syrup for the wimpy Americans!"

"Tony, did you hear the news last night?" asks Wes. "The American Dental Association has formally requested the FDA to ban the importation and sale of Vegemite in the US. Compliance seems assured as hundreds, even thousands of support letters, faxes and emails pour in to the FDA."

"Thank God for the courage of the ADA!" Alice exclaims to cheers and applause.

What little wind there is hardly moves the main topsail as we drop it while the mainmast crew makes the various halyards and sheets fast, and braces trimmed.

Wes and I along with two other Foremast crew scramble down the mainmast shrouds. We quickly walk aft and climb the mizzen mast shrouds to the mizzen top.

Tony yells out, "Foremast, hold on for ten minutes; Mainmast needs to tidy up some."

Wes looks over at me. "Ya' hear about the Sox last night?"

During the voyage we've discovered we're both lifelong Boston Red Sox fans. We've been sharing the endless tales of baseball minutia that baseball fans accumulate, particularly Red Sox fans. This year the "Bosox" have been contending all season. But for their fans that seeming success more often than not is seen very much as a "mixed blessing". Despite plenty of talent and the support of millions of hopelessly passionate supporters throughout New England, the Red Sox ultimately seem only to succeed at one thing, breaking the hearts of their fans.

"Nomar cleared the Monster in the eleventh; the Bosox now are only four games out."

"All right!" I reply. "That's great! Problem is I just don't think they've got the relief horses to catch the Yankees. If they can stay close until the series at Fenway over Labor Day…maybe."

Wes replies, "Yeah, probably right. I got tickets for the Friday game then. Nice huh? I hate the goddamn Yankees!"

"Did I tell you about fishing Bosox-style?

"During a visit to Boston, the Pope took a couple of days off to visit Cape Cod for some sightseeing. He was cruising along the beach in the Popemobile when there was a frantic commotion just offshore. A helpless man wearing a pin-striped New York Yankee jersey was struggling in a frenzy trying to free himself from the jaws of a twenty-five-foot shark. As the Pope watched horrified, a fishing boat raced up with three men wearing Red Sox jerseys. One quickly fired a harpoon into the shark's side. The other two reached out and pulled the bleeding, semi-conscious Yankee fan from the shark's jaws. Using clubs and baseball bats, the fishermen beat the shark to death and hauled it into the boat.

"The Pope shouted at the men, summoning them to the beach. 'I give you my blessing for your brave actions,' he said. 'I had been told there is bad blood between Red Sox and Yankee fans, but now I have seen with my own eyes this is not true.'

"As the Pope drove off, the harpooner asked his buddies, 'Who was that guy?'

"'It was the Pope, you dummy. He is in direct contact with the word and wisdom of God.'

"'Well,' the harpooner said, 'that may be, but he doesn't know jack about shark fishing! Is the bait holding up OK, or do we need to get another one?'"

Wes, laughing, raises his arms in triumph. "Love it! I'll tell it to the whole damn stadium! Good thing Harry wasn't here though, not a perfectly-timed joke!"

Margaret yells up at us, "OK, we're all set down here. Wes and Jack and you others go release the mizzen topsail gaskets. I'll set the mizzen course with the rest of the Foremast. Then meet at the bell before going aloft to the foremast."

The fog is finally beginning to lift as later we climb into the foretop, waiting for instructions from Tony. Alice looking forward, suddenly points. "Look at that!"

We turn, and now can see well beyond the immediate waters of the ship. A few hundred yards ahead is a sailboat sporting a huge mast. Beyond it we can see other boats.

"The start of our escort." It's the professor standing in the rigging just above us. "I forget the name of that one, but she's a famous old wooden ketch; been all around the world."

Alice looks up at him. "There are lots of boats out there. What are they doing there this early and in the fog?"

"Believe me," says the professor, "this is just the beginning. Wait 'til you see what full light brings. Newport has an incredible collection of beautiful and strange boats. They come in all shapes and sizes."

Sure enough a half hour later the fog is fast lifting. As we finish releasing the fore topsail gaskets, we can see many more boats. There are little runabouts, big fancy sail and power yachts. Off to starboard there's another tall mast. The professor points it at saying, "That's a 'maxi' ocean racer, about seventy to seventy-five feet in length. Over there is a fabulous old Trumpy yacht, built back in the fifties. See the ugly powerboat behind it? Well, at least I think it's ugly. That's the so-called 'eurostyle', glitzy and sleek. Doesn't look much like a boat though."

A few hundred yards dead ahead is a police boat, a big center console, with lights flashing on a short mast just aft of the console. Moving fast he speeds by us, wheels around and comes up just forward of our stern. One officer holding a bullhorn is standing alongside the driver. "Captain, we're the Newport Marine Patrol. We'll be your escort into harbor. We will position ourselves two hundred yards forward of your vessel, to keep craft out of your immediate way. Understood?"

The Captain has come on deck, standing near the wheel. He waves to the police boat, gives them the thumbs-up signal.

The police boat dashes off, aiming at a beautiful dark blue-hulled sailboat which seems to be getting ready to cross our bow. People are lining her rail holding cameras. "She's a Hinckley. They're famous cruising sailboats built in Maine. That one's a Bermuda 40," the professor tells us.

It doesn't seem to matter to the police. We hear the bullhorn cop bellowing at the sailboat to "come about" out of our course. Slowly the sailboat complies as the photographers jump up and run across to the other side of the Hinckley.

A handsome smaller yacht with lines like a sleek lobster boat approaches from starboard. The professor waves at the boat, "That's the Maritime Days committee boat. She's a Dyer 29, made nearby to Newport." He waves his arms back and forth to get someone's attention. Finally, a man nattily dressed in a blue blazer, red, white and blue bow tie and white pants spots the professor. He picks up a bullhorn. "Walter, we'll pick you up once you're inside the harbor, before you get to the mooring. Look for us on the Fort Adams pier. We'll come get you from there."

The professor, smiling broadly, waves his acknowledgement.

Climbing down from the fore topsail yard to the foretop to the deck I keep stopping to marvel at the boats all around us. It's an amazing show. Many are wood, burnished to a bright shine. Teak seems everywhere. A lovely antique Christ Craft catches my eye, narrow and looking very fast. Behind it bounces a smallish catboat, also wooden, maybe twenty feet or so. Well back and outside the immediate crush of boats nearest to the *Endeavour* are several large vessels. One I can make out looks like a ferry boat, another must be a tourist excursion boat, two decks high and very colorful, with lots of people aboard. Nearby are four big sailboats with "US 12" printed on their sails, another with a far larger mast.

The professor standing nearby notices me looking in their direction. "Those are America's Cup yachts. There are a half dozen or so 12-meters in Newport.

The other with the larger mast is Shamrock V, a huge old 'J boat' which raced for England in the 1930s and lost. It's also berthed in Newport. They'll have a race on a short course here later this morning, once we're on our way in. Lots of these boats are spectators out to view us, then their race."

Alice had started to descend, but stopped and is now just standing in the rigging below the futtock shrouds. "This is just so neat. We're at the center of a big event, what a grand scene!"

Harry watches her, taking it all in with a non-stop big grin spread across his face.

I agree it is certainly fun. It's so much fun nobody goes down for our award breakfast. Finally, long off watch, I go down for some pancakes, the professor right behind me.

We slide our trays along in front of the platters of pancakes. Spearing some with his fork, the professor grins broadly. "How about that, a great start! Weather looks like it'll be fine for the day, though I'm betting the fog rolls right back in tonight. That really would be perfect for us."

"Why's that?"

The professor doesn't answer as we pour syrup over our pancakes, collect a mug of coffee for him, tea for me, and start toward the tables. "Let's sit over there," he says, pointing toward an empty table in the corner. As we sit, he turns toward me, his back to the rest of the galley. "Remember my saying a couple days ago that for me it's the experience of the eighteenth-century sailing that is important, not your sailing challenges?"

As I nod, he goes on now speaking fast and quietly with almost manic energy. "When we sail at night, hopefully tonight, the fog will help blot out our surroundings. It'll make the sail more authentically an eighteenth-century experience."

"But Walter, let's get real here. Frankly it's like you're working yourself up into some kind of illusion, a magic trip, I don't know, a kind of floating séance or something. It's just a hopefully charming night-time sail in an eighteenth-century tender."

"True, but I've learned a way to make it possibly better, more real. There's no danger. But, if it works, you'll never forget it!"

"What are you talking about?"

"Jack, just trust me here. I'll tell you and Harry all about it tonight. As I said, there's no danger, you guys can even veto it if you don't want to go ahead. All I ask is that you sail with me and give me the chance to explain what we can do."

I start to respond, but the professor holds up his hand. "Jack, did you know you are a classic empiricist? I'm sure Harry is too."

I look at him blankly. He nods. "Oh yeah, I'm certain of it. It is a philosophy that claims that all knowledge is based on experience. It has had a very long historical presence. I'll refresh your memory!" he laughs.

"Empiricism first emerged in ancient Greece among the Greek Sophist, later was prominent in the Middle Ages. It really got going from the writings of Francis Bacon, later John Locke and the Scotsman David Hume. More recently, John Stuart Mill in the nineteenth century and this century, Bertrand Russell, were well-known empiricists. Essentially it is a philosophy that holds that everything meaningful is so because it is conclusively verifiable, or confirmable by observation and experiment. Actually as a philosophy it is long out of favor because it rejects reason or theory and relies solely on observation. But, many of us—and I think you included—are to some degree empiricists. To us the experience is everything, not the theory behind it or the reasons for the experience, just the event, the moment, the things we see and do, especially what we do. It is just so obvious you are thriving in the experience of the *Endeavour*, you just soak it up, keep grabbing for more. Given that behavior, I'm absolutely sure you'll jump at the experience that I'll explain to you guys."

I hesitate, finally weakly respond. "Walter, this is beginning to sound like a lot of 'mumbo-jumbo'."

He chuckles, "Maybe now, but give it a chance. I'll see you later. I don't want to miss any more of our escort fleet."

He's up and moving quickly to the stairs.

I'm no longer hungry for pancakes. I sip my tea wondering what the hell I've gotten myself into this time.

As I reach the weather deck, Harry and Alice are standing arm-in-arm at the port railing just beyond the companionway. "Hey, Jack, look at this guy!"

He's pointing at a tiny little wooden sailing skiff with a gaff rig. The skipper is an elderly man with flowing white hair, and a full beard. His skiff can't be longer than fifteen feet. "Harry, you better get moving; you need to pull him aboard before he's swamped!"

"Crap no, he's sailing faster than we are! Look up ahead, that's apparently the outer channel marker. We just tugged on braces to shift our course more northerly. I got a dollar that says he'll beat us to that mark."

"I'll take that bet," smiles Tony mischievously. "He's about to be covered by that big yawl running up behind him." Sure enough, the little skiff stalls as a gleaming black-hulled yawl roars by the skiff taking away her wind. It quickly starts to overtake the *Endeavour*, all passengers waving, tooting horns, snapping pictures. The skiff falls behind, the skipper never looking up, just concentrating on his little boat.

Alice turns to say something to Tony. I nudge Harry. "Walter's Weird Adventure gets weirder. Now we're going to have the experience of a lifetime! Catch me later when you get a minute."

"I will," he answers, "but whatever it is, it seems to me we should go along to see what he's got going, although with eyes wide open."

Jesus, another flaming empiricist!

Another police boat swings alongside the first. The two boats settle their respective courses even and about 25 yards apart, thereby giving us a wider path free of our ever-growing entourage.

I walk forward next to the "best bower" anchor, on the port side, to get a better view. A moment later Harry stops by. "So what did the professor say?"

I repeat his claim to make the night-time sail a special experience, but omit the philosophy comments.

"I don't think it changes anything," Harry responds. "Except to make me more interested. What the hell is he talking about, can you tell?"

"I have no idea, but he sure is excited, I'll tell you that."

Harry turns to walk back toward Alice and Tony. "We'll find out soon enough."

The spectator fleet has settled around us, for the most part keeping to our stately pace. The diesels are shut down. All sails are set except the fore-and-aft staysails and the spritsails. We're making maybe six knots, so for many spectator boats, barely idle speed. The fog still shrouds the sun, but visibly is distinctly better. I can dimly make out the headlands of the island—Aquidneck—that includes Newport. A few hundred yards ahead is a large red channel marker. That must be Brenton Point beyond it.

"Hey Jack!" Spasiano is smiling at me from his spot straddling the bowsprit just inboard of the bow, with Wes alongside. "What a fantastic collection of boats! I mean it's almost absurd, there are so many spectacular boats here!"

"Wherever you look it is some scene," I reply.

Moments later Tony is standing next to Spasiano. He puts his arm on his shoulder. "What perfect position! Captain wants the spritsails set and here you are ready to lead us out. Let's go to the sprit topsail first, shall we? Wes, go with our leader here; you too, Jack. I'll join you directly. Just get in position for now, Jack with Spasiano on one side of the jib-boom; I'll meet Wes on the other. Off you go!"

Spasiano looks stricken, eyes wide, mouth open. He makes no attempt to hide his fear. He turns toward Tony, who already is walking away talking to Christopher, the professor and two other Foremast crewmen, giving out other assignments. Spasiano looks at me, then Wes. "I'm not sure..." his voice trails off.

Wes, flushed and scowling, whirls around toward Tony.

"No, Wes, don't say anything, it's OK." Spasiano starts crawling forward on the bowsprit. "I'll go. Gotta' get beyond this."

Wes angrily retorts, "That's nonsense, there is no need at all to go out there."

"I know, but the voyage is almost over. I have to end it in a good way."

"Vincent, you've done fine. We've all had a terrific trip."

"You have, Wes, and you, too, Jack. But I need to try to get into the rigging one more time."

Damn, what an awkward little mess. I feel more than a little sorry for him. He looks so scared. I can see he's trembling a little, his voice has a slight tremor to it, his eyes, still wide, blink rapidly. Yet I agree he needs to try to make the rigging experience work for him to get by his evident fear. "Why don't we all go together? We can be on either side of Spasiano...Vincent, and work through it. All we're doing is untying gaskets, shouldn't be a problem."

"Thanks," says Spasiano, "that would be great."

Wes nods and climbs up on the bowsprit, stepping over Spasiano to head out first. We quickly reach the jib-boom mounted on top of the end of the bowsprit. Wes slows down as he starts to shnny along the jib-boom. I slide along right behind Spasiano. We can hear the fore-and-aft staysails being sheeted home while we shinny slowly along the jib-boom. They'll give *Endeavour* a little more maneuverability, which certainly is needed as we approach the harbor channel surrounded by dozens of boats.

Wes arrives at the sprit topsail yardarm. He turns back to Spasiano. "Stay right here for a moment. I'll get on the foot line. Then you can get on next to me." Spasiano nods, his jowly neck moving slightly.

Just then someone taps me on the shoulder; it's Tony trailed by Christopher. "Hello there, we're here to help you worthies." He points east. "See the helicopter out there? Captain says it's likely carrying TV cameras. So, we need to look nice and shipshape. You're being very nice to friend Spasiano here, but it won't do to drop one side of the sail then another! I'll step onto the foot line here first. Then Spasiano can visit with me, followed by Wes. You two release the gaskets on the starboard side. Let's dance, mateys!"

Tony steps over our little group and onto the sprit topsail foot-rope left of the jib-boom. As Wes shinnies forward along the jib-boom to clear the way, Tony turns toward Spasiano. Pointing out a line he tells him to grab it while stepping on the foot line. Spasiano slowly reaches out and grabs the line. Tony firmly commands, "Put your left foot here next to my foot, then bend your body over the yardarm."

Seeing Spasiano's foot touch the line, Tony steps on his foot, and pulls him gently toward the yardarm. He snaps his safety line onto the line running along the top of the yardarm, and pushes him down and forward so he's bent over the yardarm holding on. "Welcome, matey, you have arrived."

Wes steps onto the foot-rope and together, literally shoulder-to-shoulder, they slide out toward the outboard gasket. Christopher and I gingerly step onto the starboard side foot line. We too slide out to the outboard gasket. Quickly both teams untie gaskets as we slide back toward the jib-boom. Just as the first time handling the sprit topsail, for me its foot line is far too close to the yardarm. But now I thank my previous experience for enabling me to cope. I know I have to crouch slightly, keep one hand gripping the yardarm safety line and the other working the gaskets. Christopher is several inches shorter and has taken the outboard position, so the portion of the line I stand on has somewhat more droop, thereby more distance below the yardarm. The sprit topsail falls evenly and is sheeted home below.

Tony is sitting on the sprit topsail yardarm. "Jack and Christopher head for the spritsail yard. Wes, climb onto the jib-boom. Spasiano, slide over next to the jib-boom."

Worried about Spasiano, Christopher and I shinny down the jib-boom a few feet to get out of Wes's way, and turn around to watch. Tony tells Spasiano to turn toward Wes, now sitting on the jib-boom, unhook his safety line and hook on the line running along the top of the jib-boom. "Next," Tony continues, "holding onto the yardarm, lift your leg up and over the jib-boom." Spasiano releases the snap hook of his safety line from the yardarm line, leans over and clips onto the jib-boom line. Tony is now straddling the sprit topsail yardarm right in front of him. As Spasiano lifts his right leg, his left starts to tremble violently. Tony reaches down grabbing him under his left arm and twists him up toward the jib-boom, almost trying to throw him. At the same time, Wes is grabbing at his belt. Spasiano's left foot slips off the foot line, but his hold of the jib-boom safety line and Wes's hold on his belt steady him for a second. Tony lifts him slightly again which gets him a bit higher on the jib-boom. Another strong tug by Wes and Spasiano is draped across the jib-boom.

Incredibly, he's laughing. "'The Eagle' has landed! I made it...thank you...I made it!" He lets out a whoop of laughter.

The rest of us stare dumbly, gradually joining in Spasiano's infectious laughter. Wes and Tony get him up, straddling the jib-boom and headed back toward the ship. Tony says, "Well, wasn't that wonderful! Let's do it again! We've still got the spritsail to drop, one more chance."

Spasiano is still laughing. "I'd love to, but I don't want to have too much fun at your expense! Let's do it again some other time. Thank you all though!"

We shinny together down the jib-boom to the bowsprit. One by one we step off on the spritsail foot line, each giving Spasiano a jab or pat as he slowly slides by on the way back to the ship's bow.

"That was some scene." The professor is standing next to the port side "seat of ease". Thankfully not used on our replica voyage, this and another wooden seat nearby hang off the bow. They represent the original *Endeavour's*—and all other ships of the era—only toilets. "Spasiano took a crazy chance going out there after all his misadventures."

I agree, "He wanted to end on a high note. How high definitely was in question."

The professor smiles, "That's for sure. Anyhow, now his *Endeavour* experience is better, so that's good, right?"

"No question."

The professor gestures in the direction of the starboard beam. "That lighthouse is the Castle Hill Light, and just beyond it the building is the Castle Hill Inn. The inn is lovely, with a delicious Sunday brunch. Pretty soon we'll round the headland it sits on and pass Fort Adams. In its original form it was a revolutionary-era fort. It turned out to be of utterly no use when the English took Newport in December 1776. The Maritime Days boat will pick me up as we pass offshore of the fort. I won't see you 'til later today, after the welcoming ceremony."

He hands me a folded piece of paper. "I've put together a little note, for you and Harry. It explains our sailing trip some more. We can talk after dinner. Harry's up in the foretop with Alice. I'll give him his copy once he's alone for a minute. The notes are the same for each of you. See you later, Jack."

As the professor walks away, I turn my back on the deck to read his note.

Together we have the opportunity to do something breathtaking, almost magical when we embark on our night-time sail.

The opportunity does not require great courage or the acceptance of great risk. It does however require that during the sail:

We open our hearts, minds, and eyes to accept the opportunity

We have the courage to take a stand—we have a specific purpose and we will accept nothing less than its accomplishment

We will support each other without reservation

We will be in harmony together—a shared focus to achieve a common desire, through trust and commitment

We will honor the utter necessity of our absolute commitment to succeed. We are making a promise of the heart to do so.

Humans are sensory receptors. We select and process from incalculable numbers of stimuli constantly bombarding us. That which we select collectively becomes our reality. What we don't choose becomes invisible to us.

During the sail you will be asked to select something new, something you never thought possible to select. By mastering a few simple skills you'll be able to "see" this new option.

Our perceptions of what we believe to be true and real are entirely derived from our learned experience. We make our selections from those perceptions. In effect, making selections in this way also teaches us our limitations. We tend to fear or mistrust anything that is new or outside what we have determined to be our reality.

On our sail, you will be asked to suspend fear, mistrust and disbelief. We will go "outside the box", beyond the limitations of conventional reality.

Together we will make the invisible visible.

In his small, neat handwriting, the professor has "upped the ante" considerably. No longer a simple night-time sail, he now is suggesting it is something much more. Exactly what is still unclear, but its importance to the professor is plainly evident.

I look up to see Spasiano heading toward me. Smiling and waving, I interrupt his approach saying, "I'll be back right back, just have to go below for a few minutes." As he waves acknowledgement, I trot down the companionway into the crew mess, seeking a quiet place.

Settled onto a bench in the corner I re-read the professor's note. One thing seems certain. If I'm to go on this now apparently very special sail, I will need to accept its importance to the professor. But more than that I'll need to subscribe—or least be honestly open-minded—to his passion. That seems to mean I'll have to go along—at least in the beginning—with his explanation of how he thinks we'll see whatever is invisible. His assertion that there is no risk helps, but the mystery of it all makes any real acceptance difficult. I don't even know what I'll be asked to accept.

Deep in thought I'm startled when I realize Harry is standing in front of my bench talking. "Sleeping on the job?" he smirks.

"No, I'm not asleep."

"The hell you're not. You're head down and motionless. What else is it? Spasiano found you here after looking for you when you stiffed him…nice guy. He said you told him you'd be right back. You didn't show and he went looking for you. He was very upset when he thought he found you asleep."

"It's my perpetual state—half awake, always hungry, usually tired and dirty. How's that for an endorsement of this voyage?"

"Catchy! How about adding another part…'never a dull moment'? The professor's note fits neatly in that part. That was an attention-getter."

I sit up straight, rub my hands over my face and hair. "Yeah. I'll tell you one thing it did for me. I now think we have to honestly accept his premise or not go. It wouldn't be fair to him."

Harry nods, "I agree. We have to be willing to make his commitment, or forget it. I know you think he's a little bit nuts, but still I trust him enough. It's got to be something about making the experience authentic. I can't imagine much or any risk. Frankly, I must admit I still don't even know what his premise is. But, let's at least be sure we'll clearly be with him.

"One thing he said to pass on to you. After the welcoming ceremony this afternoon, there will be a big dinner on board. During the night each watch is for one hour only and is manned by three volunteers. He told Alice to sign her, you and me up for the 11:00 p.m. watch, one of the watches assigned to Foremast. She's doing that now with Tony. We'll have plenty of time to get fully briefed then."

"Good. Then I guess we're in with the professor. While we can't make a commitment to what we don't know, I think we tell him we support him, appreciate the opportunity and understand how serious it is. I'll try to tell him before he goes off in the committee boat."

I'm aware we have slowed down. A few moments later we hear a sharp bump against the port side hull.

"Oops," says Harry. "You may be too late to tell him."

I rush up the companionway only to see the professor standing on the accommodation stairs amidships. He is holding onto a rope ladder draped over the stairs. The committee boat is alongside *Endeavour* with crewmen reaching out to the professor. He carefully steps across to the boat's deck, turns and waves to the Captain. All I can do is give him a thumbs up. After a few attempts he spots me and beaming, shakes his fist high in the air.

Maintaining her slow speed, *Endeavour* is barely making way as we turn past Fort Adams and creep toward a vast mooring field of boats just off the dozen or so wharves and piers sticking out into the harbor from the Newport waterfront. Thousands of people are watching our stately progress and the menagerie of boats all around the *Endeavour*.

While it hardly seems necessary, the First Mate commands, "All hands on deck! Form up by watch please."

Tony explains to us we'll be in the rigging for a while as the Captain sets all sails again apparently for any filmmakers who might have missed us earlier. We'll then furl them up before arriving at our mooring.

I dash below to find my stored hammock. Realizing I could have several hours ahead of me standing on foot lines, I hurriedly change out of deck shoes for my heavier-soled sneakers. By the time I regain the deck most of the Foremast watch is scampering up the foremast rigging. Margaret is watching from the foretop. "Come on up, Jack, we've missed you! Join us at the t'gallant!"

The *Endeavour* is virtually at a dead stop as we go through a long, tedious process displaying the sail plan. The wind in the harbor is so light it barely luffs the sails. Margaret and I, along with two others, set and furl the fore topgallant and fore topsail, while other Foremast crew handle the fore course and spritsails. The unlucky mizzenmast watch wrestles all the lines for both foremast and mainmast watches aloft in the rigging. Finally, apparently having satisfied all photographic demands, Tony tells us to furl all sails one-by-one. Now with all sails furled, I stand in the topmast rigging watching as we come around into the wind to approach what apparently is our mooring. The mooring is only a few hundred yards off the piers. A big grey inflatable runabout with twin outboards is at the mooring. As we nose our way in slow motion toward the mooring buoy, a man in some sort of naval uniform—representing what I have no idea—lifts a large boat hook with the mooring hawser (large rope) securely dangling from the hook. An Aussie crewman reaches over the ship's bow railing grabbing a small line attached to the hawser. Using the line he lowers it to a hole in the bow railing alongside the bowsprit. There another crewman reaches out his boat hook, snares the mooring hawser and brings it inboard to the deck. Quickly he and Tony secure it to a deck cleat. The engines are reversed for a moment, then stopped. The *Endeavour* tugs gently on the mooring hawser.

All hands are due on deck at 5:00 p.m. for the welcoming ceremony followed by an elaborate dinner in the galley and crew mess. Finally finished the endless wait for shower and shaving, I've put on my cleanest "Endeavour World Voyage" shirt and reasonably clean shorts. Shortly after I arrive on deck, I hear Harry shout my name. Looking up I see him and Alice in the foretop. "Come on up, we've saved you a spot in the front row of the balcony!"

As I reach the foretop, they're looking off in the direction of the piers. Harry says, "I think the professor is on his way. A little sailboat with oars has cleared the wharf and is setting sail."

I look along the wharves for a moment, not seeing a sailboat. Then I spot it. I can see two sets of oars moving rhythmically and a small, gaff-rigged sail luffing in the light breeze. Soon the sail is hauled in to stop the luffing and the little boat heads smartly toward us.

"There's Weird Walter and his magic boat," laughs Harry. "She's actually kind of cute."

She's approaching us fairly quickly. As I stare at the little craft I don't think

I'd call her "cute". She has a solid, serviceable look to her. The mast is stepped all the way forward, right through a tiny little deck on her bluff bow. It can't be more than fifteen feet high. The boat is lapstreak (each plank overlaps the one below it), seems to ride high in the water, quite beamy, painted white with blue trim. Two sets of oarsmen are sitting in pairs amidships, each man pulling on one long oar, rowing in unison. They're wearing white pants and collarless white jerseys with blue horizontal stripes. Each has a blue hat looking like a flattened boater with ribbons hanging over the brim on the side. The professor is sitting in the wide stern holding the tiller. He's wearing a faded blue jacket with white piping and bright brass buttons. Under the jacket he has on a white dress shirt with frills. His pants are white pantaloons to just below his knees where they are joined by high white stockings. On his feet are low black shoes each with a gold buckle. On his head he wears a blue cocked hat sideways, the points of the hat over his shoulders. Just in front of him is a very stout older man with a blue frock coat with twin epaulettes. His coat has a high collar, two long lines of brass buttons down its front, and three brass buttons on each cuff. He also has on a white waistcoat, white pantaloons and stockings. He wears a similar cocked hat but his has gold trim, and surprisingly is worn "fore-and-aft". He carries a sword in an elaborate black and gold scabbard.

Within minutes the professor and his crew have collapsed the sail, and pulled alongside our starboard accommodation ladder. The inboard oarsmen put their oars straight up as the outboard oarsmen pull the jolly boat up against the ladder, guided by the professor steering the tiller. The older man dressed—as the professor had told us—as a full-grade "Post Captain" in the British Navy, stands in the boat waiting for the accommodation ladder to be draped over the side. He then carefully climbs onboard *Endeavour*. The professor follows. Our captain escorts them up the stairs to the quarterdeck, where they are joined by all the key personnel of the *Endeavour*. There's some awkward standing around for a few minutes. Soon the Maritime Days committee boat bounces alongside, dropping off a videographer, followed by several men and women in eighteenth-century costume. The videographer immediately starts filming the ship, gradually working her way up the quarterdeck steps.

Finally, the Post Captain opens a leather bound book and in a booming voice welcomes the *Endeavour* captain and crew as guests of honor for the 1998 Newport Maritime Days, "due all the privileges and honors suitable to your high rank and esteem." We cheer loudly, offering numerous unsolicited suggestions of the privileges and honors due us. "We're due five days' 'grog' ration!" "Free room and board in your best tavern!" "Wenches, mutton chops and ale!"

The Captain, dressed in dark blue slacks and an *Endeavour* shirt, laughing roars out, "Just what I'd expect of the scurvy lot we pressed for this voyage! Actually the galley crew has prepared a vast 'chop-house' feast of celebration featuring beefsteaks and 'cabinet pudding' with a local 'beach plum' sauce. Sorry, no grog, beer or wine. The heartless, greedy and mean-spirited insurance companies have no sense of 'privilege and honor'!" His announcement is met with a predictable chorus of boos and jeers. He continues, "Against our better judgment and the normal ways of British naval discipline, all will partake of the feast. The voyage crew will remain onboard overnight so we can give our dear *Endeavour* a good scrubbing in the morning. We'll tie up at Brown & Howard Pier at noon tomorrow presuming the tourists get off the American Coast Guard cutter cluttering our berth! Voyage crew will then be dismissed to chase down the grog they think is due them, stray wenches who make the mistake of being nearby, and other distractions their poor minds' desire. All of Newport should beware!" A louder cheer rises up from the crew.

The dinner was delicious, boisterous and jammed. The permanent ship's crew, volunteer crew, the "gentlemen" guests of the ship, all the local re-enactors were far beyond the capacity of the galley. Many had to settle for the crew mess area. Alice, Harry, Wes and I wedged our way into a corner in the galley. Loud and good-natured kidding among the Aussie and volunteer crews and Newport guests led to a sea shanty singing contest. Not surprisingly, the Aussie songs were funny and ribald. The voyage crew's attempts quickly degenerated to raucous college drinking songs. Harry dragged a reluctant Alice up to sing the old Kingston Trio standby "The Sloop John B". Harry knew all the words but could barely carry the tune. Alice's knew only some of the words but her voice was lovely and clear. The crowd cheered, asking Alice to sing some more, but without Harry. She stirred the crowd with a quiet and charming rendition of the British "proms" favorite, "Land of Hope and Glory".

Finally, the dinner and singing over, the festivities started to break up. The Captain said it was his sad duty to close the party. However, it was his joyful duty to report that the Coast Guard had relayed the hospital's opinion that Lennie, the crewman, certainly would survive and that so far there was a fair chance he would not lose his leg.

Anticipating a likely long night I headed for the pile of Foremast hammocks in order to get a couple hours' rest before my 11:00 p.m. watch. As I bent over searching for hammock 10, the professor slapped me on the back.

"Now that was great fun! I loved the Aussie drinking songs, outrageous stuff! And Alice was remarkably good don't you agree?"

"Sure was. Walter, tell me, why did you wear your hat one way, and the Captain the other?"

"Well, at the time of the Revolution oddly enough in the strict British Navy, officers could wear them either way. Mine was the old-fashioned way. Did you go up on deck, see the weather?"

"Nope."

"Thick fog! I'm staying onboard, as is the jolly boat. It's tied up alongside the starboard accommodation ladder, where we left it. The others who came out with me are going back in the committee boat, leaving shortly. We're on for tonight! I'll be up on deck for your watch."

FIVE

"Hey Jack, every time I turn around you're asleep. You're about to miss the big adventure!" Whispering in my ear as Alice gently rocks my hammock, Harry pokes me in the ribs. "Get your raggedy ass up! Coming up on 'Weird Walter' time…meet you at the helm."

I struggle slowly up into a sitting position grabbing the hammock with both hands to steady myself. I feel utterly drained. Damn, what I wouldn't give for some real sleep. I slide off the hammock and stand there wobbling slightly. Better put on jeans and the sweatshirt. It feels cool and sure as hell will be a long night. I pull on my sneakers and gingerly walk down to the galley to get a caffeine-and-sugar jolt from tea and any left over cabinet pudding.

Arriving at the helm I hear the First Mate telling Harry and Alice to keep their eyes open for anything potentially harmful to the ship. He hands each of us a big flashlight. "Basically just watch the waters immediately around us for boats coming too close or about to bang into the ship. Disperse yourselves so you cover port and starboard. No one can board except a few permanent crew coming back from town. Fog is very thick so it's not likely there will be much activity. Anything you're not sure of come to the aft companionway and give me a yell. I'll be right up. It's now 11:00 p.m., your watch ends at midnight." He nods and turns to head down that companionway.

Looking around the deck, I spot only a few people, most of whom are forward leaning on the bow rail, the professor among them. I noticed when I came back up through the crew's mess at least half the hammocks were occupied. Like me, many of the volunteer crew are worn out, badly in need of sleep. The galley still had eight or ten occupants chatting and reading.

For a while I parallel Harry and Alice on the port side as we slowly amble up and down the ship's deck. Eventually Alice turns toward me. "You guys obviously need to be together. Why don't you take the starboard side. The boat is there. I'll be on the port side."

Harry and I stop. We step over to the starboard rail, peering down at the jolly boat. The mast has been un-stepped and is lying across all three thwarts. The long oars lie alongside the mast. The boat moves slightly in the light swell, bumping softly against the accommodation ladder and hull. The tiller is tied down. It creaks and moves a few degrees left and right. There is an inch or two of water barely covering the floor boards.

After a while, Harry breaks the silence. "Remarkable this little boat is still around after more than 200 years. How the hell is that possible?"

"The power of money, how else?" grins the professor walking up behind us. He's still wearing his British naval lieutenant uniform. "The maritime historians have placed it in the American Revolution era. We don't know its fate in the early nineteenth century, but we do have family letters of a prominent textile mill family mentioning it in use at their mill in 1815. Later it was used by several generations of family children. Apparently it was lucky enough to be a part of family life and tradition. After the Civil War it ended up in the family's barn just off what is now Memorial Boulevard. Fortunately, it was put up on blocks and wrapped tightly in an old sail. In the 1880s when the Victorians of the 'Gilded Age' 'discovered' Newport for their 'summer cottages', they bought huge chunks of land and buildings. 'Cottage' was a neat little conceit. They were of course ludicrously large and sumptuous, many were virtual castles. The barn was torn down to make way for one of them. The architect apparently convinced the homeowner, a railroad financier, to save the boat. The firm's records describe— with considerable evident pride—a careful restoration using materials and methods 'true' to the eighteenth century. She was used as part of a prominent historical display in the home's solarium. It was there for decades in a fairly temperate environment, periodically restored and preserved. It was given to the Maritime Museum many years ago. We've been displaying it in Maritime Days programs for some time now. The only problem is always the need for authenticity. Every year before putting her in the water we caulk her planking thoroughly with oakum and pitch to prevent leaking. Obviously we still haven't quite mastered that skill. But, she floats, rows and sails pretty well for such an old gal."

The professor leans against the railing. He folds his arms over his chest, looks at Harry and me. "So I assume you read my note. It's time for me to explain what this is all about.

"Exactly 220 years ago right now, the original *Endeavour*, by then a troop ship named the *Lord Sandwich* and contracted to the British Navy, was anchored one mile from here. She was a prison ship. All her sails, spars, all her rigging had been removed. She was prepared for scuttling to help block the harbor against the approaching French fleet. Here's a picture of how she would have looked."

He hands us a photo of the *Endeavour* without masts, sails, rigging. "That simply is a photo of our *Endeavour* for which I had everything above the weather deck airbrushed out.

"Tonight we will do something it is likely you never have even dreamt of doing. Guided by the theories of Albert Einstein, yes *the* Albert Einstein, while at the same time completely opening our minds, we will observe another reality. We will take this jolly boat out see her. We'll only look from a distance, then return to the here and now. But, you'll see the *Lord Sandwich* of 1778."

"Oh man, professor, what nonsense are…."

Harry's scowling at me as the professor cuts me off. "Remember, the note said I'm offering a breathtaking opportunity. To seize it you need to be fully committed to understand my explanation and while doing so suspend your disbelief. You have no chance of succeeding if you don't fully believe you will. This takes discipline and intense focus. But there is no question if you believe and follow my lead we can do it. Join me! For a little while take a small chance. Make the leap to belief for the most momentous experience of your life! You both live for the tangible experiences of your lives…this will be the biggest of all!

"For now, just look at the photo. Then imagine an identical hull—one you're entirely familiar with—but with nothing above the deck. Focus your imagination on it, Jack. You've nothing to lose tonight. You will be in absolutely no danger. But with commitment and absolute focus together we can do this."

Harry murmurs, "Go ahead, professor."

"Let me explain the premise and how we'll be able to do it. I've planned and prepared for this moment ever since a year ago when I first learned of the replica's visit."

He's clearly in his element—nervous, charged with excitement, he's a believer. His face is flushed, eyes wide and sparkling, that slight amount of spittle I saw the other day again visible on the left corner of his mouth.

"As I'm sure you know, Einstein created many theories to measure and understand the physical properties of matter and energy. Arguably though, his greatness lies in the fact that his theories not only solved fundamental problems, even more importantly, they created new ideas. Most of his theories stemmed from his work on relativity. They were developed first in his 'special theory of relativity', later in his 'general theory of relativity', along with numerous other papers. For example, one spectacular revelation in his 1916 general theory of relativity was his assertion that light has weight. That flew in the face of all physics knowledge then current. However, in fact a British astronomer, during a solar eclipse in 1919, detected the bending aside of starlight by the sun's gravitational field. This only could mean that light has weight. It was pulled by the sun's gravity. In this and other theories found in his major physics papers, Einstein modified the previous rigid perceptions of space and time.

"Years later, after he fled Nazi Europe and came to the US, he devoted all his work to connecting his theories together into a comprehensible whole. At one point he wrote that his relativity theories enabled him to conclude that we do not correctly understand the continuum of time. In simple terms, we do not properly appreciate the true reality of past, present and future. We mistakenly believe the past is over and gone, and the future hasn't actually happened. Only the present exists because that's all we can see."

The professor stops for a moment, running his fingers through his thin, sandy hair. "Remember the note. In it I said we will make the invisible visible. Einstein used a simple analogy to explain our misunderstanding of time. It is as though we are in a boat drifting in the current of a winding river. We can only see that which is visible around us. We cannot see what is beyond the river's bends behind us or ahead of us. Yet the past back behind the bend in fact actually exists, even though we can't see it. It is there. The same is true of the future."

The professor stops again. Looking out into the fog he seems to be collecting his thoughts to continue. Harry and I stand motionless beside him, watching. Finally, he re-focuses on us. "Can you see it? Can you see the river? It's meandering through fields and woods, bending back and forth around bluffs, sand bars, rock cliffs, as it flows along. See yourself sitting in a kayak floating with the winding river."

He stops again, looking into the fog. "Go ahead, take a minute and picture yourself in that kayak."

After a few minutes of silence, "Have either of you ever read a wonderful book, called *Time and Again* by Jack Finney?"

We both shake our heads.

"It was published back in 1970. Many years later he wrote a sequel, *From Time to Time*. Over the years they have been read by a huge number of devoted fans. In them Finney uses Einstein's assertions about time to create a very compelling story in which his principal character is able to get from his present location to the same location in another time. He must satisfy highly specific, very rigorous conditions. He must open his mind fully to suggestion. Using visual references and physical items that link him to that other time and his imagination, he is able to connect himself to the time he wants to reach. In both novels the character makes the time transition several times. He and others in the novel soon recognize he has a kind of knack to accomplish this transition. In effect, Finney takes a step beyond Einstein's river example and enables the character to get out of the boat and walk back along the river. That's what we're going to do. We'll do it by creating similarly precise conditions to allow us to observe the *Lord Sandwich* in Newport harbor in July, 1778."

Alice waves to us from the stern, "We've got some visitors approaching port side."

It turns out to be the committee boat coming alongside. The professor explains, "They're picking up the last of the committee people and re-enactors who were aboard. That reminds me, I have the authentic uniforms. Pretty clever, I put them in a sail bag on the jolly boat after the re-enactment crew changed out of them. Nobody said a word. Not bad, huh!"

"You're a crafty one, Walter."

The professor looks over toward Alice, the only crewperson at all near our little group. In fact, there now are few people on deck. The damp, cool, foggy conditions don't encourage lingering. Alice has moved forward off the quarterdeck, well out of earshot.

"You guys seem to be focusing more...thanks. Let's talk a little bit on what we have to do here. It's all about commitment and energy. You need to be a racehorse with blinders on, unblinkingly focused on doing what you need to do in behalf of our jolly boat trip. All that matters now is what must we do to see the *Lord Sandwich*. For a brief time we will ignore all thoughts and memory of our contemporary world. We'll concentrate only on the era we want to visit.

"Why you guys? Unquestionably what counts for you is the actual experience, to encounter, to taste, to feel, touch, even to suffer a little. For you, satisfaction with something seemingly must come not second-hand, but first-hand. The experience of observing a 220-year-old ship in its reality is beyond anything we can comprehend. When you come to terms with its likelihood, my God, how wondrous, even miraculous! To attain it certainly it is worthy of our absolute commitment. We will need to focus entirely—without distractions—on what we want…no doubts or worries, absolute conviction."

He stops again. Quietly, Harry and I, still motionless, wait for him to go on. It's been quite a performance so far. His lecture skills are evident, he's knowledgeable and unhesitatingly articulate, but it's far beyond a lecture. He's fiercely intense, fully engaged, his excitement is contagious. I wait, anxious to hear what's next.

He continues, "What are the consequences of commitment? The worst consequence would seem to be failure and disappointment—despite our effort and commitment we don't find the *Lord Sandwich*. Another one might be that we have to give up something to make this commitment. Here we will have to give up our skepticism, completely suspend our disbelief. Actually, that's not so easy to do. Skepticism and disbelief are comfortable positions, easy to adopt and defend. It's far safer to doubt because it carries little risk, no commitment. It's much harder to commit and believe. Yet, to have the courage to try as hard as we can to believe something for a little while doesn't seem a difficult task. Especially if the reward for success is an experience that takes us far beyond the limitations of our normal life!

"What about danger? Suppose somehow we get to see the *Lord Sandwich*. Can we get back to the present? You'll see it is far easier to get back. But if you're convinced there's danger, the solution is simple. You don't have to go.

"In *Time and Again* the main character in effect is told that in the end all he has to do is to take a chance, to just go ahead and do it. That's good advice, it applies for us.

"By now I'm sure you're bursting with questions and comments. Just let me take one more step. I'll set the stage for the trip. When we embark in the jolly boat we will be aligned with the *Lord Sandwich* in several important ways. We will be in a boat which is authentic to its time. We will each be wearing clothing which also is authentic to its time. We will have nothing with us other than things that we know can link directly to 1778. Everything about our little journey will be in sync with the *Lord Sandwich's* time. Most importantly, we know it is there."

Harry has been standing flatfooted facing the professor. He steps over next to the railing, leaning against it with his left side. He puts his left elbow on the railing, next rests his head on his upturned left hand. Looking up from staring at his photo of the stripped *Endeavour* hull, he says, "Professor, you obviously believe we can do this. I'm not sure what to think. Its incredible stuff, I'll give you that. I'd like to believe, but I'm not sure...."

The professor gently touches Harry's left shoulder. He quietly says, "Of course, that's exactly where I expect you to be. All I'm asking is to let go of that disbelief, open yourself to the fact we can do it. Let go, Harry, just let go."

I can feel the tug...to let go and believe. If I let my mind just drift restfully I feel receptive...let's try. But in a blink I'm back to reality. Am I kidding? Einstein or not, this can only be...what?

"Jack, your brow is all furrowed. You're thinking so much that smoke soon will be coming out of your ears. Stop for a moment. I'm actually not asking for much. Be willing to let go for the sake of the greatest experience of all, to see another time. Give up a lifetime of viewing only the present. Work with me to shift gears, to allow us to see things our conventional limitations won't let us see. Give yourself the prize of going on this short trip. There's nothing to lose and astonishment to gain."

That may be true, but my conventional worries and fears keep getting in the way. I suppose much of it comes down to trust. Do I trust the professor enough to place myself in his hands? "Walter, obviously it's immensely appealing if I accept your description of the trip at its face value. But, no offense here, we're just not going to row out into the fog and see the *Lord Sandwich*. Much as on one level I'd like to believe that, I'm having a whole lot of trouble accepting that it really is possible."

"I understand, Jack," he replies. "Remember, Einstein has taught us that the past exists. We have to figure out how to get there. One part is to know where to go to see it. Another is to actually be able to get there. Do you accept that we—I should say I—know where to go to see it?"

"OK, that seems the clearest part. I've no doubt you know pretty much where it would be, though the fog will make it interesting."

"All right, then the next step we must do is to temporarily disconnect ourselves from our present moment. We remove all visual connections in order to allow us to believe we can link ourselves to the past. The three of us will do that by being in a boat and wearing clothes that are actually part of that past. We'll row out through the fog well north of Fort Adams. There the pitch darkness of late night and fog will serve as a blanket. It will reduce the visibility of our current world as well as its sounds to little or nothing. We will already be aligned with the past we seek in our clothing and the jolly boat. We then will put ourselves in a frame of mind to be able to see the past."

"What frame of mind is that?"

"We need to reach a heightened state of awareness through relaxation. When we really are relaxed we enable our subconscious mind to be open to receiving suggestions. Our suggestion will be our goal of seeing the *Lord Sandwich*. We must be very clear, so we'll support our goal with visualization. We will use our photos to exactly visualize the *Lord Sandwich* with such focus that it will seem our seeing it had already happened. We will be complementing our physical alignment with a fully receptive state of mind. A few simple techniques of self-hypnosis will let us reach a receptive state.

"Before I go any further, let me clear up a few myths about hypnosis. It has nothing to do with sleep. While this year I earned a certificate as a clinically-trained hypnotist, I not only won't, but can't put you in a trance and make you bark like a dog. Doing so would be against your will, and you must be willing and fully awake. In fact, all hypnosis is really self-hypnosis. It has been used for decades as a therapeutic tool. Millions have been helped in stress reduction, weight control, memory improvement, smoking cessation, and all sorts of other self-improvements. Hell, I know a guy who used it to improve his golf game. It has been accepted as a science by the American Medical Association since 1958.

"Here we will use it to be receptive, to accept that we can see the past by visualizing it while being physically aligned to it. First we'll relax, then we'll visualize, that's all. What's important here is that using self-hypnosis is our entry to a state of mind in which we believe we can see the past we seek. By the way, everybody, literally everybody, has been in a hypnotic state at some point in their life. You can enter it reading a book, watching a movie, listening to a story. Think of driving a long distance on a monotonous highway when you realize to your surprise you're some exits farther along than you thought you were. I used to do it regularly listening to books on tape while driving. We all occasionally find ourselves in a 'zone'. That's a state of hypnosis."

The professor looks at his watch. "It's nearly midnight. You'll be off watch momentarily. I have an idea. How about if we do a little trial first? We'll get in the jolly boat and row well out in the harbor. You'll get some experience with what I'm talking about, see if it feels right. I'll take each of you through a little exercise in self-hypnosis. That will help you both by having a valid experience of what I'm proposing, OK?"

Harry agrees immediately, "That works for me, let's do it."

I nod agreement.

The professor goes on, "I'll tell the watch I received a message that the jolly boat now must be back at Brown & Howard Wharf, not overnight out here. I'll say you two will help me get it back there and the committee boat will bring you back onboard later. When we actually return in the jolly boat, another watch will be on duty. By the way, Jack, please bring along the sleeping bag that caused you so much trouble the second day. How about meeting here in half hour?"

"OK, we'll see you at the boat," replies Harry.

A few minutes later the First Mate dismisses us off watch. As Harry, Alice and I stand amidships, we hear him briefing the next watch. Alice looks at Harry. "You guys must have had quite a conversation with Walter. Although, from what little I could see it seemed more of a lecture. You look very somber, maybe a little stunned. Can you tell me anything about it?"

Harry glances at me as he answers Alice. "Yeah, he talks a lot. He wants Jack and me to go out with him in a few minutes for a short trip. We'll just row a bit, maybe see if we can sail her a short while, then come back."

Alice is watching me, "You OK, Jack?"

"Yeah, I'm fine, thanks. It's late; I'm a little tired. Think I'll go down to the galley and get some tea. See you in a few minutes."

"We'll probably see you down there," Harry replies.

As I walk toward the crew companionway then down the stairs to the galley, whole chunks of the professor's words and images replay in my head. Jumbled, they race by—"just do it"; "be willing to let go"; I see a horse with blinders; the little lapstreak jolly boat; the professor's uniform. I keep visualizing the winding river, then the *Endeavour* hull. Startled, I realize I'm still holding the picture in my hand. I fold and stuff it in my pocket as I squeeze my tea bag into the cup of hot water.

Whatever else, what an incredible experience this would be! However crazy, the possibility of seeing that hull is chilling. No matter how unlikely it seems, I keep coming back to how not only stupid, but forever haunting it would be to walk away from this if it makes any sense at all. But I don't want to be pushed into going, argued into it. I have to decide for myself. I need to find some rationale to help make sense of the professor's plan. Maybe the answer is to lower the risk to finding out.

I stretch my legs onto the bench, lean back and sip my tea. A few minutes' quiet and motionless rest will help.

As I begin to doze off, Harry sits down. Alice is at the counter getting mugs of coffee and a platter of what look like cookies. Harry nudges my shoulder. "You OK to go?"

"Yeah. I'm actually a little more positive. Basically, I'm not at all sure this makes sense, but by the same token, I just can't refuse. Suppose, just barely suppose, he's right and it's possible to see it. I've got to try, what else is there? But I have an idea to make this track better. I'm going to insist that the self-hypnosis test is one-at-a-time. I'll feel—and you probably will too—better if I know you're in a regular state when I go through the hypnosis stuff with him, and vice-versa."

"OK, that makes sense…good idea. While I'm not worried about the professor's intention, I always like having a little backup precaution."

Alice puts the mugs and tray down in front of us. I grin at her. "A lifesaver! I could just inhale those cookies. I can't believe how hungry I am."

"Brain must be working overtime," smiles Alice.

Harry puts his left arm around her shoulders, kneading her left shoulder gently. "So, we'll go out with the professor for a little while. I'd guess we'll be gone for a couple hours, maybe less. The professor will tell the watch he's been instructed to take the boat into Newport. When we get back the watch will have changed so we won't have to explain why we're back. We'll just say the professor took us out for a short familiarization ride, practicing for tomorrow morning."

Harry pulls Alice close to him. "Do you mind staying up for a while? Don't bother to stay on deck, just kind of be aware of what's going on. Probably nothing, but I'd feel better with you awake while we're gone."

Alice laughs as Harry kisses her sweetly on the cheek. "Believe me that's not a problem! There's no way I could sleep anyway."

*   *   *   *   *

The professor is standing alongside the accommodation ladder as I arrive. "Ready to go, Jack?"

"Yeah, I am, Walter. I guess I'm a little slow, but this is taking me a while to absorb enough that I can deal with it. But, I'm getting there."

"That's great news and certainly understandable. This plan is so far outside our experience base that some struggle, rejection, incomplete understanding, and lots of doubts clearly have to be expected. We'll make real progress when we go out now. By the way, I already told the First Mate. No problem, he knows the jolly boat is entirely my responsibility."

"You guys going out in this 'pea souper'?"

It's one of the voyage crew on watch duty. He's a tall, thin guy with heavy-rimmed glasses, curly black hair and a huge, thick mustache, dressed entirely in black. I'm fairly sure he's a member of the Mizzenmast crew. Although I've seen him several times during the voyage, I don't know his name.

"First Mate told us you're headed out, to give you a hand if needed. I'd say what you need is to have your head examined to go out in this crap."

"Thanks, mate," says the professor, "appreciate the offer, but we'll be fine."

"Have fun…." We can hear him muttering about us to his watch mate on the port side. They snicker as their muttering continues.

Harry steps out of the crew companionway on his way toward us. He's changed into jeans.

"I thought all you possessed were shorts."

"Going out on this loony trip in the fog with you guys wearing just shorts didn't seem to make a lot of sense!"

The professor is headed down the accommodation ladder. "I'll climb in first and release the tiller. You guys climb in, each take up an oar and sit on the middle thwart. The boat's bow line is tied off to the accommodation ladder. Give us a good push off."

Holding up a small, hand-held compass with a fluorescent yellow strap, he smirks. "To make you feel better!"

"That it does, professor. Believe me, that it does," I retort.

Kneeling on the little forward deck, I push the sleeping bag underneath it. I release the bow line and push off on the *Endeavour's* hull making the jolly boat drift away.

I join Harry, sitting to his left on the middle thwart. He and I each lift a long wooden oar and place it into a wooden slot next to us in the boat's gunwale. We each place both hands on our oar and pull at the same time. The first few pulls are badly out of sync so we surge ahead raggedly. The oar handle is surprisingly thick, hard to grip. It is smooth, badly worn and slightly slick. I widen the space between my hands to gain a better grip. The professor steers us fully around as though to head east toward the waterfront. Almost immediately the *Endeavour* is lost to view in the thick fog. After a few more strokes the professor steers us back around. He whispers, "By my stroke count we're back very close to the ship. We'll head out on course 260. We'll make two changes onto short courses, then have our test. We'll come back on the reciprocals, eventually on 080. Let's be sure to note a few boats to remember for the return trip."

It's very quiet as we steadily row the jolly boat. She's heavy, but cuts through the water cleanly, without as much effort as I'd expected. We're causing a little stern wake, probably making at least walking speed. The professor steers by some boats. Gradually the number of moored boats around us thins out. Few lights are visible except an occasional high light attached to a mast or spreader. He whispers to us as we pass a chunky, double-ended sailboat that bears more than a passing resemblance to an oriental junk, "Remember this old Cheoy Lee." A few minutes later he grunts, "Here's the Bermuda 40 we saw this morning." We glide slowly by the handsome, dark blue sailboat.

I hear a muffled clanging sound. Moments later the professor tells us to stop rowing as we glide by a sizeable green buoy with the number "3" on its side. We resume rowing as the professor changes course well to the left, heading more south. Very soon a tubby-looking powerboat looms out of the fog. She seems to be riding slightly low in the water. I can't see her waterline at all. The white hull is scuffed and smudged as though the boat has had no attention in a long while. She has a low fly bridge topped with a bright blue bimini cover. The cover sags down in the middle as though it had a puddle of water in it. On a line trailing off her stern is a sizeable, light grey inflatable dingy with an outboard motor on her transom (vertical part of the stern).

"This Luhrs 32 is owned by a friend. He's currently on a year-long sabbatical in Turkey, studying ancient Christian relics found at Ephesus. When we actually go to the *Lord Sandwich* we'll leave some of our things here and retrieve them when we return. That's my dingy. From here we'll row on course 330 for ten minutes. That will put us roughly in the middle of the outer harbor to have our test."

We resume rowing. At one point the fog disperses a little and I see a very faint, highly diffused light. The professor whispers, "That must be one of the houses at the southern end of Goat Island."

What seems like at least ten minutes later, I glance at my watch to see it's 1:05 a.m. We must have been rowing for a total of at least twenty, probably twenty-five minutes. We haven't passed another boat since we left the Luhrs.

The professor quietly says, "OK, that's good…far enough. Ship your oars."

We place the oars alongside us lengthwise and across the thwarts, the oar handles on the forward thwart. The blades rest on the stern thwart where the professor sits steering the boat. We slowly drift to a stop.

"The tide is heading out, so we'll have to make a slight course correction when we return on the reciprocal course."

After a few moments' silence, the professor goes on, "It sure is quiet. I hear very little, just tiny noises from us and the water lapping at the jolly boat."

The silence seems almost complete except for the moaning of a distant foghorn. No birds, engine noises, none of the quiet rumble, as well as the even softer, indistinct ambient noise common to any populated area.

We are nearly engulfed in fog and silence.

The professor finally murmurs, "Let's go through self-hypnosis for a while. I'm going to both demonstrate hypnosis and teach a few basics of self-hypnosis. It is critical that we tune our attention to the specific target of July 24, 1778, and not think at all about our present. Harry, how about I work with you first then Jack, OK?"

Harry glances at me arching his eyebrows. "Sure, that's fine. Jack's already picked up enough new gray hair tonight."

"OK. Jack, let's you and I change places. Harry, move forward and sit on the forward thwart."

We shift around to our new assigned seats.

"Jack, certainly you're welcome to observe. In fact, how can you not? But, please minimize your presence by being still and quiet…thanks. Harry will need to really focus and follow along with me."

The professor reaches under the little forward deck, pulls out a sail bag, putting it between Harry's back and the thwart he's sitting on. "Lean back, Harry. Get as comfortable as you can. Adjust the sail bag any way that makes leaning back against it nice and comfortable. There's a second, smaller sail bag also under the deck, use that if it helps."

Harry retrieves that bag and puts it on top of the first so his head and shoulders are supported. He looks comfortable. He wiggles his butt and back pushing and nudging the bags to fit his body contours. "There, that's nice and cozy." He grins.

The professor leans forward. His face is very close to Harry, about three feet away. "We're going to totally relax now. While we relax together, just watch this strap from my compass. You don't have to stare at it. You can blink or look away for a moment if you want. But keep looking at it." He's holding the little compass at eye level. The compass itself is covered by his hand. The yellow strap is dangling down about six or eight inches.

"OK, first, take three breaths, deep and slow—inhale through your nose and exhale through your mouth. Silently count slowly to four, both when you inhale and exhale."

Harry does just as he's told, inhaling and exhaling deeply and slowly.

"Fine, that was just right, Harry." The professor is speaking very quietly and it seems, a little more slowly than usual.

"Next, Harry, I want you to focus on your whole body and relax. We'll do it together section by section from top to bottom. Focus on your forehead…and relax."

There's some up and down movement in Harry's shoulders as he evidently tries to relax.

"Focus on your face muscles…and relax.

"Focus on your jaw…let your mouth hang open a little.

"Focus on the back of your neck…and relax.

"Focus on your shoulders…and relax them.

"Focus on your upper left arm…and relax it.

"Focus on your lower left arm…and relax it.

"Focus on your left hand…relax the wrist, the front and back, the fingers."

The professor slowly, methodically guides Harry through the rest of his body, stopping only when he tells Harry to relax the last body part, his right foot. By now Harry is looking a little goofy, a slight grin on his face, his eyes not particularly focused. He is looking in the direction of the strap though.

"Really well done, Harry, now imagine a color that represents relaxation for you. Imagine that color flowing over your body slowly like a gentle stream of relaxation covering you from head to toes. Very slowly and quietly count backward from ten to one as the soothing, gentle stream flows over you.

"Harry, you are doing a wonderful job of accepting this. It feels very pleasant doesn't it, refreshing and restful.

"We'll stop here." He gently claps his hands once.

Harry blinks, shakes his head slightly as he lifts his back slowly off the sail bags. He smiles sheepishly.

"We'll get to this same stage before we set out to see the *Lord Sandwich*. Beyond that I'll take us a little further together. I'll help by giving us a kind of shove in the right direction, an assist to being in the time and place of the ship. Together we'll make ourselves powerfully receptive to seeing it. How do you feel, Harry?"

"Fine...really relaxed...loose. I feel like I had a great rest, but it was only a few minutes. I'm usually a little groggy after a rest, but not now. Also, I was surprised. I could hear everything you said. But it was as though you were in the distance, not right here."

"Good. You were terrific Harry. You accepted my suggestions, did a great job of relaxing your body. You were very receptive. Now you probably can see this state—I hate to call it a trance—this very relaxed but also very aware condition is not hard to get to. Do you think you could do by yourself what we did together?"

"Yeah, sure, maybe with some help, but I think I could do it."

"Jack, let's you and I do the same thing. Change places with Harry."

Once we've changed seats, the professor tells me to locate the sleeping bag he asked me to bring along. I pull it out of its carry bag, fold it in half and, like Harry did with the sail bag, lean back into it. I take the little sail bag Harry had used and put it behind my head which is resting on the jolly boat's little foredeck. The sleeping bag is acting like a cushion for my butt and back, and I've wrapped myself in it...cozy and warm.

The professor starts me out just as Harry, having me take three deep inhales and exhales. This seems to serve to slow me down a little, especially as I follow instructions, focusing on his compass strap. I find I have to blink frequently, to stop from staring fixedly at it. Maybe it's because I'm so tired. I'm always tired, but now not only is it absurdly late at night, but the professor is deliberately trying to coax me into complete relaxation.

The professor is telling me to focus on my forehead and relax it. I can't get that at all. I try wrinkling my brow, twitching it a little but to no avail. Similarly I can't do anything to relax my face muscles. I'm not even sure what my face muscles are. When he gets to my jaw though, hanging my mouth open a little does feel like a relaxing position. Next he starts on my left upper arm, then lower. Now I can glance quickly at the part, shake it slightly as I hang the arm down. That seems to work. Rolling my head back and forth helps to relax the back of my neck. Raising and releasing my shoulders to drop down definitely works. I wiggle and gently shake my wrist and fingers. I stop a minute to repeat the process so far. I droop my arms down, roll my head, raise and drop my shoulders, wiggle my wrists and fingers. I do the sequence again several times. I breathe slowly, deeply inhaling and exhaling. As I proceed down my body, I get better at sensing each part, particularly after glancing at it. Sensing it helps to focus on the part, trying to make it feel relaxed.

I can hear the professor saying, "You're doing very well, Jack, an honest effort at relaxation. I'm very impressed. Pick your relaxation color. Close your eyes and feel the color flow slowly over you."

I try to picture an aqua blue liquid flowing slowly over my shoulders and down my body. Gradually it covers my knees, ankles, toes. I can't get a particularly clear image of the liquid, it's more a thought than an image. I hesitantly count backward. "10, 9, 8…" down to "…3, 2, 1."

I'm still looking at the professor's strap, but his voice seems distant. Then in place of the strap I see a picture. Blinking I see it's a ship hull…the *Endeavour* hull with no masts, sails, rigging. "What is this, Jack?" I hear the professor ask. He sounds slightly distant and down a tunnel or shaft. His voice seems to echo slightly.

"It's the *Endeavour* hull. We think that's what the *Lord Sandwich* would look like."

"And the *Lord Sandwich* is…?"

"That's the *Endeavour* in 1778. We think we have an opportunity to see her here in Newport Harbor."

I hear a sharp clap sound, blink and sit up. The professor is holding the hull photo. Harry is watching from the stern thwart, leaning on the tiller.

"Jack, I got to tell you I'm very grateful. I know you've got some skepticism blocking you. Yet you were terrific setting that aside now. I'm inspired!"

"I'm glad you're inspired, but be careful not to confuse my receptivity with being dog-ass tired. I think I could sleep anywhere right now."

The professor replies, "That's a fair point actually. Obviously we don't want you to fall asleep now. But we all need to go through this relaxation process. You were right there. I introduced the hull photo. I was going to take you through the photo as a suggestion of what we want to attempt, but you jumped right to it."

"I know, I guess you've beat me down and I'm already in a hypnotic trance."

The professor smiles, "No, that doesn't appear likely. You're more ready than I would have thought though, I'll give you that."

Harry says, "I guess the point is, either we're going for this, or not. There's no apparent middle ground."

After a moment's more silence, "All right then, why don't we go for it now?" The professor looks first at Harry then at me.

Harry puts his watch up close to his eyes, "Take us through what we'll do. It's nearly 1:30 now."

"The first thing we'll do is turn around from here and on a reciprocal course head back to the Luhrs 32. We'll tie up and go aboard. You two will change into the best-fitting old clothing I've brought in the sail bag. We'll leave all our twentieth-century things there—watches, any jewelry, shoes, socks, all clothing. We'll keep the sleeping bag and compass for a short while. Then we'll row on a course I've established as the one to get us to the *Lord Sandwich* site. It's very similar to this one, but another ten minutes beyond. To help us get there, we'll row to a green can buoy just off Rose Island. We'll follow this same course directly to that buoy. It has a gong, so the harbor swells should enable us to hear it. The buoy is about 500 yards west of the site. Local archeologists have spent lots of time identifying the location. They know there are partial, fragmentary remains of numerous eighteenth-century ships buried in the sand and mud below. Their early research seems to indicate as many as a dozen ships were sunk, among them the *Lord Sandwich*. Records suggest it was sunk just off the north end of Goat Island. That's how I fixed the site. I've got the course from the green can to the site. We'll once again go through our relaxation, then our visualization. We'll need the sleeping bag for that. When we're done we'll attach the sleeping bag to the buoy. I'll then set our course to the site. I'll attach the compass—our last twentieth-century item—to the buoy. We'll set out to row quietly to the location. At this point, we'll have severed all contact with 1998. We'll be wearing clothing of the time of the *Lord Sandwich's* scuttling and in a boat actually in use at that time. Nothing tangible will connect us to now.

"This is a critical act. Just as explained in *Time and Again*, reaching back to the past can only occur if we sever our ties to the present. We know we are in the present by our countless ties to the objects and information that make it the present—things like specific television programs, the news of the day, the taste of McDonald's hamburgers, Microsoft's Windows 98, Viagra, Monica

Lewinsky and Kenneth Starr, the movie *Titanic*, the last episode of *Seinfeld*. In other words, the endless number of tiny threads which connect and bind us to the present. However, right here, right now in our clothing and in our jolly boat, we're in what in *Time and Again* is called a 'gateway'. It is a place that exists in both times. Like the principal character in *Time and Again*, Simon Morley, we can reach the time we seek only by making ourselves believe we can be part of it. We must erase the present and see ourselves in that time.

"Referring back to my note, we'll do this by selecting a few stimuli from the late eighteenth-century era. We do this to make the invisible visible. With the help of self hypnosis, we'll welcome our temporary absence from our current ties in exchange for links to the eighteenth century. The boat, clothing and a sharp mental picture of the hull will serve as our gateway to July 24, 1778, enabling us to believe and to reach out and be a part of that day. Simon Morley had the knack to concentrate entirely on his destination time. He'd feel himself drift away from the current time to the intended time. I may or may not have Simon's knack, but based on careful preparation and some partial trials, I am convinced I can do it and take you with me...both ways.

"When we see her, we'll only look at the *Lord Sandwich* through the fog and from a distance. We can't be seen by anyone on board it or any other nearby ship. In no way can we risk being connected to that historical moment. I'm sure you understand. We can't have any role in the past at all. Because any role we might have then could alter the future which stems from that past. That, of course, is utterly wrong and absolutely unacceptable.

"Once we've had this momentous experience we'll be done. We'll spin this boat precisely around and row well back on our course out of sight in the fog. We'll settle ourselves to focus on the here and now, particularly the green buoy.

"At the buoy we'll row the reciprocal course to the Luhrs, change clothes and finish back at the replica *Endeavour*, none the worse for wear."

"Jack, I think for us the principal issues have been, does this seem at all possible, and can we test it while being in enough control that we are in no danger?" Harry is now sitting on the thwart just behind the professor. "Agree?"

"Yeah, OK. But now it's much more. We can't possibly know if Walter's scheme will work. But right now, where we are, it is nothing less than mesmerizing. We've come to a point of no return. My guess is, Walter, you've planned it this way. But it doesn't matter now. We owe it to ourselves to go ahead. To use Walter's Einstein point, not to get out of the boat and peer around the river bend when maybe we have even a chance, is just an impossible choice. We have to go ahead."

"Let's 'rock n' roll', professor!"

The professor beams, cries, "Yes!" and raises both fists high above his head shaking them furiously. We jump back into our original seats, Harry and I at our middle thwart rowing positions, the professor sitting in the stern holding the tiller. He opens the little compass. Looking at it he steers us off on a course we all hope will take us to the Luhrs powerboat.

"We're still on 330. Let's assume we've drifted north a little on the incoming tide. I'll steer the 150-degree reciprocal with a slight favoring higher to compensate for the tide."

Harry and I are steadily pulling the oars through clean strokes. The professor looks up. "I timed us at eleven minutes from the dingy 'til when I had you stop rowing. We'll row just under eleven minutes from right now and stop. We'll listen carefully for boat noises, like lapping water or creaking sounds."

Absorbed in our own thoughts we row the jolly boat silently. I'm amazed how much I want this to happen. I visualize the hull, try to visualize what little I can think of that seems part of the Revolutionary War era—swords and long bore muskets, tri-corner hats, powdered wigs, a flag displaying a curled snake with the expression "Don't Tread on Me", the scarlet jackets of the British Army and Royal Marines, men's stockings, the *Endeavour's* red ensign, long black iron cannons…scattered, disjointed images.

"Almost eleven minutes…ship oars."

Nothing is visible, fog still envelopes everything. We glide slowly to a stop. The professor has us make a few more strokes. We drift some more. The professor puts his index finger vertically over his mouth asking for quiet. A moment later we all turn toward a slight sound. The professor points diagonally over my right shoulder, steering us that way as Harry and I make two short strokes. Before we can react, we glance off a white hull at least three feet high. "Made it," hisses the professor as he grabs the hull while the jolly boat stern swings toward it.

Sure enough, I now can see that bright blue bimini cover above us.

The professor grabs the sail bag containing the antique uniforms and clothing. I tie off the little bow line to a cleat amidships on the powerboat and scramble over the side into the modern boat. Harry steps over the side and holds out his hand to help. The professor grabs his hand as he sits on the boat's gunwale (the upper edge of the boat's side) to swing his legs over. Once in, he very gently places the sail bag on the deck. The three of us kneel over the bag, barely able to see it in the dark. Slowly he pulls out several shirts and pants, one squarish dark hat.

"Here," exclaims the professor, "here's the shirt I thought was big enough." The shirt is more like a jersey—long-sleeved, quite faded, but has distinct horizontal strips of blue or black. The shirt's neckline is sharply scooped.

"Jack, here's a couple that are somewhat smaller and should fit you OK." Peering through the darkness after a moment I can see one that seems virtually identical to Harry's striped jersey. The other is white, but badly stained, sleeves rolled up. It has a string of wooden buttons in the center and no collar.

"Here's another jersey." This one also is badly stained, long-sleeved like the striped jerseys but without any color, similar wooden buttons. Interestingly it has a badly faded red kerchief pinned to it with its two ends knotted together.

The professor is still reaching into the sail bag. "I think these will fit you, Harry. The guy who rowed in them today is at least your size, probably heavier." He hands Harry white pants with wide bottoms made of a coarse material.

"This is canvas, isn't it?" asks Harry. "The thing must have been homemade."

The professor looks up from his bag, "Actually the pants are made of flax, the material used to make sails then. Virtually all sailor uniforms were homemade. Most had made a kind of dress uniform of white 'ducks' and jersey and hat. But they had lots of other clothing they made for themselves, usually of fabric and material bought from the ship's purser. All sailors had to be handy with needle and thread."

Harry reaches for the square hat. "Ah, it's a boater. Look at the little red ribbon around it, tied in a nice neat knot. The ribbon probably will fall apart if I touch it, it's so threadbare." He gently puts it on his head. Though it's somewhat small and seems to perch on the top of his head, he has it at a rakish angle, looking quite jaunty.

I laugh aloud, "That's got to be you, Harry."

The professor has handed me garish trousers. They have blue stripes every few inches running the length of the legs. "I have one more pair of blue pants, but these should fit fairly well. I also have a very fragile short blue jacket which was a common garment then. I think it will fit you Jack. Please be very careful with it. What are you, maybe 42 regular?"

I nod as he hands me the jacket. It doesn't look like a uniform, more of a civilian pattern. It's quite short, made of coarse cloth, has a small collar, big lapels, no cuffs on the sleeves.

"Both of you, take all your clothing off—underwear, socks, everything. Then carefully put on what you've got. Remember each piece is ancient, so please wear it as loose as you can to avoid damage. Put your regular clothes back in this sail bag for now."

After I undress, I pull on the striped white pants. The material is a heavy cloth with irritating stitches up and down the inside. The front has a flap about six inches wide held up with two buttons near the waist. The waist itself is very high, well above my natural waist. It fits very snugly. I select the stained white jersey, fearing even in the eighteenth century, vertically striped pants and a horizontally striped shirt would be too much. The shirt is stiff and very musty. I carefully pull it over my arms and shoulders. As I button the few front buttons, one falls to pieces in my hand, another falls repeatedly out of a too-big button hole. Two buttons work. They'll have to do. I remove the kerchief's pin, drape it around my neck, and tie an overhand knot in front of me with the two ends. The jacket, when unbuttoned, happily is quite loose. I get into it easily, only to find the sleeves are very short. I'm glad I have it on, given the fog and cooling night air.

"Jack, the very model of an eighteenth-century able seaman!" grins the professor.

Harry still has on the boater, complemented with the blue striped jersey and flax pants. The pants are so loose they billow when he walks. The jersey, though, looks tight. Harry has a broad, thick chest and muscular arms. The jersey clearly is strained.

The professor looks at the jersey. "Breathe with great care, Harry, please." He then climbs to the fly bridge. We hear him fumbling around forward. Suddenly the boat's running lights forward and a light on a transom pole come on. "Leave a home light burning we're told," he smiles.

We fold and put our clothing in the sail bag, cinch it up and leave it in the Luhrs' cockpit, next to the ladder to the fly bridge. Once we are back in our assigned jolly boat positions, we move hand-over-hand along the mooring line to the mooring buoy. Here we pause as the professor reads the compass for the proper course. "By the way, there's no need for shoes, sailors seldom wore them except in cold weather months.

"It's just under a mile to the green can. Once we get close to the buoy you'll hear the gong. It will be faint because the swells are so small, but even small movements should sound the gong."

Aligned the way the professor wants, Harry and I start our regular oar stroking. Minutes go by as we move quietly along our north-northwest course. There is not a sign of wind. We don't bother to discuss using the sail.

"Take a short break," murmurs the professor. "Shake out your arms, take some deep breaths to get more oxygen into your muscles. Bring your mental vision to bear on the hull. I can see it out there in the fog. You can see it too."

A few minutes go by and the professor quietly says, "Resume rowing."

Several more minutes pass. "Jack, you're fading on us. I have to steer constantly to offset Harry's pull. Just a couple more minutes and we'll stop to listen for the gong. Suck up a little more effort and we're there."

I resent his criticism, but nod slightly.

Hardly a minute later, the professor stands up gingerly, bracing the backs of his legs against the stern thwart. "Ship oars and listen."

I can hear nothing. My heart is pounding too hard for me to hear anything but its thump, thump, thump.

Harry lurches forward, raises his hand to point directly off to our port. He pulls mightily on his oar, as we spin toward the left. The professor holds out his hand palm up. After a moment I can hear the gong. It seems to come from our bow. We sit silent and motionless trying to detect the faint sound's direction. Finally he points to me. Gesturing with his fingers he points at me holding two fingers up for two strokes. I perform this little move and the buoy drifts into view.

The professor partially folds the compass, pulls some electrician's tape from his pocket, apparently to use to attach the compass to the buoy. After tying off the painter he says, "We'll spend the next few minutes tied to the buoy getting into our relaxation and visualization. Let's first rest, to calm down and start to concentrate on our goal. Breathe deeply and slowly. For now picture the winding river and the hull just beyond the bend in the river."

A few moments later, "Let's get comfortable. I'll lean against the stern and rudder post, stretching my legs out onto the next thwart. Jack, drape your sleeping bag entirely over yourself and straddle that thwart so your lower back can slump against the gunwale. Get into to your original rest position, Harry. Lie back against the forward deck, use the little sail bag for your head rest. Keep your eyes on the top of the buoy as it sways back and forth while I go through our relaxation steps."

As Harry stretches out with his back on the forward thwart and head on the sail bag, I pull the sleeping bag out of its case. I put the bag over my shoulders and legs creating an enveloping cocoon. After a moment I realize the professor is right, the most comfortable position is with the small of my back propped against the gunwale, my head and shoulders slumped forward. For better balance I cross my legs Indian-style and cover them with the bag. I cross my hands over my stomach. We sit for several minutes watching the buoy and listening to the silence.

We float almost motionless next to the buoy. The professor softly chants "inhale…exhale" repeatedly. Next he slowly takes us through relaxing each part of our body. Once again, I glance at the parts I can see to help focus my attention. If I can I move the part slightly, gently shaking out its tension. Most of the time, I keep my eyes on the buoy and listen to the professor talking quietly.

Once we finish relaxing our feet, he quietly continues. "There's no need for you to talk. It's so nice here, right now. Let's enjoy it without you having to talk, just listen and feel the serenity of the moment. We feel our nerves and muscles relaxing. It feels wonderfully comfortable and serene, a little like floating on the river, calm and warm. You can feel tension sliding away. For a moment we'll drift away from 1998."

He pauses, then, "We'll just take a look, that's all. It will be well before dawn on July 24, 1778. We'll see the hull of the *Lord Sandwich* floating in the distance, barely visible in the fog. We may see hazy outlines of one or two other hulls also ready for scuttling. You may see or hear a few men on board, mostly guards. It's OK, for the moment you're part of July 24, 1778. Everything you are connected to at this moment is part of that day—your clothes, your boat. Where you are right now is all about that moment."

He unties the jolly boat from the buoy. The professor gently lifts the sleeping bag off me and pulls a folded object from under his thwart. "Jack, I'm lifting the sleeping bag off you. I'll put it in this sack and attach it to the buoy." One more look at the folding compass and he folds it shut onto a strip of tape which he attaches to the buoy. We start to drift away. The professor wiggles the tiller a few strokes, propelling us out of sight of the buoy.

"We'll close our eyes now. We're each very tired, but we want so much to see that hull. In a moment we'll sleep a wonderfully restful and dreamless sleep. After we wake, we'll go to see the *Lord Sandwich*. It will look like the picture we've been studying. Nothing else matters, nothing back there where we came from…just the hull and the moment, the *Lord Sandwich* and late night July 24, 1778. We'll be there shortly. When we wake we'll row close enough to see the hull. We will speak to no one, in no way will anything we do impact the moment. Then we will return to the buoy."

"Rest…let go…and sleep. I can feel the time of the *Lord Sandwich*. We're drifting into it. It's here. Feel it."

I'm floating in a soft current. Almost asleep I expect to see the hull. I'm certain it's there, sure I'll see it. This is going to work. I feel suspended…waiting to arrive somewhere. Soon I'll see it. Keep peering into the fog…it's there, for sure, it's there.

I jerk up a little and blinking, open my eyes. I must have dozed off. The professor is watching me with a slight smile. Harry stretches his arms wide.

The professor leans forward, taps Harry's left foot resting on the edge of my thwart. "Harry, sit next to Jack. Both of you put your oar out ready to row. To get to the hull we still need to row for a few minutes—should be about 500 yards almost dead ahead. Ignore the distance, think what you're about to see!"

Pointing over Harry's right shoulder he says, "On my word, slowly, very quietly, row together…now."

Taking long, slow strokes we begin. The professor pulls the tiller barely to the left to head the jolly boat where he pointed. For a few minutes I row in cadence with Harry. Then, even my exhilaration can't overcome my exhaustion. I'm so tired that I'm starting to feel dizzy. I must be on the very edge of collapse. The professor holds up his hand to stop rowing. He's straining to look forward, his head jutted forward. I watch him looking for any sign. My heart is thumping again, mouth so dry I can't seem to swallow. The boat rocks a little as Harry turns around trying to look forward.

"Five more strokes, nice and smooth, then stop."

Harry and I just finish our first stroke. "Stop…lift your oar silently onto your lap. Don't move…no noise at all!"

The professor groans, closes his eyes tightly shut, one hand grabs his chest.

His face, blotchy red a moment ago, is pale and moist, like he has a sudden fever. His lips move slightly, but no sound. Then, *"My God...Oh, My God...!"* He drops his head as his other arm pops up toward his chest. I lean forward to grab hold of him. As I get hold of his shoulders he opens his eyes looking over my right shoulder, I barely can hear him, *"Jack, look!"*

I turn and see nothing for a moment, I can't seem to focus. Some deep breaths and I look again. After a moment, through the fog a big hull is just visible. I'm utterly unprepared for the shock. Instantly I feel dizzy, I put my hand on the top of my head and press down. I feel myself toppling over backward. I grab the gunwale to keep from falling. Is that it? Is it really the hull? Has to be...doesn't it? I glance at Harry, he's staring out at the barely visible hull his mouth open, eyes blinking furiously.

Finally, Harry fiercely whispers, "You OK, professor? Is that it? That's the *Lord Sandwich*, professor? *Goddamn it...is it?*"

Silence. I turn toward the professor who's now sitting up straight, his hands no longer on his chest. Blinking and breathing heavily, he stares into the fog. "No question, no question at all. *Incredible...incredible!*"

Nothing else. His lips are moving, but there's no sound. Tears are flowing down his face.

My heart is pounding and I'm breathing way too fast. I try to take a few deep breaths while staring at the barely visible hull. I lose the hull repeatedly through the heavy fog, barely staying focused on two widely separated faint lights. Then it's gone...nothing.

Harry whispers, "Let's row forward a little. I've lost it."

The professor finally murmurs, "Two strokes."

Slowly we lift our oars with both hands, placing them further out in the oar locks. We gently pull two strokes and drift forward, oars held above the water.

"Got it," points the professor.

Harry and I turn around. Yes, its there, slightly clearer now. The lights are more distinct. I can barely make out a little boat alongside. The hull looks to be slightly more than 100 yards away. For a moment the thick fog lessens and it becomes more distinct. I can make out the quarterdeck railing.

Movement. A red patch of motion catches my eye. There it is...a man in a red jacket carrying a long rifle. Must be a marine, possibly a guard. I sit there stunned. My instinct is to hide, lie on the floor boards out of sight. But I can't move, staring at this figure walking forward from behind the light which seems to be on the quarterdeck railing. For the moment his red jacket is clear, even the white belts crisscrossing his chest, and funny-looking, tall black hat, almost a top hat. His long rifle is fixed with a bayonet. Am I just hallucinating? *This is an eighteenth-century Royal Marine for God's sake!* Blinking and shaking my head doesn't change things. He's still there. I glance at Harry and the professor. They're staring too, both with mouths open, motionless, seeming not even to breathe.

Suddenly the marine stops, seems to be waiting. I hear a faint grumbling, indistinct voices. The guard slams the butt of his rifle on the deck again and again as he walks to the amidships waist (center) of the hull. "Silence, you scum!"

The grumbling grows louder. While I can hear no distinct words, it seems to be many voices. The guard again yells, "Quiet damn you! Shut your foul Yankee gobs!"

Then a piercing hoarse yell, "Water, lobsterback, gives us water!"

Harry points toward the hull's bow. Another red-coated figure is hurrying toward the first. "Give'm water, Henry. Piss down the grate!"

The grumbling grows louder. I hear shouted oaths—"bastard", "filthy oaf", "limey pigs". Now the grumbling turns to shrieks and screams. The two guards are standing together, rifles slung, hands at the front of their pants.

"Goddamn it, they're pissing on them!" says Harry, not whispering.

"Quiet. Good Lord, be quiet!" The professor grabs Harry violently shaking his shoulder.

The guard from the stern jolts abruptly around. He stares out in our general direction.

"What you looking at Henry?"

"Heard something." He continues to look out toward us, but searching, not focused.

"Ahoy, who goes?" he yells.

"Quiet, not a sound," hisses the professor.

We sit motionless. The fog is drifting by, some patches almost obscuring the hull.

"Don't see nothin'," says the bow guard.

"Nah, sure sounded like a voice though," answers the other.

Slowly they turn and march back toward their respective positions.

"On my word reverse row, we got to get out of here *now*. Get ready to push your oar forward when we get the next fog patch." The professor is squinting over our shoulders.

"OK, here's some fog, push…quiet…long strokes."

He holds the tiller straight as we start to push the oars through the water. Very slowly we start to creep backward into the fog.

.

SIX

"Keep rowing…a few more strokes. OK, stop now. Listen. We've got to figure out if they're going to do anything." The professor stares off toward the hull.

We drift slightly backward in silence, straining to hear anything from the direction of the *Lord Sandwich*. Nothing. The only sound I hear is our heavy breathing, not only from our exertion, but the excruciating tension and an overwhelming awe of the last few moments. I feel a desperate need to gather my wits, to try to slow down, to think a moment to try to make some sense of it all. I have a splitting headache.

"Quietly, let's turn the boat around. We're probably a little off course to the buoy, but not too bad. Jack, make a few more short push strokes, Harry short pull strokes. I'll watch to see that we turn 180 degrees to head off in the right direction."

We take a few strokes as directed, the professor whispers, "Stop. Hold your oars in the water to stabilize here."

After a moment, he again whispers, "OK, let's row a minute or so to get well clear of the area."

We stroke slowly along for a few moments. Harry seems agitated, finally says, "Wait, stop here. Those were American prisoners in that hull, right? Sounded like a lot of them. The British are going to sink her?" Glaring at the professor he continues, "Any precise idea…?"

I interrupt, "Wait a minute, Harry, please. First, let's be sure what's real here. Help me. I don't know what to believe. Tell me what you saw. Did we see the same thing?"

Harry turns abruptly to me, "Jesus, Jack...yes, we saw the same damn thing—the hull, the two redcoats, heard the noise from the prisoners, the lights. Come on, for Chrissake, we all saw it!"

"Please, please stop this." The professor is leaning forward toward us. "First we have to get further clear of the area, in case the fog lifts, or unlikely, the guards use the boat we saw to make a patrol out here. We can't go too far because we have to get ready to return to 1998, then to the buoy. We'll row for a few minutes. I counted seconds and minutes when we left the buoy and got to seven minutes, forty seconds when I said stop.

"Of course you understand the buoy doesn't exist to us now. We have to regain July 24, 1998. We'll row a little over seven minutes. That will get us well clear of the *Lord Sandwich* but still not overshoot the buoy. We'll then proceed through our series of steps to reconnect with 1998. Once there we'll organize a little search plan to find the buoy.

"The answer to your apparent question, Harry, is yes, the marine historians have access to British Navy records. The records state numerous ships, including the *Lord Sandwich*, were scuttled on July 26, 1778. That's the day after tomorrow."

As the professor softly counts we row on and on. The fog is thick on all sides. We're in silence except for the minimal sounds of our boat in the water. The professor tells us to stop for a moment. "Can you keep going, Jack?"

"Yeah, give me a moment, I'll be all right." I know Harry must be doing much of the rowing because the professor constantly adjusts the tiller against his stroke. Just as long as I keep going...do not stop.

After what feels like an instant, we resume rowing. The pain in my arms and legs seems beyond tolerance. To survive another stroke I have to think of something else. I drift back to see the hull, hear the commotion there. I'm barely pulling the oar through the water.

Finally the professor says, "OK, we need to prepare to return. As I said earlier, it's much simpler than connecting to the past. We need to visualize and feel the future, our time and place here in 1998. See the green can, hear its gong, see the Luhrs 32, the *Endeavour* replica, Alice, even Tony and Margaret, the

134

twentieth-century galley, the feel and look of the clothes you left behind on the Luhrs, the feel of your hammock. Jack, you can think of your wife and daughters, this year's Boston Red Sox, the search assignments you're working on. Harry, think of the Potomac River. What does it look like, how does it smell? See and feel your day sailor.

"First, let's find comfortable positions, then fix our gaze on something. Here, look at this halyard." He releases a few feet of the coiled line next to the mast. He holds it up with its end dangling in his right hand, arm outstretched.

"Hold on damn it, hold on!" Harry remains agitated, his face grim, angry. "What about the American prisoners on the *Lord Sandwich*? We're just leaving them there…not doing a fucking thing?"

Leaning forward, the professor looks at Harry. Softly, almost whispering he says, "Harry, you know we can't. I made that absolutely clear. *We cannot interfere!* What is past is reality, we cannot alter it. Frankly, I didn't expect prisoners on board. I assumed they were off by now. But regardless, the past is immutable. The past shaped our present, events from then to now formed us and all that derived from them. To do anything would be to change things without any knowledge of the effect of our actions. Not only do we have no right to do that, it is impossibly fearful to even think about."

"So we leave them there to drown?"

"You don't know that any more than I do," the professor fires back angrily. "They may be transferred to a land prison, a labor camp, to another prison ship, sent to Canada or to England. Who knows? We can't assume anything. However, I will tell you I know of no record of prisoners drowning."

"Yeah, it sure is likely they kept meticulous records of drowning prisoners," grumbles Harry. He pauses, takes a deep breath. After a moment he asks, "Are you sure of the date it actually was sunk?"

"It's not me, the local historians and archeologists claim to be."

Harry pauses, rubs his neck. "OK, let's go back."

I'm surprised how quickly Harry's anger and passion evaporates. What's that all about? He's not one to suddenly cave in or lose interest when aroused. He glances at me, as he scrambles forward to sit on the forward thwart. He twists his torso and leans his side on the little forward deck. He puts his right arm on the deck, and lowers his head cradling it in his arm. The professor is relaxing his body, slumped over the tiller. I go back to my Indian-style sitting position, the small of my back propped against the gunwale.

Speaking slowly and quietly the professor begins to repeat the relaxation process. "Keep your eyes on the halyard. We just had an astounding few minutes. Now we have to momentarily minimize, even better block that memory as we re-connect to our present. Let's take a moment to remember the green buoy and its gong. Let your auditory memory hear the gong. Listen to it."

A minute or so later he continues. "Feel and visualize your clothing left behind in the Luhrs. Mentally put them back on. First put on the underwear, your socks. Harry, see and feel your *Endeavour* shirt, Jack, your sweatshirt. Both of you had jeans on. Feel them, look at them as you put them on. Remember your shoes…mentally put them on.

"Now, just relax, keep your eyes on this halyard as I take you through our relaxation steps. Think of your life and images of the end of the twentieth century—the feel, smell, taste, sound of today in our time. Hum a tune, taste the great meal we had earlier tonight, feel the kiss of a loved one, see the Cheoy Lee sailboat we passed on the way here. It's time to go back. I badly want to go back. I'll deal with the wondrous minutes in the fog with *Lord Sandwich* later. Right now, let's just get back."

As the professor quietly tells us to relax our bodies step-by-step, I listen, while obediently thinking of what he suggests, the buoy, the meal, my clothes. As I do, again I feel that drifting sensation of earlier. I'm in a kind of borderland.

A small sharp noise startles me out of it. The professor is sitting up, leaning toward us. "Let's go find that buoy," he says.

Harry is stirring. He stands carefully and steps over the thwart to resume his seat to my left.

The professor continues, "Starting here, let's work out a search pattern. We're still about twenty to thirty seconds short of the buoy, by my time count. So, let's row in fifteen-stroke blocks. Fifteen strokes forward, stop; turn ninety degrees, row fifteen strokes, stop; turn ninety degrees etc. That will give us a fifteen-stroke square. When we complete the four sections of the square, we'll stop and go to seven-stroke blocks, thereby working within the first square. Make sense?"

"Walter, are you sure you're not a geometry teacher?"

He awkwardly slaps my knee, smiling happily. We could be in big trouble here but he's having the time of his life!

The first two fifteen-stroke blocks yield nothing, not the hint of a foreign sound. On the third block Harry swears he hears something, though he's not sure what. We stop and listen while hardly breathing, but hear nothing. Finally Harry concedes and we continue to finish the big fifteen-stroke square. Once we arrive at the start point, the professor tells us to take a five minute rest.

The rest over, he says, "Let's row backward eight strokes then turn right ninety degrees to start our smaller, inside block." We push the oars through the water for eight strokes. We turn the boat ninety degrees to the right. We row seven strokes, turn right. As we start the next seven strokes Harry blurts out, "Stop! Same sound!" After a moment this time I hear it too, behind my back, off our bow.

"Two strokes forward, gently please." The professor stands carefully. I only can hear the sound when there is absolute silence, but there it is again. Yeah, I've got it, very slight. Did we make it back so easily?

"Yes, Yes, there it is, I see it…I'll be damned, I got it! We're back!"

The green buoy is rocking quietly in the small swells, the gong making slight metallic pings as it moves back and forth. Harry grabs the buoy and gives it a big kiss. We laugh long and loud, with more than a touch of hysteria mixed in. We made it! After so much laughter I'm exhausted, so tired I just slump in my seat…drained of energy. I simply have to sleep…now, right now.

Harry and the professor are silent, also slumped in exhaustion. Harry coughs, mumbles, "We've got to get to the Luhrs. But now I'm not sure we can. Professor, you row for Jack for a bit, then Jack and I will switch, giving us each a little break."

The professor removes the tape from the little compass, pushes the button on the side to illuminate its face. He then hands me the sleeping bag. "Change places with me, Jack."

Handing me the compass he tells me to use the 150-degree reciprocal course to the Luhrs. "It should be easy. We'll see the lights I left on just by rowing this course. It's just less than a mile away. We're going slower now, say, twenty maybe twenty-five minutes' rowing. Switch at fifteen minutes, OK?"

I mumble agreement as I sit down on the stern thwart and wait for the compass needle to settle. I place the compass on the seat next to me, the face illuminated. Harry and the professor start rowing slowly as I turn the tiller to set the boat on a 150-degree course. As always I can't keep the course firmly on a specific heading, so I settle for slightly above and slightly below 150 degrees.

Nobody says a word. It's been a momentous few minutes. In fact, it now seems far longer. For the moment though, as if by silent consent, we know first of all we've got to get back to the Luhrs. It represents a kind of home base outpost. Our clothes are there, it's a twentieth-century boat, part of twentieth-century life. We know we can reach the *Endeavour* from there. Silently we plod along our course. Maybe it's a hangover from so much excitement, or the realization it's over, plus the exhaustion we all feel. Whatever, I'm falling into a funk, feeling more than a little depressed. It seems like an extreme version of my mild depression at going back to work after a nice vacation, or a great weekend.

The professor says, "I'd say that's fifteen minutes; Jack and Harry to switch."

I can't believe it! I just got to the tiller. Can't be fifteen minutes! How could it go so fast?

Wordlessly Harry gets up, crouching by the thwart as he waits for me to take his place. OK, I move by him and sit down. Still, doesn't seem possible, but what choice do I have? I hand Harry the compass and get my oar set to row. Harry watches the compass for a moment than nods his head for us to stroke. The oar feels like a heavy iron bar. My forearms, legs and now my back are killing me. I shuffle my feet around trying to find the base of a thwart or a deck "stretcher" board to brace my feet against, thereby to get my legs into the rowing. I had that in my seat where the professor now sits. Why can't I find it here? There it is. I snug the arch of my heel up against a stretcher board. Then I place my other foot right next to it on the same board. Now I can push off with my legs. That's better, less strain on my back, little less on arms. Maybe I can survive the next ten minutes or so. Each stroke is an effort. I have to concentrate fiercely just to keep rowing, keep pace with the professor's stroking.

"I think that's it," says Harry, pointing over the bow.

I turn, yes, there's definitely a slight glow ahead, getting brighter as we glide through the water from our last strokes. Thank God. I'm not at all sure I had many strokes left in me. We slowly drift up to the now brightly lit Luhrs.

"Check the time."

I look at my watch. "3:15. Damn, we'd better get moving."

"Jesus, I guess so, need to get there before dawn for sure. There's some light before five, so time to go," says Harry.

We carefully strip off the historical clothes, handing them to the professor who gently folds and stacks them back into their bag. The professor clearly is the freshest of us as he scrambles around the Luhrs and puts the clothes bag back in the jolly boat. He turns out the lights, climbs back into his rowing position without discussion. Harry joins him leaving me to the stern steering position. I push off as I step into the jolly boat.

A moment later the professor says, "Jack, the course will be 020 degrees from here back to the green bell buoy '3', then 080 to the *Endeavour*. Also should be easy. We'll see landmark boats along the way, and be able to pick up the big light on *Endeavour's* maintop. It should be about ten minutes, or a little less. You and Harry switch at five minutes."

Harry looks up. "No, that's a waste of time. I'll row the rest of the way. I'm fine."

No argument there. Harry's determined. He obviously intends to finish the task. Fine with me.

I steer us onto the 020 course, once again illuminating the compass face and placing it on the thwart next to me. For two or three minutes we row along without a word. Should I suggest I break at the buoy? Harry and the professor must be as tired as I am...totally drained and deflated. We all hear the bell well before we reach it. I say, "Quick break, couple minutes."

No complaints or arguments. Two or three minutes of silence, then Harry looks up at me. "Sorry Jack for snapping at you back there. I was just totally blown away with the *Lord Sandwich*...and the prisoners. I wasn't ready for the impact of all this...over-friggin-whelming." He looks away, then back at me.

"No sweat, not to worry. I...."

Harry breaks in, "I just can't get over the prisoners, stuck below decks on that hull. To hear them and to just row away is killing me. I know...I know we're not supposed to do anything. I understand the no-interference bit, believe me. But to do nothing is just wrong, it goes against every instinct, everything I know I'm supposed to do...at least do something!"

"Walter, tell us what you know about the prisoners."

The professor nods. "Actually not much. While we have no record of drowning prisoners on the *Lord Sandwich*, Harry's right. If it did happen that record is not too likely to exist.

"Who were the prisoners? Probably a significant number were crew off privateers. Rhode Island was a hotbed of them. Privateers were armed private vessels that fought for plunder. The American leadership sanctioned and encouraged them to harass British merchant shipping. They drove the British crazy all through the war, particularly around Newport. It was the principal

British port outside of New York, so an important target for the Americans. Other prisoners would have been local patriots or sympathizers. Some prisoners probably were shipped here from other sites. Remember the British controlled only two important northern cities in 1778, New York and Newport. So prisoners captured in other parts of New England may have been sent here. Some probably were sent to Canada, to England, some to New York. I imagine there were a few American soldiers there too. In 1778, Brigadier General John Sullivan had 1500 regulars and varying numbers of militia in and around Providence. They had regular encounters, occasional skirmishes with the British Army. The Americans had outposts all around Narragansett Bay to watch and harass the British occupiers. Some could have been captured and put in the *Lord Sandwich*. I'd guess there were local common criminals, thieves, maybe drunks in there as well."

The professor pauses for a few seconds then continues. "I should tell you since you ask about prisoners, that their lot was terrible in the Revolutionary War. The treatment of prisoners—if they survived the circumstances of their capture or any wounds they suffered, both fairly unlikely events—was appalling by both sides. Arguably though, the British were the worst. They tended to think the Americans were rebels. In fact they generally referred to Americans as 'the rebels'. Thereby, as rebels they did not deserve the treatment due to regular prisoners of war. In fact they housed prisoners in some pretty awful places. Two were in New York, one on land called the Sugarhouse, the other the infamous '*Old Jersey*.' That was a black-hulled hulk of a former 64-gun man-of-war. Reportedly it housed 1200 prisoners at a time, and thousands died there. I read a famous account of conditions on the *Jersey*, by a Thomas Dring, himself from Rhode Island. He describes it as a grim, even grotesque place. Prisoners were filthy with dirt, matted long hair and beards, sores all over, clothing disintegrated into rags. He scares the reader with the frightful noises all night long of prisoners groaning and screaming, the agony of the sick, dying, and delirious. He goes on to describe the prisoner diet of wormy bread, oatmeal and beef cooked in seawater. Ravenous hunger and extreme thirst were the common fate of all. The prisoners couldn't resist diseases that spread unchecked—smallpox, and yellow fever especially. He writes of the suffocating heat, the hateful malevolence of the prison keepers. He tells of the Dante-esque ordering of decks, the lower the deck the more horrendous its conditions.

"In another story, a Captain John Trevett of Newport and the Continental

Marines rails at the British jailors in his journal. He describes them as so evil that Black Beard, the notorious pirate, was 'a Christian' compared to the—wonderful expression—'billingsgate villains' who commanded there. His brother, the commander of a Rhode Island merchant vessel died 'of hard treatment from the British pirates' on the *Jersey*.

"Since we don't have such documentation on the *Lord Sandwich*, it may be that it wasn't as bad. In fact, it wasn't a prison ship very long before it was scuttled. Still, given its time and purpose, it probably was pretty horrid. Our little glimpse seems to concur.

"We better get going, Jack."

The professor starts to stroke slowly, as Harry quickly joins him. We glide slowly along.

"Pretty nasty stuff…about the prisoners, professor," mumbles Harry.

"Never a good deal to be a prisoner, but especially so before the Geneva Convention or twentieth-century laws started to have some impact," replies the professor.

Finally several minutes later I spot a thick mast looming out of the fog. Steering around it I remember the boat that looked a little like a Chinese junk. Wasn't the Bermuda 40 after that on the way out? We must have somehow missed it in the fog.

The professor looks at the Cheoy Lee and holds up his hand. "Better stop for a moment to get our story straight. If we're missed we'll say we went for a practice row and got badly lost in the fog. It took us a long time to find our way back. If we're not missed, we just have to say we went out to practice and get used to handling the jolly boat."

Harry and the professor resume rowing. Once we again are plodding along in exhausted silence. Shortly, I see a patch of light directly ahead and high. I quietly say, "Slow down, hold your stroke for a moment. I think we're here."

The *Endeavour's* hull and rigging quickly take shape, emerging from the fog.

A voice above us says, "Here they are! They're right here, Andrew!"

Oops, bad sign, Andrew has been looking for us. Damn, what a pain in the ass! I can see Alice standing next to Andrew. "Told you they'd be back. They must have gotten lost."

"For three hours?"

The professor scrambles up the accommodation ladder. "Alice's right. We will have no time in the morning so I asked Harry and Jack to row for a bit tonight to get comfortable with the boat for tomorrow's ceremony. We got turned around in the fog. Finally we nearly ran into the Number 3 channel marker. We tied up there for a long while waiting for the fog to lift. Eventually we decided to try again and here we are! We're tired as hell. Harry and Jack would have mutinied if they'd had to row much further! I've had it, going below, good night."

Smart move…just say your peace and leave.

As I climb the ladder, Andrew watches me. "I can't believe you were lost for three hours. What happened? Where'd you go, really?"

"Just like the professor said. It was like rowing around in a can of pea soup. In a way we're lucky to be back even now. See ya'." Trying the professor's strategy I walk away along the deck. But no….

"What a load. You did something you won't talk about, didn't you."

Alice grabs Andrew's arm and walks him away. "Andrew, they're exhausted. Let them alone. They've told us what happened and that's it. You're not on duty are you? I didn't see your name on the watch list. Tomorrow's a long day. Let's get some sleep."

She walks him toward the companionway into the crew mess. "I'll help you find your hammock." While he keeps looking back at us, she guides him down the steps.

"She's the best, the *best!*" smiles Harry. "Very smooth, she saved the moment. One of us likely would have thrown that asshole overboard."

"Or fallen asleep trying!"

He laughs. "Too true, too true. Here, you forgot your sleeping bag."

We lean on the railing above the jolly boat looking into the fog. "What an unbelievable night we had, Harry. Unreal, literally unreal. It'll take me a helluva long time to get over. I don't know, maybe I'll never get over it. Awesome, just goddamn awesome."

"It's too late, now we've got to get a little rest. But, Jack, we've got to talk tomorrow morning. Let's have breakfast together. After that we'll have to clean for a while then back to the jolly boat, then we're off. I'll meet you at 7:30 a.m. in the galley, OK?"

"Sure." I turn to leave, as Alice walks up, apparently having delivered Andrew to his hammock. "Nice job, Alice…you really handled our favorite messmate, thanks."

She touches my arm as she listens while watching Harry. She kisses him hard and flush on the lips, backs up, looks at him. "Jesus you scared the hell out of me! After two hours I was coming unhinged. I had no idea what to do! I couldn't come on deck because Andrew had been pestering me the whole time. I had no answers and no idea where the hell you were. I couldn't just lie in my hammock. I finally climbed into the mizzen top to be left alone and watch for you. That jerk even found me there. God, am I happy to see you! *Please* don't do that again, there's no way I could cope!"

Crying softly now, she leans into him. "I missed you. I was scared at the end, really scared. You can't believe how good it was to see you three suddenly appear from nowhere. It was so weird. I started shaking like crazy. I'm still shaking." She puts her arms around Harry, squeezing hard. He puts his arms around her shoulders and head and she seems to disappear into him. His eyes stream tears. Time for me to leave.

I head for my hammock, hoping it's still strung up in the dark of the crew's mess deck. I have to lie down, or I'm sure to fall down. There it is, still up, thank God. As I pull my left sneaker off, a figure looms up next to me. "Jack…."

It's the professor.

I hiss toward him, "No, no talking, not a word. I have to rest now. I want to talk…what did we just do…what should we do…whatever. Just not now. Night, Walter."

"OK, I understand. We'll talk later."

I'm falling, I'm falling! I wake up hanging half in and half out of my hammock, with somebody next to me. Dazed and totally confused I hear a voice behind me say, "Easy man, take it easy." It's Archie, my arrhythmic hammock mate. "You were twisting and turning so much, I knew you were gonna fall. Shit, I thought you'd break your leg inside the hammock you were so tangled up! Were you dreaming or what?"

I realize he's got hold of my left elbow. He must have kept me from falling.

"Yeah, I guess. Thanks." I start untangling my legs in the hammock. What a mess! Archie probably saved me from a nasty fall. "Thanks Archie, hope I didn't wake you up. Sorry for all this."

"Jack, it's after seven, everybody's up. Actually you weren't making any noise, just turning back and forth, moving your legs a lot in your hammock. Eventually you got so twisted you were about to fall. So I just grabbed you before you landed in a heap on the deck. I gotta go wash up, see you later."

Brutal headache. Got to find my toilet kit and get some Advil in me. Carefully I descend to the head area to wash up and swallow the pills down. Back at my hammock I put on my dark blue shorts and second *Endeavour* jersey, fresh socks, sneakers. Where are my sunglasses? Got 'em, need those today, for sure. Down to the galley for a big glass of orange juice, that'll help. As I fill my plate with fruit, toast and eggs then pick up a cup of hot tea, I see Harry watching me from a table in the corner. As I turn in his direction, he asks me to bring a couple bananas. Moments later I arrive at his table and sit down. Harry's wearing the same clothes as last night, very wrinkled and grimy. We have most of the table to ourselves.

"I know I must look like you, Jack, and that's not good. Your face looks like somebody must have used it as a chart plotter. Lines are all over it, deep and scary. I'd say we need a little rest."

"Sweet Harry, a sweet way to greet a fellow sufferer after all of three hours of sleep! Where's Alice?"

"She's the smart one. Asked me to save her a couple bananas and she went for a hot shower. I probably look like someone I arrest every other day in the District, and she'll look like she just stepped out of an Ann Taylor catalogue."

I mumble, "Maybe there's some sort of 'opposites attract' thing going on here. You're lost if you clean up and she discovers the real you."

"Right," he laughs, "got to be what'll happen."

After gulping down orange juice, blueberries and two slices of watermelon, I pause for a moment. "Harry, I must be obsessing. I was cooked last night, utterly done. I go to sleep only to dream of the *Lord Sandwich* going up in flames right in front of me. I don't do anything, just watch it flame. This whole deal is getting out of control. I apparently damn near fell out of my hammock tossing and turning during the night. But in my memory of the dream, I did nothing, not a damn thing, just watched."

As I attack the eggs and toast Harry rubs his huge hands over his face, down his neck, stretches his arms, cricks his head back and forth. "You got any more of your Advil?"

I nod, "I'll get you some."

He takes a sip of his coffee. "I'm just as screwed up. The whole thing does seem like a crazy dream. My problem though is I'm hugely pissed at it."

I start to interject, but he raises his hand. "Yeah, I know we went through that last night. It did happen, we were there, whatever 'there' means. It was over so fast, the whole thing is so…what…unfinished. Wham, bam, done. What we did see was so incredible that I can't talk about it. I don't know what to say. Would anybody believe this stuff? I started to tell Alice. We've been going up into the foretop at night. So we're lying under this little blanket she has and I started to tell her. I started, but it sounded so dumb after a minute I stopped. All I could do was tell her we had an amazing experience, that all of us had glimpsed another time. I asked her just to accept that for now and I'd figure out how to explain it to her. She listened, looked at me for a long time, kissed me, put her head on my chest and went to sleep. I can't believe she has that kind of control…incredible patience."

"Harry, it's not my business, but like she said, I think Alice is just relieved to get you back. It's getting to be a serious thing…you two."

"It sure is. Jesus, how lucky am I! She shows up here of all places. Can you believe it? By the way, it dawned on me why the professor seems not to want her involved. Number 1, what would a woman be doing in that boat in that time? Number 2, I didn't see any women's clothing in the professor's sail bag. So he's got to keep Alice out of the loop. She doesn't fit so he can't use her in his plan. Unfortunately, she and I are spending more and more time together making it harder and harder to cut her out."

"Probably right."

"Anyhow, I'm really outa' joint on this. We get this little glimpse of the *Lord Sandwich*. We hear what we guess were American prisoners and we run away. The professor tells us how really shitty the British were to POW's. Then he tells us they're going to scuttle the hull the day after tomorrow. He tells us over and over we can't interfere. But what we witness can only lead us to the possibility that some unknown number of men, many of whom likely are patriots to a cause we hold sacred, may be drowned by their enemy. I'm telling you this…not to act if they're going to be held in that ship when it is scuttled is *flat impossible, will not happen*! Sorry, Jack, anything else is out of the question. I cannot, will not argue ethics and logic in the face of murder. I understand we'd raise hell with their future and our history. But frankly I don't give a damn! It is inconceivable to do nothing when we know what might happen. We, or at least I, have to get back there."

"OK, I hear you. What would you do?"

"Have to figure out how to go back tonight. I'll be prepared to do something if the prisoners are still aboard. We know this hull and can study it. Figure out some way to get into the original below decks and release the prisoners."

I'm not surprised at Harry's passion, but I am impressed at his conviction. I always see multiple sides of an issue and thus sometimes hesitate to act. Harry is firm and sure, he knows where he is. "One thing here seems important, Harry. As long as no one is killed in an interference from outside, in at least that respect we'd not be corrupting actual history. Those alive then stayed alive then."

"You'd go...you agree?"

"Have to. I'm not at all sure we could get there. I'm especially not sure the professor would go along and he's our guide. Even if he went I don't think we can trust him since he's so certain about non-interference. But, once again we have little choice here. Since we have been given knowledge of a possible terrible crime, ignoring that knowledge is itself a negligent act, almost as bad as the murders themselves. We're in a box, we've got to act. Not acting is impossible when we could—maybe—do something to prevent it."

I pause, looking at Harry. Over his shoulder I see the professor headed to our table. "Here comes the professor. What a crazy mess we're in—a five-day cruise that turns into a time travel soap opera!"

Harry slaps me on the back, "And I met Alice!"

The professor rushes up. "Morning! I have a meeting in a few minutes with the Captain and the re-enactment committee who are due aboard shortly. The bag of antique clothes is at the foot of the companionway to the gentlemen's quarters. Two of the guys who rowed out yesterday will join you. Be at the companionway at 11:00. At least this time you'll get some help! We'll shove off at 11:30 sharp. The ship will drop her mooring exactly at 12:00 noon and head for Brown & Howard Wharf. One of the 12-meters has just cleared the dock, the Coast Guard cutter is getting under way."

He leans over the table toward us, quietly he continues. "This afternoon, let's have lunch ashore. I've got some thoughts on last night, and I'm sure you guys do. I'll treat. We can go to one of my favorite spots, *The Black Pearl*. It's not far; we can walk there. We won't get a chance to talk much 'til then. That OK with you guys?"

"Sure. What time?"

"To be safe, let's say 2:00 p.m., the docking and welcoming ceremonies should be over by then. I'll meet you on the dock next to the accommodation ramp. See you later."

He strides quickly over to the food line, grabbing some rolls and coffee before heading upstairs.

The First Mate is standing alongside the entrance to the galley. He loudly whistles to get attention. "All crew to the ship's waist in ten minutes, 8:00 a.m. I'll give out cleaning assignments. You have one more chance to give the dear *Endeavour* a good scrubbing!"

I get up. "Catch you later, Harry. My gear is in a mess, got to square it away."

I toss all my gear—filthy clothes for the most part—in my sack. Tony has been nice enough to leave my "pig" foul weather gear next to my hammock. I stuff it in with the sleeping bag. I carefully roll and tie off the hammock and place it in the pile with others. I tie my sack and sleeping bag together and align them with other volunteer crew gear along the edge of the crew's mess deck.

As I step out on the main deck in the waist, it's still cool and damp from the dense fog. But the sun is boring through. Soon it is likely to be a hot summer day. Will the fog come back in tonight? Seems hopeful, even likely—there's little breeze; it's already humid, air is heavy.

Tony comes over to me. "My spies tell me you went cruising in the fog. That must have been as much fun as driving a bumper car in an arcade!"

Andrew overhears Tony. "Ask him where he went!"

"Andrew, it is not my task—however rewarding it may seem—to be your spokesman, or grand inquisitor. You may ask him yourself. Or a better idea, don't ask. Somehow he doesn't look especially responsive to your query."

I reply, "Let it go, Andrew. We just picked the wrong fog bank in which to practice. You'll see later this morning, we became ace rowers, avoiding all the boats in the fog. Good practice." I can't stop myself, and give him a wink, as he flushes red-faced.

I catch Alice's eye and walk across the waist. She joins me on the port side. I ask her, "Why do you suppose he's so curious? Just being a pain, feeling left out, general nastiness, what do you think?"

Speaking softly, she says "He must have seen you leave at least he claims he did. Maybe that guy who was on watch when you left told him. They hang around together. Kept asking me what you were doing. I gave him the practice rowing answer. For whatever reason, he doesn't believe it. He obviously can't know what little I know, but something about it bugs him. Maybe it's only that he is easily bugged, I don't know. I just hope he leaves when we get to the dock. He's just impossible."

The First Mate is standing on the quarterdeck looking down at the assembled volunteer crew. "Foremast, your station will be here, scrub the entire weather deck. Also you're to clean, then repaint the accommodation ladders. Mainmast, your station is the crew's mess deck, cleaning everything there. Mizzenmast, your station is the galley and heads. Cleaning will stop at 11:00, when we will break for clean clothes, then to sailing stations. By then our beautiful *Endeavour* will be 'Bristol-fashion' clean, and ready to sail regally in to her dock, an overwhelming presence to the awed colonists."

Tony's still standing nearby. "Jack, I know you and Harry have to leave early. One of you paint the starboard ladder, the other port. Alice, clean the helm area, polishing the wheel, the binnacles and the instrument desks."

Harry joins Alice and me standing on the waist port side. "Good man, Tony. He sure gave us easy jobs."

After some standing-around-and-waiting, a highly unusual event in the well-organized *Endeavour*, we collect our cleaning rags, paint, brushes and Alice's sponge, clean rags and can of cleaner-polisher. As Alice readies her materials, I walk along with Harry toward the port accommodation ladder. Once we're far enough away I put my hand on his shoulder. "I realize it's not exactly my place, but what about Alice if we go? I guess she was pretty close to the edge when we got back."

He turns to lean on the railing. "I know, I know, I've got to figure out what to do. No way I'm going to slide it by her. But, just the same, there's no way she can go...won't work. Is there something in the middle? I don't know. I just haven't figured it out yet. Any ideas? Are you OK with her being involved somehow?"

"We've got to be very careful. Let's think about it."

Climbing down the starboard accommodation ladder I run my rag all over it, rubbing at grease, dirt, scuff marks, etc. I retrieve the paint and two different size brushes to start slowly and carefully painting the steps and railings. Soon it is largely an absent-minded effort as my mind drifts toward our *Lord Sandwich* predicament.

Some things seem clear. Presuming the professor's marine archeologists are right that the scuttling will be the day after tomorrow, we have to go back. Harry's ironclad position is right. The prisoners' fate cannot be ignored. It seems important though that no deaths occur. Certainly we will have to take some action to release them. Yet if no deaths occur we haven't cheated a person's future and lineage. On the other hand, if in fact they were to be drowned in the actual scuttling, obviously we will have added whatever number we release to survive on history's rolls. Since it is probably a significant number—at least dozens, maybe many more—the release will have a powerful impact. Yes, it's disruptive, but it seems—with no deaths—there is no loss, only gain. Is that somehow sufficiently virtuous to be OK? Who decides? Is there a decision? Are there historically negative consequences of releasing men who would have drowned? Certainly, that's the rub. We cannot conceivably know what the downstream effect would be. Thereby the professor's absolute insistence on no interference.

Alice. She and Harry are in deep with each other. No question, Harry won't lie to her, or avoid her, or somehow exclude her. So, she's in. What does that mean? She really can't make the jolly boat trip. Like Harry said, she doesn't fit our alignment with the past. But she made it very clear she will not sit still just waiting for Harry. In effect she has asked for the right to participate, though for now she actually has only asked that Harry not leave her again. Harry certainly will agree.

The professor. Right now he seems tough to clarify. I have no doubt he'll be sorely tempted to make one more visit. Can he be convinced a no-death interference is an acceptable act? I suppose there is a slight possibility, but he has insisted categorically on no interference over and over again. Moreover, it seems that his insistence is more about the unknown consequences than it is likely to be about the absence of death. If he came with us, can we trust him? After ruminating for a while, I can reach no conclusion. It would seem likely that his fear of interference would simply be overcome by compassion for the prisoners' dire straits; the immediacy of death by drowning too much for the refined rationale of non-interference. Maybe true, but the even remote possibility of his unexpectedly blocking the rescue is such that some precaution seems essential. Somehow we'll have to test his resolve before we set out tonight. If he fails do we go on our own? The argument for going does not change, but the degree of difficulty certainly does.

Harry. I admire and envy his purposefulness and directness. Harry is a man of action and reaction. His is a direct, transparent style and personality. While with Alice he seems loving and nurturing and quite emotional, for the most part he has what I think of as a senior cop's mentality. He has an absolute belief in law and the rule of law; wrongs must be corrected; society must be protected against bad people and dangers, and assisted when assistance is clearly required. He's seen so much nastiness, crap and misery he can be world weary and cynical as hell. He's not nice when it comes to discussing human motives. But here, the prisoners' predicament seems clear and the correct response to Harry must seem self-evident.

Can we do it? Who knows? I have to admit I dread all that rowing again. Hopefully they'll be gone when we go back. If not, rescue may be possible because the number of guards seems small, therefore vulnerable. Or, maybe we can pull off a distraction to get them off the hull. First, we'll have to figure out how we can release and remove the prisoners. The hull has numerous portholes, hatches, even windows in the great cabin, so maybe there is some access. Yet as a prison ship any access must be secured. Another question has to be, can we get to it? Assuming we decide to exclude the professor, can we again go through all that we did with him? Can we know the courses, sustain the alignment? Can we follow the relaxation steps, make ourselves shift focus and references from today to 1778? Then, can we repeat all the steps to necessary return, all on our own without his dominating leadership? As a start, I better spend some time trying to remember the courses. Generally we went out heading west, a little south to the Luhrs, then north-northwest to the gong buoy. The *Lord Sandwich* was east of that. We then returned on reciprocals. That helps, but I better spend time getting my recollections to be more precise. I'll buy a detailed Newport harbor chart, that'll help.

As I finish painting the topmost step I hear some talking. Looking up, I watch Harry and Alice laughing about something they've shared. It's fun to watch them together. They're so connected to each other it seems almost contagious when with them.

Alice sees me. "Jack, your friend Harry is being mean. He says I'll have to get a 'learner's permit' to drive his precious old sports car. I'm too young to understand it, and I might endanger the poor thing."

"He's not my friend if he's being mean to you, Alice. I'm afraid though, he may have a point for once. The car is a '56 Porsche Speedster right, Harry?"

He nods. "The finest little roadster ever built. Alice will love it so much she'll pass the learner's permit test first time, I have no doubt."

Alice tosses a rag in his direction. "It's older than I am for goodness sake! Can they even devise a test for such an ancient car?"

Smiling, I collect my painting materials and inspect my work as they banter back and forth. Tony has joined them, jabbering away about noisy rhesus monkeys while they laugh along with him. He talks with them a moment longer, then walks over to tell me, "Thirty minutes to your costume cue!"

"A quick shower, OK boss?" I ask.

"My word, these actors expect too damn much! They all have to be pampered. Yeah, I guess you've got to be pretty and clean for your performance…well at least clean. Go ahead."

Feeling nicely refreshed from the shower and even a quick shave, I dress. I have a few minutes to spare so I sit for a moment in a corner of the crew's mess deck. There's plenty of hubbub from volunteer crew cleaning the ship above and below me, but little activity nearby. For the first time in days, I realize the cruise is almost over. In one, or at most two days I'll be headed home. Home? I've hardly thought about anything other than the voyage. I've been consumed by the *Endeavour* and my trials on board, the engaging cast of characters I've met, and most of all, our passage to the *Lord Sandwich*. What will tonight be like? I feel doubts and misgivings creeping in. Should we go back at all? After last night there is no escaping the presence of some risk, even danger. Is it sensible to put myself at risk to extend an experience I've already had? If—as seems likely—we probe further into the past for the sake of our passion about the prisoners, the risks certainly won't diminish, they'll increase. Yet, look what happened last night! An absolutely transcendent experience, like nothing I've ever known. I was never so in the moment, so totally connected, spellbound. I never have, and certainly never will, realize anything remotely like this again. There is no decision here, no reason to re-think going out again. I cannot escape the same rationale for going…*not to* just isn't an actionable option. I'll do it again…see the hull again, be there again, even engage in that world a tiny bit! Sure there are doubts and fears…but they're no match for the thrill of returning to the *Lord Sandwich*!

As I climb the companionway stairs, Harry passes me dashing down. "See you in a minute; going for a quick wash up."

Alice has resumed her polishing task at the helm, now working on the wheel. The professor is back in his Royal Navy lieutenant's uniform. He's hauling in the jolly boat painter bringing the little boat close alongside. Cleaning continues all over the deck. Reaching Alice, I admire her polishing, "The helmsmen will need sunglasses to stand next to this beauty!"

"Thank you, sir. You are so kind...I think." Putting down her polishing cloth, she looks at me, "Harry invited me to go to lunch with you and Walter today." She's watching me closely, evidently to gauge my reaction.

"Great, glad to have you...you should be there."

A big smile crinkles her pretty face. "Thanks, Jack. I wonder if Walter's answer will be the same."

"Yeah...we'll see." The sun is rapidly transforming the day into a hot, muggy mid-summer New England day. I walk down the companionway to the gentlemen's quarters. Two middle-aged men are already there. I recognize them as rowers from yesterday. They introduce themselves as John and Carl. John carefully pulls the antique clothing out of the sail bag. He puts on the clothing I remember he wore on the row out from the waterfront, white shirt and white canvas pants with a cap like the boater Harry had worn, but smaller, a very slight brim. He's chunky but the clothing fits him comfortably. Carl is heavy, broad shouldered. He seems to be wearing eighteenth-century clothing already. He's not changing into clothes in the bag. On second glance, his shirt and pants must be replica material. They are neat, not frayed and faded as all the clothing in the bag. He does put on the scarf I had worn last night, and he's carrying his own boater with a bright green paisley ribbon tied to it. It must be his special hat. It fits in with the other costumes though.

I quickly change into the same clothing as last night, cringing a bit as I put on the shirt still damp with sweat from last night.

The professor is standing at the top of the companionway. "We'll put the mast up, but mostly for show. No wind to speak of."

We make small talk, mostly about last night, laughing about Harry's monotone singing voice. Carl asks numerous questions about life aboard as a volunteer crewman. He laughs at my story of the defeat Harry and I suffered at the hands of Margaret and Alice.

"Sure, sure, when you have the ten-thumbed man as your partner, what do you expect?" Harry punches my shoulder. "Hi. I'm Harry Cassis, the aggrieved plaintiff suing to break up the failed partnership."

Smiles and handshakes around as Harry casually selects his clothing from last night. He nudges me as Carl and John climb on deck. "Jeez, how nice it is to put these things back on…ugh!"

The professor is in the jolly boat busily sliding the mast hoops attached to the canvas sail up from the bottom of the mast. After all the mast hoops are in place, he follows with the mast hoops attached to the boom. He ties the sail's halyard through a pulley attached to the gaff of the sail. He then threads it through a single block belayed to the top of the mast. He carefully coils the halyard and loops it over a small wooden cleat on the little forward deck. Carl joins him in the boat. Together they lift the mast, Carl holding the mast hoops from sliding down off the mast. They step it through the deck down onto a little wood collar underneath. The professor pulls a long wooden trunnel (nail) out of his pocket. He crawls under the deck and inserts the trunnel into a hole in the collar. He and John twist the mast back and forth slightly, seating it in the collar. Eventually the trunnel slides all the way through the mast to the other side of the collar.

"I like that, secures the mast…clever." Harry nods appreciatively.

"We won't raise the sail for now, probably not at all," says the professor. "Let's get ready to shove off. John and Carl sit on the aft rowing thwart, Harry and Jack forward." He steps over the two rowing thwarts and sits on the aft thwart next to the tiller. "Jack, untie the painter. Let's settle ourselves, row a few yards forward. It's time for us to head for the wharf."

We watch the same big inflatable from yesterday hovering around the mooring. Aboard the *Endeavour* crewmen are untying the mooring line from the starboard forward cleat to which it had been attached. They drop it in the water as a man on the inflatable pulls the line on board and attaches it to a large pickup buoy.

"OK, mateys bend your backs into it," gleefully shouts the professor. I've positioned my feet against supports for the aft thwart. It doesn't help much though. My soreness seems to have overwhelmed my body. I'm sore everywhere, even places that don't seem to have anything to do with rowing. My neck is sore, so are my feet; my left elbow aches; arms and legs are entirely sore. I need a bath in ibuprofen. Thankfully, the addition of two more rowers makes it far easier as we pull toward Brown & Howard Wharf and the waiting throngs.

The *Endeavour* crew has set the topsails and topmast staysails on the main and foremast. We watch as the crew sheets home the mizzen course. The ship is moving nicely thanks mostly to the quietly rumbling diesel engines. Once again we're being escorted by two Marine Patrol boats, one a center console Boston

Whaler, the other a sleek, but older Bertram cabin cruiser, both madly flashing red and green bursts of light. I smile at the *Endeavour*. She looks terrific, absolutely the queen of all around her. People on dozens of boats surrounding our path to the wharf are smiling, snapping pictures, even applauding. I glance over at Harry who is smiling broadly. Over my shoulder I can see people crowded on all the nearby wharves and docks, roof tops, decks, seemingly wherever space is available. We're headed for a big wharf. Directly behind it is a large shed with a colorful sign announcing it as the International Yacht Restoration School. Another sign on the wharf proclaims "HMB *Endeavour* in Newport Sponsored by the Newport Historical Society and the International Yacht Restoration School."

The professor loudly commands, "Portside oars up." John and Harry hold the oar straight up, as Carl and I make a few more gentle strokes.

"Starboardside, oars up. Jack, toss the painter to the gentleman in the marine uniform." I turn and nearly fall out of the boat. I double take wildly on the man standing above me with arms outstretched. He's dressed as a Royal Marine, the red coat with crossed white belts too familiar from last night! He watches me, waving his arms as others yell, "Come on, come on…throw the line!" Finally I weakly toss the painter toward him. The professor tosses a stern line to another colonial costume, this a heavy-set man all turned out in frilly white shirt, bright blue jacket, yellow pants and white tri-cornered hat.

Harry whispers too loudly, "Looks like a giant fat parrot, for Chrissake!"

Carl, John and I roar with laughter as we ship oars, and climb onto the wharf amid pats on the back, shouts of "Well done!", "Hail Britannia!" and "Welcome to Newport", along with other indistinguishable whoops and cheers, applause and more picture-taking.

Minutes later the *Endeavour* glides slowly in behind the jolly boat. Lines are passed ashore and made fast to several pilings. As her sails are furled, Carl spots a nearby coffee stand. John, Harry and I follow him. Standing on chairs, drinks in hand, munching on hot dogs from which all taste has been cooked out, we watch the proceedings.

Soon the professor again escorts the costumed Post Captain aboard the *Endeavour* as the throng surges forward to watch and listen. The Post Captain welcomes the ship with a similar welcome to yesterday's, then proclaims Newport Maritime Days officially open. He adds the *Endeavour* will be open for visitors and guided tours at 2:00 p.m. Two permanent crew members fire off the ship's cannon in response. It makes a loud boom and for a moment fills the air with paper fragments.

Watching the crowd thin out, Harry and I climb back aboard. He goes in search of Alice as I descend to the crew's mess deck to retrieve my sleeping bag and clothing, change back into my "Endeavour World Cruise" jersey and blue shorts. I carefully fold the antique clothing into an outer pouch of my clothing sack. Tony and Margaret are talking animatedly with several Foremast crew. I join the conversation waiting for a chance to thank them. After a few minutes the conversation pauses. I reach out to shake Tony's hand. "Thank you, Tony. Quite literally I couldn't have done it without you and Margaret!"

"For a day or so that was all too true, matey! I told Margaret to encase you in a fully inflated rubber suit and attach a permanent safety line!"

"No, don't listen to him, Jack…typical Tony nonsense." Margaret gives Tony a little shove.

"You guys have some time off now, right?" I ask.

Tony answers, "God Bless the schedule, yes we do! Four days for yours truly. Tomorrow, I'm headed for Cape Cod, to hang out with the Kennedys and pick up some 'sheilas' on the beach!"

"Tony lives in a complete fantasy world," laughs Margaret. "I'll be going with him to attach the safety line that he wanted on you!"

I reply, "I suggest renting a sky writer; 'Get off the beach, Australian shark spotted!'"

"No problem," says Tony. "A meaningless challenge to a man of my wondrous social skills."

"Good luck, Margaret. Clearly you'll need massive doses of it. Seriously, thanks, you both were terrific." I turn and walk back up on deck. Checking my watch I see it's nearly time to meet for lunch.

I thank the Captain and First Mate, chatting with them near the gangway to the pier. Wes comes over to exchange email addresses and phone numbers. We promise to cheer on the Red Sox together. A few more handshakes and best wishes with other Foremast crew, including hammock neighbor Archie.

"Jack, over here." Alice is waving, the professor and Harry with her.

"Sam Adams regular draft, bowl of clam chowder and coleslaw, please." I'm the last to order as Alice, Harry, the professor and I sit at a corner table inside the Black Pearl on Bannister's Wharf. Most patrons are sitting on the restaurant's outside patio. The inside is only half full. "You better bring another basket of rolls. This man next to me has given in to his flour addiction."

Harry is devouring what must be his third roll. "Take a moment to breathe, Harry," urges the professor. "It's an important part of the process."

Harry pauses, picks up his beer glass, draining it. A slightly suppressed burp, a sigh, he glances at the professor. "Ah, the envy we who gulp full tastes of life must suffer from those who merely sip at it. It can be difficult to be patient with lesser beings."

Alice puts her arm around Harry's neck. "This one needs a spanking!"

She blushes and laughs as Harry turns to her. "An intriguing thought. How should we explore that?"

He pauses then continues, "But, on to the matter at hand. Before we get started, Walter, I have told Alice most of what happened last night. I did so with the premise that it is absolutely private, and that she would not, could not accompany us if we were to return. But, as I guess is obvious, she and I have struck up a relationship that is now important to both of us. I will not mess it up with secrets and stories not told."

"Harry, let me say something." Alice puts her hand on Harry's. Turning to the professor and me, she quietly says, "Harry is being wonderfully considerate. However, I do and will respect your confidentiality here. Whatever happens, even if nothing happens, I will tell no one. I only want to help if there is any help I can provide."

The professor looks glum. "No offense, Alice, but Harry, that wasn't fair. I asked you and Jack to keep this between us. Alice clearly is a fine person, but we agreed to a promise between the three of us made together."

We sit silently as the waiter brings two baskets of rolls and another round of drinks, Sam Adams for me, Bud for Harry, glasses of pinot grigio for Alice and the professor.

Uncomfortable with the silence I say, "Walter, I have no problem involving Alice in whatever is left about the *Lord Sandwich*. Certainly we intended to keep it among ourselves. But I have to respect Harry's right to explain it to someone who's become very important to him. Especially because it seems that was happening almost simultaneously with your run-up to our adventure together. I don't think it actually compromises the intent of our promise if you think of her promises as a commitment not to disclose it to others outside our little group. Maybe even, as she said, there will be some way Alice can be helpful."

"Like what?" the professor asks.

"Right now, I don't know. But it doesn't seem inconceivable."

"OK, OK, let's set it aside for now. Alice is welcome to stay on the basis that she can't make the same journey…if we make it at all."

Harry and Alice, still holding hands, nod together.

"I assume you guys want to go back tonight?"

Surprised at his bluntness, all I can do is nod.

Harry says, "It was too brief, all it did was whet our appetites. It feels unfinished…a glimpse at something important, then nothing. We've got to have some finish, some closure to seeing the *Lord Sandwich*."

"Harry, with due respect, that sounds like baloney. You want to go back to rescue the prisoners or at least to make sure they're gone. But you're a cynical cop. You think they'll still be there. You need to rescue them and to hell with worrying about interfering with history. Am I right?"

I start to say, "That's a little harsh…."

Harry interrupts, "Yeah, it is a little harsh, but it's true. I understand, Professor, you say we can't interfere with history. I'm not proposing to kill anybody thereby depriving them of their life and legacy. However, it is just absolutely wrong to let men die—men who served to create the United States, for God's sake—when we can do something about it."

"Harry," the professor hisses, "you've got to think this through, damn it!" Almost spitting he goes on, "There is no possible way to determine what hundreds of men will do who perhaps weren't supposed to live. Even if you don't harm a soul releasing them, they'll have an incalculable impact on history. For one thing, most of them are soldiers and sailors. Because some will go back to fighting the British, they're likely to kill other soldiers or sailors, maybe even civilians. In any case whoever they kill would not have died in that way in his or her real history. Suppose one of them marries a woman who otherwise would have had five children with her historic husband. But she and the survivor husband have three. What about the other two? It goes on and on, can't you understand?"

"Yes, but the unavoidable fact is we can't let men die when we can protect them. That to me is the glory of last night. We can do something incredible for those men…save them. We must be bound to that duty. *It's the only right thing to do*; nothing else is possible!"

The meals arrive at the table. My chowder is delicious. The others silently focus on their food.

Halfway through the chowder, I stop. "I have an idea. Walter, it works on the assumption you want to go back to take another look, but refuse to interfere."

Without waiting for a reply, I continue. "I propose a kind of bargain. We go one more time…tonight. If we see the prisoners are still aboard, Harry and I will return you to today and go back ourselves. That way you will take us there, but not have to interfere with history. If they're not there, we'll help you have some other glimpse of Newport in July 1778, before returning to today."

The professor stares at me. I'm pretty sure I've got him. First, it seems likely he thinks the prisoners will be gone. Second, for more than a year his obsessive passion about the *Lord Sandwich* has driven him to try to create an opportunity which must have seemed—for most of the time—utterly impossible. That passion still burns and is fueled relentlessly by his endless curiosity about eighteenth-century Newport. Together they are far too tempting to turn down.

Harry smiles slightly. "That seems to work. What do you think, Professor?"

No response. Munching slowly on his lobster roll, he nods slightly. A swallow of wine, he takes another modest bite from the roll. Glaring at me he says, "Jack, that's positively Faustian. You're more complicated than I thought. OK…what can I do? I'll go along…I need closure too. But, fair warning here— I may compromise on seeing the hull again, but not on interference. I won't countenance it, won't help, I won't even be a bystander. Don't get me back to today though, that's unnecessary and too complicated.

Harry grumbles, "What the hell is this 'Faustian' crap?"

Alice, finishing her Caesar salad, leans into him. "It started as the story of a magician who made a bargain with the Devil. Today it suggests being willing to sacrifice what you believe is right in exchange for getting what you want."

The professor still looking at me says "We will have to do exactly what we did last night but with more rowing. Do you think we actually can get there and back? You were exhausted, absolutely on your last breath last night."

"As long as I—for that matter each of us—get some rest along the way we can make it. If we regularly switch places and take a nice long break at the Luhrs in both directions. Also we have a few hours to rest this afternoon. Sleep, pain killers and another carbo-load meal—that should do it."

Harry has finished his blackened tuna steak, pushes his empty plate slightly forward. "Jack's right, we need to switch off to have any chance. That's a lot of rowing. As we agreed, Alice won't come on the trip to the hull. But she can help getting to and from the Luhrs. If she steers the jolly boat the three of us can switch off at intervals. That'll help. When you're tired and sore like now, little breaks can make a helluva difference."

The professor glances up. "She may have to wait on the Luhrs for quite a while. Remember, we have to row to and from the buoy, find it twice, transition twice, find the hull, all probably in another pea soup fog."

Harry glances over at me, smiling. I guess he's thinking as I am, the professor seems to have come over to our side. He's not resisting. Maybe he just needed a little push and a rationale to jump back in.

Alice answers, "Harry said it is a little cabin cruiser, and has power. That certainly doesn't sound like a hardship, even if I'm there for hours."

Finishing our meals, I make notes as we enumerate the steps we have to take to get ready.

Each of us has the antique clothing we've worn last night and today.

The professor must get the jolly boat away from the *Endeavour*, so that without risk of challenge we can take it out tonight. We agree this evening the professor will tell the duty officer we're taking it to Bowen's Wharf for another re-enactment tomorrow. We'll meet at the ship and row it actually near Commercial Wharf, leaving it out of sight behind the commercial fishing boats tied up there. They'll largely block it from public view.

Harry has a long-held two-night reservation at the Newport Harbor Hotel. He and Alice eventually will check-in there.

I have no reservation. The professor is certain few, if any, rooms are available in the area because of the tourists in town for Maritime Days. He'll call two new B&B's he knows of, thinking they may have space. I'll check with big hotels just in case they have cancellations—the Newport Harbor, the Viking Hotel, the Marriott and the Hyatt on Goat Island.

The professor will stay in the waterfront area. He is expected to at least look in on numerous exhibits, performances, and shops.

The professor will make dinner reservations at a favorite little French bistro two blocks above the main street on the waterfront, Thames Street.

We'll meet at the ship at 8:00; the reservation will be for 9:00. We'll plan to depart in the jolly boat at 11:00. We'll take a long rest once we've reached the Luhrs, planning to be back underway to the hull after midnight.

Alice will join us at least on the trip to the Luhrs.

The professor stands up. "By the way, as my part of Jack's bargain, I'm going to want to row directly from the *Lord Sandwich* toward shore. That will take us to what then as now is an area called 'The Point'. The North Battery there protected the town and its northern wharves. We'll row along just off the shoreline staying away from the battery, nobody will bother us."

He turns and walks to the front of the restaurant and speaks to the maitre d'. A moment later he's on the phone. Minutes later he returns to the table. "Both B&B's are full. But this morning one called the Hyatt for the friend of a guest and found a room. Want to try?"

"Sure," I say standing up to follow the professor to the phone. Already dialing, the maitre d' puts me on with hotel reservations. Relieved, I'm told a single is available.

Twenty minutes later I've checked into my room. Our restaurant waiter was heading off duty. He offered me a ride. I gratefully accepted, wondering why the professor was smirking at me. Some quick goodbyes, reminders to meet at 8:00, and I follow the waiter out of the restaurant and into an adjacent alleyway. He swings his leg over a gleaming Harley-Davidson motorcycle. "Climb aboard. Sorry, no helmets, we ride free, my hog and me," he smiles. "Put your sack in my saddlebag, strap down the sleeping bag here. Hang on to the handle right behind my ass. Here we go!" He jumps down on the chrome kick-start handle and the motorcycle explodes with engine noise. He revs impatiently as I carefully pack my stuff away. Finally I swing my leg over, seating myself behind him. He reaches down and flips out a little foot pedal on each side below me. Just as I get a foot on each pedal and grab the back of his seat, off we go. We slowly pull out of the alley, down another, eventually into a main walkway thronged with pedestrians. He turns again into another narrow alley, ending up on the edge of a parking lot. Rumbling around the parked cars, we approach the ticket collector shed and gate. He waves at the shed as we skirt around the gate and onto a street thick with traffic. Weaving through cars we come to a stop light. We make a u-turn and head off in the opposite direction.

Moments later we turn onto a connector heading over water chockfull with boats, and alongside a boatyard itself full of boats on land. Some of them are outrageously large and elaborate. One that grabs my attention is a huge blue-hulled ketch. On blocks it towers above everything else. Its hull is gleaming even in the overcast sunlight. Its rudder is pure white, and looks to be at least as large as the jolly boat's sail. I yell in the waiter's ear pointing at this blue beast as we roar up the connector ramp, "Hundred feet at least, huh?"

He shrugs elaborately, "Who cares!"

Moments later we stop at the entrance to the Hyatt. Thanking the waiter, I untie my rumpled bags and walk with a slight wobble into the hotel.

I've phoned home, leaving a message of my plan to return tomorrow and the hotel phone number. All that matters now is sleep followed by a hot shower with just enough time to get to the *Endeavour* at 8:00.

The alarm is loudly ringing. Finally I find it and stop the noise. 7:30, more than four hours' sleep. Groggy and disoriented, I shuffle into the bathroom to run a very hot shower. Once again in last night's sweatshirt and jeans, I carefully wrap my antique shirt, pants and jacket into a hotel towel and put a small plastic bottle of Advil in my pocket. The doorman whistles up a taxi as I tell him, "Brown & Howard Wharf". The fog is back. Visibility is already down to just a few hundred yards.

"I hate this damn fog," grumbles the driver. "Gonna be another lousy night. Fares will disappear after 9:00, same as last night. Business sucks."

Maybe for you buddy, but I know a few people who aren't unhappy.

After paying the fare I walk past the big boat restoration shed admiring the *Endeavour* all lit up by her mainmast rigging light and lights at intervals around the wharf. There are still a dozen or so tourists milling around, gawking at the masts, talking quietly. A blue line blocks the accommodation ramp. One or two crewmen are on deck. The ship is apparently finished for the night as a tourist attraction. Somebody comes out of the gentlemen's quarters companionway. It's the professor, dressed now in a plaid shirt and chinos, a sweater over his shoulder.

"Hey Jack! We're all set. I just told the Captain he no longer had to think about the jolly boat, we're taking her away to her next duty. Apparently they had all sorts of trouble this afternoon with people trying to climb down into her. He had to put a guard on her for God's sake! Even Tony got into a scene with some drunk insisting he wanted to sit in it. Tony tried to kid him out of the idea, but the guy wouldn't quit. Finally the First Mate got on the radio to the Marine Patrol and they hauled him away. Captain's happy as hell to get rid of our boat!

"Harry and Alice are over there watching a demonstration by the students at the yacht restoration school. They're working on a beetle cat (a small sailboat with a single gaff-rigged sail)."

We head off in the direction he pointed, to the school's entrance. Harry and Alice, along with ten or twelve others are exiting. Alice sees me. "Go in, take a quick look before they close up; it's fascinating."

Moving against the flow of people leaving I peek in. five or six young men and two women—most of whom are long-haired, dressed in coveralls—are chatting and laughing excitedly. They're collecting tools, sweeping up a mountain of sawdust, shavings and pieces of wood, dusting off the little gaff-rigged sailboat. Her hull is bright yellow, her decks are orange. The sail is brilliantly white and appears to be brand new, as do the lines. Must be newly rebuilt, awaiting her owner. Nearby is a larger hull, upside down, seemingly with her hull planking about half finished. Frames, various shaped pieces of wood, clamps, molds and tools are scattered neatly around the hull and adjacent work benches. Huge windows let in large shafts of light. In the far corner what appears to be a small sailboat hull rests in a cradle. I turn toward the exit, but notice a little desk selling Newport and yacht restoration publications. I spot a Newport harbor chart. $10.00 later it's mine.

Harry, Alice and the professor are standing a few yards away as I walk through the entrance. I ask the professor, "Did you use the school to restore the jolly boat?"

"Sort of. We've had lots of volunteer talent—junior curator types, Maritime Museum members, students, even experts from Mystic Seaport. The IYRS folks gave us great advice."

Walking back toward the ship, the professor launches into another of his tutorials, this on the restoration of the jolly boat. He occasionally refers to it as "*Giggles*", apparently the name affectionately given by someone years ago.

As we approach the boat, still tied forward of *Endeavour*, Alice says, "Somehow I'm skeptical that a jolly boat named *Giggles* took you guys on your journey of a lifetime. The name definitely doesn't warrant the event."

I reply, "I agree. Walter, you never used the name before. Is that why?"

"I have to confess it probably is. To concentrate all our energies on our task while knowing we were in the *Giggles* seemed counterintuitive. We'll just have to forget it, or at least ignore it.

"I'll be at the tiller again. Alice, please sit forward on the little deck. Jack and

Harry in your usual rowing thwart positions. I found a safe and inconspicuous space this side of Commercial Wharf. It's not far; should take us little time to row there."

We settle into our places as the professor tells Alice to untie the painter. She pushes us off the wharf. Harry and I pull easily on the oars. The professor steers us out into the water just off the end of the wharf. We turn right and row slowly past one wharf after another. One or two still have people on them, several are empty. Once again the fog seems to be discouraging all but hearty tourists from exploring the waterfront. A few wave and smile in our direction, we wave back.

Harry nudges me with his elbow. "How you doing?"

I nudge him back with my elbow. "Piece of cake!"

He laughs, "That'll change!"

"Thanks, that's just the encouragement I need. I'm ready to row all night now!"

"Good, you should be," says Harry. Half turning toward Alice, "Didn't I tell you I was an inspirational leader of men?"

"You did…repeatedly. This is certainly a reassuring illustration. Jack appears to be all pumped up by your inspiration!"

We slowly pass two smaller wharves, then approach a large one, surrounded by commercial fishing boats. On it are trucks parked on the wharf, a busy complex of fishing boats off-loading their catch, others on-loading supplies. Nets hung up high and outriggers create a forest of equipment.

The professor is turning us sharply to starboard, heading into the nearer smaller wharf. "Sorry," he says, "almost went right by our spot."

A few minutes later, "Jack, ship your oar. Harry, a few more short strokes."

We slowly glide into a rickety wooden dock on the harbor side of a rusty old fishing boat, its deck a tangle of lines, nets, collapsed outriggers, a real mess. The once white hull is stained with rust lines; there's a big black smudge amidships possibly from a fire; near the bow I can see faded, indecipherable lettering. Alice ties off the painter to a splintered piling forward; the professor ties off to one aft.

I sigh, "Finally, home sweet home."

"It'll be OK for a couple hours. *Giggles* has certainly seen worse in her long life," says the professor.

Following the professor, we settle ourselves around a corner table at "Dordogne", a quiet, charming little French bistro he frequents. The professor explains, "The name comes from a river in southwestern France, famous for its robust history and bucolic charm. Now a popular tourist area, the Dordogne had a significant role in history hundreds of years ago. That early importance has made it an important historical site for generations of French and as it turns out English as well. It was a battleground between England and France during the Hundred Years War in the thirteenth and fourteenth centuries. Even before that, Richard the Lionheart captured its most famous feudal castle, Beynac, in 1189. It's a fantastically scenic place, medieval villages, huge castles, fields full of crops, stands of trees, towering rock walls carved by the river and the beautiful Dordogne River itself winding through it all. In more than one part of the river, the English and the French faced each other from opposing castles. My favorite is the English fortress Castelnaud facing...."

"Wait, professor, wait a minute...please." Harry pleadingly holds up both hands as we sit waiting for service. "Jeez, time for a break don't you think? No more lectures.... You've stuffed me so full of historical trivia my brain aches. Cut us some slack, please, I'm begging you! From Revolutionary Newport to feudal France, enough man, I'm done! I don't need any more history lessons. All I need now is for you to tell me what's good to eat here! Is that too much to ask?"

The professor laughs, "OK, no more lectures, I promise. No need to confuse ourselves. Tonight we'll have plenty of time to do that!"

Alice has pulled her chair close to Harry, taking hold of his hand. She turns to the professor. "I love your stories! Harry, let's ask Walter to walk around Newport with us tomorrow. What fun! Would you come, Walter?"

In a "sotto voce" aside, Harry turns to whisper to me, "Do you think it's possible to that my brain will seize up from too many professor stories?"

Alice laughs and grabs Harry playfully on the arm, ends up kissing him on the cheek. The professor smiles. "Let's see what tomorrow brings. Here are some of my favorites on the menu."

He recommends the duck, a sauteed tenderloin of veal, raves about their bouillabaisse with local seafood, several other seafood dishes including scallops and codfish. I order one red Rhone wine and one white Burgundy. An hour and a half later all our plates are clean, the wine bottles are empty, even the last crumb of French bread has disappeared. Coffee and tea come to the table as we reluctantly sort through a startlingly high bill. Harry growls, "These river folk sure as hell aren't bashful!"

Walking slowly down a hill toward the waterfront, Harry stops next to a bench on the edge of a sizeable park. "Let's sit for a minute. I've got 10:40, so we have a little time yet.

"Everybody OK with the plan? Professor, you all set; you're with the program?"

"Sure, we've got Jack's bargain and the steps we agreed to this afternoon. I think, though, we've got to start focusing on our objectives. There have been so many distractions since last night we need to start excluding things from our attention. There's no way we can assume since we got to the *Lord Sandwich* last night we can just up and go again. Thankfully the fog is back and seems just as thick as last night. Let's take a moment here and reach back in our memory to last night...see the hull, hear the voices, see the Royal Marines. Close your eyes and bring it back."

After a minute or so, he continues, "Let's try to hang on to the memory at the front of our consciousness. Think about it as we walk to the jolly boat.

"Thanks, Alice, thanks for being sensitive just now. I'm sure you wonder what that was all about, but you didn't interrupt."

"Harry's told me what I guess is most of what went on, so I understand what you're trying to do."

Harry looks down the bench toward me. "You OK for tonight?"

All the memories have come flooding back during the professor's little reminder moment. I can see the *Lord Sandwich*, the lights and the guards, hear the prisoners, see the guards pissing on the grate...everything. It is crystal clear in my memory...vivid, even scary. My heart is racing again. I'm nervous, excited, frightened, all mixed up into an emotional stew. All I can get out is, "Good to go!"

What a stupid thing to say! I sound like a goddamn astronaut launching off into space! I'm excited, but also worried as hell, not feeling remotely heroic.

We walk silently down the hill, cross Thames Street. A few minutes later we're standing on our decrepit wharf staring down at the jolly boat bouncing gently off the two pilings.

One more time to the *Lord Sandwich*. Will we see it again?

SEVEN

The professor pulls out his hand-held, illuminated compass. "I make the course from here to the #3 bell buoy as 265 magnetic; the distance to be just over a half nautical mile. From the buoy, like last night, we'll row a couple hundred yards southwest to the Luhrs. Since the fog is as thick as last night, we'll have to row slowly. Probably take us fifteen to twenty minutes to make the Luhrs. I'll row this leg with Harry. Jack you steer. Alice, sit forward to be the lookout, mostly for boats, moorings and buoys. When you spot something tell Jack where it is by saying its position, using the hours of a clock. So, dead ahead is twelve, next off to the right is one o'clock, followed by two o'clock, etc. Jack, get on the 265 course as soon as we clear this wharf."

"Aye-aye, Captain!"

"Just as we did last night, we need to remember a few boats along this course to help coming back. Once we've rowed for twelve minutes we'll pause regularly to listen for the bell."

Alice's sharp eyes, the steady stroking of Harry and the professor, and the little compass make the first leg to #3 bell buoy, then the next leg to the Luhrs happily uneventful. Several boats along the way provoke commentary. One we all admire is a charming, old sloop of about twenty-five feet, with a very sleek cabin barely two feet above the water. She has a disproportionately high mast and a giant American flag hanging from her back stay. The professor explains she is a Quincy Adams made in the 1920s. Another that evokes considerably less admiration seems more than twice as long. In huge script letters on her stern she proclaims herself to be *"Fish Stud"*. Bristling with huge outriggers, gleaming poles protruding from her fly bridge, a huge bow and small cockpit outfitted with a fighting chair large and elaborate enough for an admiral, she seems to crouch in the water waiting to explode into roaring action.

Finally we arrive alongside the Luhrs. We agree to rest here for forty-five minutes, departing just after midnight. The professor reminds us the break must be used to concentrate on last night's experience. He insists we put on last night's clothing—again with no article from the twentieth century—and to use its appearance, feel, even smell as a reminder connection. We remain in the Luhrs' cockpit. Alice goes into the cabin, apparently assuming her presence does not help Harry's eighteenth-century concentration. The professor claims the cabin is both forcing us to be surrounded by the twentieth century and is a little warmer than outside. Thereby staying in it will mess with the authenticity of the moment. No argument. We're each ready to do what we're told to again reach the *Lord Sandwich*. It worked last night.

The professor stirs and stands up. Moments later, Alice emerges from the cabin, now wearing the bulky dark blue cotton sweater she'd had draped over her shoulders earlier. Reaching into its pocket she brings out a handful of what look like candy bars. "I brought along some crunchy granola bars for energy. Anybody want one?"

That was thoughtful, but no takers.

Harry's sitting on top of the boat's transom. "Professor...one more thing. I'm a cop. Cops are addicted to backup. We've got to have backup for everything—mandatory on patrol, backup procedures in the station house, paperwork in duplicate, triplicate, quadruplicate. Alice can be a backup for us. She stays here, but it would be helpful if you would give her the course to the gong buoy of Rose Island and the key to your inflatable. Just in case something happens—what, I don't have any idea—she can head there at some point."

"What could happen?" asks the professor.

"Like I said, I don't know. This is just backup, something to help our odds. We've got to deal with the fog, a very old boat, whatever happens at the *Lord Sandwich* hull, the possibility of getting lost, probably other stuff. Knowing she can power up your inflatable and go along our course makes me feel a whole lot better. Jack, does it make you feel better?"

"You bet it does. We'd appreciate it, Walter."

"What would she do?"

"At some time, if we're not back, she cranks up the inflatable and follows the course to the buoy and back. It'll be tough to spot in the fog but she can get close, then shut the motor off and on to listen for the gong. We're a little ahead of last night's time. It was well after 3:00 a.m. when we got back to the Luhrs. We won't need less time tonight. So, if we're not back by say 3:30 a.m., she could head for the buoy."

The professor asks Alice, "Have you ever run an outboard before?"

She laughs, "Yes Walter, dozens, probably hundreds of times. In fact for years my family had a little rubber inflatable. Not fancy like yours. It was a tender for our sailboat."

The professor sits next to Harry. "Obviously this only applies if I stay with you at the hull. The inflatable is simple enough…. Sure, let's do it. Alice can be backup."

He tugs on the inflatable painter trailing off the Luhrs' stern. The inflatable emerges from the fog as the professor pulls out a small flashlight. "Alice, it's a center console type. Ignition is on the little control panel next to the wheel. Push the key in a few times for choke. Just a little is all she'll need. The shift lever is now in neutral. Push it forward to go forward, back to go in reverse. The farther you push the lever once you're in each gear, the faster you'll go."

He climbs into the inflatable. It's surprisingly big—two small seats directly behind the center console and a small bench behind them. She seems to be about eighteen to twenty feet in length. The motor is fifty horsepower. "First, just open this door." He reaches directly below the wheel and twists a latch.

"Reach up and back toward just above the door and you'll feel a key on a nail, that's it. Insert the key in the ignition and remember to slide the other part of the key assembly onto the twin slots. That's the 'dead man's connection'. Have you seen that before?"

Alice nods patiently.

"There's a Narragansett Bay chart, including Newport, folded into a flat plastic case on a shelf." Reaching down below the operator's seat, he unlatches a drawer and pulls it open. "In here is a floodlight, and flares." He turns the floodlight on and off, stands back up facing the wheel. "Here, just below the wheel, is the marine radio. Next to it are toggle switches for the console and running lights, including a stern-mounted pole light."

Alice climbs into the inflatable, reaches into the compartment to get the key, puts it in her sweater pocket. She then opens the door, takes out the folded chart. "Reading material to pass the time," she smiles.

The professor takes the chart from her, lays it on the driver's seat. Pointing onto the chart he says, "It's folded open to the Newport portion. Your course from here is 330 degrees magnetic to this green channel marker here, just before Rose Island. Last night the fog was so thick we never saw the lighthouse beacon on the island. You may see it, a high light flashing at six-second intervals behind and to the left of the channel marker as you're approaching it. The channel marker has a gong which sounds in most swells."

Climbing back aboard the Luhrs, he says, "I'll turn on the running lights here. Then we better get underway. We've got a full nautical mile to row and it's getting well past midnight."

Alice joins us. Threading her arm through Harry's she looks at him, then each of us. "So, you want me to stay here until 3:30 a.m. If you're not here by then I'm to track along your course. I may go nuts waiting that long. Do come back earlier if only to save my sanity." She's a little teary, lower lip quivers slightly. Thrusting her candy at us, "Please, each of you, take a damn granola bar!"

The professor hands the little compass to Harry. "You steer, we'll row. After twelve minutes, you and Jack switch. You know the course."

The professor and I step into the jolly boat. I go through my little ritual of finding a fixed support on which to place my feet. Harry turns his back on us to wrap his arms around Alice. He strokes her hair while she whispers to him, her eyes wet but concentrating fiercely on his face. Harry kisses her hard, both hands covering most of her head. He turns to go, but she pulls him back for one more moment just staring at him. Harry finally steps into the jolly boat and the professor pushes us off. Harry sits on the stern thwart and fiddles with the tiller. Alice raises her right arm halfway, giving us a little wave. Quietly she says, "Good luck, come back soon!" Harry's ignoring the tiller, just watching Alice, swallowing repeatedly.

"Hold your stroke, Jack. I'll row first to get us swinging toward the heading." Looking at Harry, the professor says, "Tell us when we get past 300, Jack can start stroking then. Harry, hello Harry, are you with us?"

Harry blinks a few times, nods. "Yeah, yeah, 300, got it."

Moments later, Alice and the Luhrs are lost in the fog. "OK, start rowing,

Jack." Harry adjusts the tiller slightly back and forth as the professor and I stroke slowly along.

Twelve minutes later, Harry and I change places. Nobody has said a word. Once we're settled into our rowing the professor whispers, "Let's concentrate entirely on seeing the hull. Join me. We'll look at it together. I see the two lights, bow and stern. I remember some kind of little structure aft, maybe a guardhouse. There are two redcoats on board, one in the bow and one in the stern. There was a little rowboat alongside the accommodation ladder. The British battle ensign hung limp from its stanchion on the taff rail. We heard a murmur of voices, followed by one loud voice pleading for water. The guards walked amidships pounding their musket butts on the deck. They then pissed on a grate. There were screams and curses from the voices which sounded to be below the weather deck. One guard turned to look in our direction and we backed away into the fog. See it. Hear it. Concentrate entirely on that scene. We're here solely to see it again. We were in it last night. Shortly we will be in it again. Same hull, same jolly boat, same clothing, the next night. That is all we can think about from now on, except finding the channel marker up ahead. Nothing else...nothing else matters now...nothing."

Harry and the professor resume rowing. I settle the boat close to the 330 heading, wavering slightly above and below it.

After a few minutes, in a near whisper the professor says, "We should slow down. Harry, stroke with me; I'll slow the pace. Seems to me we're going slightly faster than last night. Let's stroke and listen, stroke and listen."

We keep rowing slowly forward minute after minute. Did we miss the buoy? The professor has stopped stroking entirely. No sounds. Finally he starts up, "Stay on 330 for another minute or so, Jack. Maybe we didn't quite get up to the channel marker yet."

Moments later I hear a sound. Again. Harry says, "That's no gong; that's water lapping on shore."

We listen, each straining to hear. The professor says, "Yeah, I agree, its water breaking on rocks. We must be closing on the little rocky point on the southeast side of Rose Island. Turn us around Jack. Use the reciprocal of 150, but subtract twenty degrees, to 130 magnetic. If that's the point I think it is, we must have gone by the buoy to the west. To get back to it we've got to head more easterly. Harry, you back row. I'll pull us around. Jack will put us on 130."

As we turn I can feel there's more motion in the water here. The current is tugging on the tiller. The water we can see has some swirl to it. There are sticks and leaves floating on the surface. The boat jolts a little, followed by a bump. Harry grunts, "Here, we just hit this."

He pushes a good size log away from forward of his seat. We watch it drift astern as Harry and the professor stroke slowly. It must be six feet long, a foot in diameter. It probably has been in the water a long time. There's very little bark remaining. Its branches have been reduced to sharp little stubs. It floats low in the water, two-thirds of it submerged. I say, "That's a visual on the word, 'waterlogged'."

"You on 130, Jack?"

"Yes, right on it."

"Harry, let's make just a few slow strokes and stop, say five or six. We should hear the gong then." The professor starts a slow stroke, as Harry catches up to him. After the sixth stroke, they stop. Still no sound. We make a few more strokes on the same 130 course.

The professor says, "It's very calm; the swells aren't much. The gong must be just tapping the side of the buoy. It's going to be hard to hear. Let's drift here silently."

For an impatient minute we hear nothing. "OK, it has to be right around here. Let's do our little square like we did last night. Three slow strokes per side. Use right hand turns."

Finally, after completing the first three sides, on the last side Harry hears "something metallic". We stop, wait silently for what probably is a minute but seems far longer. We hear the sound, but can't agree from which direction it came. I say forward, Harry and the professor claim it was starboard. Outvoted, I steer us sharply right. After two strokes the green buoy silently appears. The gong makes a muffled, light metallic sound as we tie the painter to it. I pat the buoy, "Got to do better than that, buddy!"

We agree to rest for fifteen minutes, tied to the buoy. But first, the professor insists we align the bow east. "The course I used last night from here to the hull is just south of due east, 095 magnetic."

When he's satisfied we're aligned, he ties the jolly boat to the buoy to secure the aligned position. A few minutes later, once again he holds up the dangling compass strap as he tells us to concentrate on last night's scene…we'll soon be there. "We'll pretty much repeat what we did last night to relax and visualize the hull. But now we can actually see it. We don't have to guess.

"First, let's relax. You can do it, just like last night. Keep looking at this strap and relax your facial muscles, next your neck muscles...." Whispering now, he finishes taking us through our muscle relaxation and ends saying, "We feel calm and at ease, thrilled to be heading once again to the *Lord Sandwich*."

He unties the painter. Checking our heading once again, the professor tapes the compass onto the buoy. He moves to the stern thwart and taking hold of the tiller, tells us to stroke out of sight of the buoy, stop rowing and drift. As we do he keeps checking our visual alignment with the buoy.

Once again in thick fog with no landmarks, no noise other than our own, we row for several minutes and stop, floating motionlessly. The professor continues to murmur to us. "We're fully relaxed. We can see what we saw last night—the hull, redcoats, ensign. We can hear the redcoats talking, next we hear a murmur, then the shouts of many voices. There it is...I can hear the voices. Once again we're all aligned. We're drifting into July 25, 1778. Close your eyes and welcome it; you're coming back to the *Lord Sandwich*. You'll see it in just a few minutes...be ready."

That unmistakable feeling of light-headed drift is making me drowsy; I'm floating...waiting to see the hull...once again certain it is there...any moment I'll see it on the edge of the fog.

I jolt upright. "Let's row to the *Lord Sandwich*, Jack. We're all ready to return."

The professor is standing alongside the tiller. I pick up the oar and sit down next to Harry.

No fog. We were in dense fog, now there's none. How'd it all of a sudden get so clear? I can see thousands of stars. In fact there seem to be many more than I'm used to, many thousands. It seems warmer than it was a moment ago. There's a quarter moon giving us some reflected light. What happened?

Jesus, we must be there! What else could have happened? Obviously the weather won't likely be the same on days 220 years apart! Last night's fog was just chance, though fog is common here. This is their weather tonight. *My God, we're back, we made it back!*

"We're back, right Walter?" I whisper.

We stroke along for a few minutes. The professor holds up his hand. He's staring in right over my shoulder. He nods his head up twice, gesturing us to turn around and look where he's staring. Clearly visible in the distance is a hull. Is it the *Lord Sandwich*? It's too far away to see clearly enough. But there are no lights on her. It's just a dark shape on the water.

"No lights, could it be something else?"

"No," whispers the professor. "I'm pretty sure that's the little guardhouse I saw. Let's row at an angle to her, not directly in. So we can veer off into the dark if someone is onboard. May not be, because if someone were there I'd think there'd be a light. You guys row as quietly as you can, very slow strokes, careful into and out of the water so there's no noise."

After eight or ten strokes we're much closer, but rowing obliquely to the hull. I agree that it is the *Lord Sandwich*. I even see the stump of the mainmast amidships. It's quiet and empty. The prisoners must be gone.

"They're gone. There's no one there." The professor stands slowly and peers into the dark.

"We need to be sure," growls Harry. "No mistakes here."

"We're really exposed in this moonlight, just a little closer. Row five or six strokes more. I'll angle us in a little."

"Professor, let me be clear." Harry leans slightly forward on our thwart. "We need to know for *certain* there's no one onboard. There doesn't appear to be anyone and there's no boat in sight. The best thing is to quickly row right up to the hull; get in its shelter. Then we can listen carefully to know for sure. Since it's my issue, I'll quickly check the hull. Won't take a minute. Let's go."

"That seems unnecessarily risky."

"Professor, that's the way it's got to be."

The professor shrugs slightly. "OK. After that we'll row toward the Point for a quick look."

"That's the deal," I reply.

Stroking quietly we glide into the hull's side, bumping amidships. I grab two frayed and repeatedly knotted hemp lines. At several points the lines are knotted together. I hold the jolly boat to the hull. Hardly breathing, we listen. Nothing, not a sound.

Without a word, Harry pulls himself up the two lines, using it like a rope ladder, stepping where it is knotted together. Maybe that's its purpose. He disappears as he steps onto the deck. We can just hear his bare footsteps as he scurries around the deck, apparently looking down the forward companionway, and the aft companionway on the quarterdeck.

He's back. Carefully he turns around, grabbing the two lines. He bangs off the hull once as he slowly climbs down the lines.

Back in the boat he sits down. Sitting next to him I ask, "Well?"

He rubs his face and neck, the same gesture I've seen before. I notice he looks very tired, with deep lines all around his eyes and mouth. "What a shit hole. Rats everywhere, some food scraps, torn pieces of cloth, a few what I guess were mats to lie on, just crap all over the place. It stinks something terrible. I can smell it out here. Like one of the condemned dumps in DC; like a fucking un-flushed toilet."

I smell it now, his description seems right on.

He looks up toward the deck. "There are two bodies aft below decks. Probably were prisoners—just scarecrows, naked, face down. I threw some mats over them."

The professor steps over right in front of him. "Right now, wash your face, hands and feet in saltwater. Please do it right now."

Harry nods, leans over to repeatedly wash his face and hands. Next he balances with a hand on my shoulder swirling first one foot then the other back and forth in the water.

A big sigh, turns into a huge yawn. Harry turns toward me. "I think we're outa' business here. Professor's turn."

"Right, thank you, Harry." The professor says, "It'll be best if I take the tiller again. We'll row around to the other side of the hull. It's fairly clear so we'll be able to see Goat Island. Once we do we'll follow the shoreline north, keeping our starboard side to it. We'll round its northern end, turn slightly to starboard and be just a few hundred yards off the Point section of Newport."

Sure enough, moments after we reach the other side of the hull we can see the faint outline of low-lying land. There are several small fires.

"Sentry posts, I'd say," whispers the professor. "The British had a small fortification on the island, with a battery of guns. That may be it. See off to the right where there are several campfires close together? Some eighteenth-century charts call it Fort Liberty, a rather odd choice of names given they were an army of occupation."

Some slight movement is visible in and out of the shadows of the fire nearest to us. We glide away at a northwesterly angle. Almost immediately we spot the northern tip of Goat Island. We cautiously swing widely around it to starboard.

Just as we pass the tip I see a large shape about 100 yards off our port side.

A ship…no a hull, stripped of all rigging just like the *Lord Sandwich*. I point it out. "Another hull to be scuttled?"

"Incredible! I thought there might be more. The research seems like it may be right!" stammers the professor.

I whisper, "There are more?"

"Yeah," he replies, "if I remember the research paper I read, there were four or five 'transports' scuttled near the *Lord Sandwich*, off Goat Island. They were supposed to block access to landing on the island to attack Fort Liberty. Then there were more scuttled just north of the island to protect the North Battery which is on the north end of the Point. In front of them, just north of Rose Island were frigates to fire on the French fleet when it tried to attack the North Battery. We haven't seen them. If the research is right, they're probably just out of sight in the dark."

"So, we have frigates—maybe with crews on them no less—on one side of us and the *Lord Sandwich* plus eight to ten other transport ships all around us." I gesture back toward the hull, still slightly visible in dark.

"I'd say that's likely," says the professor. "The record as I recall is very fragmentary, a few documents from British Navy archives, one or two old charts with notes on them. I certainly have no idea the disposition of British ships here, just a few tidbits from the research papers I saw. I can't imagine anybody in our world knows anything but pieces of the whole. I don't even remember all the details of the research. I was just focusing on where the available documents suggested the *Lord Sandwich* was located."

"So here we sit, apparently in the middle of the goddamn British Navy! But, in fact, you don't know for sure where the ships actually are! Moreover, if we do happen to bump into one, we really have no idea if it will have a crew or guards or patrols or nobody protecting it! *Now* I get why you don't want to interfere! What a goddamn mess. Let's go, get us outa' here!" Harry spits over the side. "Come on, come on!"

Flustered, the professor repeatedly glances around. "Look, the safest place will be to head into the middle between Goat Island and the mainland, directly away from the transports and frigates. They're likely to have patrols or at least lookouts. Goat Island is about five hundred yards offshore, so in the middle we shouldn't be seen in the dark."

We row slowly, carefully dipping the oars in the water. I can see the inner shore of Goat Island—no fires, what few we see seem to be the same ones we saw earlier, on the outer side. I can barely make out a few low lights on the mainland. We stop to carefully listen and look for boats, any movement at all. Nothing is evident except around the few campfires on Goat Island.

"Just take a moment to row a little closer to the town. Let me take my look and we'll get out of here, back to the *Lord Sandwich* then to near the buoy off Rose Island, to get home."

"You want to row into town, for Chrissake?" Harry is glowering now. "Are you out of your goddamn mind? Jack, where are you man?"

"Still is the deal. There's no boat traffic. We'll scoot in a little, drift a moment, stare at whatever, and take off. But Walter, Harry is right. This is too close for comfort...in and out fast."

Harry looks at both of us. "We are seriously pushing our luck. No sightseeing, professor, or we'll be interfering, like it or not!"

"OK, OK, let's just get a little closer. We'll angle south toward the mainland. What I'd really love to see is the Point section, but maybe it's just too risky. The transports are awfully close. Plus, we certainly can't go anywhere near the North Battery. I'm sure that's a pretty formidable place, nearly a little fortress. Its walls enclosed twelve cannon. In a few minutes rowing as we are, we'll be more or less opposite Long Wharf, the center of Newport's maritime commerce. It's probably that long, black shape up ahead. Let's head there, then turn around and head back toward the tip of Goat Island. Please, just a little closer to shore so we can at least see the wharves and a few nearby buildings behind them."

Harry resignedly shakes his head as we start angling toward the long black wharf.

"Who goes there?"

Where'd that come from? Damn, a sentry is now clearly visible at the end of the pier off Long Wharf. The familiar white belt across the chest is easy to spot. Never saw him. We were concentrating on getting the jolly boat turned back north.

"Ahoy, what vessel goes there?"

"Wait, just a second," mumbles the professor. "The research report named some of the frigates, one name was the same as a Newfie I see every day...'Juno', that's it...Juno!"

He stands up, whispers, "Here goes...." He cups his hands around his mouth. "Dispatches for the frigate *Juno*!"

176

The sentry waves and walks along the pier. The professor nearly collapses into the stern thwart.

"What the hell is a Newfie?" I ask.

"A Newfoundland, you know, big black dog that looks like a little bear. My neighbor has one—great big gentle creature. I think Juno really aspires to be a lapdog but no one has a big enough lap."

"We better head for the *Lord Sandwich*. We got lucky with that stunt, but I'm not real anxious to depend on our luck here." Harry gets ready to stroke his oar.

The professor says, "What a shame, *look what we see...look!* It's overwhelming...we're actually looking at 1778 Newport! We can't just leave...*look at it!*"

I lean forward toward the professor. "Walter, we have a deal. We've taken your look. I agree it is astounding, the moment of a lifetime, no question. We'll remember it forever. But it is also way too dangerous. We cannot stay any longer. We will not pass muster with people who live here. If we're caught or even challenged, we'll been in one very big mess. We don't sound right, probably don't look right, we don't know what we're talking about. They'll wonder who or what the hell we are! And they sure as hell won't just let us go on our way. You said the British are getting ready for an attack from a French fleet. That means they've got to be wired tight right now—nervous, jumpy, distrustful of anything strange, looking for spies, saboteurs, doing everything to protect themselves. They'd lock us up or shoot us.

"Your whole idea was just to look, not to interfere in even the smallest way. Staying any longer represents far too much risk and violates your own rule."

The professor is standing up again, staring at Long Wharf. "This is too much to leave! Look where we are, we've got to see more. *It's insane to leave!* I won't go. I can stay, look around and leave later. There are other "gateways" to get me back home. I just can't leave now...!" He's rocking the jolly boat, gesturing repeatedly toward Long Wharf and the other wharves nearby.

Harry, carefully watching the professor, stands up. I grab his arm, "Harry...."

He gently pushes my hand away, puts his hands on the professor's elbows and says quietly, "Walter, please sit down. Let's take a moment to relax together. We can work this out." Gently, slowly he barely tugs at the professor, getting him to sit on the stern thwart.

"Let's take a deep breath and blow it out. Man, this is something, huh! What a scene! Actually, I think that response—carrying dispatches to the *Juno*—might work for one very short trip along the wharves, as long as we're well off and don't get too close to the transports and especially the frigates, or the North Battery. If we see any other boat though, we have to head fast in the other direction. This way you can see a little more. But then it's only fair that we leave. We need to be fair to all of us. Remember, we first came with you in part because you said there would be no danger. I need to get back to Alice, Jack to his wife and daughters, and you to record the astounding experiences we've had. It won't be easy. We'll have to be strong to get back. But for a few minutes now, like you've taught us, we will concentrate on what we're able to see, set it in our memories.

"OK, Jack, let's you and I stroke slowly. Walter, steer us well off the wharves."

No response from the professor. He's staring, fixated on the waterfront, now getting slightly more visible as we drift closer. Despite the loss of light as a large cloud covers the moon, we're still able to discern the outlines of many low buildings. Most do not look in good shape.

In fact, Long Wharf was in existence as early as 1685, called "Queenhithe" on an antique map. The name is a medieval English word for boat haven. For much of Newport's early colonial history, butchers would drive cows onto the wharf where townspeople would crowd around. Buyers would mark the steer with a piece of chalk describing the portions of the animal they wanted cut for them. In 1723, twenty-six pirates were hung just south of Long Wharf, their bodies later buried in tidal sections of Goat Island.

Long Wharf is far longer than any other Newport wharf. Scattered all along it from its land end to farthest point in the harbor are "market houses" in which merchants sell their wares to townsfolk, or account for product they purchase from sellers' vessels on the wharf or product they sell to buyers' vessels. By 1778, most of the market houses are ruined by the British troops' insatiable need for firewood. Surprisingly, there is a small drawbridge less than halfway along its length. Long Wharf as the central feature of the waterfront is very much at the center of Newport public life. Just beyond it, almost visible to the twentieth-century visitors is the Court House and the Town School House directly up the road from Long Wharf. The popular 2nd Congregational Church is just off to the right. In fact, 1778 Newport physically is very concentrated. It doesn't sprawl out much from the waterfront.

The professor continues to stare at the shore. He's not looking, he's staring. His eyes don't seem to shift at all.

Harry whispers, "I think we need to get him being a professor again. Get him to explain what we're seeing." He taps the professor on the arm. "Tell us about those buildings. What are they used for? The wharves I can see look pretty beat up. What happened? Is that an inlet or a pond right behind Long Wharf? There's no inlet there in 1998, is there?"

The professor blinks several times. He turns toward Harry. "Sorry, what did you say? What about an inlet? Give me a moment, please."

He rubs his eyes again and again, runs his hands through his hair time after time. Speaking very slowly, he whispers, "I'm so tired I think I'm going to collapse. I think preparing for this, then actually doing it has created so much turmoil for me that I'm now just overwhelmed by being here. I feel out of touch, awake but not awake, like a trance. Maybe I've just run out of gas, or I'm in some kind of stupor. I've pretty much had it." No longer staring at the shore, his head has slowly bowed forward so he's now looking into the bottom of the boat.

I lift his shoulders. "Harry was asking you to describe what we're seeing. Look at the small pier next to Long Wharf. It's hard to tell at this distance but it looks ruined. The one next to it looks just as bad. I thought you said Newport was a powerful, rich port."

The professor stretches and yawns, exhales loudly. "Yes…right. The wharves…yes, right, many were ruined. We know the British even before the Revolution repeatedly bombarded Newport with 'hot-shot' torching the wooden buildings. A particularly nasty fellow named Captain James Wallace terrified Newport and other Narragansett towns threatening to burn them 'to the water's edge'. He regularly seized ships returning from trade cruises. Thousands fled Newport in 1775 and 1776 because of his terrorizing actions. Much of the damage you see came from him. Later the occupying soldiers ripped many up wharves and homes for firewood. I'm sure if we got closer we'll probably see many of the buildings on the wharves are ripped apart, also used for firewood. I would expect that some wharves are useable, those used by the British. Long Wharf must be useable. I can see some masts there. While I can't see from here, there are a few or at least a couple buildings on Long Wharf that likely are still functioning…the brothels. Prostitutes loitered about Long Wharf, selling their services to sailors. Probably there are some 'ladies of the evening' over there right now. Any interest?" He smirks at us. "Wait…listen."

Relieved to watch the professor start to recover his senses, I listen. The clatter of horse hooves on cobblestones is distinctive. I can barely see several horsemen passing the land end of Long Wharf. I can't tell anything more than they appear to be moving slowly.

The professor says, "That might have been a patrol. We're not really close enough but I've sort of expected to see lots of milling around on the wharves. All the sailors—they called them 'tars' then—on shore off the ships to be scuttled must have made a nasty nuisance of themselves. They supposedly roamed the town drinking their rum rations—called 'kill grief'—carrying various weapons with which they were supposed to fight the French."

The professor leans over the side, splashes seawater on his face.

He points to the right of Long Wharf. "See that light high up? That must be the lantern in the steeple tower of Trinity Church. What a beautiful place…lots of paneling and a fantastic three-deck pulpit. It's behind the waterfront, well up a slight hill. That's why we can see it from here. It was the establishment church, Anglican, all the best people worshipped there. Its roster of parishioners was largely a list of Newport's royalists, even some Quakers so desperate to save their positions they converted to Anglicanism. Obviously the British forces will have left it alone. I've been told its bell was the first church bell to ring in New England. It was given by Queen Anne in the early 1700s. She also donated the communion service."

We row slowly for two or three minutes. Harry keeps looking, regularly checking each direction. I'm captivated as we slowly pass along the shore. Now well past Long Wharf, we're approaching what appear to be numerous large, often square homes, several very close to the harbor. In front of them though just like so many of the wharves we've passed, the waterfront appears partially destroyed. "Looks like some pretty good size houses there."

"Yes, the Point was quite a place leading up to the war. Problem is the occupying British troops just overran it. In the winter, most of those big houses probably housed soldiers, sailors, marines, even the hated Hessians. The troops bivouacked in the summer. They declared martial law right after they arrived, took over many private homes." The professor seems once again to be fully warming to his subject.

"Before the British made an awful mess of the Point, it had somewhere around 100 homes. Some were ostentatiously opulent. Many rich Newport merchants lived there. The big houses facing the harbor were largely owned by merchants. That street to us is called Washington Street, but then was named Water Street.

"Many homeowners there were Quakers, sometimes mocked as the 'Quaker Grandees'. The houses flaunted spectacular architectural features and possessions—large circular stairways, paneled walls, mahogany doors, marble fireplaces, large 'widow's walks' on the roof, beautiful furniture, glimmering displays of silver and gold dinnerware, candelabras, collectibles…all manner of stuff. The famous Townsend-Goddard cabinetmakers were Quakers then building their fabulous walnut and mahogany furniture—hall clocks, secretaries, tables, chairs, chest of drawers, desks, on and on. It all seemed to fly directly in the face of the demand for simplicity of personal appearance required by the 'Society of Friends'.

"There is a kind of delicious irony to all this wealth. In especially the seventeenth and early eighteenth centuries, Quakers were widely considered dangerous. England at that time regularly flogged and deported them, even hanged some. The Puritans in Massachusetts were utterly intolerant of them. Most who survived in New England did so only by fleeing to Rhode Island, after being expelled or otherwise driven out of Massachusetts, as well as Connecticut. Rhode Island's religious tolerance made it their obvious haven. So, here they arrived desperate and fearful. Some prospered fabulously and in the face of both their religious strictures and the animosity of non-Quakers, brandished their wealth for all to see. They were among the first colonialists to subscribe to a style we mock two hundred years later—'if you've got it, flaunt it!'

"There are dozens of simpler homes and shops behind Water Street. They were owned by ship captains, shipwrights, and various craftsmen, especially candle makers and silversmiths. Ships from all over the world tied up to those wharves. The houses we're looking at—along with shops, chandlers, distilleries and warehouses which we can't see from here—were largely destroyed or damaged by the occupying British by the time they were ordered to New York in 1779.

"Newport's commerce never truly recovered. Soon after they left, Newport slid into being a backwater port. It didn't recover in any significant way until well into the 1830s and '40s, when a surge of summer visitors caused a flurry of hotel building. Then it rapidly evolved into the Newport of its fabulous 'Gilded Age', starting shortly after the Civil War."

"OK guys, time to head for home," Harry says firmly. "I can make out the end of Goat Island, so the other transports must be just out of sight in the darkness. If I remember, we row from here keeping the end of the island to our port. As we turn around the island, keeping it just in sight, the *Lord Sandwich* should be dead ahead. Agree, professor?"

"Yes, that seems right."

I've stopped rowing, while Harry turns us onto our new course rowing on his own. After a shove from Harry, I resume rowing. The professor is turned around watching the waterfront recede out of view in the dark, except for a few lights scattered along the shore in both directions.

Pausing his stroke, Harry says, "Walter, let me just say something here. Remember what you said in your note? I give you credit, you did what you said. You were right…it was unimaginable, almost like a miracle. In fact words, at least my words, can't do it justice. Like you said, we did something 'magical'. The 'invisible' became 'visible'. It's been an incomparable experience. You have my lifelong gratitude for making your dream come true and allowing me to be part of it…my deepest thanks. But, *now* it's time to go home."

The professor nods. His eyes are tearing, I'm sure he can't speak at all. Neither can I.

Within a few minutes we're several hundred yards offshore, abreast of the island's northern point. We can see a campfire near the point, and another several hundred yards south. The professor whispers, "I'd guess those are small unit patrols, squads or less. They might be on guard for infiltrators or small raiding parties. But it was well known the French fleet was approaching, so it's likely the main concern of the British was to get ready for that. The Americans under General Sullivan were well north of here in Tiverton, so are not at this time a factor. While they must be preparing for ship bombardments and attacks landing from the French ships onto the shore, they probably were not too concerned about night attacks in force. I don't see any motion, men walking the beach, patrol boats. Nothing seems to be going on. Generally, the French and British tended to fight 'set piece' daytime battles."

"We've got to keep moving. I'd guess it's very late," I add. "It was well after

12:00 when we left the Luhrs. Bet it is after 2 a.m. Alice probably is already fidgeting with the inflatable."

"I wouldn't be surprised." The professor points forward over our shoulders. "That should be the hull."

Harry and I turn around to see it looming up in the dark just to starboard.

The professor continues, "We approached on her port side, pretty much on a right angle to the hull. She's anchored bow and stern, so doesn't move much. Let's go around to the other side. We can get ourselves headed out of here on a reciprocal course as close as possible to our approach."

"There's that goddamn smell again," grumps Harry. "You can exclude that from my gratitude...gross and awful."

We reach the bow. I hear a rustling noise, metal clicking on metal, scraping steel, the creaking noise of a small boat. *"Who goes there? Stop in the King's name!"*

Approaching us from the shadows of the hull's port side are the red jackets of Royal Marines, muskets leveled at us. An officer in the stern is pointing a sword at us. "Release the oars, hands in the air! We've been listening to you! Who the hell are you?"

There are eight marines, two still at their oars, the others aiming their muskets at us. Their boat is considerably longer than ours. Now they're close. I can see the officer is very young, no more than a teenager. He's not wearing a redcoat, but a blue frock coat, without epaulettes. He has on a tri-corner hat. One marine reaches out to grab the painter on our bow.

The professor stands up. "Midshipman, have your marines put their weapons to rest, we are carrying dispatches to the frigate *Juno*."

Way to go, Walter! Can he pull that off?

No....

"Sorry sir, I cannot do that. You're nowhere near the *Juno* and well off course to reach her. I have precise orders to detain or shoot anyone approaching or boarding the transports."

One of the marines nearest the young officer has two chevrons on his sleeve. I can hear him speak to the midshipman, in a thick Cockney accent, "May be more, sir. Better have a look 'round the other transports."

"By all means. Corporal, take Jenkins with you. Have the prisoners board the *Lord Sandwich*. Tie them on deck. We'll then patrol the remaining transports in this anchorage and return for them."

The professor tries again. "Midshipman, I'm an officer in His Majesty's Navy. These men serve in the fleet. You are making a grave mistake. If you confine us, I will bring you up on charges, do you understand?!"

"Nonsense, stop your gabbling! Half of it is gibberish! I can barely understand you. You may be a trick, some sort of artifice. You could be an imposter. Or possibly you just escaped an asylum and are play-acting." The marines snicker and guffaw.

The professor makes one more try. "We are loyal servants of King George. We are local citizens loyal to the crown!"

"Enough, sir, enough! We will bring you ashore for others to sort you out. Corporal, if you please!"

The corporal salutes the midshipman by pressing is knuckles to his forehead. The marine holding our painter pulls us alongside while the others continue to point their muskets directly at us.

Harry whispers, his lips hardly moving, "Careful, move slowly, do what they say."

Two marines climb up to the hull's deck and point their muskets down at us. Two others, including the corporal, clamber into our boat. They repeatedly poke us with the bayonets mounted at the end of their muskets. The corporal pushes me toward the rope ladder earlier used by Harry. He has long, thick, sandy brown sideburns down to his jaw. His hair is filthy and tied back in a greasy club knot. His face is pale and deeply pockmarked. Deep wrinkles splay out from his eyes, nose and mouth. I'm surprised how old he appears. His blue eyes are watery and bloodshot. The red jacket is heavily stained. It buttons high on his neck. He wears that strange top hat we've seen before. "Move along madman, up the bleeding rope!"

I climb on deck, closely followed by the professor, then Harry. One of the marines hands the corporal a coil of rope who growls, "You buggers sit down with your backs to the mainmast stump here. Put your arms behind your backs...move, damn it!" He roughly ties the professor's elbows together behind his back. He next takes a wrap around the stump, knots that off. Pushing me hard to the deck he does the same to me, after first viciously kicking my left thigh to make me move up against the stump. Almost immediately I'm in agony. I'm tied so tightly in an awkward position—my arms bent at the elbow and thrust behind me—that the arthritis in my right shoulder and elbow is inflamed. With the same line he similarly ties Harry to the stump. Harry keeps his eyes averted,

184

looking down at the deck throughout. The corporal uses his bayonet to cut the line after Harry is secure to the stump. The bayonet must be razor sharp, as he effortlessly slices what appears to be at least a quarter-inch line. He then wraps first the professor's feet tightly together and ties off a knot. He then runs the line to me for the same tight wrapping of my ankles together and finally to Harry.

He steps back to glare at us. "I for one don't trust you bleeding cullion! You're spies or saboteurs. We should just throw you overboard and be done with ya! Slimy buggers!"

From over the side, we hear the midshipman, "Corporal, leave Jenkins as a guard."

"Aye-aye, sir. We're done here. Jenkins, you heard the midshipman. We'll be back quick like. Watch 'em close. If they diddle you, you'll cop it, by Heaven!"

After a few minutes we hear the oars splashing in and out of the water as the patrol boat heads south from the *Lord Sandwich*. I try to adjust my position slightly to ease the severe pain in my shoulder and elbow. I can't move enough to gain any relief.

Jenkins the guard squats down about twenty feet away. Like the corporal he has long sideburns, his very dark. He has no badges of rank, so must be a private. Younger, his uniform is much cleaner than the corporal's. He repeatedly licks his lips; must be nervous. At first he points his musket right at us, actually at Harry whom he's directly facing. Eventually, he lays it across his lap, though he stays crouched. He remains motionless in that position as minute after minute ticks by.

Finally, many minutes later, slowly he stands up. Ambling over to the side, he unbuttons the flap on the front of his white duck pants. He starts to urinate over the side.

Harry whispers, "Jack, fake like you're out cold. We've got to get the guard to come look at you. I've got my arms free."

The professor replies, "I'll handle it."

I close my eyes and flop my head down onto my chest. Peeking up, I watch the guard button his pants and resume his squat position twenty feet in front of Harry. The professor says to him, "Private, one of my men appears to have passed out. May I look after him?"

"No...sir...whatever you are...shut your gab."

"Could you just tell me if he is breathing?"

"Who bloody cares," grumbles the guard.

The professor sighs and catches his breath sharply, sobs slightly for good measure. "He's my uncle…please, I beg you!"

Silence. Then there is a slight metallic noise and shuffling sound. Is the guard coming to me? I shut my eyes, take a deep breath.

THUD! I jerk up and open my eyes as the guard slumps heavily onto my knees. Harry, his feet still tied, is touching the guard's neck. "Has a pulse." He leans over and unties the knot at his ankles. Rubbing the meaty part of his right hand, then his ankles, followed by his elbows and shoulders, he bends over me. Quickly he runs the loose line through my elbows, next through the professor's. He rolls the unconscious guard off my legs. "Jack, you looked in bad shape. You OK?"

"I'll be all right. Old age crap kicking in, I guess. How the hell did you get loose?"

"Old amateur trick we've been teaching police recruits forever. When someone ties your arms, flex your arm muscles as much as you can. When they're done tying you, relax your muscles and the line will be a little loose. I've been slowly working it down my arms by slightly rubbing the line against the mast stump. Finally I got it to my fingers a few minutes ago."

I laugh, "You are one sneaky bastard! But we love you even so.

"It's late as hell. Damn, we were tied up a long time! Who knows when the lovely corporal and his friends will be back. We've got to fly! Walter, so now I'm your uncle?"

The professor laughs as stumbling over debris on the deck, we reach the lines hanging amidships that should lead to the jolly boat. Fearfully we peer over the side. Did they take it on patrol? Is it still there?

Yes, it's there! Thank God!

"We love you, *Giggles*!" hoarsely whispers Harry. "Jack, you better steer. Walter, take starboard. I'll row port."

The professor says to me, "Line us up with the transom flush on the hull. Keep checking that we stay on that course until the hull is out of sight. Then we'll row basically the same course as well as we can. Right now we have to assume the patrol will be looking for us."

Once in the jolly boat I grab the two lines dangling off the hull. Harry and the professor push and pull on the oars. Eventually the transom is flat on the hull. "OK, row," I say and turn around to give us a push off. "Long strokes, pull hard, dip the oars in the water quietly."

I steer, turning around repeatedly to watch the hull, keeping our slight wake lined up as best I can.

"Jack, I think you should bear slightly left." The professor is breathing heavily. "We've got to keep as far from the frigates as we can. If they're patrolling the transports, they must also be patrolling the frigates."

I make a slight adjustment. Turning around, the hull is fading from view. Moments later, it's gone.

Far off, behind us and slightly off to our right there's a distinct horn sound, possibly a bugle. "Shit," exclaims Harry. "Probably it's an alert. Row hard, Walter, row damn it! Jack, steer straight; get us outa' here."

Harry and the professor are in rhythm, pulling the oars strongly through the water. I'm impressed with the professor. Nearly fifty, small, thin frame, he's keeping up with the much bigger, stronger Harry. The boat is not being pulled slightly to one side or the other, but tracking straight.

Minutes later, the professor says, "OK, OK, stop for a moment. Let's listen."

For a moment we hear nothing. Then, not far away, the clear screech of a seabird, probably a gull.

"Damn...*damn*! It can't be...*it just can't be*!" The professor looks crestfallen.

"What...what's wrong, Walter?"

"Gulls don't fly late at night. It must be very close to dawn. We can't be caught out here. We'd have no chance. Not only are there the ships and at least one or more patrols, there are probably British on Rose Island. They had a gun battery there to fire on the French. We are going to need shelter now. No way we can settle ourselves, go through all our relaxation and concentration steps to get back to 1998. It's just too much risk. With any sort of daylight they could see us. They'd likely then shoot at us like sitting ducks! We're escaped prisoners for God's sake!"

"Where do we go?" I ask.

"Only place close enough that makes any sense is Rose Island. We know Goat Island has a fort, sentries and probably patrols. The only other land close by is Rose. We need to hide in among the rocks and bushes on the east side. Thick bushes, a slate covered beach, some rock outcroppings. It's not likely anybody goes there. Maybe there's some sea grass there to hide us. Who knows about two centuries ago. The battery would be on the other side of the island. I think the remnants of a later French fortification—eventually on which the

Rose Island Lighthouse was built—were built overtop the British battery. The remnants are on the southwest corner of the island. We have to head for the east side and hope for the best."

"Can you find this island?" Harry is watching the professor.

"If we head in the same direction we're going, maybe risk a slight turn to starboard, I should think we'd run into it. It can't take very long. If we row more than ten minutes, we missed it."

"Right, no other choice. Let's row for five minutes, stop and listen, repeat. Make sense?" Harry looks turns to the professor.

"It's as good as any. Jack, steer a little off to the right."

While he's been talking, the professor keeps putting his hands in the water. Harry takes his kerchief off, rips it in half. "Wrap these around your hands; it'll help."

"Thanks," mumbles the professor.

I turn us slightly starboard as we resume rowing, now at a slower pace. The silence has returned except for heavy regular breathing from Harry and the professor. I'm just about to announce "five minutes" when we hear another bird noise. Not a welcome sound.

"Look," whispers the professor, pointing in the water, "grass. Lots of it. We must be close."

Yes, I can feel a slight push of current on the boat, maybe a small tide-rip. We must be near land.

Harry crouches and turns toward the bow. "Jack, take my place. I'll look for rocks and hopefully a piece of shore we can land on."

The professor and I make short, slow strokes.

Harry whispers, "We're coming up to some grass, not much but some. Hold up, there's a rock well out of water just ahead. Professor, give me a short stroke; let's see if we can go inside it."

There is a slight scrapping sound on the bottom of the jolly boat. "Stop, stop! She's too fragile, you'll hole her." The professor's voice is high-pitched, frantic.

Harry steps out into knee-level water. "This might do for now. We're slightly behind this rock from the open bay."

He turns back to the boat. "Everybody out. I'll walk a few steps in this direction. Jack, walk off the stern. Walter, the other direction."

I gingerly step one leg over the stern. I can't touch bottom. "Must be deep here. I see just a few stalks of grass, over there to the right."

The professor is walking in knee-deep water. "Small rocks, wait, a bigger one up ahead. There's a bush behind it, no, several bushes. There's a beach covered with pieces of slate just ahead."

Harry turns around. "Let's try to lift the boat forward a little more behind this large rock. We can't lift it much, but we've got to try to get it a little farther behind this rock."

We manage to shove it forward a few feet with minimal scrapping.

"OK. We have a little shelter—this rock, some sea grass and the professor's bushes. Let's wait for a little daylight and see how we are." Harry sits gently on the gunwale, swings his dripping legs into the boat.

The professor looks utterly dejected. "Sorry guys, but I'm sure we'll see we're way too exposed here. As we get a little light we'll see the frigates anchored off the island and later the transports next to the *Lord Sandwich*. We probably can't be seen by the British gunners on the other side of the island, but we'll be almost in plain view of the ships. The rock is nowhere near large enough to shelter us. Once they see us, there's no way we can outrun them. We might even be able to hide ourselves by pushing the boat deep into the wild shrubs and bushes here, but if we're spotted we're done." The professor starts to continue, but Harry interrupts him.

"I agree. Look, we got to face it, we're in a box. The ships by now must be alerted to three escaped prisoners in a jolly boat. They're certainly nervous as hell about the French fleet. The British garrison must be frustrated by regular harassment from local militia and privateers. It all adds up to a very edgy situation. That, plus all armies—certainly the British Army then, or maybe I should say now, the most formidable in the world—go on patrol…always go on patrol. No way the gunners on the other side of the island are just going to sit on their asses. No non-com will ever let that happen."

The professor takes over from Harry. "Right. So, we're faced with being spotted by the frigates, the transport patrol, or a Rose Island patrol. To any of them we're either escaped prisoners or caught hiding on a British-occupied island just before being invaded by an enemy fleet. We've got to get out of here right now."

"To go where?" I ask. "Our options don't look like much."

"Our only choice is to get out of this area, maybe over to the Jamestown side of the bay. But it's a long way and it'll be light very soon. At least there we're away from the defense of Newport…and it's quite rural."

Harry again interrupts, "That actually might work. In my world it's sometimes called 'hide in plain sight'. The bad guys try to blend in, not be noticed, to be inconspicuous. We could simply be three British Navy men in a boat, as long as we stay well away from the transports. Sail around, find a place to rest, sail some more…nice day on the water…sounds like fun!"

I've developed a nasty headache, can't breath easily, am anxious and very irritable. "Jesus, this isn't some little goddamn Sunday sail! We don't even have any wind! You want us to sail around playing some kind of crazy, over-the-top stupid game of 'chicken'?"

Harry puts his arm over my shoulder. "Jack, if you have a better idea I'll definitely listen. But that's all I have."

The professor agrees, "That's our best bet. We can't feel any wind here, but I think its likely we'll get some later. Most summer wind comes from the south and southwest, slightly behind the island from us. We could row out of here, directly away would be roughly south. Once we're well out and away from the British battery on the island, we can raise the sail. If there's not enough wind to make way, we'll row until there's wind. I assume just like in our time, the wind will come up some in the early morning. One way or the other we'll get on a course to eventually work our way to the Dumplings and Old Salt Works Beach area, well south of Jamestown. We passed there as we made the turn around Brenton's Point toward Fort Adams on the way in yesterday. We'll have to be careful because there are lots of rocks and tidal rips, but once in we'll be hard to spot. We probably could get some mussels and quahogs to eat."

"What the hell are quahogs? Sounds awful. Like something dropped from the wrong end of a browsing animal."

I respond, "I even know that. Walter, we should be gentle, not to offend the simple vocabulary of Potomac folk. They're clams, Harry, delicious clams."

"Thank God, I thought you were asking me to eat…."

"All right Harry, we get it. Then we're agreed?" asks the professor. "We'll head out of here now…right now, before any more light creeps in."

"Yeah," I reply as Harry nods. "Let's get going."

Carefully we lift and gently shove the jolly boat afloat. We resume our positions, Harry and the professor rowing, me at the tiller. Once turned around we stroke along the edge of the island, steering around some sizeable rocks just offshore. As we approach the largest rock island, a racket of gull screeching

190

explodes in the night-time quiet. "Jesus, go ahead announce our arrival, goddamn birds!" Harry swears colorful oaths at the unseen gulls as he and the professor row long, hard strokes.

"Jack, steer a little off to your starboard. We need to be sure we head for the middle of the bay, but stay well south of the island." The professor can barely get the words out through his heavy breathing.

We row for several minutes. While all I see is water in all directions, it definitely is lighter. I can see farther, no question. For the last minute or so I feel a little air movement on my face. "Do you guys feel that…a little wind?"

They both stop rowing and turn around. The professor raises his hand slightly. "Not much, that's for sure. Right now though, anything will do. We can always keep rowing. We must be at least several hundred yards south of Rose Island. Let's try to sail. Harry, go forward and sit on the deck. Pick up the base of the mast and the fork of the boom. They're wrapped together with line. They're lying together on the thwart just aft of the deck. I've got the middle of it. Lift it onto your lap. Then place them next to the hole in the deck. First, untie the line wrapping the mast, sail and boom together. We'll step the mast into the hole. Be sure to keep the mast hoops from sliding down and off the mast. The sail is attached to the mast hoops. It'll move a little when you lift the sail, but stay mostly folded down along the base. It's attached to the boom with smaller hoops. When you're ready, I'll lift the mast up. As I lift it, place the base in the hole, holding off the hoops. I've got the halyard in my hand."

I can see Harry holding the bottom of the mast in his lap. He shifts it onto the deck. It's painted white, easy to see so close by. Slowly the professor stands up, lifting the mast as the sail flops down. Finally the mast is upright. "Harry, hold the mast as straight upright as you can." The professor kneels down next to Harry, starts to feel around under the deck. "Got it. Twist the mast slightly clockwise…little more…that's it. Pin's in place."

The professor stands up, holding the boom, the sail attached. "Harry, grab the fork portion of the boom. Hold it against the mast, fitting the fork around the mast about two feet above the deck. Push the mast hoops up as you do it." The professor is holding the middle of the boom and a line, apparently the halyard, which leads to a block at the top of the mast and down to the top of the sail. "Hold the fork in place." He gradually, slowly pulls on the line and the sail lifts up along the mast. "Use one hand to help the hoops slide up the mast." The sail reaches the top of the mast. The professor bends down to tie off the halyard to a little wooden cleat next to the mast. Stepping aft, he tells me to sit in the next forward thwart, as he takes my place in the stern. He loosens a half hitch in a line at the end of the boom, holding it—apparently the sheet—in a coil. The sail is flopping listlessly. "Jack, use the port oar to paddle us around to starboard. Let's see if we can pick up any wind."

As we gradually turn, the sail luffs a little, finally fills slightly, still floppy, but clearly picking up a little wind. The professor is watching the forward portion of the sail, moving the tiller slightly back and forth to find a course that can fill the sail more.

"Jack, one more paddle stroke please."

The sail fills slightly.

"Let's try this course for a bit. We're moving, not much, but see…a tiny wake."

Moments later, the professor says, "Get ready to duck, right now, coming about!"

"What's up?" Harry asks.

"Look ahead, damn it, a frigate!"

Several hundred yards ahead of us is the distinct shape of a three-masted warship. The professor explains quietly that it must be a British frigate. The British stationed warships in the east and west passages that lead out of the bay to the ocean. The idea was to prevent American ships from getting out of Providence and other towns along the northern portion of the bay. The British had them bottled up in the northern bay, by controlling its southern entrances at Newport and Aquidneck Island. Probably the frigate also was a lookout for the French fleet.

More disturbing than the presence of the British frigate which is at anchor, sails furled, is the fact that we can see her. We slowly come about, starting to sail a course away from the frigate. Looking back we can see her all too clearly. Dawn is arriving to Narragansett Bay.

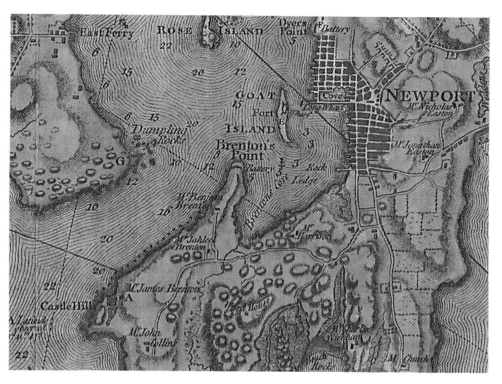

Map of Newport, Rhode Island, drawn by Charles Blaskowicz in 1777 for the British Navy. Note Castle Hill inlet on the lower left.

EIGHT

The little jolly boat has no jib (triangular sail set in front of the mast), so cannot "point" up near the direction of the wind. Unfortunately, as the professor explained, the wind is mostly from the south and slightly west, too near the direction to our destination to sail there directly. So far we've made several tacks (straight runs during which the sail is set obliquely to the wind) as we attempt to reach the Dumplings. At least we have steady wind now. In fact the bay is now slightly choppy.

We have been silenced by the onset of dawn. I have an uneasy sense of foreboding, imagining dangers in almost all directions. Behind us is the frigate which either ignored us or in the gloom missed us. In either case it's not very comforting. They can see us now, we can see them. Thankfully no rush of activity is apparent on the ship and we're putting distance between us every minute. More ominously for the moment we are approaching the southern end of Goat Island, now clearly visible on our left. Any close approach is absurdly risky as it certainly will provoke a reaction from the nervous British sentries. Looking behind us I can just begin to see the hulls alongside the northwestern shore of the island and beyond toward the Point. Soon we'll be able to see the anchored frigates off Rose Island. The only direction that seems not to hold obvious danger is our destination. I wait nervously as the professor continues a course toward land. Finally, I can't keep quiet.

"Walter, we're too close. Let's come about."

He seems to snap out of a reverie. "Oops, my mistake, coming about." As we turn he gestures toward the land we've been approaching. "That point has on it what today is Fort Adams. The locals built a fortification in 1776, but it didn't serve any purpose during the Revolution. Maybe some British troops are stationed there, I don't know. I don't see anyone. In any case, there's no point in risking contact. We'll clear by it, then head for the Dumplings. We should make the Dumplings on this tack."

Ahead I now can make out a rocky headland, with several sizeable rocks just offshore. Two of them appear fifteen to twenty feet high or more, maybe sixty to eighty feet in length. I see the professor's point. They likely will provide considerable shelter if we can make our way behind them. On the other hand, they're very prominent and can be seen for miles. Once behind the rocks, we may be sheltered, but approaching them, we'll be easily visible. Nervous British sentries or patrols may want to know what we're doing there, particularly since the Dumplings are virtually at the entrance to the harbor.

"There's a small sailboat coming out over there." Harry is pointing well up the shoreline from the Dumplings.

"Probably it's the ferry that sailed between Jamestown and Newport. Keep an eye on it to make sure it's making for Newport. Look, I can make out Rose Island now, vaguely the ships behind it and over alongside Goat Island. This is fantastic, an incredible scene! Look at all the ships, some barely visible in the distance, some closer. The one closest to the northern end of Goat Island must be the *Lord Sandwich*. Many others, mostly hulls, all with their masts cut low like the *Lord Sandwich*. It's just phenomenal to see all this! Amazing what the British are sacrificing to protect Newport."

"Walter, no more tour guiding, please. Remember, we're not supposed to be here. We've got to find a damn good hiding place in one helluva hurry." Harry turns to me. "Jack, let's row some, pick up the pace."

We settle into our familiar positions and start stroking. The jolly boat's speed quickly improves. Something over on Brenton's Point catches my attention. Movement...one, no two people standing on the shoreline watching us. Even at this distance they appear to be small...must be children. One is wearing a long straight dress. The other has a wide sun hat, shorts, a big shirt with the sleeves rolled up. "Look, on the shore, couple of kids watching us. What do you suppose they're doing there?"

The professor glances toward the shore. "Just kids on the beach. Must somehow be part of one of the big farm estates out on Brenton's Point."

He waves. After a moment the figure in the dress gives a small wave in reply. "That estate is...wait!" The professor is straining to look beyond the Dumplings. "Pick up the pace, row hard, let's go, let's go!"

We're now only a few hundred yards off the first, nearly rectangular rock.

The professor exclaims, "Go full speed. I saw something glinting on the hill that slopes into the water behind the big square rock. We've got to get ourselves into the rock's lee. First, let's lower the sail. We'll be harder to spot behind the rock. Harry, reach behind you and release the halyard from the cleat. Let it run slowly through your hand so you can drop the sail softly. It'll fall on the gunwale next to you, Jack. Just lift it into the boat. Harry, you may have to give the hoops a little push down the mast. Don't know what I saw, but I'm pretty sure something's on the hill."

The sail down, we approach the rock. The water shallows quickly. It is crystal clear, the bottom strewn with rocks, weed, shells, a few scattered sand patches. Harry jumps into the shallow water. "Come on, professor, show me where you saw whatever you saw. Jack, hold *Giggles* off the rocks." It's now full light as they climb the rock, and carefully peer over its top. Some gesturing and conversation ensues, followed by another peek. Grim-faced, Harry scrambles down the rock and sits on a waist high boulder on the water's edge. "There's at least one small cannon there, with a few British soldiers. Professor knows nothing about it, has no idea what it's doing there. Doesn't really matter...it's there. But, I'm really goddamn tired of his surprises, let me tell ya'."

"Here he comes."

Harry slaps his hand on his sitting rock. "This sucks. There's no way we can stay here. If we try to leave, those gunners can take their goddamn time, and just blow us right out of the water."

The professor is irritated. "Yes, but they didn't on the way in, why would they when we're on the way out? And maybe they can't train on us from that angle. Maybe they don't give a damn about us, we look harmless enough. Maybe they didn't even see us. Who knows? I'll take my jacket off so we'll look more like fishermen. There are lots of mussels around, clinging to the moss on the rocks. Collect a bunch of them to eat later or to show if we're asked why we're here."

Harry scoffs, "Yeah, we did so well the last time we talked to the British!"

Mussels are everywhere. We pick dozens in a few minutes, putting them under the little deck. Harry works his way back up to the top of our rock, climbs back down to announce no one seems to be coming out from shore toward our rocky island.

"OK, then let's get underway." The professor is wading toward the boat. "We'll sail out just as we came in. Gradually we'll work our way south along the Brenton's Point shore. There's a little cove there where in our time there is a Coast Guard station and some private boats, all just down the hill from Castle Hill Inn. Maybe that will work for us. Far removed from Newport, there should be few if any people around, maybe a farmer or two. It will be a helluva lot better than here. And I don't think sailing north past all those ships and harbor activity makes much sense. What do you guys think?"

"No disagreement from me; let's get it over with."

Harry nods agreement. "Let's both sail and row. The more speed the faster we get past the range of that goddamn cannon."

The professor disagrees. "That would look too suspicious. Why would innocent fishermen be rowing and sailing? Let's just do what seems logical—sail now because we'll be tracking across the wind, row later when we're headed into it. If for some reason they open fire, we can always sprint for land over there south of the fort, to get out of range."

I ask, "What do you suppose is the range?"

The professor replies, "I think we should assume pretty much the width of the passage between here and Brenton's Point. Anything less seems unlikely, as the cannon would serve little purpose guarding the passage. In any case if they fire our only choice will likely be to run for the far shoreline."

"Walter, how about once we reach that shore—assuming we do—we stop and gather up some more mussels? If we make a few stops we might sell our shellfish act."

"I like it, good idea, Jack. Going into the Castle Hill cove will make more sense doing that...another shellfish stop."

As I hold the boat in place, the professor with help from Harry once again steps the mast and sets the sail. Nervously we sail out from behind our house-sized rock, stealing glances toward the cannon beyond. Plainly we hear a shout from its direction, but the words are indistinguishable. We wave back, hoping that will satisfy the shouter and gun crew. Another shout, another wave from us.

Minutes go by as we keep sailing away. Each of us holding our breath, we bounce through the increasingly choppy water toward the Brenton's Point shore. Occasionally, I remind myself to breathe, gasping as we approach the shore. No sign of the children.

"We need to take the sail and mast down again. We'll be headed almost directly into the wind. Let's use Jack's suggestion and go ashore. After that we'll row along the shoreline. Jack, take the tiller. Steer us directly into the wind."

"Practice makes perfect." Quickly the mast and sail are wrapped in the halyard and lying next to us along the thwarts. I stay at the helm, heading us to shore for an easy soft landing on a beach of sand and small rocks. There is a sharp bluff full of wild flowers and shrubbery just behind the beach. We step out of the boat, wading around, bending over to pick up more mussels. The professor goes ashore. Regularly he kneels down to dig in the dark sand. Occasionally, he pulls grayish, heavy-shelled clams from the sand. "Quahogs, to find 'em just follow the air holes in the sand!"

Harry heads up the hill to look around.

Soon our stash of shellfish has grown to several dozen mussels, nearly a dozen quahogs. We sit in the boat resting. "I think it's time for some rest and food. I'm beyond tired. We've had no food for I don't know how long. It's really catching up with me now. And I'm so damned thirsty...."

The professor interrupts, "We're all in the same fix, Jack. We need to find a fresh water stream. I'd say it's likely at the cove, because the land is higher there, with more slope than here. So rain collecting and streaming off into the cove seems probable. We could eat the mussels and quahogs raw—in fact I guess we'll have to. But, the saltwater in the shells and the meat will just aggravate our thirst. So, let's hold off eating for a while.

"Few more minutes' rest. We've a long row ahead, at least a nautical mile or more."

Harry slips and slides down the hill above us. "Can't tell much, the shrubbery is dense. It does seem to flatten out on top. Let's row a little ways and try again to see what's here."

The professor organizes us into twenty-minute watches. He and I start rowing, Harry steers. Twenty minutes later we again pull into the shore. The professor and I bend into the water to gather shellfish, as Harry struggles up another shrubbery-covered hillside. He disappears from view. Twenty or more minutes later he reappears, yells "grazing land." Moments later he's leaning on the boat, lifting one foot onto the gunwale. Little specks of blood are oozing from several cuts. Numerous thorns and burrs stick to his foot.

"If I get home, I may never go barefoot again!" He removes numerous irritants stuck to his left foot. He puts that foot down, raises the other. "Land is slightly rolling, grassy; quite pretty; lots of exposed bedrock and rock outcroppings. Tree stumps are scattered all around. Someone has cut down most of the trees, very few remain. Judging by the grass length just above the ground, and the hoof marks all over the area, there's a big plot of pastureland above us. The hoof prints are small. I don't think its cattle, maybe sheep or goats. Surprisingly though, I didn't see any animals, or people. I didn't even see any houses, though I spotted a little lean-to. Nothing else down the sloping hill I was on and up the hill opposite it. It must have been a half mile or more over to the next hill, all grazing land. There was a falling down, roughly made rail fence along the bottom. I'd say the animals were driven through or over that fence. Hoof marks have turned that whole area into a quagmire. I didn't see any water, though it's so green and lush, there must at least be plenty of subsurface water. I'd bet there's a pond or some sort of water collection area somewhere nearby."

"Let's take a few more minutes here, give Harry a chance to rest. No doubt the British cut down the trees. They endlessly needed firewood. Remember, by now they've occupied Newport for two winters so have felled much of the island's trees. They even regularly send ships to offshore islands like Block Island and Fisher's Island, even to Long Island in New York for wood." The professor sits in the boat. He makes a show of prying open a mussel, placing the meat inside into a sail bag, all with great flourish. "Just in case the battery has a glass (telescope) on us. They might. At least I'd think they would have a glass to study ships and boats in and out of this passage."

Back in the jolly boat, Harry and I are rowing with long, slow strokes, the professor tending the tiller. The wind has freshened still more but is of no use to us, right on the boat's nose. Little whitecaps push at the boat slowing our progress. The professor announces we're approaching a slight indentation in the coastline, where we can pull in for our next stop. "I cut the rowing time down. I counted roughly fifteen minutes. It's getting hot and sunny, so I'd say less is better. Cove can't now be too much further."

He steers into the indentation, but the bottom scrapes off a rock near the surface. Again we climb out to enable the boat to be floated around the shallows.

I dig numerous holes in the dark sand beach, retrieving the occasional quahog. Harry sprawls at rest across the three thwarts of the jolly boat.

Finally, we hoist ourselves back in the boat. Now, I'm at the tiller. No rowing for a while. My hands, forearms, shoulders, back and neck all ache. My shoulder and elbow haven't recovered from being tied up. Now, though, I'm nearly giddy with relief to just hold onto the tiller. For a few minutes I have to concentrate not to smile. Once again, just as last night, time flies when I'm at the tiller. My first thought is the professor has cheated me when he gasps, "Into shore, Jack; fifteen minutes are up."

Reluctantly, I gradually head in.

The shore is no longer the sloping hillside we've been gliding by. It's much lower. Moments ago we passed a tidal salt meadow. Sandpipers skitter away from us as we slide into the sandy bottom of the shallow water in front of a little beach. The professor quickly climbs a pine tree just off the rocky shoreline, on a small knoll. "The land slopes away and down, so I can't see much. I have to believe the cove is close."

Harry growls, "I'm about ready for that prediction to come true." The professor rests, leaning against his tree, as Harry and I continue the shellfish ruse.

"OK," Harry announces, "let's get underway. I'm at the tiller."

I can feel the professor's stroke pushing the bow toward my side. His strength continues to hold up much better than mine. It's a struggle to keep to his pace. Harry steers against him constantly, to keep the jolly boat tracking straight.

"Harry, steer offshore a little," suggests the professor. "Let's try to spot the cove."

Once we're off about 100 yards, we spot a clear break in the shoreline ahead. It's not large, less than 100 yards wide, but its there. A few small trees and a mass of wild, tangled shrubs covered with scruffy little vines grow right to its edge.

Harry steers us directly to the opening. "Looks good, professor—very sheltered from the coastline and the bay. If we can get well up into the cove, might be a good spot to rest and to hide for hours. Sure as hell hope so."

Minutes later we're in the cove. It looks more like a little river. Widest at its mouth, it narrows quickly, ending just a few hundred yards in. Scrub brush and fields of daisies on the east side, the west side is a hill gradually sloping way from the cove, dotted with tree stumps. Like Rose Island, there's thick shrubbery along the shore at the entrance. Inside is a rocky, slate beach. Well in, the shrubbery overhangs the water's edge. We row along the shrubbery, finally find a gap into which we push the boat in knee deep water. Stepping out, we get our first look at our hoped-for hideout.

I start undressing. "I'm going for a swim…anyone else?"

Harry replies, "I'm with you. But, let's first set up a simple watch system. We can do roughly one hour shifts, one on duty as sentry, the other two off duty swimming, exploring, resting, most of all looking for water. The one on duty will check the cove entrance and walk the hills. There is very little cover so we'll really need to stay alert."

Harry has been stripping as he talks. I wade into the cove water. Pleasantly cool, it instantly refreshes me.

"Since Jack is already naked, thereby useless as a sentry, and I'm almost there, looks like you're it, professor." He strides into the water and dives underwater.

The professor snorts, "Easiest decision we've made. OK, I'm off. I'll head to the cove entrance, have a careful look around. I'll see if I can spot the jolly boat from there."

I'm too tired to swim. I simple float looking up at the sky and occasional bird. For a moment I watch an osprey just outside the cove entrance. It hovers high in the air, suddenly plunging into the water. It emerges with a small fish, ten or twelve inches long, clutched in its talons. A magnificent bird with a wing span that must be four feet or more, it is white underneath, dark brown on top and has a beautiful brown-and-white pattern under its wings and tail. If we weren't in such a mess, this would be a pleasant moment, quiet and peaceful. The sun is hot, the sky clear, a breeze ripples the water's surface. A few bird calls, distant screeching gulls, are the only noises. Harry is floating nearby.

"What do you think is happening on the *Endeavour*?"

I reply, "Well, all the volunteer crew is supposed to be off. For now it's mostly a tourist site. We've not seen any mates since yesterday. Some are probably scattered around Newport, but most are home by now or on their way. Tony and Margaret are headed for the Cape. Other than the chambermaids at the hotel no one will miss us yet. That is, except of course for Alice."

"Yeah, she's on my mind constantly. Can't stop thinking about her—scared, trying to decide what to do, wondering what the hell happened to us. What a screwed up situation. It drives me nuts, thinking about her worried, having no idea about us. Hell, we could be dead for all she knows! I feel seriously shitty about getting her into this crazy nonsense. Just when we really connect, I up and disappear. What a goddamned stupid thing to do!"

"From what I could see, there was no way she was not going to be involved. She wanted in; you wanted her in. She strikes me as pretty resourceful and resilient. I doubt very much she'll just roll over and give up. What we've got to do tonight is get back somehow."

"More to the point, now we need is to survive and not get snatched before then," Harry replies. "Thanks, though. You're right about Alice. But this minute, I badly need water, you must too. Let's get on the stick." He swims a few strokes to the shore near the jolly boat. Wading through the grass he reaches in and loosens the wrapped up sail. "Here's your towel sir, time to find water."

Dried off and dressed in my now tattered and very dirty ancient pants and shirt, I walk to the head of the cove as Harry climbs the incline on the western side. We agree to walk large loops, meeting back at the head of the cove. I decide to skirt along the heavy growth of tangled shrubs and little trees, walking up another gentle incline on the eastern side, away from the cove. I walk slowly, listening carefully, stopping occasionally to look around. I notice Rhode Island Sound not far ahead down a gentle hill. Turning back to the cove, now well below me, I see no one. Finally, I spot Harry halfway up his side, stopping and starting, changing direction, constantly looking left and right, occasionally behind.

Turning back, I start to resume my walk. Standing just off to my left are a boy and a girl, watching me. I'm so startled by their sudden appearance I gasp. I start coughing from the violent intake of air. The boy jumps backward behind a small tree. The girl doesn't move a muscle, just staring at me. She's dressed in a coarse linen dress, really more of a sack, what, if memory serves, is called a 'Mother Hubbard'. Long, tangled blond hair tied back with a string, dirt-smudged face, no shoes. She couldn't be more than nine or ten. She hasn't flinched, just stares at me. The boy appears years younger. I can't see much of him as he peeks from behind his tree. We stand motionless, looking at each other.

Finally, I hold my hands out to them, palm up. "I am a friend. Don't be afraid."

"I'm not afraid," the girl says. "My name is Hannah. What is thy name?"

"Hello Hannah, nice to meet you. My name is Jack."

"Are thou a Britisher?"

I pause for a second…what will make sense to her? "No, I'm an American from another place."

"Are thou here to take our sheep and cattle?"

"No Hannah, I promise. Did the British take your animals?"

"Yes, and my Mommy and Ezra. But they left Curley and Hopper behind."

"Who are Curley and Hopper?"

"Our baby sheep. I take care of Hopper and Isaac takes care of Curley."

Gesturing toward the boy, I ask, "Are you Isaac?"

Hannah turns to face the boy. "Yes, he is. Come here, 'fraidy cat'."

He doesn't move.

"When did the British take the animals and Mommy?"

"Yesterday. We were in the lean-to with Curley and Hopper. We heard lots of yelling and shouting. When we ran over the hill, the Britishers were kicking and hitting our sheep with sticks heading out to the road."

"What did you do?"

"We ran home but Mommy and Ezra were gone." She starts to cry a little. She stops, her shoulders heaving up and down as she whimpers a moment longer. "They clubbed Barker…he died."

"Barker was your dog?"

She nods.

"Is Ezra your brother?"

"No, he's a Negro who works for my Mommy. But we don't own him, the Brentons did. Now he works for us. He's very old. He's my friend."

I squat down in front of Hannah. "You and Isaac were down on the beach a while ago. I was in the little sailboat you watched."

"Oh, yes the boat was headed to the Dumplings."

"We decided to come to Brenton's Point for quahogs and mussels and to find some drinking water. Can you and Isaac take me to some water?"

"That's easy, there's a stream right over there." She points behind Isaac. "Come, I will show thee, Jack sir."

I follow her into a dense patch of shrubs. After a minute, she stops, pointing down. Sure enough, a small stream gurgles down toward the cove. Thirsty for hours and hours, now I'm overwhelmed. I drop to my knees, thrust my face into the cold spring water and gulp as fast as I can. I start coughing and sputtering. I can't get enough.

Hannah kneels down next to me. "Do it like this, Jack sir." She cups her left hand just under a rock where the stream tumbles over it. Following her instructions, I drink gulp after gulp. Leaning back on my haunches, I'm happy to see Isaac is standing slightly behind Hannah. Then, looking just behind them I see Harry. He's sitting on the ground, smiling.

I sit up turning toward Hannah and Isaac. "I have a friend. He is a very nice man. His name is Harry. He wants to say hello."

Very softly, Harry says "Hello children. My name is Harry. What are your names?"

Hannah turns as Isaac jumps behind her. "My name is Hannah. This is Isaac. Would thee like some water too, Harry sir?"

"Thank you, Hannah, I would." Slowly Harry stands up and kneels next to me at the stream. He's learned his drinking lesson. He cups his hand just where Hannah did and drinks slowly and fully.

I say, "Harry, I told Hannah and Isaac that we were in the sailboat they watched from shore. We came here for quahogs, mussels and water."

"Yes that we did." Before getting up Harry turns toward Isaac. "Will you shake hands with me, Isaac?" Harry extends out his right hand toward Isaac. The boy eyes the hand, then darts his hand out to touch Harry's. Instantly he's back behind Hannah.

"Thank you, Isaac," smiles Harry. "It's nice to meet you."

Isaac looks from Harry to me and back, but no smile, very serious.

Harry turns to Hannah. "I bet you know all the shortcuts and trails here, Hannah."

Her eyes brighten. She rocks forward on tiptoe, "Oh yes, Harry sir! Deer trails, and trails Father used to drag logs on, and little trails the sheep use to run away and hide, and special trails that only me and Isaac know."

Harry continues, "I bet you know when the British soldiers are coming here long before they see you. You are probably very good at 'hide and seek'."

"Yes, I always beat Isaac."

"Do the soldiers come here?"

"Yes, they come and cut down trees."

"Where do they take the trees?"

"To the hospital."

"Is the hospital near here?"

"Yes, it's two hills past our house on the main road to Mr. Collins' house."

"I bet you know secret trails hidden by bushes and hillsides and the few trees that are left, so if we wanted to see the hospital we wouldn't have to go along the main road."

"Yes, Harry sir."

"Would you and Isaac like to take us there?"

"Yes. Then we can go to our house. Isaac is hungry. Would that be all right?"

"Sure," I interject. "You lead the way as far as you can without going along the main road or the shore. I bet you can pop us out right at the hospital. Can we do that together?"

Hannah rocks up on her toes again, "That will be fun. Come on Isaac. Let's take Jack sir, and Harry sir."

Harry pauses, "Is it a hospital for soldiers?"

"Well, it used to be Mr. Brenton's house…it's very big. Now it's just a hospital."

Harry and I have to walk fast to keep up. Hannah trots and skips along their trails, Isaac right behind her. He's wearing short pants of apparently the same linen material as Hannah's dress, and a dirty old white shirt with the sleeves rolled up into huge rolls at his elbows. The shirt is many sizes too big for him. He has on a wide-brimmed cloth hat, with the brim sagging down below his face. A few strands of blond hair stick out. He must be about five or six years old. Apparently fascinated by us, he can't go more than a few paces without turning to look at us. He doesn't say a word, but his face is less serious now.

We're skirting along just inside the dense patches of wild scrub brush, shrubbery and little pine trees. The rolling pastureland is clearly visible just to our right. Finally, just as I spot a little lean-to well away in a grass field, we head farther away to the left. The pasturelands no longer are visible. The scrub brush is thicker now, the path narrow. We walk along in single file for several minutes. Suddenly we slow down then stop.

Hannah shouts out, "The bay is right here."

Approaching her, I quickly crouch down. We're standing on a small hill, with scrub brush all around us, and down the side of the dune to the water ten feet below. "Let's all sit down and look around from here."

The scrub brush is thick enough to conceal us easily. However, I feel exposed to the British on the hill behind the Dumplings. While it's hundreds of yards away, their position is directly across the water.

"Hannah and Isaac, please sit down next to me. Harry and I want to tell you a secret. Can you keep a secret?"

Hannah sits down next to me and beams, "I can, I can, I promise! And I will make Isaac keep it too. What is the secret?"

"First, do you like the British soldiers?"

"No, no, no! They took away Father a long time ago. Mommy says he was made to go on a boat. Now they have killed Barker and taken our sheep and they have taken Mommy and Ezra. I hate them, I hate them!"

Isaac is closely watching Hannah, nodding his head up and down faster and faster.

"Well, Harry and I don't like the British either. We have been running away from them, because they want to put us in prison. We have another friend at the cove. They want to put him in prison too. When the British soldiers came out here to your farm, do you know where they took your Mommy?"

"No sir."

"Which direction did they take the sheep?"

"They took the sheep toward town."

Harry slides over to sit next to Isaac, who slides closer to Hannah. Harry grins at him. "Jack and I can only stay until dark. Then we have to leave. But we want you two to be safe. After we look at the hospital and go to your house we will decide together what is best. One of us will stay there with you for a while. Would you like that?"

Hannah nods her head. "Yes. We should go home. Isaac is hungry and so am I. Maybe Mommy and Ezra will come back. Isaac, we can have some johnnycake with sugar on it!"

Isaac smiles ear-to-ear, bounces up and turns back up the trail.

"Follow Isaac!" shouts Hannah.

"Wait, Isaac," says Harry. To Hannah, "Remember, first we look at the hospital, then we will go to your house. That is our plan, right?"

"Oh, yes, Harry sir, that is our plan."

We continue on, making several turns onto different trails, finally emerging onto a small field full of white daisies with a little house in the middle. Hannah and Isaac run down the hill yelling for "Mommy" and "Ezra". Harry slows me down. "Jack, I think one of us needs to get back to the professor. He's probably worried as hell right now. We also need some food if the house can spare it. After we check out the hospital we'll come back here. Will you stay here?"

"Sure, I'll stay for a while. I imagine there's food at the house, but obviously I'll only take a little and make sure the kids understand that. Hopefully we're outa' here tonight. Also, I've been thinking about what to do with them. They need shelter, food and adult companionship. I have a feeling we're it for the latter. I'll find out if any neighbors or friends are around."

Harry nods, "Right. We really need to be careful going to the hospital. All I want to do is figure out what if any threat it is to us."

Hannah and Isaac are trudging back up the hill approaching us. "Nobody is there! Mommy is not there!"

I put my arm around Hannah's small shoulders. "When we come back from looking at the hospital I'll stay with you for a while.

"You said you and Isaac like to play 'hide and seek'. We want to see the hospital but not let the British soldiers see us. Can you help us do that?"

"Yes, sir. We can hide behind the rock wall on the hill above the house. We also can climb a tree and look at it. Isaac likes to climb trees."

I stand up and turn away from the water. "It's time to go to look at the hospital. How long will it take to get there?"

"Not long," says Hannah as she runs up a trail. Panting, I grimace at Harry.

"Thank God, she has the stride of child! Think how much fun this would be if she were as tall as Alice!"

"We'd be giving you last rites, Jack! Keep the faith. Pretty soon you'll get some johnnycake, whatever that is!"

We skirt the high ground above the house, later descending a gentle hill behind it. Harry reminds Hannah to stay away from the stump-filled open fields. After ten minutes of fast walking, interspersed with brief moments of jogging to keep up with Hannah and Isaac, we come to a stone wall. Crouching down, Hannah skitters ahead to a small stand of trees a hundred yards out. Isaac is slightly bent over. He turns, looks directly at Harry, and surprisingly grabs his hand. He tears off along the wall, Harry duck-walking as fast as he can to stay down. Laughing then sputtering, I crouch and after several near stumbles join them behind the trees.

We carefully look over the stone wall. In the far distance is a large, two-story home with three chimneys and two entrances. There's a road leading to it from what appears another road in the distance. Three horses are grazing in the overgrown grass immediately in front of the house. A carriage, two carts and several large boxes are strewn around in front of a dilapidated porch off the right entrance.

Harry scans the house and fields around it. "Nobody in sight, no patrols are evident, no troops, not even a sentry. No point in risking being spotted. Let's go. Hannah, please take us back to your house."

This time we crouch and run single file along the stone wall. Quickly our view of the house stops as we crest a slight ridge in the land. Isaac now in the lead, we set off for the house.

"Harry has to go back to the cove. Can you tell him the best way to go?"

"Yes, sir." Hannah points. "Thou go over two hills, that one and the next one. Go to the dead tree up there, see it? Then thou will see the lean-to in the valley of the next field. Walk right by it to the end of the old stone wall at the top of the next hill. Walk along the stone wall until it turns this way," gesturing outward with her right hand. "There turn the other way and walk ten paces five times. That's where we met thee, Jack sir."

I turn to Harry. "Can you handle that?"

Harry starts to reply, "I don't...."

Isaac tugs at his left hand pulling him in the direction Hannah has been pointing. Off they go.

Hannah yells after Isaac, "Turn back at the stone wall."

I can't tell if Isaac heard. He's running up the hill, Harry lumbering along behind him.

Hannah and I walked toward the house's entrance. The house is a little one-story box, with a gently sloping roof. The roof has uneven, obviously hand-split wooden shingles. The exterior wall is unpainted clapboard. The house sits on a foundation of simple rubble masonry. There is a large, thick, stone chimney. She steps on the stone stoop and pushes on the door, roughly made of pine board and batten. Something caught my attention. I step back and am surprised to see a simple casement window of multiple small panes next to the door. Stepping inside, I'm expecting a gloomy, dark interior. In fact, it is surprisingly light. I notice another casement window on the back wall. The house is cool, at least six to eight degrees cooler than outside.

Hannah wants to take me on a tour. "This is where we eat our meals. Father made the table and stools and the cupboards and the windows, and lots more."

The table is at least five feet long, made of three long, well-used, stained oak boards joined together. Square legs anchor each corner. Two three-legged stools are next to the table. Next to them and far out of character with the primitive simplicity of the room, are two handsome American Windsor chairs. Hannah sits in one, "My Mommy sits in this one. The Brentons gave it and the other one to us for Christmas when I was five years old! They were made for their wedding years ago by somebody famous in Newport! The other one is Father's chair. Isaac and I get to share it on Sundays. I also sit in it when Mommy is reading me my lessons."

There are two cupboards each with two shelves. One contains stoneware cups and simple white plates, two or three glazed stoneware jugs. The other is for food, including eggs in a little wicker basket, a pile of some sort of cakes under a cloth cover, slices of ham with a cloth draped over, a dozen or more potatoes in a large wicker basket, smaller baskets of apples and plums. Several candlesticks are placed around the table. At the far end of the room next to the window is a simple, square two-drawer bureau. Directly under the window is a little wooden box containing scattered grasses and a little cut down stoneware cup full of water. Inside are two small turtles with spotted shells.

"Those are Isaac's turtles. There is a little green snake in there too." Hannah makes a face to show me her opinion of Isaac's amphibian and reptile collection.

Looking around, I stare at the huge stone fireplace. Surprised, I notice a sheet of wrought metal in back of the fire area. It must be used to radiate heat into the room. There are several iron pots hanging from iron rods protruding from the fireplace and other pots on the hearth. A huge kettle contains clothing, probably to be washed. Looking down, the floor is made of long planks, close to a foot wide. At relatively even spacing, trunnels fix the planks to something underneath, probably heavy floor timbers. Looking up I see sturdy exposed rafters and cross beams. The interior walls are rough- hewn timbers notched together.

"Jack sir, come into the sleeping room. Father added the whole room when I was little…I remember. He brought up the great big logs he cleared for the cornfield and made the room. This is where me and Isaac sleep."

The room has two low, unpainted post beds, one half again larger than the other. Each is roughly made but obviously serviceable. Both have lumpy straw mattresses on them. Both have simple head and foot boards, and thick square legs. The larger one is partially screened by sheet material hanging from a cross beam. Another bureau sits at the far end of the room. The room is lit by yet another casement window. On one wall is a piece of sheet iron cut into a crude oval and fitted with two candleholders each containing a partially-melted candlestick, to make a simple sconce.

"Ezra lives in the back." Through the window's uneven, distorting glass I see a lean-to attached to the main room. Its roof is an extension of the rear roof slope. Behind it is an old wooden bench and work table. An iron scythe leans against it, along with a mattock used for digging and grubbing, a long-handled axe, and big wooden rake. Farther back is a simple shed made of clapboard and the same hand-made roof shingles. It must be the outhouse.

"Your father and mother have made you a wonderful home, Hannah." She beams up at me.

The door bangs open as Isaac skids to a stop next to the fireplace. "I want johnnycake and sugar!" His first words...he wants food!

"Me too," exclaims Hannah. "Would thou like some, Jack sir?"

"Yes, Hannah, I would like that very much."

She reaches on tiptoe up to the second shelf of the food cupboard, pulls down the plate of cakes covered with a cloth. There are two squares of cornbread—"johnnycake" in Rhode Island—each about a foot on a side. One is untouched, the other half consumed. Hannah places the latter on the oak table, using a tarnished old knife with a wooden handle, she cuts three sizeable pieces. Reaching to the lower shelf in the other cupboard, she uses two hands to pull off a small stoneware jug. She pulls a wooden stopper out of its neck and slowly, carefully pours coarse brown sugar on each cake.

Isaac races over to the table and grabs a piece. Holding it in two hands, he chomps an enormous bite spilling cake crumbs and sugar down his over-sized white shirt, grinning all the while.

Hannah scolds, "Thou are a silly pig, brother!"

"Harry sir, would thee like some ham with the johnnycake?" She again rises on tiptoe to pull down a platter of sliced ham. Thickly sliced, cooked to a medium brown color, it smells delicious. Immediately I'm completely distracted by an overwhelming hunger as the smells of the johnnycake and ham tease and remind me how famished I feel. "Hannah, thank you but I don't want to take food you and Isaac will need."

"Oh, we have lots of food. There is a whole ham wrapped up in burlap in the root cellar, and flour to make johnnycake. I know how. My Mommy says I make better johnnycake than she does!"

"Hannah, maybe then you would be really nice and give me three pieces of johnnycake and three slices of ham, one for Harry, and for me, and for our friend. That still leaves a whole baking pan of johnnycake here on the plate and slices of ham too. Do you and Isaac think that will be all right?"

They both nod up and down. Hannah selects three large pieces each of ham and two johnnycakes. She puts these along with my piece of johnnycake in a little burlap sack.

"You and Isaac are very nice. You are good friends."

Isaac grabs my hand and shakes it as Hannah giggles at him. "Thou *are* very silly, but maybe not a pig!"

"Hannah, do you know any people who live near here?"

"Nobody lives here but Mommy, Isaac, Ezra and me. There used to be servants who lived at Mr. Collins house but I think they are gone. They were not nice to Isaac and me. They shouted at us to go home one time. Some men lived at the other Mr. Brenton's house a long time ago, but not now."

I sit down on a stool. "Do you and Isaac think Harry and I are your friends?"

She looks at the ground, shuffling her feet first one than the other. She peers up at me with her head still down. "Yes sir." Isaac nods.

"Good. Because I think you are my friends, and I am sure Harry does to. Because the British don't like us, and took your Mommy and Ezra away, we need to help each other just like friends do. Do you think that is right?"

"Yes sir."

"I would like you and Isaac to come with me to the cove. Harry is there now with our friend. We can all decide where the best place is for you and Isaac. We can help each other."

"We cannot live here, Jack sir?"

"Hannah, it will be better for now to find a place you can stay with friends for a little while. Then you can come back here. Does your Mommy have friends or relatives? Do you have any cousins that live somewhere near here or in Newport?"

"No." She pauses, thinking. "My Mommy talks to people when we go to meetings."

"What kind of meetings do you go to, Hannah?"

"Friends. Old Mrs. Overing lets us go to meetings in her barn at the end of her wharf."

"Are your family Quakers?"

"No, Jack sir. We are Friends. But I have heard that word, Quakers."

"Maybe going to the place where you have Friends meetings would be safe for you and Isaac. For now, let's walk to the cove to join Harry and our friend so we can all be together. Just in case we don't come back to your house today, please bring the pan of johnnycake and all the ham on the plate. Bring some plums too. Then you and Isaac will have lots of food if you stay away from your house for a night. Do you think it would be all right if you put some sugar in a cup and bring it for the johnnycake?"

"Yes, that would be nice. Why can't we stay at our house, Jack sir?"

"Hannah, we agree I am your friend. As your friend, the most important thing for me is that you and Isaac are safe. I am sure your Mommy wants you to be safe. Even though you are a very good sister to Isaac and a very good johnnycake maker, I am sure she will want you to go to a safe place until she comes to you and Isaac, gives you a great big hug and takes you back here. She knows people at the Friends' meeting barn. That means people there will know you. If you and Isaac go to the barn, they will be able to talk to other people and eventually your Mommy will learn you are at the barn. I am sure you will see Mommy soon and be able to come home. Do you understand?"

"Yes, Jack sir. Isaac, put the johnnycakes and ham in the big sack in the bottom drawer of that bureau."

He smiles at me, turns and sprints toward the bureau.

"Hannah, do you have some warmer clothing to bring in case it gets colder?"

"Mommy made me a sweater with blue buttons and a blue flower on the front! I will bring that. Isaac has a 'smock-frock'. It is very tatty."

She yells, "Isaac, bring thy coat. Mommy put it in the upper drawer of that bureau." He pulls out a stained, oversized, stiff-looking linen overcoat with rope loops on one side, little wooden ties on the other.

"Before we go to the cove, both of you please finish your johnnycake and have a piece of ham. Do you have some water or something else to drink with the food?"

Hannah nods, runs outside and brings in a big stoneware jug to the table, carrying and lifting it onto the table with both hands.

Both are watching me with bright, excited faces as they wolf down their remnants of cake and ham. I pour some of the water into an empty smaller stoneware jug. I guess—hope—they see all this as having fun with new friends. I collect her tightly stitched, clean, white sweater with a big blue daisy adorning one side; Isaac's coat; the big sack of plums, cake and ham; my smaller sack; and the water jug. Hannah carefully cleans up, picks up the sugar cup, and pulls the door securely shut. Off we go up the hill along the same path Harry and Isaac walked an hour ago.

Hannah and Isaac regularly turn around and impatiently wait for me as I trudge up first one hill, then another. I am gradually approaching the top of the second hill, when I hear Hannah talking excitedly. Looking up, Harry is waving, making expansive gestures for me to speed up. Finally, he pumps his fist up-and-down in the classic military "double time" signal. To no avail. I continue my slow, set pace eventually into the little gathering of Hannah, Isaac and Harry.

Hannah giggles, "Jack sir, Harry sir says he wants thee to give him a piece of ham. He also said he was afraid thou would not make it up the hill. He asked Isaac to give thee a push, but Isaac shook his head 'No'!" She giggles on for several more seconds.

I try to talk without gasping, but fail. I raise both hands and give Harry the "time out" "T" gesture. A moment later, "Harry, Hannah, Isaac and I are friends. Friends share everything. So, we will wait to see Walter—that is our other friend, Hannah—so we can share the food equally among friends."

Harry smiles, "Jack—sorry, Jack *sir*, is right. We will share the food with Walter. He's asleep in a clump of tall field grass, just above the boat.

"Did you ever go all night without sleep, Hannah?"

"Just the night Isaac was born."

"Well, I bet you were very tired that night. Your Mommy probably let you take a nap the next day. Last night we didn't have any sleep at all. So, I think we should let Walter continue his nap for a while. Do you agree?"

"Yes, Harry sir. If someone needs to sleep, my Mommy says it is important for that person to sleep."

"OK, then let's let him sleep. We will save his food for him in a safe place."

There are some more nods of agreement from Hannah and Isaac as we descend toward the cove. There we point Hannah and Isaac toward the jolly boat. Harry and I each inhale a large slab of ham and a square of cake four inches on a side. Most of the water in the jug is consumed in moments. Harry takes it up to the small stream for refilling. For a moment I have motionless peace and quiet, sitting on a rock on the water's edge, munching on a plum.

Hannah climbs onto the rock I'm sitting on, dangles her feet in the water next to mine. "Isaac is playing at steering the boat."

"Hannah, Harry and I will need to sleep for a while. You and Isaac can play in the boat and around the cove for a while, but please be a little quiet so we can sleep. Once in a while I want you to come say hello to either Harry or me, whoever is not sleeping. Later we will introduce you to Walter so you can tell him also. Just tell us where you are. After that we can have supper together."

"I will take Isaac to the place he likes to fish for crabs, just over there." She points halfway up the cove on its eastern shore. "Isaac always has string in his pocket. We will tie a piece of ham to the string to catch the crabs."

"Good, that's another good plan." I smile at her. She beams back and jumps up to "fetch" Isaac.

While there is no doubt in my mind, I hope Harry and Walter will agree we have a clear obligation to find a safe place for Hannah and Isaac. Actually, now that I think about it, I remember Harry saying to Hannah we will be sure they are safe. The combination of an apparently brutal occupation by the British and Hessian troops, the imminent arrival of the French fleet, American militia harassment and maneuvering, and jumpy, probably fearful occupiers, all create a particularly menacing predicament for two children on the loose. But, I have to admit for me it's more than simple kindness and duty to children. I've been touched by them. They're not only vulnerable kids. I like them, and they reciprocate. I have a strong sense of being bound to them, and they to me. It seems that Harry feels somewhat similarly, though probably not as strongly.

No doubt there is risk helping them. We'll have to dream up some sort of handoff to a responsible person with enough interest in the kids that they're motivated to help. The only possible solution for now seems to use the Friends' meeting house connection. Unfortunately, that means going into Newport somehow, somewhere. Not an attractive thought. In fact, a damn scary thought.

Will Walter know enough details that we can come up with a workable plan? Will he cooperate and help? My guess it's the same predicament for him as the second trip to the hull. No interference, but an overwhelming fascination with 1778 Newport. Maybe the solution is the same…do it with him or without him. If the latter, we get the kids to safety, pick him up and try to get ourselves home.

Home. I close my eyes to think of my daughters Dottie and Gina, and wife Pearson. I easily visualize where I last saw them, the girls sunning in lounge chairs alongside our small in-ground pool, Pearson busily watering, pruning, cleaning...as usual, high-energy multi-tasking. Can I risk all I have with them, all I owe them, to yet again take a chance for strangers? I don't see any choices. Not to help the kids certainly is just irreducibly wrong. So, helping them is the only right thing to do. But, let's be honest here, it's exciting too. There's the challenge of weighing and accepting the risk, devising a plan, executing its steps. All directed toward winning the outcome. Sure, the purpose is to get Hannah and Isaac to a believably safe place. But, undeniably, it also is successfully responding to a challenge.

Am I getting dangerously close to the professor's observation on the *Endeavour* which upset me so? Am I just being selfish here, once again grabbing for an experience without thinking of the consequences? Enough...no more ruminating! Act...decide and act!

Once again I close my eyes. The poolside image of Pearson and the girls instantly returns. My sense of self is sinking fast. What am I doing here? This whole damn nonsense is wrong. What a mistake! What if I can't get back home? What then?

Come on...*stop it!* We've transitioned before. Surely we can do it again. We'll make it back...right?

I stand up and bend over toward the water, splashing water on my face.

"Why splash thy face, Jack sir?" Hannah, trailed by Isaac, is walking toward me in the shallows, weaving around slabs of slate rock.

"It helps me to stay awake, Hannah."

"Me and Isaac are going to catch crabs. Did thou know, Jack sir, the boat is more than half full of water?"

Bad news! If we can't use the jolly boat we're in trouble...nasty trouble. It's our ticket out of here, to help the kids, to get home. Standing up, I slide off my rock, into the shallows. I see Harry approaching the head of the cove, carrying the water jug. Waving, I wait on the shore. "We've got a problem badly in need of a solution. Come on, we've got to check out *Giggles*. Hannah says she's got a lot of water in her!"

"Shit! Age or too many landings last night and this morning."

We push our way through the thick shrubs to reach the boat. The water is almost up to the thwarts...well over a foot deep.

"Let's turn her over, see if we can see the leak."

At first we can barely lift one side of the boat. She's heavy and water-logged to begin with and the extra water weight is too much to lift, especially since she is in less than two feet of water, so hardly buoyant. She's tilted to one side. We lean in and splash half the water out the low side. Finally, barely, we lift the high starboard side enough to get most of the remaining water to flow out to port. Moments later we twist and turn the boat entirely over onto its gunwales. The stern section is still in the water, the bow resting out of the water on a crushed-down clump of shrubbery.

Harry spots the problem right away. Running his hand along the edge of a lapstreak board next to the boat's chine (the intersection of the boat's bottom and sides) he says, "This seam is wide open; I can see right through it." Still running his hand along the same seam, he adds, "Also here...and here. The caulking for half or more of this seam has failed. Could have been scraping the bottom, or who knows what. But it has failed. How do we fix it?"

We hear a voice from up the slight hill, "Oakum, but that's the easy part." It's the professor. "You guys could wake the dead! That may, in fact, be necessary. What happened?"

"You better come take a look," I yell back.

The professor appears, wrinkled and dirty, hair straying every which way off his head. "Not surprised. I've been worried this would happen all along. Ever since I've known her, she's leaked a little. We've been gone so long that we've asked way more of her than I ever thought she could handle. Let's see."

He slowly runs his hand along the exposed seam, stopping occasionally. "We can caulk all right, but the question will be how to seal the caulking to make it last."

He stands motionless staring at the offending seam. "To be sure we can get back to our time we have to retain its authenticity. We'll use something called "oakum", which is made from old rope. We have plenty of rope onboard. We will have to untwist it, picking it into shreds as much as possible. We will then stuff the shreds into the seam. But, that's not much good without some type of pitch to make the shreds stick together and to seal the caulking."

"Like what?" Harry asks.

"Tar is best. Maybe we could get by with tree sap, but we're way past the season for sap. I have no idea how we'll get tar. We'll just have to pack the seam really tight and hope it holds for a while."

After a moment, I say, "Maybe there's some tar at the kids' house. If you use it to seal things, seems likely there'd be some around."

"What kids?" asks the professor.

I reply, "We met two young kids—a girl named Hannah and a boy named Isaac...."

The professor interrupts, "Oh yes, Harry told me a little before I fell asleep."

"Well, the British apparently took their parents, their herd of sheep, and a slave. Hannah and Isaac gave us some food, showed us around...nice kids. They're playing in the cove now. We have some of their ham and johnnycake for you."

The professor, listening responds, "Thank God, I'm starved. Actually, their farm is likely to at least have some tools to shove the oakum in tight."

"I'll get the kids." I walk to the head of the cove, and around onto the eastern side. Hannah and Isaac are a hundred yards along. I shout to them, "Hannah and Isaac, we need you at the boat. Please come with me." I watch as they look up, turn and run toward me.

"We need your help to fix the leak in the boat. And you can meet our friend Walter."

The professor is sitting on the ground devouring a big slice of ham. He stands up to shake hands. As usual, Hannah looks at him unflinching, while Isaac steps back behind her. The professor bends over and extends his hand to Hannah. "Hello there, my name is Walter. What's your name?"

Hannah shakes hands, introduces Isaac, then herself, saying, "Pleased to meet thee, Walter sir."

Glancing up at me with a smile, the professor replies "Well, thank you, Hannah. I'm pleased to meet you and Isaac." Touching the upside down boat, he crouches down. "Hannah, this boat is very important to Jack, Harry and me. But, see here, there is a big hole in the seam, so water comes into the boat. Boats with holes in them like this don't work very well, do they?"

"No sir."

"So, we need to put oakum in the hole, and put tar on the oakum. Do you have a boat? Have you ever seen your father do that?"

"Yes, my father has a boat for fishing. Me and Isaac used to go fishing in it with Father. I caught a flounder once. Isaac just catches crabs."

"That's very good. And Isaac, crabs are good to eat, aren't they."

Isaac slides further behind Hannah.

The professor, still crouching, kneels down. "For us to be able to fix the holes, we will need some tools and some tar, and help untwisting and shredding rope. Does your house have some tools we could use for a little while, like knives and maybe a chisel or something else with a flat point to push oakum into the hole? Do you know if there is some tar at the house?"

"Father has a whole drawer full of tools in the shed. When Father was with us, Isaac followed him around all day. He can show thee the tools. Maybe he knows about the tar. Isaac, take Walter sir home to look for tools for the boat."

Isaac, still partially behind Hannah, shakes his head. He points to Harry.

Harry laughs, "My new little buddy Isaac! I'll go with him. I gather you need a tool with a small, blunt end, to push the shreds of rope into the hole, and most of all, something to seal it with. If not tar, maybe grease would do for a while, must have grease around."

The professor agrees, "Tar is far superior, but thick grease might do as a substitute. Don't forget a couple knives. We can use them to cut and shred the rope."

Isaac is already tugging at Harry's left hand. They trot off up the first grassy incline toward the family home.

I lean down to Hannah. "If I give you a piece of rope, will you untwist it into separate little strands for us?"

"Yes sir."

The professor walks around to the bow; with some grumbling about an "impossible damn knot" unties the painter. Handing it to Hannah, he shows her how to untwist the main strands, next to pull apart each main strand, leaving the rope reduced to small filaments. The painter is about twenty-five feet long so awkward work for her small hands. But with lips pursed and a look of intense concentration she slowly starts to untwist the line.

I pick up the stoneware water jug and hand it to the professor. We walk a few yards away and sit down.

"So, Jack, fill me in. I don't think I've been asleep for long but things are happening. Harry told me about the kids, but you've spent more time with them and been to their house. Tell me about it."

I recount details of the house, what I've learned of the family and its trials from Hannah, and describe the farm area. "What do you make of them, Walter? Are they squatters who took over from some fancy landowner somehow?

Maybe they are farm hands working the land for the owner? One thing, they're not getting any favorable treatment from the British. Not only was the mother taken away, but I gather so was the father quite a while ago. He might have been impressed into the British Navy. Hannah says he was taken in a boat."

The professor takes another gulp of water. "It does seem likely. The British impressed locals all over the world. They never had enough shipboard complements. As far as the family and their homestead, the key fact seems to be its location. I'm pretty sure it must sit on the large estate owned by a guy named Jahleel Brenton. He was a prominent man just before the war. In fact he later ended up an admiral in Scotland of all places. The Brentons were a major Loyalist family. In the run-up to the Revolution, the rebellious factions in Newport and elsewhere really went after the Loyalists, especially in response to the Stamp Act. Remember I told you about the British Navy Captain Wallace and how he terrified the locals? He was acting to repress the anti-British population. These rebels-against-the-crown—later they are in fact 'rebels', but then they were called 'Whigs', after the name of their political party—attacked Loyalist and British properties and ships, especially in 1775.

"Brenton was run off his estate. He fled to Boston where he was branded a traitor to the colonies and his properties sold at auction. He made it to England and managed to come back in command of a British warship against the rebels. Years later, in 1799, Brenton commanded a small, three-vessel British convoy off Gibraltar in a famous, heroic action. His convoy was attacked by a French privateer, ten Spanish gunboats and two schooners. His schooner, the *Speedy*, successfully fought off the attackers and brought the convoy into Gibraltar. The *Speedy* was badly shot up but survived. Brenton later left the sea and became Captain of the Naval Post in Edinburgh, Scotland until he retired.

"Back to Newport in 1775. I think a mob seized all his sheep and cattle. Since his property was sold at auction, there must have been some form of Whig ownership of his estates. So the kids' parents might have been involved there. But, it seems unlikely. Why are they still on the land? After all, the British have been here since 1776.

"I'd guess they worked for Brenton. They may have received some sort of nominal rental deal from the Whigs to continue to work the estate for the period right after the auction. Since they probably didn't have a house of their own under Brenton, they may have built the one you saw after they were able to rent the land. Once the British occupied Newport in 1776, they probably made them stay on providing sheep, crops, maybe some cattle to the garrison.

"The big landowners and merchants all had numerous indentured servants brought over in virtual servitude to work off their service—seven years was a light sentence—for their eventual freedom. I'd guess they were indentured. The British Army would have re-instated their indentured servant status when they took over Newport and made them work for the garrison.

"As far as the mother and the sheep being taken away, we have accounts of that. The British are pulling everybody into Newport as the French fleet approaches. They are turning the town into a fortress. Remember the crews off the ships to be scuttled supposedly were all around the waterfront, though we didn't see them? I assume the mother and all were herded into town.

"There's one more fascinating element to all this. You know what Brenton's estate is called today...today being our today not this today?"

"What?"

"Hammersmith Farm...Jackie Kennedy's little girl playground and where she and Jack were married."

"You're kidding! Hell, let's go back to 1958 instead of 1998. We can meet the rich and famous! No...on second thought, let's go home please, the hell with the rich and famous.

"Walter, walk with me a minute." The professor stands up and follows me toward the cove, away from Hannah slowly untwisting the jolly boat painter. "Do you know where to find a wharf owned by a family named Overing?"

"Sure, it's the southernmost big wharf, not far from what for us is now a park and the famous old Ida Lewis Yacht Club. It's long been known as 'Coddington Wharf'. The Coddingtons were another even more important Loyalist family. I've seen their name on lists of prominent merchants so clearly they were merchants, maybe distillers as well. What's with you and your interest in these Loyalists?" He laughs, "Shall we sing 'God Save the Queen' together?"

"Let's hope we don't learn all the verses soon enough. No, apparently Hannah's family is Quaker. They occasionally go to meetings in a barn at the end of the Overing wharf. She referred to an 'old Mrs. Overing'."

"Fascinating," the professor's interest has clearly perked up, "many of the powerful merchant families were Quakers, including the Coddingtons, maybe the Overings as well, though I don't know for certain. But as they achieved greater wealth, and tensions between the ordinary colonists and the British government got worse, many Newport merchant Quakers converted to become Anglicans, in our time Episcopalians. It seems it was both a prestige thing and making sure they were on the right side. Again, I don't know for a fact about the Overings, but like the Coddingtons they were prominent merchants, likely part of the 'Quaker Grandees'. Seems highly possible that when the family became Anglican, an older member of the family retained her Society of Friends faith or at least support and gave the barn for Quaker meetings. Why are you asking about the Overings and Coddingtons?"

"I'm trying to find a safe place for Hannah and Isaac. Assuming *Giggles* will float, we're going to leave here tonight. But to me there's no way we can just leave them behind to fend for themselves. You know better than I, but its obvious this is a scary time to be that young and on your own. So, before we try to head back to 1998 Newport, we could get them to the sanctuary of the Friends' meeting house."

The professor picks up a stone, with a violent throw tries to skip it across the cove's surface. He's thrown it too hard. It sinks with a big splash. "Damn, you guys and saving people! Is it some sort of hero complex? First you're going to save the poor prisoners, now the poor children! I told you Jack, you are not allowed to interfere! Whatever is going to happen, must be allowed to happen…*get it?*"

"So, once again you throw some cosmic rule against interference at us! I think we can surmise that whatever might happen to Hannah and Isaac is not likely to be good. Yet, your cosmic law insists we ignore our ability and obligation to protect them…ignore the dangers they'll face, ignore doing the *right thing*! What nonsense! My solution is the same as we agreed at the Black Pearl. You stay here. Harry and I take care of the kids and return for you."

"Jack, damn it, you don't have the right to interfere!"

"No, Walter you've got it wrong. We don't have the right *not* to interfere. We're not dealing here with pure, clean logic and ethics. We're dealing with messy, confusing reality. Once again, for me I don't see a choice. I certainly understand I'm not supposed to interfere and I don't want to. However, Hannah and Isaac are real people that I really care for and likely can really help. So the right thing to do is clear…help them. That's it, no other choices."

The professor puts up his hands toward me palm down. "OK, OK, I get it. Let's leave it for now. We were lucky at the hull, the prisoners were gone. Here, the interference is clear and certain. It's a far different problem. But for now though, first things first. We need to concentrate on repairing *Giggles*." He strides back around the cove toward the boat.

Hannah has managed to untwist one major strand from the painter. The professor takes it from her and starts to pull it apart. I take the end of the painter opposite from Hannah and begin to unwind it.

We've accumulated the start of a little shreds pile as Harry and Isaac return. Breathing hard, Harry drops several tools at our feet. "This commuting home is getting tough," he laughs through gasps. "Why is it that little boys must run everywhere?"

The professor bends over to pick up two knives, an awl used for piercing holes in leather or wood, a small pick, a finely sanded, rounded piece of wood, much like the stopper on the sugar jug. "Good work, Harry and Isaac. These are useful. Two of us can work together, from outside and inside. Did you find any tar?"

Harry has stopped gasping. "Yes, an old iron pot of it. Problem is we'd need a fire to heat it up. It's tough as an old street now. That seemed to pose two problems—how to make a fire and should we risk one? I think we're much better off if the British don't think anyone is in this area. If we announce our presence with a fire, they might send someone to look around. So, I brought along a tub of heavy, thick grease Isaac dug out of the shed. Hopefully it will somewhat seal the shreds stuffed in the hole. Several coats probably should do it.

"I'll help you shred. Jack, get some sleep. I'll wake you and change places after a while. Up the hill, there's a good place to sleep away from the noise of the boat repair crew."

I nod to him, grab his arm and quietly say, "Show me the spot if you don't mind."

He glances at me, nods and walks back in the direction he arrived. Catching up I say, "Thanks, just need to chat a minute." I summarize my intent to find a safe place for the kids, and my conversation with the professor.

Harry again goes through his familiar face, scalp and neck rubbing ritual. "Yeah, I agree, the kids come first. It doesn't sound like the wharf with the meeting house is too far. We can probably make it all right tonight. Hannah can steer. Maybe the professor can be left off and picked up at some place close by. Once we've got them to safety, we're not too far from getting home. Let's just get this done and get home. I've got to admit I'm very uneasy about staying around here much longer. We are way off base. We've got to get going before we're tagged off base for good."

Looking more than a little absurd in his ripped, filthy sailor's outfit, I notice Harry is now walking with a definite limp. "I don't think we're going to get a lot of chances to get home, Jack. Got to get the first one right, buddy…first one." Scowling he stares at me turns and limps back toward the cove. I lie down on thick grass.

I wake up sore. My right shoulder aches. I feel exhausted. If I roll over into a more comfortable position, I'm sure I'll fall back to sleep. But directly above my head several birds are shrieking at each other. They're small, look like sparrows. Probably what woke me. I lie on the ground scratching insect bites. Finally I sit up. Surrounded by tall grass I can barely make out the cove. No one in sight. Feeling vaguely alarmed, I stand up and with awkward, stiff steps walk down the slope toward the cove. I reach the shore. Moments later a high-pitched voice comes from the eastern shore. It's Hannah. Scrambling along in the shallows I reach a little indentation in the shore where she and Isaac stand in knee deep water.

Hannah's holding her right hand in her left, sucking on her index finger. She turns as I approach. "Isaac's crab bit me…look, Jack sir."

There's a small red mark on the finger; no skin is broken.

"No damage. Slosh your finger back and forth in the water. That will make it feel better."

"What does 'slosh' mean, Jack sir?" She hesitates, looks down at the water, then back up at me. "Sometimes it is very hard for me and Isaac to understand thee, Jack sir."

"Hannah, Harry, Walter and I come from a faraway part of the colonies. We speak English a little differently from the way you speak it here."

"Do you live on a farm like Mommy, Ezra, Isaac and I do?"

"No, I live in a town, so does Harry. Walter lives near a school where he is a teacher."

"My Mommy is my teacher. She said maybe someday I could go into town to the real school. It is at the meeting house. She let me attend three times this year."

"I hope you can continue on and on."

Isaac is tugging on my left hand. Hannah scowls at him. "He wants you to come see the crab house he built."

Isaac splashes off toward the shore scattering three sandpipers poking their beaks into the patch of sand right at the water's edge. The kids have piled up pieces of slate to a height of four or five inches. As I move closer, I see there are four piles forming four walls, all touching at right angles, higher than the water lapping around them. Isaac is bent over the walls poking a stick down inside the square formed by the piles of slate. Inside are three crabs. One, a blue crab, is considerably larger than the other two.

"Isaac, good for you...three crabs...that's terrific."

"He lies on the rock over there," says Hannah pointing at a large rock that forms a little promontory into the cove. "He drops his line with a piece of ham into the water. When he catches a crab he has to pull the line up very slowly because the crabs usually just drop off. He threw that one at me. It bit me when I picked it up and put it in the crab house."

"Can I go with thee, Jack sir? I don't want to crab anymore."

"Sure you can, Hannah. I'm going to look at the boat."

"I helped make lots of rope shreds, Jack sir. Harry sir and Walter sir were stuffing the bottom of the boat with them."

"Isaac, we'll be back in a little while." I start to walk back toward the head of the cove to turn there turn toward the jolly boat. Within a few strides, Isaac has splashed up alongside Hannah apparently not wanting to be left behind.

A voice from above warns us to "shhhh". Startled, we look up to see the professor a few feet above my height, in the crook of the lone maple tree in the cove. "My watch tower. No sign of any movement anywhere. Please be quiet. Harry's still asleep just above the boat."

"How *is* the boat, Walter?"

"We've caulked her, I think pretty tight. We used two tree branches to lever her up on her side, then braced her. Harry and I pushed shreds into the seam, Harry from the outside, me from the inside. We twisted the shreds against each other. Each shred we lightly dipped in the grease, so its consistency was thicker. A while ago I started coating the seam inside and out with grease. I've done two coats since Harry went to sleep. My guess is as long as we don't step on the inside of the seam, and we don't ground on it, we may be OK. But, we haven't tested her."

Looking at the boat I tell Walter how impressed I am with all he and Harry had finished. I ask him how long Harry had been asleep.

"Harry, probably well over an hour; you've been gone for several hours, I'd say."

"You're kidding! It felt like nothing."

"Jack, I think we need to do some patrolling, just to be certain nobody's around. Maybe the kids would like to climb up in the tree with me, as long as they're quiet. You could then check the shoreline west of here over Castle Hill, and walk back a little along the paths toward the hospital. What do you think?"

"Will do. Hannah, you and Isaac climb up in the tree with Walter. Would you like to have a plum before you climb into the tree?"

"Yes, Jack sir," replies Hannah, but Isaac is already climbing above Walter, high in the old maple tree.

Retrieving the food sack, I hand plums to the other tree dwellers and head off up the western slope toward the water.

Hungrily eating my own plum, I walk up the hill. As I climb, I notice the sun, while still high in the sky, definitely is no longer above me, but now at a slight angle over the western horizon. It must be mid-afternoon or so. Walking steadily I realize while not refreshed, I feel fairly good. The general feeling of achy exhaustion has diminished. The rest, the plum and a little walking have energized me somewhat. I approach the crest of the hill slowly. It is nearly barren, a few low grasses and patches of bare bedrock. Feeling all too exposed, I lie down and crawl the hundred yards or so up and over the crest of the hill. Below me is the familiar shrubbery along the shore. Looking right up the bay, I spot a small boat with several oarsmen leaving the headland just south of the Dumplings. Must be from the British cannon position that so scared us early this morning. Beyond them is the frigate anchored in the same position as last night, between the Dumplings and Rose Island. I turn back to watch the small boat, then immediately look left, down the channel toward Rhode Island Sound. My peripheral vision has picked up something. A schooner—flying the British battle ensign—is swooping along on a fresh southwesterly breeze up into the bay. She's not more than three hundred yards away. She's moving very fast, pushing a big bow wave and trailing white water. Look at the sails on her! She has two very tall masts, with huge fore-and-aft courses on each. The mainmast has a big staysail atop the main course. The foremast has two square-rigged sails—topsail and topgallant—stacked on top of the fore course, with a big fore-and-aft jib attached to the forestay (a strong rope extending from the head of the foremast to the bow). She's an awesome sight, a big, bulging black-bottomed cloud tearing up the bay. I see crewmen clinging to the topmost yardarm. The foot (bottom) of the topgallant sail starts to rise.

Quickly it is apparent what she must have been doing. Far off in the southwestern distance I can make out the outlines of several ships…big ships. They likely are part of the French fleet readying itself to attack Newport. The big schooner must have been out spying on their preparations. Now she's racing back to Newport to report. I can read the name on her transom, "HMS Janna."

There's a lone, scraggily pine tree halfway down the slope toward the shrubbery and the water. I wait a few minutes to let the ship fully pass by. Half crawling and crouching, I scramble down to the tree. Breathless, I wait for a moment then climb ten or fifteen feet up. Clinging to the trunk and several branches I traverse fully around. I can spot no movement at all on the hill and the parts of its slopes I can see. Well up in the bay I spot several boats moving about beyond the frigate. I look southwest toward the French fleet. Staring for several minutes, I can only spot modest movement. From my distance it almost seems like "milling around", though that seems highly unlikely. In any case, I can detect no organized movement in my direction. The fact remains though, the fleet has arrived. The window we hoped was open enough to get Hannah and Isaac to safety and us to the twentieth century now looks to be closing. Harry's right. Our only chance is to get through that window tonight. After tonight, it well could be impossible.

Fifteen minutes later I'm passing the head of the cove. I wave to the tree dwellers, spotting the professor and Hannah, but not Isaac. He's probably too high in the big tree to see. Walking up the gentle incline east of the cove, I recognize a few landmarks, enough to direct me toward the stone wall we've been using as a reference point. Arriving at the wall, I turn to follow the little path just inside the dense underbrush. I follow paths that give me slight cover by the wild shrubbery and occasional scrub pine, but still on the edge of the estate's pasturelands. I've seen the shoreline well up into the bay and south into the Sound. There's no apparent threat to us from the water. Now I need to walk at least toward the army hospital to be certain there's no movement on land threatening to approach the cove. Finally I can see the kids' homestead as I crest the next gentle hillside. Sticking to the now wider path, I pass the house. I watch it for several minutes lying under a blueberry bush above the house. Three pheasant are stalking around a garden, steps away from the house. No other movement at the house; no sound in all that I can see, except for chirping birds, wind in the trees.

Looking past the house, I reluctantly continue to walk toward the hospital. The path turns into heavy scrub brush so that I get only glimpses of the pasture. A nagging worry creeps into my conscious—how easy it would be to get disoriented and lost here. I decide to stay on this one path. It's headed in what I think must be the general direction of the hospital. Better walk slowly, stop regularly to listen, look well ahead. Feeling slightly foolish, I stop and start my way down the path...Jack the scout. While I continue to hear and see nothing out of place, my growing fear and worry is pricked by anything I can't instantly identify. This is useless. There's nothing around. It's time to head back to the cove. No, I've made it this far, go a little farther. The more ground I cover without seeing any threats, the safer we are. Nervously, I stop-and-start my way along the trail for several hundred yards.

What's that? I hear creaking, clanking noises...well distant but clear...horses snorting. They're off to my right. Taking note of a stubby little pine tree, I turn beside it off the trail, heading into a patch of scrub pine, most six to eight feet tall. Moments later I arrive at a small clearing. Across it are more wild shrubs and one droopy old pine tree. Gathering my nerve, I crouch and trot the fifty yards across the clearing. I jump slightly to grab the tree's lowest limb. Dangling from the limb I heave myself up, while twisting my right leg up and over the limb. The inside of both my calf and thigh are scraped and skimmed, the pants torn. Finally, I stand wobbling on the limb. With one high step and grabbing at a nearby small branch, I step up onto the next limb above. Turning toward the sound, I'm looking at the side of a large house. Two four-wheel wagons each pulled by two horses are out front. I realize it's the hospital, from a side view. Two soldiers come out of the house carrying a body on a stretcher. They place it in the first wagon, followed by other soldiers carrying stretchers. Must be patients being taken from the hospital. Likely they are being moved into Fortress Newport. A mounted soldier canters around from the distant side of the house. Shouting something in the direction of the wagons, he turns his mount to gallop down the house's driveway toward the road clearly evident several hundred yards off. More stretchers come out of the house.

OK, it seems clear they're headed for Newport. This retreating group of patients, and attending soldiers, orderlies, doctors, and others appear to be no threat to the cove. I descend from my perch, cross the clearing, walk quickly through the scrub pine, and regain the trail.

Don't be sloppy…keep doing the "scout" walk. Got to know what's going on around me. Cautiously, stopping and starting, I walk back along the trail. Once I reach the little homestead I sit for several minutes, watching and resting. The three pheasant have come out of the little garden and are now marching abreast toward the shelter of the wild shrubs and grasses. High above, a hawk again and again circles the house and adjacent pasture. I start to feel drowsy as I lazily watch this simple pastoral setting. That won't do. I stand up and continue along the now familiar trail toward the stone wall and shortly thereafter the cove.

"See anything, Jack?" The professor is still in his tree, though I don't see the kids.

I recount viewing the French fleet and the fast schooner, the apparent retreat of the hospital patients and staff.

"If our accounts are accurate, the fleet will not run up the bay firing on Newport for several more days. They're waiting on the American militia under General Sullivan to get in place for their attack from the north. But it really doesn't matter. The British now know they're just offshore so they've got to be primed for attack. Our problem is they've got to be ready for attacks from almost anywhere. While they can keep track of the French fleet from the cannon site across the way, and sending out your sloop, I've got to believe they'll patrol out here too. The Sound is only a few hundred yards south of the cove. They get a better view going all the way to the southernmost point, but it's quicker to go right over there to the beach." He's pointing at the ocean visible in the distance. "Plus they'll have to be worried about infiltrators or harassment actions coming ashore on the beach or somewhere on this point. We'll have to watch from now on, at least until dark."

"Where are Hannah and Isaac?"

"With Harry in our sleeping grove. I told them they should go take a nap. They'll be up late tonight. I think Harry's trying to settle them down now."

I start up the hill toward the sleeping area. Harry is walking down toward us. "Don't worry, Jack, they're fine. Isaac is probably already asleep. He made me promise to check on his crab trap! Walk with me. Then I'll relieve Walter-of-the-tree."

He chuckles happily at his new name for the professor. "I heard you briefing him. This place is no longer looking good…now it looks bad. 'Time to boogie.' As soon as it gets fully dark, we're gone."

We walk through the eastern side shallows to Isaac's crab trap. All the crabs are gone. One side of stones is partially down. Probably wave action or tidal current collapsed it and the crabs scurried away.

"Too bad," I say, "Isaac will be disappointed."

"Well, at least the crabs are happy," smiles Harry. "I hope I can be as happy as one of them tonight. Right now I feel as trapped as they must have." He pauses for a moment. "I must admit once again I'm not sure about the professor. He said the wharf you described with the meeting house at its end is easy to find, even in the dark. But he wasn't committing himself to going with us…even for the kids. He takes his interference hang-up it so far it's just stupid. He's a purist who wants to avoid being corrupted by reality. But shit, what about two little kids? It's nonsense to deny helping them. I told him so. He didn't say anything except he didn't want to argue about it anymore."

I answer, "So you and I will go. We can sail until we're near the old fort. Put the sail down so even in the dark we're less obvious. You and I row and Hannah can steer with our checking on her course into the harbor. We drop the professor off somewhere, put the kids on the wharf and head back for the professor then into the bay to set up for going home. I know it won't be that easy, but it's a simple plan at least."

Harry smirks, "Simple…if and until we get challenged…then not so simple."

We splash back toward the tree. The professor is a few yards up the hill. "Shhh, they're asleep."

Harry climbs into the tree to the third limb up, the favorite perch of Walter-of-the-tree.

Speaking quietly, the professor says, "Obviously we've got to get out of here tonight. I've been keeping an eye on the tide. Now it's starting to come back in. So tonight it should be pretty high to help get *Giggles* re-launched."

He continues, "One more thing. I know saying this is almost silly, but I need to. My plan, as I said, was just to take a look at the *Lord Sandwich*. That was all, just to take a look. I certainly never envisioned all this." He smiles slightly. "I mean I know how much you guys love to experience life, but this is a little excessive." He chuckles, but stops quickly when he sees we're not sharing his little laugh. "'Best-laid plans' and all that…. There was no way I could guess the variables that would occur, or the consequences of acting on one or another.

The idea of a passive, distant observation made sense. But there's no way I could anticipate what we saw and how we'd react."

I reply, "Walter, we get all that. All that matters now is we get the kids into a hopefully safe situation and get ourselves home. But please understand, Harry and I will deal with the kids first, with you or not."

Once again the vision of Pearson and the girls looms into my consciousness. "Those are the only two things that matter. Nothing else will be allowed to interfere. I don't know about you guys, but the longer I stay the more desperate I feel about getting home. For me this is no longer a great and wonderful event. It's more like being overwhelmed by a great play. Now I want to leave the theater and go home. But this world is blocking me from going home to my *real* world. I've got to get by it to get back to my life...whatever it takes. But, first a place for the kids."

Harry has climbed down one limb to hear. He lurches to his feet and quickly steps up to the higher limb, then the next. "Horseman.....redcoat...300 yards, maybe more."

I crouch and crawl through the heavy shore growth up the incline toward the sleeping kids. The professor asks Harry, "What direction?"

"Toward the beach, moving fast."

The professor whispers, "Probably got word of that schooner sighting the fleet. The horseman likely was sent to take a look."

Hannah and Isaac are breathing peacefully as I arrive. No sense in waking them, so I return to Harry and the professor.

Harry is saying, "Can't see him. He must be beyond the ridge and down the slight slope to the beach. Better be quiet for now, in case anybody else is around."

A few minutes later we hear galloping hooves of a horse running hard. Harry watches and explains the red-coated horseman is racing in the other direction, toward Newport.

Harry returns to the lower branch. "Probably we're OK now, though we need to keep a lookout for a patrol to check out the French from the beach. I'll keep the watch. Let the kids sleep for a while, and you guys rest. After that we'll eat, then get ready to head out after dark."

Silence for a few minutes. I try to visualize tonight's attempt to take the kids to the meeting house and then to again make the passage home. As the professor taught us, first we have to *see* it happen before we can *make* it happen. Seeing us make the passage to our time is easier than finding a hoped-for sanctuary for the kids. We've made the passage; I can't visualize the dock and meeting house. *Keep trying both…from now until we are done!*

The professor stands up and paces back and forth for a few moments. "I'd like to get back to what I was saying earlier. The idea was not even to be a witness, just a silent and distant spectator. We didn't do that. Once we got close, we couldn't control events and our reaction to them. What had been the greatest experience of my lifetime and I think yours as well, has now been transformed into a real danger. I'm sorry, really sorry for the danger. Yet, still I'm thrilled at the experience."

Harry's back in the lower branch of the watch tree. "Walter, what's up? You need our approval, our thanks? We gave you that. You did what you said, showed us to the greatest experience ever. Although you did say there was no danger. Nevertheless, the danger we did, and likely will, encounter has come from our choices to get closer and closer to what we've seen. That's not your fault. Jack's right now though. All our focus and all our energies have to be devoted only to getting home…after getting the kids to church."

The professor sits down next to me on a knee-high slate outcrop jutting from the eroded soil next to the water. "You know, Jack, you were the guy who really made me think we could do this."

"How…."

"I had already talked to Harry some, and thought he was a good fit for our passage to now. But, days ago I was struck by your real respect for the power of experiences. What clinched it for me was when you said something about all of us being to some degree a product of our experiences. Therefore it is natural and certain that our personalities and even our behavior will necessarily be shaped by them. The unspoken conclusion was we should seek and select experiences because they make active contributions to who we are."

"Right, Walter, I do think that. But don't simplify it. Don't exclude the really important stuff like genes, hereditary traits, parental love and training, physical environment, on and on."

"Sure, sure…obviously. But there's not much choice available there. Selecting, immersing yourself in, learning from an experience is a deliberate choice. You know, thinking like the historian I'm supposed to be, there's an interesting point in here." The professor has that glazed look again. "Here we sit at the dawn of the US. The Declaration has just been written; the Constitution not yet. But the unique propositions of United States are emerging. Think about it. One of them can be framed as the choice of experience. You can frame it as opportunity, but that's more focused on jobs and money to be earned. Unlike the rest of the eighteenth-century world in which everybody's choices are largely proscribed, here you can choose your experience. That's one of the US's unique propositions to the world. Yet, we don't directly or precisely make that connection when we consider our founding values.

"It's kind of an unspoken expectation now…the right to choose our experience. We expect government to insure that. But we don't evaluate governments or elected officials in the context of that specific value. I suppose we do in terms of the elements that enable our right to choose our experience, but not the value itself."

Harry breaks in. "I agree. My problem is we expect that, but we don't do much to earn it. We pay some taxes…not everybody that's for sure…and that's about it. Hell, half of us don't even vote. What gets me is we have all these expectations, but deliver little or nothing in return for them. Nobody is linked to the notion of 'quid pro quo'. Nobody gives back anything to Uncle Sam. Some give to their community, but not to the US itself. I served in the Marines back during 'Nam. No big deal, I admit, and I'd have been drafted if I didn't enlist. But at least I served. You serve, Jack?"

"Yeah, I was Army ROTC at BU in the early '60s. Then I got lucky, no 'Nam, two years in low-level NATO staff jobs in Italy and some temporary duty in Turkey."

"Point is you served. You and I are in the minority of that time, believe me. I always can rile up the young guys in the department by zapping them that everybody loves to chant 'USA, USA, USA' during the Olympics, loves to show the flag, wear red, white and blue on the Fourth of July, other show-off crap like that, but serve…nah, no thanks.

"At least cops are different. Some did serve, more probably than other organizations. I tell the guys in my division I think everybody should serve the country at least somehow, some time in their life. Drives them nuts when I say it might give them some real appreciation, something more than cheers, slogans and flags."

The professor picks up Harry's point. "In my post-grad seminar on 'Life in Colonial Rhode Island' our discussion sidetracked one day last spring onto your point of national service. I tried to get the class to see that there is a link between our common ground as Americans, and the obvious value of proactively acting to enhance the common good. Not only would well-planned service do that, maybe more importantly it would give us common linkages. I tried to get buy-in from them that national service could well be a 'feel good' thing. I was getting nowhere, because they all saw it as a waste of their time. They couldn't see any personal gain. They'd fall behind in the competitive world they can't wait to enter, but are afraid of. I told them OK we'll take away the 'fall-behind' issue, and hypothetically make everybody serve for, say, eighteen months sometime between high school graduation and age thirty. I got some grudging 'well maybes' but nothing else. Would be a hell of a selling job, but it's the right thing. It's the one way to start bringing some focus to our sense of national community, to all together honor an obligation to serve the common good, and…to get back to where we started…have a common experience."

"Jack, we better kick over the professor's soap box before he marches on British Army headquarters demanding the right to serve the common good."

"Ah, thank God, we don't have to. Here comes Hannah to set us straight."

Hannah, rubbing her eyes and stumbling, arrives to sit next to me on my slate rock pile. "Jack sir, Isaac is hungry, me too. Are we to stay here all night?"

"I'm hungry too, Jack sir," chortles Harry. "Can we eat now…please?"

"Be careful, or you won't be given a plum for dessert."

"Sorry, Jack sir." Harry stands up. "The food sack and water jug are in the boat. I'll continue in the watch tree if someone will bring my food…including my plum. Hannah, can Isaac join me?"

"Yes, I am sure Isaac would like to join thee, Harry sir."

We wolf down some more johnnycake, most of the remaining plums and would have wiped out the ham slices except for Harry's insistent reminder we were to save some food reserves for the kids. Hannah and I walked back twice to the little stream to refill the stoneware water jug. On the last return trip to the cove we sat for a while and watched the setting sun and low-lying, fair-weather clouds turn the western sky a wispy pink.

"Hannah, we will take you and Isaac to the Friends' meeting house after it gets fully dark tonight. You will be safe. We will take you right into the meeting house. I am sure someone will be able to tell your mother that you and Isaac are there. Even if it takes a little while for her to come to the meeting house, you have friends there."

"I like Missus Carr, she sits with the girls and talks to us. I have met old Missus Overing and Missus Myrtis too."

"Good. When we get to the cove, please put on your pretty sweater and tell Isaac to put on his jacket. It will be much colder when the sun sets. We will sail the boat to the wharf in front of the meeting house."

We arrive at the watch tree, to find the professor back in his perch, Harry playing a stick game with Isaac. After a minute, I realize Harry has taught Isaac to play "pick-up-sticks". It's all Harry can do to keep the long-silent Isaac to stop shrieking with laughter and excitement. Hannah steps in and takes a very reluctant and unhappy Isaac away up the hill, telling him they need to pray for Mommy, Father and Ezra.

Silence again. The western sky has lost its pink hue, as dusk takes over. Quietly I say to Harry and the professor, "If it weren't for the strange world that lies all around us, I'd say we were on a little camping trip together. That reminds me of a little story. Did you know that the famous old detective Sherlock Holmes and his faithful Dr. Watson often went camping together?

"After a good meal and a fine bottle of wine they lay down in their tent for the night to sleep. Several hours later, Holmes awoke and nudged his faithful friend. 'Watson, look up and tell me what you see.'

"Watson sleepily replied, 'I see millions and millions of stars.'

"Holmes asked, 'What does that tell you?'

"Watson pondered for a minute. 'Astronomically, it tells me that there are millions of galaxies and potentially billions of planets. Astrologically, I observe Saturn is in Leo. Logically, I deduce that the time is approximately a quarter past three. Theologically, I can see that God is all-powerful and that we are small and insignificant. Meteorologically, I suspect that we will have a beautiful day tomorrow.'

"'Is that all?' Holmes asked.

"'Yes,' Watson replied. 'Why, am I missing something?'

"Holmes was quiet for a moment, then spoke: 'Watson, you blithering simpleton, someone has stolen the goddamn tent!'"

The professor chuckles lightly, "Is there a message there?"

"No message. Well maybe a little one, slightly relevant…something about paying attention."

Harry shifts his position in the tree. "Jack and his jokes. Got another one? I could use a good laugh."

"Here's one that will help us connect back to 1998. Several men are in the locker room of a golf club. A cell phone on a bench rings. A man engages the hands-free speaker function and begins to talk. Everyone else in the room stops to listen.

MAN: "Hello."

WOMAN: "Honey, it's me. Are you at the club?"

MAN: "Yes."

WOMAN: "I'm at the mall now and found this beautiful leather coat. It's only $1,000. Is it OK if I buy it?"

MAN: "Sure…go ahead if you like it."

WOMAN: "I also stopped by the Mercedes dealership and saw the new 1999 models. I saw one I really liked."

MAN: "How much?"

WOMAN: "$60,000"

MAN: "OK, but for that price I want all the options."

WOMAN: "Great! Oh, one more thing…the house we wanted last year is back on the market. They're asking $950,000."

MAN: "Well, then go ahead and give them an offer, but not full price, offer $900,000."

WOMAN: "Wow! Glad I called! I love you!"

MAN: "I love you too."

"The man hangs up. The other men in the locker room are staring at him in astonishment.

"Then he asks, 'Anybody know who this phone belongs to?'"

Harry throws his head back and laughs loudly. "That'll work."

The professor has been tearing up stalks of sea grass during the jokes. "Before we run out of daylight, help me make a path of sea grass for *Giggles*. We can slide her along it into water deep enough for her to float."

For a half hour, we pull up sea grass as well as remove some shrubs to clear a path. Finally, the path several inches thick with grass, we slowly push the boat along it toward the cove. The bow is in inches of water. Heaving and straining we lift the stern off the grass path and into the shallows. We tilt the boat away from the damaged seam as we push and twist it along a slight trench we've dug in the shallows with tree branches. Moments later the boat is floating freely.

Fearfully we lean over the gunwales to check on the leak. Almost immediately water is seeping into the long patch of stuffed and greased rope. After a few minutes it seems to slow, even stop. There's not more than an inch or two of water in the bottom.

The professor slaps the boat. "*Giggles*, you're back in business, girl! Keep your act together now!"

It's dark. A half moon behind scattered clouds affords some light, other clouds obscure much of the dark sky. Harry and the professor busy themselves with stepping the little mast and raising the sail.

I realize we haven't decided what to do about the professor's non-interference insistence. I put my hand on his left shoulder. "Are you with us about the kids or not?"

"I have to be consistent. I'll only help you get to the Friends' meeting house."

Harry tosses the halyard he's coiling onto the ground. "Walter, that's crap! You can't go there then choose, on the spot, what you will or won't do! Suppose we're challenged, or there's a fight, or for some reason we have to get the hell out of there, or the kids are grabbed, or whatever might goddamn happen? I can't have you in the middle of things and not know what you'll do. Certainly you believe this nonsense, but now it's a luxury we can't afford. I refuse to put myself, Jack or the kids at any more risk than we're gonna be in already. We'll drop you somewhere and come back for you. That's a promise, but you're not coming with us to drop off the kids...no way."

The professor is surprisingly calm. "OK. You can drop me close by. It's a place we probably should go first. On the eighteenth-century charts I've seen there's a marshy area with a little river running through it not far from the Overing wharf. It's roughly where today there's a small park. The marsh and grasses along the little river should hide us a little while we look over the wharf and the water around it, sort of a recon site. After we see there's an opportunity to head for the wharf, I'll stay there while you take the kids. The wharf should be only a few hundred yards away."

"Fair enough," growls Harry.

They resume rigging the boat. Where are Hannah and Isaac? I haven't heard them for a while. I assumed they are in the sleeping grove just above where the boat had been pushed into the bushes. They're not there. Softly I call their names. Nothing. I walk around the head of the cove toward the spot Isaac caught his crabs. Several times I call their names. Nothing. What happened? Where are they? Anxiety flooding in on me, I start up the incline toward the stone wall.

"Jack sir," barely audible.

"Where are you, Hannah?"

"Here we are."

They're sitting on the ground, with their jackets on. At first they're hard to see, just behind what I remember is a large wild beach plum bush. Isaac has his head down, looking sad or scared, I can't tell. I can tell in the dim moonlight that he's been crying. Tears streak his dirty face.

"What's wrong Isaac?"

He turns away from me.

Hannah is scowling at Isaac. "He is afraid. He wants to go home. Isaac is afraid of the dark and he is afraid of going in the boat in the dark. Mommy told me it is because he fell in the water one night with Father."

I sit down next to him. "Isaac, we are taking you to a place where soon you will be able to be with your Mommy. We will go by boat, but you will be safe. We are your friends and we will keep you safe. I tell you what…you can sit on Harry's lap in the boat. Would you like that?"

He looks up, slowly standing. Not a word, but he accepts my offered hand. He slowly trudges back toward the cove.

The jolly boat is floating, sail slightly flapping in the light breeze that finds its way into the cove.

Approaching the boat after first nodding to Harry, I quietly say, "Isaac wants to sit on Harry's lap. Harry can take the tiller. Walter, you and I row us out into the bay. Hannah can sit on the foredeck."

The professor adds, "Once we clear Brenton's Point let's sail toward Goat Island, then change course toward the wharf and nearby marsh. That way hopefully we'll look like just another boat going back and forth between town and Goat Island. I think that's safer than going all the way along the shore. Also, if the wind holds like it seems now, we can sail most of the way."

I lift Hannah into the bow. Harry puts Isaac in the stern, next climbs in after him. The professor lifts one leg onto the port gunwale, next awkwardly rolls himself into the boat. I follow with little more grace, being careful not to step near the leaky seam which runs along the bottom on my starboard side. Settled, we set off along the cove. A dozen or so pulls on the oars and the wind picks up the sail. The little jolly boat picks up speed. The professor and I ship oars.

We're under way, sailing back into British-occupied Newport. No one speaks. Hannah sits cross-legged on the deck facing forward. The professor and I are half-turned around on the middle thwart. He's looking to starboard, me to port. Harry keeps looking at the sail, occasionally makes small corrections with the tiller, feeling the wind. He is gesturing quietly to Isaac. I watch him put Isaac's hands on the tiller. Isaac stares at his hands until Harry points at the sail. Then he stares at the sail.

More and more lights are clearly visible as we sail steadily along the coast—a flickering light to our left across the entrance to the bay likely is the British cannon site; the cluster of several lights up the bay a short way must be the British frigate still on station. The more distant lights of the town come into view as we angle slightly away from the shore toward Goat Island. None of the lights are bright, more like little yellow dots in the general darkness.

I'm surprised. I'm anxious, but not fearful. In one thought I concede many things could go badly for us, preventing sanctuary for the kids, or passage home for Harry, Walter and me. The next thought is yet another glimpse of Pearson and the girls. I try to visualize a pier and barn for the kids. Mostly though, it seems I just want to engage, get this adventure underway.

We're now a few hundred yards west of Goat Island. Happily, for now clouds obscure the moonlight. Harry whispers, "Changing course for shore. Professor, give me a landmark."

We've been running before the wind, the sail on the port side. Harry slowly hauls on the main sheet to change our course slightly closer to the wind and aimed at the shore.

The professor has turned all the way around on the thwart, facing forward. "See the last light just off our port bow? Apparently that is the last pier, probably Coddington's, sorry, Overing's. Use that as a reference and point the bow twenty or so degrees to the starboard. I should spot the river and marsh as we get closer. Hannah, please keep looking at that last light. Tell us if you think it is on the Overing pier. Have you ever come to the meeting house by boat?"

"No, Walter sir. I have been on the pier though. We watch the older boys fish there in the summer."

The little jolly boat slows. As we approach the shore—still at least a quarter mile distant—the rolling hills of the Brenton estates partially block the wind.

Silence again. Finally, the professor points forward. "There's the river. It's small, more like a stream. Harry, I'm going to release the halyard, drop the sail. We'll be less obvious rowing the rest of the way. Once I un-step the mast, Jack wrap the halyard around the mast and sail."

Staring forward, I can see the vague outlines of a little stream, high grasses, and what appear to be mud banks on either side.

The professor is under the little bow deck, Hannah peering down at him. He whispers, "Jack, pull the mast. I'm pulling the stepping pin out."

I lift the mast and lay it on three thwarts, folding the sail on top of it. Next I coil the halyard around the collapsed sail and mast. As I finish, the professor returns to his seat on the middle thwart. I join him and together we pull each oar through the water. Harry steers with Isaac still sitting on his lap. Now the marsh and river are plain to see. The nearest light is the one well to our left that we've been using as a reference. Two indistinct lights are far behind and slightly above the marsh we've just reached. They appear to be exceptions to a clear pattern. The marsh is the southern end of the town. All the lights except those two are to the left (north) of our reference light. While Hannah hasn't said anything, it is apparent that light is on the end of a long pier. Other lights are now visible on the shore side of the pier. From that point to the left numerous lights appear both on piers and adjacent buildings, as well as buildings well behind them. All of the lights flicker, some appear to sputter. There is one actively traveled road just behind the piers. Horses, wagons, carts travel back and forth; groups of red- and blue-coated soldiers can be seen moving in both directions along the road. Now and then a horseman or horse-drawn carriage canters down the road scattering all before it.

We turn the jolly boat to face out. The professor grabs a clump of sea grass and pulls us next to a low, muddy embankment. Pointing to the right, "Jack and Harry, look over there. Fifty yards away is a steep embankment, so it must be dry or at least drier than this marsh. I'll wait for you there, but meet you right here.

"I have no doubt the pier light we've been looking at is on Overing's wharf. Can't logically be anything else. Hannah, can you tell if it is the wharf with your meeting house at the end?"

"I do not know, Walter sir. I think I can see the meeting house, but it is all so strange from here."

"Please keep looking. It is very, very important to find your meeting house."

Partially hidden by the marsh grasses and river embankment from the nearby wharf and remainder of the town, we concentrate on the water immediate nearby. From my port seat I look along the shore and out toward Goat Island. The professor studies the wharf and north toward town. Harry scans back and forth looking at the dark waters directly in front of us. We can see and occasionally hear small boats going to and from Goat Island, especially using a small pier at its southernmost end. Several boats are evident around the wharves near center of the town. The closest is a large boat with six rowers on a side and a gaff-rigged sail. She emerges out of the shadows of a wharf about a quarter mile away, headed away from us toward Long Wharf in the distance. Finally, I break our watchful silence. "Pretty quiet...let's go."

The professor carefully steps out of the boat, and first balancing himself and testing the embankment on his hands and knees, finally stands looking down at us. "I'll see you here hopefully very soon. One suggestion—if anybody challenges you, try to speak in full words; don't use contractions like...well, 'don't'. Instead use 'do not'. Explain that you are Canadians, off a wood transport ship out of Halifax. The British in Newport always needed wood. That story might buy you some time or just be accepted. It's likely most listeners wouldn't know how a Canadian might sound different to them. Your ship is stuck here because of the French fleet in the Sound. You were sent to find more wood, and are bringing in children you found along the way."

Harry reaches out to shake the professor's hand. "Not bad, that might work. See you soon. Be sure to be here in no more than half hour. Keep an eye on us from shore."

Harry turns to Hannah. "Please come back here and sit next to Isaac. Jack, you and I will row, steer by adjusting our rowing. It looks like only a few hundred yards to that pier light."

I glance at Hannah and Isaac sitting together on the stern thwart. Holding hands, they stare at me with wide, frightened eyes. I give them a big smile, but get none in return.

We stroke for the pier.

NINE

We stroke slowly along, regularly glancing over our shoulders to be sure our course is aligned with the pier light. Suddenly I'm struck by something I don't know.

"Hannah and Isaac, we don't know your family name. Would you tell me your full names?"

She looks down a moment than up at me. "My name is Hannah Eliza Ellis. Isaac is just named Isaac Ellis."

Breathing harder with each stroke, I smile at her. "That is a pretty name, Hannah. And Isaac is a good strong name. My name is Jack Ashburn, and he's Harry Cassis."

Harry gives them a grand low bow without slowing his stroke. They both show the hint of a smile at Harry's theatrical gesture.

We're now a hundred yards off the pier. The light is a small torch lashed to a piling at the end of the pier. Well up the pier are two similar lights, one next to a small shed; the other, behind it, lights a little courtyard in front of a large, square building. It looks like a storage building or maybe a barn.

Hannah exclaims, "Jack sir, there is the meeting house! The little building next to it is where the older children go for lessons." Isaac nods his head rapidly.

Harry murmurs, "Yes! OK, let's just float here for a moment and take a look."

A woman in flowing skirts walks in front of the courtyard light, then another. We hear several female voices talking. Too far away to make out what they're saying. No sign of guards. From the meeting house, female voices again; a light in the meeting house barn goes out.

"Jack, let's row quickly right to the side of the pier away from the torch. As soon as we get there, you climb on the pier. I'll lift the kids up to you. Walk directly to the meeting house. Hold their hands, but move fast. I'd guess its fifty yards to the courtyard. Walk the kids into the doorway there and walk right back here. I'm going to tuck the boat as far under the pier as I can. Got it?"

My throat too dry to talk, I nod.

"Ready...row!"

I just dig in and row. Harry, stronger, steers the boat by constantly turning to look at the pier, then adjusting his stroke to direct us in.

Thud...what's that? We're at the pier.

"Grab that piling, pull us along to the next. Pull yourself up."

I reach up to the pier surface, about head high. I heave myself up chest high, I feel a powerful push on my butt, grab the piling with my right hand and wrench my body around, just getting my hips onto the pier. I scramble up, crouch, look fleetingly around and turn toward the boat. Harry has Hannah lifted up slightly above pier level, his arms fully extended. I take Hannah from him, turn and sit her on the edge of the pier. I tussle her hair and try to smile. She looks up at me then down as Harry lifts Isaac to me. I sit him next to Hannah.

Facing them, I put one hand on Hannah's shoulder, the other similarly on Isaac. "We're here. Each of you hold my hand. We will walk to the meeting house."

They're both shaking, Hannah closer to a shiver, Isaac far more violent. Hesitatingly they stand up. Hannah takes Isaac's hand, reaches out for mine with her other hand. OK, that seems to work. Isaac shuffles down the pier, Hannah and I slightly behind, all hand-in-hand. Another light comes into view on the courtyard side of the little shed. A stooped, heavy-set woman with a large white apron over her black dress is framed in the doorway of the meeting house. She's facing away from us toward the shed light. Without thinking, I head the three of us toward her. She turns as we approach, studying us.

"Hannah Eliza Ellis and Isaac, is that thee, children?" She rushes up, grabbing both to her waist in a fierce hug. "The Lord be praised! Where have thee been, children? We were sore afraid!"

"Hello Missus Myrtis. Can we see Mommy now?" Hannah has pulled away looking up at her.

"We will get word to her right now." She hugs the kids again then looks me up and down. Unshaven, barefoot, my sailor's clothes are torn, stained, and filthy. What will she do? Should I run for the jolly boat?

"What is thy name, sir?"

"Jack Ashburn, ma'am."

A long pause. "Thank thee, Jack Ashburn…thank thee."

Blinking, choking back unexpected tears, I turn to Hannah and Isaac. I grab their hands in mine. "Go find your Mommy. Give her the biggest hug you have ever given her. Everything will be all right then,…everything." I give each a kiss on the head and turn to force myself to turn and head back down the pier toward Harry and the jolly boat.

Someone's walking fast toward me. Frozen, I stare at the figure. It's Harry, his shoulder-rocking gait and slight limp unmistakable. Scowling, "The professor…I saw him walking along the shore and up the rocky embankment right over there." Pointing, he continues, "He's headed toward town."

Stopping, he seems to see Missus Myrtis and the kids for the first time. "Kids OK?"

"Yeah, they're fine. This is Missus Myrtis. Ma'am, this is Harry Cassis."

Harry nods his head, "Will Hannah and Isaac be safe here, ma'am?"

"Certainly," she smiles.

"I'm sorry, ma'am," Harry nods again. "Since you will be able to take care of the children, Jack and I must attend to our friend who is headed for trouble." He bends down to Hannah and kisses her on the cheek as she cringes a little, but smiles shyly up at Harry. He squats in front of Isaac, "Goodbye, my little friend. You are going to be a good sailor, and you are the fastest johnnycake eater I know." He grabs Isaac by the shoulders and shakes him gently, messes his hair and pats him on the back. Isaac stares at Harry, then wraps his arms around Missus Myrtis' skirt, still looking at Harry, blinking furiously.

"Ma'am, it's late. If you could take Hannah and Isaac into the meeting house, we will be very grateful."

"Yes," Missus Myrtis replies, "but it is we who are very grateful." Gently pushing and guiding, she manages to get the children to walk backward into the meeting house, as all the while they look back at Harry and me.

"You OK?"

"Yeah," I reply, "little shook up, but OK."

"The goddamn professor must be certifiable. Probably up on that street by now. I'm sure as hell tempted to leave him. Right…I know, I know. He can't be far. I'll walk behind a few houses toward town. Then back in the shadows along the street to the meeting house. You check the street right in front here. Let's go."

Harry ducks behind the little shed, crosses an alley between the shed and another tumbled down building, and disappears in the dark. I walk around the meeting house on the dark side. It takes a moment to be able to see much as my eyes adjust from the dim light of the courtyard to the nearly complete dark on the side of the meeting house barn. No radiant lighting here, just the dark of a barely moonlit night or the dim, shadowy light of a simple torch. Stumbling occasionally over who-knows-what, I emerge on the dark street. A street lamp casts some light well up ahead. A figure holding a square lantern crosses the street to my right. Up the street a figure hurries in my direction. He's backlit by the street lamp. It's Harry. He points repeatedly at a low, seated figure, leaning against the windowless building next to the meeting house.

I reach the figure steps ahead of Harry. The professor turns to me with a pleading look. "I'm staying. I can't leave now. This is more than I ever dreamed of."

Harry arrives red-faced, about to explode. I put my hand up to him, gesturing with my index finger for a minute. Harry spits, steps back two paces.

In a kind of stream of consciousness burst, I blurt out to the professor, "Walter, you're risking everything, literally everything, for a form of fantasy. At most it's just a glimpse into another world. It's only a moment. It means little in your reality. It's closer to a thrill than a meaningful event. You lecture us about being driven by our need for experiences. We need new thrills and excitement, action. But you're the one who's now going over the top. What's got to happen now for us and if truth be told, for you, is to *honestly* grasp reality. What matters for me is Pearson and the kids, our friends, my work, figuring out how the hell to retire, our next trip, all that kind of stuff. Harry understands his realities— Alice, his boat *Cop Out*, I don't know, probably most of all doing what a cop does. What must realistically matter for you? Teaching, learning, researching, stuff like that? Not this! You're risking everything for a moment!

"As Harry said yesterday, it's goddamn time to go right now! We're done, not another minute."

The professor looks back at the street. Not far away is a squad of red-coated soldiers, muskets on their shoulders, marching along the street toward a nearby building. "Jack, no…this is…."

I grab him on his bicep as hard as I can. "No, not another word...we're leaving." I feel him sag just a bit.

Harry shakes his head at me. "My job...let's go Walter. We started this together, we go home together."

Harry stands the professor up and guides him into the alley between the building on whose stoop he's been sitting and the meeting house barn. I follow, looking back to see if we've attracted attention. As we pass the barn, I clearly hear Hannah, "Jack sir...Jack sir."

A woman's voice says, "Thou are safe now, Jack will be soon." I hurry down the dock.

At first my heart nearly stops. I don't see the jolly boat. But Harry wordlessly passes the professor to me and climbs down a seaweed-covered ladder to which the boat is now tied. He nudges it into view. The professor climbs down and I follow.

"Professor, this has been your show. Jack and I know you will finish it right."

The professor nods slowly. "OK Harry, I will...I will." With one glance back he settles onto the stern thwart. He shakes his head back and forth several times. Tears roll down his face. I take the port rowing position, Harry the starboard. "Ready...row."

Facing aft, I watch the pier slowly diminish as we stroke away.

I repeatedly replay Missus Myrtis' simple thank you in my memory. Each time it triggers an emotional response. Again and again I become slightly choked up and teary. What is this all about? Eventually I decide it has a combination of causes—affection for Hannah and Isaac, the loss of never seeing them again, the intense stress and anxiety of the moment, and the realization that I just did a good thing. That last cause soon overrides the others in my replay. Its hypnotic power to trigger emotions over and again soon is mesmerizing.

Finally I disconnect from my repetitions as someone grabs my right arm. "Damn, Jack, pay attention!" Harry laughs a little. "Where the hell are you? Stop rowing, we're going to step the mast and sail. Take the tiller."

"Harry, we did a good thing then."

He stares at me. "Yeah, we did a good thing."

Shortly the mast is up, the sail is fluttering its way to the top in a light breeze coming over the Brenton estates. The professor has scrambled forward. He pulls slowly on the halyard, as Harry pushes the sail's attachment hoops up the mast. The professor ties off the halyard to the little cleat on the foredeck. I fall the jolly boat off the wind for a moment to pick up momentum. Gradually, I pull the main sheet back in to get closer to the wind. I steer our course to split the middle between Brenton's Point and the southern end of Goat Island. I head up at a closer angle to the wind knowing that *Giggles'* lack of a keel makes her side slip badly when sailing close to the wind. By sailing this course, I hopefully will get well clear of Goat Island. Once we are roughly south of Rose Island, I'll fall the boat off and be able to run before the wind toward the southeastern corner of Rose. That would put us close to the twentieth-century site of the green gong buoy we struggled to find last night. Last night? It seems unimaginably longer ago than one night.

I announce, "I'm headed eventually for roughly where the gong buoy will be off Rose Island. Anything closer to Goat Island is too risky. Agree?"

Harry nods, as the professor says, "We still have to set up as best we can and prepare ourselves to make the passage back. We can't do that while sailing, so we'll first have to take the mast and sail down again. For now we should just start reacquiring the memories we will use to help reconnect to the twentieth century. Stay alert, but get the memories to the surface of your conscious."

That's not hard—the family pool scene, my clothes on the Luhrs, the Luhrs itself, the restaurant, the yacht restoration school...for some reason New England style baked beans crowd their way into my thoughts. I can feel myself already drifting home...stop! Not now, not now.

Harry has been looking to all points since we left the pier. "I'm surprised there's not more boat traffic. Maybe it's late, maybe they're concentrating on just guarding Newport. Whatever...I haven't seen much activity."

I add, "We're heading away from Newport, so we're not likely to attract much attention."

"Probably true," agrees Harry.

Several minutes later, the professor says "We've cleared the Fort Adams point. You can fall off for Rose Island."

In moderate wind, to "fall" a boat off the wind takes only moments to reach a new course headed farther away from the direction of the wind. Now, as typically happens in the late evening, the wind has diminished so much it takes nearly a minute for me to settle the boat on a course running before the wind. I can't yet see Rose Island, though Harry claims to see a vague outline of land just off the port bow. Slowly, and silently, we sail on.

Minutes go by. Abruptly the light improves noticeably. The partial moon has emerged from behind a large cloud, whose edges are now illuminated by the moonlight. Other clouds are visible all around. It's too light. The British troops on Goat Island, even on Rose must be able to see us. It almost feels like we're in a spotlight; I feel so conspicuous. Now the outline of Rose Island is clearly visible. Beyond it are a few pinpricks of light. Most likely they're from the frigates at anchor, maybe even the transports to be scuttled, if they haven't already gone to the bottom.

I whisper, "Let's put the sail back down. We're too easy to spot now."

Harry and the professor nod and wordlessly go forward to drop the sail and un-step the mast. A few minutes later they are settled onto the rowing thwart. All of us strain to see the full outline of Rose Island. But it's harder to see now, as thankfully the moon again is covered by a cloud. The professor breaks the silence. "We should head just to the port of the way we're drifting now. Jack, you'll need to find some reference for steering in the dark. Maybe you can use that light far off the port bow, probably one of the anchored frigates just behind the island. I'd judge we're something like five or six hundred yards off the southeastern point of the island. If you aim just to the right of the light, we'll end up far enough off the island, hopefully, to be near the buoy. Seems like our best bet."

I start to count time. I estimate it will take us ten minutes to cover the professor's distance guess. I count the seconds as Harry and the professor settle into a stately stroke cadence. Carefully I concentrate on the professor's suggested tiny light. It's so tiny I'm afraid to blink. The two acts keep me focused. No other thoughts are allowed to intrude. Ten minutes of silent rowing, counting and staring.

"OK. In two minutes we should stop. We'll then be very close to our guess point for the buoy." Harry and the professor are breathing hard. They both nod acknowledgement. Two counted minutes later I quietly tell them to stop.

For several minutes we say and do nothing. My mind tricks back and forth between the day's events in and around the cove, the scene at the meeting house barn, the marching soldiers in the street, especially Hannah and Isaac. I try to get back to visualizing 1998, so easy minutes ago.

The professor must be having a similar difficulty. He seems almost to be reading my mind. "We have had a powerful experience. It likely will dominate our conscious for a while, although sometimes other memories will slip in. Let's try to help our 1998 visions by talking about them. Each of us should describe the visions we'll use, and concentrate on those memories. First though, as we do each time, we need to find relaxing physical positions. I suggest, Jack, you curl yourself onto one side and drape over the tiller. Harry, last time you were lying partially on the foredeck. Try to find that comfortable position again. I'll find a nice position here."

The boat rocks and bounces as we shuffle around finding as much comfort as we can. The professor, while still restlessly moving around, says, "I'll start. Keep it very simple. Only concentrate on a few strong, highly sensory memories."

Eyes closed, very quietly he begins. "I see my inflatable tied to the Luhrs. I feel the dense ribbed rubber on its pontoons, the cold smooth feel of the stainless steel wheel on the center console, and see the gauges behind it. I hold the handle of my ancient briefcase, and heft the case, feel its heaviness. It's always heavy. I put too many papers in it. I can smell its slightly sour smell. I see the musty old stacks upstairs in my home-away-from-home, the Newport Historical Society. Old documents bound more with dust than book binding; working at simple, stained, rectangular work tables; no pens allowed, only pencils. I'm leaving the Historical Society, driving my trusty old Volkswagen bug down Bellevue to Farewell Street, through the cemetery and onto the Pell Bridge. No, wait, I stop before the bridge and get a clam roll for the ride home to Jamestown.

"Go ahead, Harry. Don't mind me as I keep this up some more." I can hear the professor's indistinct mumbling continue, then stop.

I have to strain to hear Harry. "Alice…. I see her, remember her feel and taste. Her hair is very soft…kissing her is incredible." Long silence. "I remember feeling sore as hell from lying on the floor of the foretop. Alice would lie on my shoulder, my arm around her. Christ, my arm and shoulder ached something fierce after that. I can feel the pressure on the middle of my feet when climbing ratlines, and especially standing on foot ropes." More silence. "I can see my marina in Alexandria, as I sail *Cop Out* in from a night sail on the Potomac. I can smell my old Police Special when practice firing at the range."

The professor interrupts, "OK. Keep going Harry, but silently, to yourself. Jack, your turn."

"I go back to seeing my little pool at home. For once, Pearson is asleep. The girls are floating in the pool each on a green raft. Pearson looks pretty good. She's wearing a light blue one-piece bathing suit. Still has a lovely body, little muscular legs. There are streaks of grey in her short brown hair. She seems fully asleep, breathing slowly, a magazine face down on her stomach." I stop for a moment. Blinking, concentrating, I shift to the view from a little cottage we rent every summer on the south coast of Vinelhaven Island, in Penebscot Bay, Maine. "I'm headed off on vacation soon. We rent the same place every year. It's a little house which sits halfway up a windswept bluff overlooking the ocean. I'm sitting in the one Adirondack chair that has survived over the years we've rented. As always it's windy, now from the southwest. There are a few small islands offshore. I can see Isle au Haut well off to the east. Sometimes I can see Matinicus Island to the south, but not today. A lobster boat passes by, pausing to pull traps right below me. The crewman has on bright yellow slicker pants with suspenders. A trap dangles from the pulley as he quickly replaces the bait in the trap's mesh sack and releases the trap back into the water. A big sailboat is heeled over, driving along well offshore, outside the little islands. A group of four hikers stride along on the adjacent bluff. One seems to be wearing a bush hat. Pearson waves from the Volvo wagon as she drives off toward the little nearby village. Gulls ride the wind coming up the bluff, hardly moving their wings. I can hear the waves ceaselessly breaking on the rocky shore just out of sight below me. I taste another swallow of Sam Adams beer."

"OK, keep connecting to places, people and things in 1998, but quietly for now." The professor stretches his legs across the width of the rowing thwart.

Thoughts of Hannah, Isaac, the meeting house scene, flow into my conscious. I shake my head, concentrate. Finally I see the foremast shrouds of the *Endeavour*. I'm climbing in them, reaching the foretop futtock shrouds. Hanging backwards, I climb slowly up and onto the foretop. Looking forward, I feel our slow, rolling progress looking out through the ship's maze of head sails and lines. Familiar things, concentrate on stuff I know well. Work. I slowly take a visual tour of my office. Big old desk, with attached table, files all over it. A glimpse of the Connecticut River flowing under the I-84 bridge. I tour the pictures on the wall—a team portrait of the 1986 Boston Red Sox, an autographed picture of Carl Yastrzemski coiled motionless in the batter's box, a set of three clipper ship paintings. As my mental tour continues, my attention is drawn to my computer monitor. On its screen is a half-written memo I'm going to attach to a client email. It describes the career of the latest candidate I'm recommending for a superintendent's job on a highway project in the Berkshire Mountains of western Massachusetts. Still on my mental tour, I look left toward my secretary Rosie busily typing away just outside the doorway to my office....

A thunderous *CRASH, BOOM...BOOM...BOOM*. I'm in the water! My head feels like it's going to explode. I can't open my eyes. A fierce, piercing light, then pitch black. *CRASH, BOOM...BOOM...BOOM*. It's raining furiously, stings like little pellets slamming into my face. I feel motion in the water...waves, water gets in my mouth. I cough again and again. *FLASH*, then immediately, *CRASH, BOOM...BOOM...BOOM*. I try to breathe. There is a shrieking noise...incredible wind. The water is a wild turmoil of crashing waves. Salt water floods into my mouth, I cough violently again and again. I'm starting to sink, sliding down into the dark...sliding, sliding. Something grabs my right arm, but I'm slowly falling, falling away.

"Jack, Jack, get with it, goddamn it...look at me!"

I cough and cough, finally squint open my eyes. Harry is crouched low in the boat. It's rocking wildly back and forth, first away then down toward me. Another fiercely bright white light is followed by booming crashes. The wind shriek is deafening. Lightning and thunder again. Harry is leaning over his left hand still with a vise-like grip on my arm. The boat is rocking so much it looks like it will topple right over onto me.

"Jack, nod if you hear me. Nod, damn it, nod! *Jack...nod, NOD...do it!*"

I nod slightly. My head is killing me, all of it, but most intensely on the right side.

"Grab the gunwale and slide along to the stern, hang on there...both hands. I'm afraid these seas and this goddamn wind will flip her. Professor is unconscious, I hope. Could be dead, but I don't think so. Don't know what happened, he just slumped and damn near rolled out of the boat. Maybe a heart attack, I don't know."

Another brilliant burst of light, followed by loud claps of thunder. This time there's a slight pause between the lightning and the thunder.

"Jack, come on man, hang onto the stern. Put your hands as far apart as possible. It might help stabilize her a little."

I reach the stern and hang on. It doesn't work; I can't hang there. My head splitting, I hoist myself to hang over the transom at my armpits. No sea water in my mouth, a little more balance. I can't keep my eyes open...head hurts too much.

250

"Jack, you'll make it. Lot of blood. You must have hit the side of your forehead when the first thunder crash nearly knocked us all out of the boat. You just slammed into the gunwale and flipped over into the water. Thank God I heard you coughing."

A violent blast of wind lifts the boat, she's about to turn over but Harry smashes onto the windward gunwale as I lean feebly down on my left armpit. Just before tipping, the jolly boat barely rolls back to windward, as the wind blast passes by.

Again and again, blinding flashes are followed by crashes and booms. Without a word, Harry and I try only to survive the storm's violence. I hear a howling noise. Finally, I figure out its Harry screaming at the storm. The noise is maddening…Harry's howls, the crashing thunder, wind shrieking.

After a few minutes, an hour, I have no idea, the interval between lightning and thunder seems greater. The lightning's brightness and thunder's loudness are reduced, even the terrifying wind is gradually diminishing, the rain closer to a shower.

Harry peers through the dark at me, "Storm must be moving away."

For several more minutes the thunder still echoes around us, but less loudly. The lightning seems ever more distant.

"Jack, stay there if you can, OK?"

I nod.

"There's a helluva lot of water in the bottom of the boat. I need to scoop as much out as I can right away. I'm afraid that seam will just let go. She'd sink like a stone."

I watch dully as Harry cups his two hands together and powerfully sweeps them through the water in the boat, up and out. Rhythmically he scoops and sweeps, over and over.

Taking a break, his shoulders heaving as he regains his breath, Harry says, "I can't believe that storm. Where the hell did that come from? We had a light breeze, some clouds, some moon. It doesn't make sense."

Back to scooping, sweeping.

He's right. What was that storm?

A light flashes. The storm has stalled? Is it coming back? No…wrong direction. There it is again…darkness…again…darkness. A lighthouse? What else? Yes, what else! A lighthouse. Rose Island Lighthouse…*We're back…we're back!*

"Harry, look, *look*! That light has got to be Rose Island Lighthouse! It didn't exist in 1778. That means we're back, Harry, back, goddamn it, *back! We made it...we made it. Thank you, thank God, thank you.*"

Harry stops bailing, looks at me, looks where I'm pointing toward the light. A few seconds later it shines toward us. "Jesus, you're right.... You Are Right!!...Yes!"

Swinging at each other, we miss several attempts to "high five", finally hitting each other's right hand a glancing blow.

"Problem is," Harry scowls, "I'm not making any progress with all this bailing. I think more water is coming in than I'm pushing out. And I'm afraid to have you get in the boat. Might just be too much weight for her. *Giggles* is sinking."

"How about we take a chance? Help me in and we row as quickly as we can toward the light. There must be shallow water between us and Rose Island. Maybe we can make it."

"Get in. That's probably our only chance. I'll grab you under your arms and lift, you kick. Once you're up to your stomach, roll over and try to get a leg over the transom. Ready...heave!"

Harry nearly jerks my shoulders out of joint. Kicking as hard as I can, I roll to my left and lift my right leg. Still holding my shoulder with one hand, Harry grabs my right knee as it brushes the top of the transom. I'm half in, half out. I grab for the transom with my left hand as Harry gives one more tug. I roll half on my back, my waist landing hard on the tiller. Harry's already at the port rowing position as I right myself, pushing off on the tiller and the starboard gunwale next to the transom. Finally I get turned around facing aft. Carefully I shuffle a few steps on the extreme starboard side of the floorboards. My pounding headache is far worse. I can barely open my eyes.

"Let's go...row, Jack, row! If we start to sink I'll take care of the professor. Row, goddamn it, row!"

We hardly move the jolly boat. She's sitting so low the water almost seems above us.

"Where's the light?" Harry pauses turned around looking for the light. "Got it!" He strokes mightily with his oar as I hurry to catch up.

Again and again we stroke, the boat heavier and heavier. My head is throbbing. Something warm is trickling down my face into my left eye. It must be blood. I brush at it with my left hand, quickly re-grip the oar for our next stroke. I'm feeling more and more woozy and take a few deep breaths. Harry has stopped rowing. He's looking off to port.

"I think I saw a light. Yes, there! See it? It's moving all over the place, up and down, all over. It must be on a boat. Got to get its attention! Let's both stand up, hold up an oar. Wave it back and forth. Maybe the beam will catch the blades."

Braced on either side of the floorboard he stands in a deep crouch to balance himself as the jolly boat rocks slowly, heavily, side to side. I stand but fall back down onto the thwart immediately. The best I can do is place the end of the oar on the transom and hold it upright, blade up. Finally, I manage to sway the upright blade slightly. The light beam jerks over near the oars but continues away to port. I can barely pick up the rumble and cough of an engine. Sounds like an outboard. Slowly the beam comes back, again going by the oars. It's well off to starboard when I jump and nearly fall as Harry bellows, "*Here, over here! Damn it, here, shine over here!*"

The light flashes over in our direction, goes too far, stops, comes back. It hits squarely on Harry's oar, holds there bouncing up and down. The engine noise increases. In moments a small, low boat emerges from the dark. In the glow of its stern light it's clearly the professor's inflatable. Alice is at the helm.

Wearing a red full slicker outfit, with a "Newport Maritime Days" baseball hat, Alice slowly glides alongside, nudging the jolly boat. "Harry? Harry?"

"Right here, beautiful. My God, you are something!"

"Oh Harry, you're back, Oh my God, you're back!"

Harry grabs a cleat on the inflatable's starboard bow. There's a line in it which he quickly ties into an oar slot on the jolly boat's starboard gunwale.

"Jack, jump in with Alice. I'll lift the professor's shoulders onto the inflatable's pontoon here. You and Alice pull him inboard. Careful, Alice love, I don't know his condition, but he's at least unconscious."

Harry repeatedly lifts and pulls the professor from the bow where he's been lying outstretched, alongside the inflatable. After a moment's pause to catch his breath, Harry lifts him slightly onto the inflatable's starboard pontoon. Alice and I pull him slowly onto a little seat at the inflatable's bow. We lower him to the floorboards, and lean his back against the seat.

"*Giggles* is gonna sink any minute. We can't let her disappear. Without her, we don't get here. How long is this line?" Harry is holding up the line he's attached from the inflatable to the jolly boat.

Alice says, "I don't know, maybe fifty feet."

"That should be plenty. But, just in case, I'll thread the halyard out of the mast and tie the two lines together. I'll stuff the sail under the thwarts so it doesn't float away. Jack, grab an oar and tie it off to the end I'll hand you in a minute. We'll tie it all off to *Giggles* so we or someone will have the floating oar as a mark to find her later." Harry furiously pulls the halyard through the masthead block and ties the two lines together. He ties the line to a thwart. I hand him my oar to which I've tied the line's bitter end. Harry places the oar across the jolly boat's gunwales so to be free to float away with the line once the boat sinks.

He turns to Alice, "You are fantastic...incredibly brave, stubborn, a little nuts...the best, the very, very best." He wraps his arms around her, kissing her, pressing hard against her.

She gasps, "Oh Harry, I was afraid I lost you. I had just about given up hope. Again and again I couldn't find you. I can't believe suddenly you're right here! Hold me, Jesus, hold me, I think I'm about to collapse."

"I got you babe, gotcha...gotcha." They hug and kiss fiercely.

This time Harry breaks away. "Love, we need you to drive us into Newport fast, no stops. Let me check on the professor. Let's go...I know you got it in you. If you found us, hell you can be a Navy Seal tomorrow!"

She smiles at him, seems to see me for the first time. "Oh Jack, look at your head." Fumbling in the center console compartment below the wheel, she brings out a box. "First aid stuff, find some gauze and hold it against your head. You're bleeding."

"Thanks Alice...thanks for being here. How, I have no idea, but what a sight to see your light out there...what a sight!"

Harry says, "I'll sit here with the professor, brace him against the chop. He has a decent pulse. There's a big bump on the base of his skull. Maybe that knocked him out. Try to keep the bounce to an absolute minimum, love."

I'm vaguely aware of the inflatable's motion through the water. Later I sense lights, some voices, being lifted.

I awake in a bed, slightly tilted upward at the waist. A television hangs in the corner. A tube is attached to my wrist. I turn to look and get a sharp jolt of pain in my nose. Another tube is attached there. Light fills the room.

"He lives...run for your lives...he is alive! Hey, Jack...you look terrible!"

Turning my head I see Harry, shaved, in his *Endeavour* shirt and jeans, sitting in a recliner chair, with Alice asleep in his lap, covered by a blanket.

I blink repeatedly. "Harry…what's up? Is this a hospital? You OK?"

"Never better. Yup, you guessed it, a hospital. Sharp, very sharp. You're OK. It's a sweet little concussion. No big deal."

Alice yawns, stretches and stands up. She leans over the bed and kisses me on the forehead.

Harry laughs, "All better."

Alice laughs, "Your wife can take over for that. She'll be here soon, with your daughters. Told her not to worry, little boating accident, that's all." She laughs, "'Course when they meet Harry, they may ask a few questions." She sits on the arm of the chair. "So, just in case, I'm taking him where he promised two days ago." She pinches him on the cheek and kisses him as he grins foolishly.

"Walter?"

"Apparently he'll be OK. A form of whiplash. They've got him motionless for now while they run some tests. First look seems not too bad."

Harry stands up, holding Alice's hand as she stands alongside. "We've got better things to do then mess with you half dead in bed. Not a lot of fun, so we'll make our own." He arches his eyebrows at Alice.

"You do need a spanking!"

"There you go again about spanking. Little freaky, huh Jack!"

Alice slaps Harry on the butt. "There's your spanking! Bye Jack, we'll check back with you."

She turns to leave as Harry leans over to grab my hand. "Remember to check your next tour guide more carefully!"

Harry is halfway to the door.

"Harry, do you think Hannah and Isaac are OK?"

He comes back, leans over the bed. "Yeah, I'm betting they're hugging their Mom just on the other side of the bend in the 'river'. Thanks to your 'good thing'." He turns and waves, reaching out for Alice's hand.

Once again tears well up as I close my eyes.

THE END

SOURCES AND ACKNOWLEDGMENTS

Abbas, D.K. "Newport and Captain Cook's Ships." *The Great Circle: Journal of the Australian Association of Maritime History*, Volume 23, No.1, 2001.

Bayles, Richard, editor. *History of Newport County.*

Bennett, Jenny. "HM Bark Endeavour." *Maritime Life and Traditions*. No.14, Spring, 2002.

Brown, Frank Chouteau & Whitehead, Russell F., editors. *Colonial Architecture in New England*. 1977.

Crane, Elaine Forman. *A Dependent People*. New York: 1992.

Dearden, Paul F. *The Rhode Island Campaign of 1778*. Providence: 1980.

Dring, Thomas. *Recollections of the Jersey Prison-Ship*. Providence: 1929.

Finney, Jack. *Time and Again*. New York: Simon & Schuster: 1970. Copyright permission granted.

Hagist, Dan N. *General Orders, Rhode Island, December 1776—January, 1778*. Bowie, MD: 2001.

HM Bark Endeavour Foundation. "The North American Tour." Kent, UK: 1997.

Horowitz, Tony. *Blue Latitudes*. New York: 2002.

Hough, Richard. *Captain James Cook*. New York: 1994.

Johnson, Charlotte E. "A New Perspective on Rose Island: The Evolution of its Fortifications and Defenses." *Newport History*, Vol. 59, Part 1, Winter, 1986.

King, Dean et al. *A Sea of Words*. New York: 1995.

Mapes, James. *Quantum Leap Thinking*. Beverly Hills, CA: 1996

May, Commander W.E. *The Boats of Men at War*.

McLoughlin, William G. *Rhode Island, A History*. New York: 1986.

Metzer, Milton. *The American Revolutionaries*. New York: 1987.

Nimmo, Eileen G. *The Point of Newport*. Newport: 2001.

O'Neil, Richard, consultant editor. *Patrick O'Brian's Navy*. London: 2003.

Rhode Island, A guide to the Smallest State. Boston: 1937.

Sinclair, Jacqueline M. *Captain John Trevett, His Journal, Ancestry & Descent*. Greenwich, CT: 1969.

Walker, Anthony. *The Despot's Heel*. 1996.

Various web sites available on the Internet, 2004.

Special thanks to Commander Bob Makowsky, United States Coast Guard.

Cover art by James Fleming, architect.

Research into British naval records and opinions derived from recent underwater dives actually places the bark *Lord Sandwich* slightly north of the position herein described. The French fleet in fact sailed into Narragansett Bay to attack Newport in early August, 1778, though was known to have been immediately off Newport as described.

Printed in the United States
71247LV00005B/103-150

9 781424 104017